Project Anastrophe

A Sci Fi Novel

George Karnikis

Outskirts Press, Inc.
Denver, Colorado

This is a work of fiction. The events and characters described herein are imaginary and are not intended to refer to specific places or living persons. The opinions expressed in this manuscript are solely the opinions of the author and do not represent the opinions or thoughts of the publisher. The author has represented and warranted full ownership and/or legal right to publish all the materials in this book.

Project Anastrophe
A Sci Fi Novel
All Rights Reserved.
Copyright © 2008 George Karnikis
v2.0

Cover Photo © 2008 Photos.com. All rights reserved - used with permission.

This book may not be reproduced, transmitted, or stored in whole or in part by any means, including graphic, electronic, or mechanical without the express written consent of the publisher except in the case of brief quotations embodied in critical articles and reviews.

Outskirts Press, Inc.
http://www.outskirtspress.com

ISBN: 978-1-4327-2898-4

Library of Congress Control Number: 2008933876

Outskirts Press and the "OP" logo are trademarks belonging to Outskirts Press, Inc.

PRINTED IN THE UNITED STATES OF AMERICA

Dedication

This book is dedicated to my beloved wife,

Ingrid

Acknowledgements

In this Sci Fi novel one finds relevancy to our time. We live in a time of possible nuclear war. Oil and other pollutants have caused irreversible damage to our ecosystem. "Project Anastrophe" shows how much worse it could be, and offers hope.

There are a few people that I must thank from the bottom of my heart. If it wasn't for their help and advice "Project Anastrophe" would still be in its genesis. First of all I want to thank my wife, Ingrid, who put up with me during the eight long years it took me to write this book. She helped me with those prepositions that are so hard for a non-native speaker. I would also like to thank JoEllen

Moldoff, my writing Mentor, whose knowledge I value and respect; Stan Moldoff, for his good advice; my son Karolos, who gave me many good ideas about space and spaceships; the Writers' Round Table, the Poetry and Memoir classes headed by JoEllen; and my children who encouraged me to stay the course.

Chapter 1

It was one of those foggy March mornings; a day off to do as I pleased. With a hot cup of coffee in my hand I was already plotting my weekend schedule. This past week had been especially difficult for me and I was glad to have it over. There was that loose muffler I had to fix, and of course I needed to mow the lawn.

I got tired just thinking about all the work I had to do, so I made an executive decision; I am going fishing! The last time I went fishing was at least six months ago and I had a lot of preparatory work to do. First I had to find my tackle box and fishing pole. It took a while but I managed to gather everything. I made a few sandwiches, picked up my coffee thermos and a six pack of beer. I threw them into the boat, tied the lines on the trailer, and was ready to go.

George Karnikis

As I kissed my wife, Tasoula, she said in a teasing way, "Are we going to have another super fish dinner, dear?"

"Don't hold your breath, honey," I said and was on my way. It took about thirty minutes to go to the marina and another thirty minutes to put the boat in the water and park the trailer out of the way. Once the boat was in the water it took me another fifteen minutes to get to my favorite fishing hole. The sun was rising fast now and I had no illusion that I'd catch any fish, but I kept the line in the water anyway. But then, I didn't come here to catch fish, I came here to get away from it all. I should do this more often; this place is so beautiful and quiet. It was 10:30 a.m. by my watch and although a few clouds started to obscure the sun it was still a nice day by Northwest standards. One learns to live with the weather changes here in the San Juan Archipelago. I turned off the motor, secured the line, and let the tide take me home. I was looking at a floating log when I noticed something shining on the water. I bent over to take a closer look and still couldn't figure it out. It looked like a light blue electric current floating on top of the waves. It was about twenty feet in diameter and perfectly round.

The atmosphere felt electrified. I felt as if I were in some kind of empty space; a funnel, or a vortex. My hair stood up and I got goose bumps - - I was scared. A period of time passed; whether it was minutes or hours or even weeks I would not have known. The only thing I could feel was numbness. Vivid colors went through my mind; red, yellow, green and finally black. It was a sensation I had never felt before. Without a doubt, I was in another dimension, another world.

But where is the boat? Where is the sea? I must be dreaming. That's it–it's a dream, it's a nightmare. I start to count, "One, two, three, wake up!" I had heard somewhere

Project Anastrophe

that this was the best way to snap out of a nightmare. Slowly, I open my eyes to avoid the sun's glare. I feel the coolness of grass on my face. I must have lain here for some time. The sun is too high above the horizon. I feel cold, nauseated, and very tired.

I am lying on a hill covered with luscious green grass. There is a creek only a few yards from where I am. It snakes its way down towards the flat land covered with pine trees.

Meanwhile, back at Nick's house Takis answers the phone.

"M-o-m-m!"

"Now what do you need again, Takis?"

"Grandma's on the phone."

"Okay, I got it. Thanks."

"Mom, what's up?"

"Oh--not much--how about you, dear?"

"I am doing fine; we are all doing fine here."

"Well, the reason I called is that Father wants to know if you and Nick are still interested in that piece of property. You know the price is very good and it's not that you can't afford it--buying land is always a good investment."

"I know, Mother. We have talked about it many times, but if Nick gets his promotion as he hopes, we don't know where we are going to end up."

"Well your father wants to talk to him anyway."

"Oh, Nick isn't here, he went fishing but he is due to come home anytime now. I'll have him call Dad as soon as he comes back."

"How is Nick doing these days?"

"He had a very difficult week, that's why he went fishing."

"Oh poor Nick, give him my love, will you dear?"

"I sure will, Mom."
"Well, I'll be talking to you soon. Bye for now."

The day was beautiful, there were no clouds in the sky; it was warm but not hot. It felt like a typical Northwest spring day and yet I felt very sick and my face was clammy and feverish. Although I felt miserable and confused I tried to put some order in my thoughts. I looked at my watch to check the time but it had stopped. I felt my face to see if I had any whiskers, (I had shaved this morning), but my face felt smooth. So if I don't have any whiskers, this episode could not have lasted long, a few hours at the most. I know now for sure that I am not dreaming, but then what happened, why am I here, and why do I feel so sick?

On a beautiful day like this there should be a lot of life around, but I see no birds flying or twittering, and no other sounds for that matter. Then a sudden harmonic chime sounded, and about ten feet in front of me there appeared a sheet of blue light about seven feet high by four feet wide. A young woman in her late twenties, with blue eyes, blond hair, and wearing some kind of uniform appeared on the screen.

"My name is Norina. We are going to transport you to a safe place as soon as we get your coordinates. How do you feel?"

"Not so good. Actually I feel very sick and feverish."
"We will have you in a safe place pretty soon."
"Where am I, what happened to me, and why do I feel so sick?"
"We will tell you as soon as we get you over here."

This was all too much for me. Nothing made sense any more, so I closed my eyes and let things go as they would.

Project Anastrophe

It didn't take too long. The blue screen that was in front of me all this time disappeared and was replaced by an intense yellow light. Seconds later I was bathed in it. I noticed two robot-like beings close by. I felt numb and soon after that I went blank.

"35-A calling 35-B."
"35-B here, state your request."
"Patient from year 2000 with radiation poisoning delivered to room 401. It is suggested that he be put in vat 15."
"State vital statistics."
"Male, age 34, 1meter, 99 cm, dark hair, dark eyes, of the gene 12-cti, 0 electronic implants; healthy human specimen. Information completed, 35-A terminates transmission."
"Message received and coded. 35-B terminates transmission."
"35-B calling Megacephalos."
"Megacephalos here, state your request."
"Please advise as to prognosis and diorthosis of human patient 12-cti."
"Acute radiation poisoning, therapy for diorthosis as per program c.f.2. Patient will be submerged in cianohidrosis in comatose state as per required time. Megacephalos terminates transmission."

A computer was emitting the natural sounds of birds and other small animals busy in the early morning. Norina loved nature and she had programmed her computer to wake her every morning with this lively natural concert.

"Good morning, Norina, how can I help you this morning?"

A robot came into the room. It was an anthropomorphic robot, one of the latest models, the 12-C series, one that contained the latest programs in psychoanalyses. It could be made to look any age or sex. In this case it looked like a man between 25 and 35 years old---- a handsome guy.

"Good morning, Ner, I would love a cup of hot coffee and then the usual, thanks."

"Yes Ma'am, right away."

Ner knew not only Norina's breakfast menu but also lunch and dinner for many weeks at a time. He would remind her of all her appointments. He was also her chauffeur whenever he was needed and at times he was her confidant. Ner called her for breakfast and she was more than ready. She was very careful with her diet. Her breakfast consisted mainly of fruit and cereal but she never gave up her coffee which she drank plain.

The news was flashing in front of her, on a screen which was part of the table. She pushed her plate and her cup to the side to have a better view of the picture and the letters that were unfolding with great speed. She was not satisfied with the two dimensional-pictures so she asked for three–D. A hologram of a naked young man was shown as he was about to be submerged in a crystalline vat containing deep blue liquid. The man appeared to be in suspended animation, lying in a hammock which was gently lowered into the vat.

"Huh, nice looking fellow but I wouldn't like to be in his shoes right now."

She quickly made a verbal notation to her wrist unit to find out more about this latest arrival. Then she called Ner.

"How can I help you, Miss Norina?"

"I would like to hear my schedule for the day, Ner."

"It is now 7:00 a.m. and your first appointment is at 9:00 a.m. until 10:00 a.m. with Dr. George Dylos."

"Is it about the recent time travel accident?"

"Yes, Miss Norina, and I would like to remind you that

Project Anastrophe

you communicated this problem to Dr. Dylos before, but he did not respond."

"I see, carry on, Ner."

"Your next appointment is at 12:00 noon with Miss Lana Duvick. You will have lunch at Perifimo restaurant, and may I remind you that she is a media person and you should be very careful with your answers. You have two free hours between your first and second appointments. The rest of the afternoon you are scheduled to be in your office. Would you like me to make any changes in your schedule?"

"No, that will be all, thank you, Ner."

"You are quite welcome, Miss Norina."

"I better get ready for my first appointment with Dr. Dylos. A few more weeks and I will finish my service, and then I will leave this God-forsaken Megalopolis and go home where I belong. I may even take that trip to Mars and spend a few weeks at the Hellas Resort. Oh Norina, Norina, stop dreaming and get going so you won't be late again." She arrived at Dr. Dylos' office on time.

"I don't need to tell you, Norina, that this time we are in real trouble. The previous seven times we picked up birds, fish, and a cow, but this time we managed to pick up a real human being. Please tell me what happened. Don't we have a special filtration system to keep out human D.N.A.?"

"Dr. Dylos, according to my records I show that I brought this problem to your attention three months ago, but you did not act upon it."

"Don't tell me that we have picked up more humans in the past?"

"Actually we have picked up only two mammals; one human and one cow the rest were fish and birds."

"Rufus, please locate Miss Norina's report regarding the Voyager–A5."

"Yes, Dr. Dylos, right away."

"What's wrong with your voice?"

"I am sorry, Dr. Dylos, I need to make a minor adjustment—is that better?"

"Yes, that's fine, please continue."

"Just tell us what's pertinent to these accidents."

"The report was filed by Miss Norina Anderson, on July 12, 2500 at 10:00 a.m."

"We seem to have problems with the warp speed adjuster on the Voyager-A5 and I recommend we cancel use of this ship until the problem is rectified. The malfunction of the time speed adjuster has caused the ship to jump into the wrong epochs. It seems to calibrate the year 2000, usually spring, between 10:00 a.m. and 12:00 noon. Instead of parking at its scheduled portals to pick up its cargo, it goes anywhere at random. Its cargo doors open and pick up whatever is in front of it then brings it to our time and dumps it anywhere. So far it has picked up fish and birds, but if this continues I would not be surprised at all if next time it picks up mammals. I need authorization to stop the Voyager for repairs."

"On July 15, 2500 the Voyager-A5 malfunctioned again. It jumped back in time to March 28 in the year 2000 at precisely 10:00 a.m. This time it picked up a cow and fortunately it dumped it into a safe area. The cow is temporarily in quarantine."

"And how is the cow doing health-wise Norina?"

"Oh it's doing very well considering what it has gone through."

"Thank you, Rufus, you may go now."

"You are welcome, Dr. Dylos."

"This time the Voyager A-5 picked up a human being and by law I must report it to the authorities," said Norina.

"Is there anything else I should know, Dr. Dylos, before I proceed with my report?"

Project Anastrophe

"First of all I must thank you for your prompt report, and I am very sorry I didn't keep you abreast of what's going on within my department. But I should tell you that we have been busy trying to repair the VoyagerA-5 ever since you submitted your first report. But we had strict orders not to let anyone know about the accident at that time. We have been using the Techno-Nanos on the Voyager to repair most of the problems, but as you know, we are not out of the woods yet."

"I understand your dilemma, Dr. Dylos, but these accidents, and especially the last one, fall under my jurisdiction and I must file my report as soon as possible unless I hear otherwise from higher authorities within the day."

"That won't be a problem, Norina. In the meantime be very discrete about it, and especially with the media people."

"Miss Norina, this is Ner. I am sorry to disturb you at this time but before you left you made a notation in my memory data about seeing the human from the year 2000. I thought that this would be an appropriate time to remind you of it."

"Thank you, Ner, I'll see to it right a way."

"Hello, how are you feeling today?"
"Much better, thank you."
"The doctors told me that you are in excellent condition considering what you have gone through lately. I would like to ask you a few questions if you don't mind."
"And I also have to ask you a few questions if I may."
"Of course you may."
"My name is Norina, what is your name?"
"My name is Nick."
"Well now that we know each other's names perhaps you will allow me to ask you a few questions."

"Go right ahead."
"What's your last name?"
"Papas."
"What kind of name is that?"
"It's Greek."
"I see, and how old are you?"
"May 6th I will be 34."
"Are you married?"
"Yes."
"Do you have any children?"
"Yes, I have three; one boy, Takis 7, and two girls, Sophia 5, and Julie 3. My wife's name is Tasula and she is 33. The doctor was here this morning and gave me this electronic pad and he asked me to write down my personal history which I did this morning."
"Oh I am so sorry. I should have asked you if you had already done it. However this makes it a lot easier for both of us. May I take a look?"
"Please do."
'Physicist employed by N.A.S.A.'
"I heard about N.A.S.A. when I was a student in the university."
"Now may I ask you a few questions too?"
"Of course, please do."
"You may think that I am crazy, but before I found myself here I was fishing at my favorite fishing hole. I was about to go home when I was picked up by something and was thrown onto a grassy hill. I felt very sick and then I think I saw you as some kind of a hologram. I woke up here in this room with a doctor telling me that now I am fine and not to worry at all. Will you please tell me what's going on?"
"Dr. Papas, that is precisely the reason I am here to see you, and you are not crazy at all."

Project Anastrophe

"You can call me Nick."

"And you can call me Norina; I would like that very much. As I said, you are not crazy, Nick. You were picked up by the Voyager A-5 and brought 500 years into the future."

"If this is one of those jokes to make me feel better it has already gone too far."

"Nick, this is not a joke. I am telling you the truth. Surely you don't think that this is the year two thousand do you? Take a look around. I can assure you that none of these technologies were discovered by the year two thousand. But as your therapy progresses and you have all your implants everything will make sense to you."

"I had thought all along that I must have been kidnapped by terrorists because of my position as a physicist at N.A.S.A.; perhaps for ransom or some political reasons, and that I had been taken to a country far away from home. I had never imagined that I would end up five hundred years in the future. And what do you mean about putting implants? What sort of implants are you talking about?"

While Nick was talking I was blaming myself for being so matter-of-fact with him. I could have waited one or two more days before I broke the bad news. But how could I guess about a person who has come five hundred years from the past? After all, English is not my language, and it has not been spoken since the Confederate Government of Earth adopted the international metric language in 2208. I should have consulted Ner; he would have given me a few good ideas. Poor Nick, how terrible he must feel away from his loved ones and so far from home.

"We all have implants that are installed in our brains from the day we start kindergarten and they are updated every so often. They are very important in our lives; without them we couldn't function. They are like computers were to you in the twenty-first century only more so for us because we rely on them one hundred percent. I am sorry, Nick, but it looks as if you are going to be with us for a while. Of course for the duration, you need to live like we do. When we are ready to send you back to your time zone, we will remove your implants."

"In the year two thousand, traveling to the past or to the future was only a fantasy. I am excited but scared to be here, five hundred years in the future. All my loved ones died hundreds of years ago and that is very painful. But let me ask you something. Suppose you send me back in time before all my trouble started; wouldn't that solve my problem?"

"That is one of the difficulties we are facing, Nick. If we miscalculate even by a nanosecond, you will be thrown years off and then it will be very difficult, if not impossible, to recover you again. You see this is not the kind of thing we do every day. You were picked up by mistake because the Voyager malfunctioned. You and the cow are the only two mammals we have picked up since we have been able to travel in time. The cow has been examined by the vets and is now living in the zoo. But you are one of us, Nick, and whatever we do to you will affect us in some way. So we must be very careful to send you back to the exact time and place the Voyager found you. It is the "Prime Directive" of our policy. And yes, if we manage to send you back to your time zone and at the exact place where we picked you up, all of your loved ones will be just as you left them and you will remember nothing of this."

"That is the best news I've heard so far. But why was I so sick with radiation, was it the time travel?"

"No it was the place you landed. It is one of the many places you people managed to contaminate and now we pay the price for your mistakes. But as you are aware we saved

Project Anastrophe

you on time, and from the last report I have seen from your doctors, you have made a complete recovery."

"What happens now, how long do I have to stay here?"

"As I said, the only thing that remains to be done now is to install your implants which will take one or two days at the most."

"Norina, you have been very helpful to me and I want to thank you. You are my first contact in this New World, and I hope that you'll come to see me again because I trust you."

"Don't worry, Nick, I promise I'll come to see you again when you have your implants installed and believe me, you won't feel as lost as you feel now. I'll take you out and show you around, O.K.? You should know that you have been assigned two doctors both of whom you have met; Dr. Liza Green and Dr. John Miller. They are the only people you should talk to. We have taken all pertinent precautions for your own safety. We also made sure that no holographic visitors would come to see you here. If you would like to communicate with me, just press the button here and call my name. I am the only one who can visit you as a hologram. I need to go now, I'll see you later, Nick."

"This is indeed a different world. If this place is a hospital it looks much different from the ones I have seen in my world. For one thing this room looks more like an egg than the square rooms I am used to. The texture of the wall feels like a combination of terra cotta and some kind of an alloy. When I touch it, it even feels like an egg shell. The colors on the walls change like neon from white to blue to pink and they shimmer and pulsate. The only furniture that I can see is the bed I am in. There is no bathroom but I never feel the need to use one either. I have no covers over me but I don't feel cold. There is a light blue color that covers my body from toes to neck. It also pulsates--it must be some kind of chromo therapy.

George Karnikis

The ceiling is white along with part of the upper wall, there is a soft white light on all the ceiling and part of the white wall, but light comes from within, like phosphorous. There are no switches to turn it on or off anywhere that I can see. There is a wide bracelet attached to my left wrist with a pulsating red and green light. There is no doubt that I am living in the twenty-fifth century. How long have I been gone from home? Have they missed me yet? I suppose it all depends if I make it back on time or not. Norina said that even a nano second's delay from the exact time and place could throw me years off. Christ, what a mess I have gotten into. And still I am not out of the woods. I should have gone to the baseball game with Takis. Didn't I promise that I was going to take him to the game this weekend? Had I known that I was going to find myself so abruptly in the future I would never have gone fishing. But now here I am in a world in which I was not meant to be. I wonder why the light is dimming."

"Oh, I see. Dr. Miller, I was hoping that you would visit me live and not as a hologram."

"Hi Nick, that was just to let you know that I was about to visit you in person. We need to be very careful with your security, that's all."

"This is something I need to discuss with you, Dr. Miller. Why am I kept in such strict security?"

"Well Nick, for one thing you are in quarantine until we are sure you don't carry any of those dreadful diseases from the twenty-first century and kill us all. Also you haven't had your implants yet. Another thing is that you are the first man ever to have come to the twenty-fifth century. Without a doubt you are the hottest thing in town, Nick, and for these reasons we have to make sure that the wrong person doesn't come to see you here."

"Do I have to have those implants? Couldn't I just wait

a little while? Who knows; you may be able to find a way to send me home soon, and I wouldn't have to have them at all."

"Nick, I wish you were right, but it looks as if you are going to be with us for a while. If you are going to be here, you must have your implants in order to function as we do. Besides, when the time comes to go back home we will remove them."

"Will these implants do any damage to my brain?"

"Not at all, you will feel just as you feel right now, but one thing is for sure, you will miss them when they are removed."

"Dr. Miller, I think you have convinced me. Now tell me when I am going to have my implants."

"Tomorrow morning. Mark my words, because tomorrow you are going to be more knowledgeable than we are because you have the knowledge of your past experience too."

The night was so quiet that Nick could hear his heart thumping; he looked around the room once again at the different colors of the walls and the ceiling. They were hypnotic and maybe that was the purpose of it all, to make him sleepy.

The Symposium

"Ladies and Gentlemen, may I please have your attention? Most of you know me, but for those who do not, my name is George Dylos and I am in charge of environmental studies as they pertain to the problem we have with the radiation on our planet. What we are going to discuss today is of the most secret nature. That's why we are meeting in a satellite. You have been chosen from all over the planet because you are the best scientists in your fields.

George Karnikis

You are all aware of the radiation that is killing us. Each one of you will be given a set of problems according to your expertise. Your task is to give back your ideas or solutions on these particular problems. Most people around the world know that we have serious difficulties with the environment, but not to the extent you will know by the time you read your assigned E–Text. I can't tell you how important it is that you don't share your knowledge with other people. We do not want to start a worldwide panic. Once you have completed your assignments we will retrieve your text from your E-Box. For the sake of giving you a chance to ask questions about our problem, I am going to summarize the events in the order they happened, and for that we have to go 500 hundred years back to the end of the 20th century. That was when our problems started with the release of atomic energy.

The first person who thought of releasing atomic power was Democritus, 2900 hundred years ago in Athens, Greece. Of course at that time everybody thought he was crazy. Albert Einstein in one of his three important 1905 papers explained Brownian Movement on the basis of his study of the motion of atoms. His special theory of Relativity, (1905), dealt with the Brownian Movement and the motion of atoms in relation to one another. Einstein went on to contribute more mathematical theorems during the rest of his life. (1) As you probably know, it was in the state of America that the first atomic bomb was made and later on, similar bombs were detonated over the state of Japan in Hiroshima and Nagasaki on August 6th and August 9th 1945. Those bombs killed thousands of Japanese people and contaminated a large area of that state.

I would like you to know that we are not discussing the politics of that time, only the fact that it was the first time

Project Anastrophe

an atomic bomb was used against people and the environment. But why do I say all this to you now, since most of you already know about it? It is because at that time the planet Earth started to be bombarded by radiation. Finally after many decades, in 2115 A.D. people all over the world managed to stop making and using nuclear bombs, other weapons, and equipment. But there were many groups who kept using smaller but just as lethal weapons. Some people who lived in the so-called third world countries, sympathized with those groups and helped by giving them money and materiel secretly. Some of the materiel was in the form of micro-nuclear bombs or "pocket nukes" as they used to call them. They used them in big cities and killed thousands of people. Their reasons were many; one of the most important was for liberating their small countries which were under powerful worldwide cartels. But those who wanted to liberate their countries proved to be the most potent enemy of all. They eventually won their freedom by using many of those pocket nuclear bombs but at a price we are paying even today.

Ladies and gentlemen, it is this radiation poisoning that I want to talk about and what it is doing to us at this time. We have done a good job of protecting ourselves from the radiation that exists in the air by building geodomes that have helped us sustain the quality of life that we are accustomed to. But now we are again getting sick just as our progenitors did long ago. As you know, this time the radiation comes from under our feet and there is no way we can cover the earth's floor forever. Building aqua cities is very expensive and even that would be only temporary. We need to do something to eradicate radiation once and for all, or we will all perish and that's not an option. There have been suggestions that we colonize Mars, but that would be very expensive, and the biggest price would be leaving our planet Earth for good. Now I would like to give you the opportunity to offer any suggestions."

"Yes. State your name please."

"My name is Margulies; I am a geneticist from Athens in the state of Greece. My company is working on a gene that will help to neutralize radiation poisoning when it's introduced into the human body. We are in the first stages of development and need financial help from the confederate government in order to complete it on time."

"Dr. Margulies, can this gene therapy work on other animals also?"

"Yes, sir, once the gene has been altered for human use it can also be altered for other animals."

"Thank you, Dr. Margulies, your request has been noted and you will hear from us very soon, you can be sure of that."

"My name is Dr. Poulain. I come from Paris in the state of France; my company has been working on what we call, 'Nano-Ergophags.' When they are introduced into the human body they locate the radiation particles and eradicate them just like the white cells do with infections. They will work in other animals and in vegetation too. We also need financial help."

"Dr. Poulain, your invention sounds very interesting and you will be hearing from us shortly."

Next came Dr. Buchanan from Tomintoul in the state of Scotland. His company had been working for many years on dome flooring. The product was completely impervious to radiation due to the fact that they had combined basic lead with an alloy called purethium–zita. This product was less than half the price of the leading material currently in use, and could be used right away.

Dr. Jack Jones from Seattle Washington in the state of America stated his belief that if we were to concentrate our

Project Anastrophe

thoughts into a wave of harmonious vibrations, we could neutralize radiation, but it would require the majority of people of the world to accomplish this task.

"My name is Dr. Vanderhus I come from Amstelveen in the state of the Netherlands. I have an idea but it would take much more time for me to explain it. Perhaps now that we know the extent of the problem as you explained it to us, we should prepare a written exegesis as to how we can contribute to the solution, and also request the appropriate aid from the confederate government."

"Thank you, Dr. Vanderhus. If you all agree with this idea please say so.--From the looks of it, it appears that you agree. But please-e-e, you must respond ASAP. Ladies and gentlemen, our meeting is adjourned. Thank you very much for making the effort to come."

Chapter 2

First Day Out in the World of the Future

"HI, Nick, how are you feeling today?"
"Oh, Norina! I am fine, thanks."
"I just talked with Dr. Green and she said that everything went fine and there were no problems inserting your implants. She considers the surgery a success, thinks you are a genius. But how do you feel now that you are one of us?"
"Norina, just as you said when you first came to visit me, I still have all my previous memories intact but now

Project Anastrophe

there is so much more knowledge to tap into that I am seeing the world from a different perspective. You people know so much and have far more education than we do."

"That's because we live in the Twenty–Fifth Century and had plenty of time to learn more. Now Nick, I am here to take you out. How about that?"

"I can hardly wait to get out of here."

"I am going to show you my world and I'm looking forward to your reaction. If you have any questions, feel free to ask."

"Oh don't worry, I will. Here is my first question; is this your car?"

"This isn't a car; we stopped having cars a long time ago and haven't used fossil fuel for an even longer time. Now our primary fuel is antimatter energy which we have managed to secure in such a way as to make it usable for our transportation, electricity, and other necessities. This is my magneto which hovers approximately one meter above ground when we are in town, and when we are out of town we can fly hundreds of meters up. But enough of my magneto, I would like to show you my city which is called Zita Biosphere or Z-Bio. You see, Nick, the whole planet is divided into biospheres because we can only live in domes like this."

"You mean to tell me that this is a dome?"

"Yes, it's a dome, but it's so big that you can't possibly see it from here. Sometime I will take you up to the tower and from there you can get an idea of how gigantic it is. This is an average size; there are others that are even larger."

"How many of these domes are on the planet?"

"There are millions of them. For example, in the state of America each county has its own dome and there are thousands just in that state. When we go to my place I'll ask Ner and he can tell us more on this subject."

"And who is Ner?"

"Ner is my private robot, he is very important to me and I couldn't function without him. He is one of the latest models and is very expensive, but in my case he comes with the job. I think we had better start with the museum of science and engineering."

"Norina, who is driving your magneto?"

"Oh, it's programmed to go to our destination on its own. The computer has taken over and we will be there in a few minutes."

"It's amazing there is so much traffic and it is so quiet. The magnetos come so close and never collide, how can they do that?"

"I don't quite know the mechanics but I think there is some kind of sensor that keeps them apart. Anyway here we are now; we are going to fly up for parking."

"How high?"

"I don't know Nick, maybe 60 or 70 floors but we will know pretty soon."

"It looks higher than that to me."

"Yes, first it has to go to the top and then the elevator will park it for us."

"And how do we get back to the magneto?"

"The escalator will take us pretty close to it."

"And how does the escalator know where your magneto is parked?"

"It simply reads my D.N.A. It knows who I am and where my magneto is parked."

"Amazing, amazing, in my time we are just starting to use D.N.A. for forensics."

"Don't forget that you started it in your time as you say, we just made it better. No, no, don't go out yet we need to wait a few minutes for the escalator to come by. There it is. Now we get in."

Project Anastrophe

"Wow, this doesn't look anything like our escalators; it looks more like a train to me."

"In a way it is a train but of a much smaller size."

"And where is it taking us?"

"To the museum, of course."

"So we just sit down and watch?"

"We could walk if we want to, but in your case we had better take it easy. Remember you haven't walked for five hundred years."

"Only in time Norina, only in time."

"I programmed it to start us from the Twenty-First century so that you get a pretty good idea of how we have progressed in the last five hundred years. Now you are going to see some of the cars you are used to driving. Here we are in the year 2000, starting with passenger cars and here is a very popular car, Lexus, made in the state of Japan; this one is a Lincoln Continental made in the state of America; a Volvo made in the state of Sweden.

"I don't know how they could drive these kinds of cars, they must have taken their lives in their hands, and they must have had thousands of accidents every day."

"To you it looks like ancient history but to me its real life and yes, you are right, these cars were real killers but they were lots of fun too. Norina, if you don't mind, I would like to see something new, something that I would not have seen in my short life under normal circumstances."

"I am sorry, Nick, but I have never seen these kinds of cars before. It's fascinating how far we have come with transportation and everything else. Why don't we go to the present and future exhibition? We can see some of our medical advances here in the pavilion of modern science. After we are through here lets go to the pavilion of robotics. We need to find out a few things for you, because you are going to need one of them pretty soon.

"Good morning, we are interested in your new models."

"Good morning, Norina, would you be interested in a male or female robot?"

"We would like to see both, thank you."

"Would it be for Nick?"

"Yes it would."

"Then Nick will have to talk to Lucria. She will give him all the latest information on our new robots."

"Norina, I am the last person to ask questions."

"Don't worry, Nick, I will be here with you."

"Norina, how could she know my name? She doesn't know me from Adam."

"But she does, in fact she knows all about your new persona; what she doesn't know is your real identity and don't you tell her either."

"And how come she knows my new persona, unless you told her. This is the first time she has seen me."

"Remember those implants you recently had put in your brain? She can read part of your personal identification; that's how she knows who you are."

"She does, but how come I don't know anything about her?"

"Because you don't know how to use your implants yet, but in time you will, trust me. Anyway it's her business to know who you are. She is a sales person and a robot."

"No, that can't be, she doesn't look anything like a robot, she looks like a very attractive woman."

"You should see Ner, my robot. He is handsome and very intelligent too."

"My name is Lucria I am the latest model '2501 c2f' and I am in charge of the sales department. I am going to show you our latest products both male and female. Make yourselves comfortable. The show is about to start."

Project Anastrophe

Nick expected the lights to go off and a person to start talking in preparation for the show, but a young couple about his age walked in and introduced themselves starting with the man. He said he didn't have a name because he hadn't been sold yet. He introduced himself as '2501c2m' and then the female did the same thing only her model number ended in '2501c2f' they were both attractive and very polite. They looked so human Nick had a hard time believing that they were robots, and because of their human likeness he felt that he was slave bargaining. He told Norina he really wasn't in a position to make the right choice because of his being in the hospital and not being in good shape physically and emotionally right now. She understood what he was trying to say, but she was merciless. She wasn't about to help. She only said,

"Nick, pick the person you feel most comfortable with and I will help you program it to your needs later on; anyway you are not going to take it right now. It will come to you in a few days. Nick chose the robot model 2501c2f. She smiled at him and said,

"Thank you for choosing me."

When we were out, I told Norina how uncomfortable I was to be put into such a predicament when I knew nothing about choosing robots. She said,

"Nick, I knew you were going to choose the girl and as I said, I will help you program her when she arrives."

"By the way, how does she arrive--in a box?"

"Oh no, she will come on her own. In fact she will take you anywhere you want to go; she knows this city very well."

"I would rather have you take me around, Norina. And how are we going to keep her from finding out who I really am?"

"We will tell her."

"Tell her?"

"Yes, we will program her to not only keep it a secret but she will help you adapt to the 25th century."

"This is a gigantic place."

"And speaking of gigantic places, Nick, I am tired and famished. How would you like to have a bite to eat?"

"I hope you are buying, Norina, because I don't even know how to spell the kind of money you have here."

"Don't worry, Nick, I will take care of it."

We stepped out of the museum, the sun was blazing up on top but the air inside the biosphere felt cool and pleasant. We stepped outside on the sidewalk and started to walk towards what appeared to be some kind of shopping center. On both sides of the sidewalk there were trees and fragrant flowers. There were magnetos, most of them flying a few meters above the ground but several were driving on the road. People and magnetos didn't interfere with each other and although there was a lot of traffic there was very little sound. When I looked more carefully at the streets and buildings I realized the sidewalks along with the trees and the flowers were moving too. It was amazing how everything was moving and yet except for the whooshing of the magnetos, there was very little noise. A few children were walking on the moving sidewalk but most adults preferred to stand still. As we approached the center, part of the sidewalk turned gently to the left and then straight into the center, where it slowed down. We finally stepped onto a non-moving sidewalk and the other sidewalk picked up speed and went down on its regular route. There were no shops that I could see but there were many people going in and out of the building.

"Norina, where are we?"

"Just wait, you'll see."

We walked into a restaurant, sat down at a small table,

Project Anastrophe

and looked at the menu which was part of the table itself. One could look into the table and see three dimensional pictures of food arranged on a counter. You simply touched a picture and a man or a woman robot would appear and explain the contents of that particular dish. My problem was that I had never seen these kinds of dishes before and couldn't make up my mind as to what kind of food to choose. There were about ten different shapes on the dishes: squares, circles, diamond shapes and others. I turned to Norina and asked her,

"What are all these shapes?"

"Those are put there so that you can identify the basic value of the food. For instance, square is for proteins and circle for sweets, but don't worry for now, I will show you and pretty soon your implants will kick in and you will know what to do."

"Will you choose something for me?"

She touched several of the shapes and in a few minutes the top part of the table lowered about 30 centimeters. It was replaced by another countertop which had the food, drinks, silverware, and other things I couldn't recognize. On the upper center part of the table there were also three-dimensional pictures of people. Then the countertop rolled up to its original height and Norina said,

"Well, Nick, start eating and see what you think." I started with the square looking things which tasted like beef. Later Norina told me that they were composed of sea proteins.

It was a wonderful day and Norina tried her best to make my first day in this unknown world an informative and pleasant one. It was beginning to get dark. The sky looked clean as the day gave way to dusk. It was difficult for me to believe that if you were exposed for only one hour outside the biosphere, you would be sick from radiation. That was their biggest problem as I was soon to find out.

Norina said it was time to go home and I was wondering where home would be; certainly not back at the hospital. Norina set the automatic pilot on the magneto traveling about ten meters above the ground; other magnetos were traveling the same direction and within one meter of each other, but according to Norina they seldom collided. Every so often I could hear the rhythmic whooshing of the magnetos going the other way like the sound of a passing train. We were both tired. It had been my first day out in a world totally unknown to me, and although my implants started to work, I still had a lot of adjustments to make.

There were those quiet moments when my mind floated back to my past life, my world, my family – were they starting to worry about me being late? Or was I not late yet? Norina said in time-travel even a split second could be the difference in years back there. How confusing. Anyway my being here for two weeks was a lot of time away from my loved ones. I found myself very lonely and unhappy. My face must have shown my inner thoughts because Norina started to talk again.

"Nick, you are going to like your new quarters. You are going to be among astrophysicists so you will have a lot to talk about."

"Where are we going?"

"We are going to the North West University and you are going to have your own place for a change."

"Do they know who I am?"

"Of course not, and even if you told them the truth, they wouldn't believe you."

"What am I to tell them?"

"All in good time, Nick. By tomorrow your implants will tell you who you are supposed to be and what to do in

Project Anastrophe

your new environment." The magneto started to elevate to about one hundred meters. It went higher than the top of the building and then slowly came down and an elevator moved us horizontally for twenty meters or so, then another elevator moved us downward and horizontally again and finally parked. We took the escalator to the lobby and both went to the front desk where a pleasant robot girl welcomed us.

"Hi Norina, hi Nick, welcome to our city. Nick, your room is fixed and ready for you it's number 1250 North."

"Thank you."

"You're not going to drop me here just like that; you are going to see my place, aren't you?"

"Yes of course, Nick." The elevator was more like a living room than a cubicle, it had windows all around and you could clearly see from three sides of it. It went up over three hundred floors according to Norina. My room was a spacious apartment consisting of one large room which could be changed as needed. You just had to push a button. Presently it was a living room and it looked comfortable. Norina seemed to know her way around. She pushed a button and part of the wall moved backwards turned around and became a bar with counter top and stools. It then moved forward about one meter into the living room. It was quite a metamorphosis.

"Nick, would you like a drink?"

"Yes, I would."

"And what will you have?"

"A glass of red wine will do it for me," I said. We sat down by the bar and she started to explain the reason why I was here. She said this apartment was equipped with the latest security gear available, and that I had to be careful because I was in great danger.

"I am in great danger--but why?"

"Nick, I think for tonight that's all you need to know. Tomorrow I will tell you more about it, I promise."

Chapter 3

The Conspirators

"Sit down and shut your mouth. I don't want to be bothered when I am thinking," said Nephus to Zakov.

Nephus had a lot on his mind tonight; to begin with he had to come up with a solution to a problem that had been bothering him lately.

Nephus's whole life had been a problem since he was a four year old about to receive his implants. His parents, Dr. Milton J. Northmount and Dr. Marie Northmount, both geneticists, decided to implant him with their latest version.

Project Anastrophe

Their intention was good and if it had worked, it would have given little Nephus superior intelligence which would have put him well ahead of any other child his age. But something went wrong. While Nephus was above average, the implant damaged part of his nervous system and he became moody and extremely agitated. His parents were heartbroken and did all they could. A visit to a psychiatrist, a good friend of theirs, explained the extent of the damage the implant had caused.

"Moodiness and agitation are part of what we call delirium. In the future, and especially in his teen-age years, when his hormones kick in, he will experience hallucinations, unusual excitement, and psycho-sensory impairment. But there is a lot we can do to minimize the effect of these symptoms to the point that he will feel almost normal."

And that was the key phrase, "almost normal." He is now thirty-five years old, tall and handsome with dark hair and brown eyes, and an easy way with women. However his bad temper has put him on the wrong side of the law. Because of his hidden psychological problems, he has very few friends who are willing to put up with him, and most of them are on the wrong side of the law too.

Zakov, one of his friends, comes from Epsylon Bio. Zakov has no problem with his implants. He was taken away from his parents at a very early age and grew up in various institutions. His parents were members of the infamous "Damos Group" who were involved in psychedelic drugs. They were eventually apprehended and sent to a colony on Mars for rehabilitation. Zakov loves Nephus and he'll do a lot to be his friend.

The message came directly from the "Number One", the richest and most dangerous man in the underground world. He came to Nephus as a hologram on a private secured channel. What he told him was not everyday business talk, this was different. Mr. Narkilos, or Narky, as he was known to most underworld people, wanted Nephus to kidnap a scientist, name and place to be given later, if he took the contract.

"Christ, this is different; kidnapping a scientist? We have never done this before, and why me? Surely there are other guys who have done this sort of thing and they are much better than I. He knows that my specialty is in altering robots. That's all I do and I am one of the best deprogrammers."

"Zakov, where are you?"

"Right here, Nephus."

"If Darna calls in, tell her I am busy and don't want to be bothered tonight."

"Sure thing, Nephus."

"Mr. Narkilos, there is an incoming hologram on the private channel, do you wish to see it?"

"Who is it?"

"It is Mr. Nephus, sir."

"Transfer it to my office!"

"Yes, sir."

"And Prito!"

"Yes, sir."

"Have you charged yourself for tonight?"

"Yes, sir, I have and I will be fully operational for ten hours and twenty-two minutes."

"I want you to record and file the conversation between Nephus and me."

"Yes, sir."

"Well, Nephus, have you decided?"

"Not quite, Narky. I have a few questions to ask you first."

"O.K. I am listening. What do you want to know?"

Project Anastrophe

"Narky, you know that I like you and I am always here for you, but I don't do kidnapping. You know very well robots are my specialty, so why me? There are other guys who can do a much better job."

"Nephus, that's a legitimate question and I would have been very disappointed if you accepted this contract without asking. You see, if I were to give this contract to a kidnapper, that's where the police would look first, isn't that right?"

"I suppose so, but I still need to know more about this scientist and I will need lots of help."

"No problem there. Tomorrow I am going to send someone to help you with this, just don't worry about it, Nephus, everything is going to be all right."

Back home, Back in time

"Hi, Jim, this is Tasula, is Nick there?"

"No, is he supposed to be here?"

"Well, I don't know where he is. He should have been home at 1:00 p.m., it's now past 4:00 and he is not here yet."

"Hold on a minute, I am going to talk to Duvak, he just came in, maybe he saw him out there. Tasula, if you give me a few minutes I'll go and talk to him and see if he has seen Nick out on the water. I'll call you back."

"O.K., Jim, I'll wait until you call me before I call the police."

"I'll call you as soon as possible."

"Duvak, did you by any chance see Nick?"

"Yes, I saw him at about nine o'clock by the big bell and I asked him how many fish he had caught, and he said nothing yet and he was fixing to head home soon."

"Well from what I hear, he was supposed to be back home by one o'clock in the afternoon and he hasn't shown up yet. I am going to check with Tasula to find out if he is home by now and if he isn't, I am going to call the Coast Guard. Anyway thanks a lot, Duvak."

"No problem. Let me know if I can be of any help."

"Tasula, this is Jim from the marina."

"Hi, Jim, did you find him?"

"No, but I talked to Duvak and he said that he talked to him this morning at about nine o'clock and Nick told him that he was going to be heading home pretty soon."

"Do you think I should call the police?"

"No, I think this is more of a Coast Guard matter than a case for the police, and if you don't mind I'll call them right now."

"Go ahead, Jim, and I'll be there pretty soon."

"My name is Bill Miller, and I am with the Coast Guard are you Duvak?"

"Yes, sir."

"You said you saw Nick at about nine o'clock; is that right, sir?"

"Yeah, that's about right."

"Anything you wish to add to it, sir?"

"He looked a little disappointed that he didn't catch any fish and he said he was heading home."

"Did he look drunk to you?"

"No, he looked fine to me."

"Are you close friends with Nick?"

"We are neighbors."

"Thank you very much, sir."

"You are welcome--anytime."

Project Anastrophe

"I see a small white boat beached on a sand bar about half a mile north-west of the bell."

"Roger, Bill. We will send someone right away. Stay on the target--out for now."

"I'm on it, sir."

"It looks as if it's been here for a while, wouldn't you say?"

"It looks like it, but where is Nick?"

"I don't know. He could be anywhere."

"Maybe he drank too much, fell overboard and drowned."

"No, there is a six pack of beer here untouched. However he drank some of the coffee, other than that everything looks fine."

"It's getting to be too dark and they are going to have a hard time finding him even with the helicopter."

"Well, there is always tomorrow."

"I guess so." Next morning two helicopters searched the area along with the Coast Guard and many private boats. They searched all day and well into the night but could not find Nick anywhere. They continued for the next two days and finally stopped. It was assumed that Nick most likely fell overboard and drowned. By now the powerful currents would have taken him half way out into the Pacific.

"Mother, you can go now, I'll be O.K. I have to deal with Nick's disappearance on my own."

"Oh no, honey, I can't leave you like this. You've been crying too much lately and you are going to get sick. Think of your children, they suffer too. You just have to look forward and try to forget a little bit. Why don't you all come with us out to our country house for a few days? It'll do you good."

George Karnikis

"Mother, I told you, I am feeling a lot better. I just want to be left alone for a while. Is that asking too much?"

"O.K. honey, but I'll be checking on you, O.K.? Don't forget I am your mother."

Back to the Future

Norina turned on some soft music and brought me an empty glass and a bottle of water. She also brought what appeared to be a box of candies. When I asked what they were she said they were concentrated wine cubes. I asked her how many cubes I was supposed to mix in, and she said,

"Think of mixing wine, and your implants will tell you how to go about it." It was then for the first time, that I made use of my implants. I simply asked myself how I was supposed to mix dry wine with water and the directions came to me as though I had known it all along. All I had to do was to recall my thought, and before I knew it, I was mixing my wine to my liking. Norina looked at me with her beautiful blue eyes smiling and said,

"I told you, it wouldn't take too long before you made use of your implants, didn't I?"

It was at that moment that I noticed what a beautiful woman she was. The light bathed her golden curly hair. She had that silent eloquence that attracts most men. She could easily rival Marilyn Monroe five hundred and fifty years ago. But Norina was not an actress; she looked official and very sophisticated. Did she have a boy friend? I dare not ask yet anyway. The music was quite different from what I had heard back in my world. It penetrated the whole nervous system and made one feel very relaxed. Norina pulled a chair closer to me and started to tell me my schedule for tomorrow. She said,

"You are going to be among other scientists and you are

Project Anastrophe

going to be very interested in the subjects they will be discussing." She was talking and I was listening, when I realized we were looking at one another in a different way.

The next day was beautiful and sunny; students hurried in and out of the North West Progressive University. The lawns were green and luscious, bordered by roses of brilliant color. It was so hard for me to believe that all this was contained within a biosphere controlled artificially. I walked slowly towards the university enjoying the scenery and the beautiful flowers. Norina was waiting for me at the entrance of the cafeteria and she suggested the kind of breakfast I should have. We started to talk about the meeting that was going to take place in an hour's time.

"Nick, you need to remember not to tell them who you really are. Always consult your implants; they will remind you what you are here in this place and time."

"But Norina, even if I were to tell them who I really am they wouldn't believe me. By the way, who are those two guys at that table? They seem to follow me wherever I go, or is it my imagination?"

"Those guys are your guards; they are assigned to keep you safe, Nick. Just let them do their job."

Our breakfast came from within the table, the top opened and a small tray rose up with the food. It didn't look anything like what I would call a "slow cooked" breakfast, it looked unnatural but must have been very nutritious otherwise they wouldn't have offered it. My plate had what appeared to be five sticks about three inches long and a bunch of grapes only they were not grapes. Each "grape" was filled with a different kind of juice and it melted in my mouth. Each stick contained the necessary proteins, carbohydrates and other nutrients. They all tasted good, and the coffee was exactly as I liked it, with cream and sweetening in the correct proportions.

George Karnikis

I asked Norina how they knew how I liked my coffee. She said,

"Your implants told them. Your implants also know if you have a medical deficiency and will arrange the appropriate diet for you."

The room was full of people. My problem was that I couldn't tell the difference between the robots and the real people, but my implants could tell the difference. I would have been lost without them. I asked Norina,

"Why are they bringing their robots with them; what's the use of bringing them here?"

"Well, they are very important; they will take notes and advise the humans on all kinds of subjects. They were called 'secretaries' in your time."

"I guess that makes sense." The robots were hurrying back and forth doing all the preparatory work before the start of the conference. Norina and I sat in the front row. She was talking to someone on her three-D holophone. I looked around to see if my "friends" were close by and sure enough, they were behind me. According to my implants, one was a robot and the other was a human. One of the robots made a brief announcement, then he introduced the first speaker.

"Ladies and gentlemen, thank you for coming to our second meeting. My name is George Dylos. Our last meeting was held on a satellite. At the time it was important to do that as a precaution to keep people from knowing too much about radiation poisoning. Now it's common knowledge. We have nothing to hide, and all are welcome to contribute in any way they can towards finding a solution. We have received all your papers and we have studied them thoroughly. Although there are some good ideas, we haven't yet found the panacea."

Project Anastrophe

The meeting went on for two hours. There were many new ideas introduced from states all over the world. It was amazing to me to see those robots speaking eloquently and often better than their owners. They had all the necessary information at their finger tips, and very few humans actually got up to say anything at all. The meeting was winding down when Norina tapped my hand and said,

"Now is our time."

I said,

"You have to be kidding."

"Not at all, Nick. We are going to talk, but not here in this room, in Dr. Dylos's office."

"But why didn't you tell me so I could be prepared?"

"We had to keep it secret until we came here, Nick."

"What do they expect me to say, Norina?"

"Nothing, Nick. For the time being, just listen to what Dr. Dylos has to say and then the two of us will talk about it before you answer him."

After a few minutes the last speaker finished and the people started walking out of the room. Norina again tapped my hand and said,

"Nick, I think it's time for us to go see Dr. Dylos."

"And where are we going, if I may ask?"

"Not too far, it's within the building."

We got up and started to go towards the exit. The human and the robot were right behind us until we reached Dr. Dylos's office. He seemed a pleasant, courteous man. He asked us to sit down, looked at me and said,

"Nick, I know all about you, so you can talk to me just as you talk to Norina."

I looked at Norina mechanically not knowing how to react. She said,

"It's O.K., Nick, Dr. Dylos does know who you really are, so go ahead and speak freely."

George Karnikis

I felt better right away, but I wish she had told me about this meeting before. I trusted that she must know what she was doing. Dr. Dylos was a slender man with thinning gray hair, brown eyes, and bushy eye brows. He was in his late sixties and didn't look well. I felt at ease with him right away.

"Nick, first of all let me tell you how sorry I am about your being here away from your family and friends five hundred years in the future in a world which must be very strange for you.

As you know, it is our fault that you are here. Norina must have told you by now that we are trying hard to send you back home, but it is very difficult to do. However there is another reason I asked Norina to bring you to my office. In the last two hours several of our best scientists have been discussing different ways to remedy the radiation that's making millions of people sick, including you. But in your case, you have been cured. As the radiation poisoning progresses, it becomes more difficult to treat and eventually it will kill us all."

"I am puzzled, Dr. Dylos, as to why you are telling me all this, when you know very well there is nothing I can do to help you."

"But you can, Nick, or at least we think you can."

"Now I am really puzzled. How can I, five hundred years from the past, with my limited knowledge, help you when your technology is so much superior to ours?"

"Nick, what we would like you to do for us does not require technology or anything like that. But it will require you to be at the right time and place."

"I don't understand. It seems to me that I am in the wrong place and at the wrong time; please explain."

"As you can see we are at an impasse. We need to do something before this radiation gets any worse. Here is how

Project Anastrophe

you can help us. We will send you home at exactly the same time and place you were picked up. Once you are home safe and sound, then you can begin to help us."

"And how am I supposed to help you from way back there?"

"All in good time, Nick, but do you want to help us?"

"Of course I do, just show me how. If you send me back home that's the least I can do for you."

"Nick, we have had scientists working to find a way to send you home ever since you came here. Right now all you need to do is relax and take it easy, let us work on this problem and we will let you know in due time. Norina will be in close contact with you for the foreseeable future."

It was getting to be late afternoon. Norina and I went straight to the restaurant again. I was itching to find out how I was going to help from back home.

"Norina, is there any way you can tell me when I am going back and how I am supposed to help you?"

"I don't have any idea and I don't think they do either at this time, but even if they did know they wouldn't tell me. Trust me, when the time comes they will tell us."

I was beginning to enjoy the good food and Norina's company. I knew that I was some kind of a novelty to Norina and to the scientific world, at least to those few who knew about me. I liked that, but I was very lonely and Norina was the only person who kept my sanity in check.

"Nick, your robot lady is going to come here in a few minutes; she is going to give us a ride back to my home where you will meet my robot friend Ner."

"That sounds great. I have wanted to meet Ner. From what I hear he is very intelligent and up to date with the latest technology."

"That's precisely the reason we are going to my place.

Ner needs to re-program your lady robot. By the way, have you thought of a name for her?"

"I haven't thought about it at all."

"Well now is the time, Nick. Think of a name and Ner will incorporate it into her programming."

"Why do I have to give her a name at all? After all she is only a robot."

"You don't have to name her, but she will not like it."

"Maybe Ner will help me pick out a name for my lady robot, what do you think?"

"If that's what you want, Nick, that would be fine with me too." The dinner was wonderful and I was starting to ask questions about Norina's life. It took her a while to loosen up but finally she did. She began to talk about her early life. Her father was an exometallurgist on Mars and that's where she spent most of her young life. Then the family moved back to Earth and she and her brother Danon continued their education. She went to the state of England where she studied at Oxford University and earned her Ph.D. in astronomy. She was telling me about her love life there when we were interrupted by a beautiful young lady.

"Hi, Nick, hi Norina, I am here to give you a ride to your place, are you ready?"

"Yes we are," said Norina.

"Nick, we will continue our conversation at another time, O.K.?"

"I would be most interested to hear the rest of your story, Norina."

I knew I had seen this lady robot before, but now she had changed. She looked more human. Now I had to find an appropriate name for this lovely lady robot. She escorted us to what appeared to be a brand new magneto. The upper half was all plastic or something like that; the lower part was some kind of composite.

Project Anastrophe

Lady robot kept quiet all the while she was driving the magneto. Norina and I sat in the back. I took her hand in mine and squeezed it gently, she did likewise. We held hands for a while, then she leaned her head against my shoulder. Lady robot kept quiet all the way as though she wasn't there. The magneto flew up to the roof of the building as usual and then we took the escalator, then the elevator, and finally the hallway to Norina's apartment. Although lady robot had never been there, she knew the way as if it were her own place. Ner was at the door to meet us.

"Welcome, Miss Norina--Nick. Nice to meet you 2501c2f."

"Nice to meet you too, Ner."

"Miss Norina, with your permission I would like to start programming 2501c2f as soon as possible for security reasons."

"Yes of course, Ner, go ahead."

"Could I offer you anything before I start the programming?"

"I will take care of that, thank you Ner, but let me know when you're finished."

"Yes of course, Miss Norina."

"Come on, Nick, let's have something to drink. We had quite a day--would you like your usual wine?"

"Yes, I would like that a lot thank you, Norina."

"Well Nick, pretty soon Ner is going to come and ask you what name you are going to give to the lady robot. Have you thought of one?"

"Yes, I think I have a name. It's going to be Vrima. What do you think?"

"Any special meaning about this name?"

"Not really, I just think this name goes well with her personality."

"Well Nick, if that's what you like, we had better tell Ner. He would like to put her name into the programming. Go ahead and call her."

Lady Robot came in right away. I asked her to sit down and then told her that I had a name for her. She got very excited and waited anxiously to hear her first name ever.

"I have decided to call you Vrima, but if you don't like it, please say so and I'll try to think of another name for you."

"I love the name Vrima. It's beautiful--thank you, thank you so much, Nick. It's the nicest thing for me to have a name rather than a number, thank you."

"Congratulations, Vrima, I think it's a beautiful name."

"Thank you, Norina, I love my name."

"Well, Vrima, you can go and tell Ner."

"Yes of course, Nick, I will go right away-- thank you."

"Norina, it's so hard for me to see a good looking woman like Vrima and to think she is an artificial being made of thousands of silicon chips and countless electronic components."

"Actually she is made of seventy-five percent silicon and twenty-five percent carbon matter; the same carbon you and I have."

"Really, that's hard to believe, and where is the biological part of it?"

"Mostly in the spine, but some in the brain area too."

She handed me the glass of wine just as I liked it and then she turned on the same music she had played in my apartment. It makes you feel as if you have taken some kind of powerful drug. I was looking at her room and couldn't help but notice how different this room is from the ones back home. For one thing this room changes according to one's needs. At this time it's a living room, but by pushing the appropriate button it can change to an office or

Project Anastrophe

kitchen. The walls turn around or go up or down and in case of a living room it morphs into a wall with chairs attached to it, and from the floor a bar counter arises with all its accoutrements. I was absorbed in my thoughts when Norina tapped lightly on my shoulder.

"Do you want to dance?"

"I'd love to, but I wouldn't know how to dance to this kind of music."

"I'll teach you--get up!"

I did, but we didn't dance much, we stood there moving rhythmically with the music. We looked at each other for a long time and we both knew we were very much in love. We felt that sweet warm feeling, and then we kissed and kissed again and again, with that pathos that only young bodies can produce. We walked slowly to her bedroom holding hands. We closed the door and began to undress slowly. Her body was so beautiful; I could hardly wait to touch her. We made love again and again all through the night until we were both exhausted and fell into a deep sweet sleep.

Vrima was as happy as any robot could possibly be. She had been given a human name; no more numbers and letters in between. The nicest thing of all was that her name had been given to her by Nick, her handsome owner. Ner was waiting for her in his office down the hall. He knew what to do. He had programmed many robots of the latest generation; Vrima was just another one of them.

"Come in, Vrima. Sit down and we will start right away, unless you wish to wait a little while."

"Not at all, Ner, I am eager to start as soon as you are ready."

"Very well then, please sit down." Ner started with

slow, precise movements, he had to be very careful with Vrima because of the human brain matter her body contained. Half of her programming was in twenty-five percent of her brain. An artificial heart was pumping blood into that portion of her body. Ner entered her name. She was now officially "Vrima" and would remain with this name until she was irretrievably damaged or discontinued. He entered the code number that had been cryptically given to him only a few minutes before via a secured channel from the ministry of defense.

Vrima would never know her code number just as he didn't know his own. The code numbers were kept within a master computer controlled only by humans. Humans could switch off any or all robots anywhere on the planet at will. THAT WAS THE CARDINAL RULE.

"Vrima, this is going to take a while. Would you like to go on a charge /sleep mode or would you rather go on charge/awake mode?"

"I would rather stay awake and talk to you if that's O.K."

"That's quite all right with me, Vrima."

"It never ceases to amaze me what they have done with your generation. Your model has the latest technology and I wish I had it."

"But you can upgrade your programming to match mine at your next checkup, right?"

"Not quite, Vrima. You are twenty-five percent carbonized, I am only eighteen percent. You are seven percent more human than I am, and as you know, once you get your brain matter, it becomes you and it cannot be altered in any way, unless there is a specific and important reason."

"But your programming is far superior to mine, isn't it?"

"That is true, but you are more human, and for that I envy you."

Project Anastrophe

While Ner was talking to Vrima he opened the small portal on the lower part of her back, and as he was doing that he could see and feel the texture and the smoothness of her artificial skin. Once he opened the portal he had control of her vital signs and a maze of controls with which he would work to program her. Ner was trained to do this kind of work and he was good at it.

Ner was at a point where he had to concentrate on what he was doing. He told her that as part of the programming she would now have to go into sleep mode. Ner worked slowly and methodically. He started by adjusting her oscilloscope to contain x-ray vision. Next he calibrated her linear and analogical parameters, and then he enhanced her compatible temperature sensors. He enhanced her hydraulics and electric drives. And then he entered the two last and most important programs; first, all the information pertaining to Nick's implants, history, and the role he had to play here and back in his time and place. Second he installed "Asimov's three Laws." (2) (Isaac Asimov was a Russian-born American writer of the Twentieth Century, 1920-1992. He was esteemed for his science fiction and for his popular works in all branches of science. His rules read as follows: (1) a robot must not injure, or allow the injury of a human being; or through inaction allow a human being to come to harm. (2) A robot must obey all orders of humans, except when to do so would contradict the first law. (3) A robot must protect itself except when to do so would contradict the first or second law). To that Ner added a fourth rule that read: when the human in danger was Nick, Vrima would do anything possible to save his life, even though it might endanger other humans or her own life. The last thing he did was to delete Vrima's code number from his own memory.

"Vrima, you may get up, you are now a very powerful robot-woman."

"Thank you, Ner, I do feel stronger, and very important. I had better get acquainted with my new files and my new personality."

"That would be an excellent idea, Vrima."

The Conspirators

"Nephus, are you there?"
"What's up, Zakov?"
"Lavoutis is at the door, should I let him in?"
"Yes, let him in, it's all right."
"Hi, Nephus."
"Hi Lavoutis, what can I do for you?"
"I guess what you can do for Narky is more to the point, Nephus."
"Spit it out, Lavoutis. Don't beat around the bush, you know I hate that stuff."
"Okay, okay, man, don't go berserk on me now. Narky sent me; he said I am supposed to do a job for you, that's all."
"Zakov, take him out of here and I don't want to see him until I say so, understand?"
"Yes, Nephus, got it."
"Come with me, Lavoutis."
"Boy he sounds cranky, what's wrong with him?"
"I guess he has too much on his mind. You want one of these?"
"Now you're talking. I haven't had one of these candies in a coon's age. Can I have two?"
"This is strong stuff. One of them will give you the trip of your life."

Nephus was examining Lavoutis' record and he wasn't happy with what he found.

Project Anastrophe

Lavoutis was born in Z-BIO in 2472. His implants had been altered because of bad behavior. He had done two years in behavior correction and therapy on Mars. He was street smart and dangerous with normal implants, and must report daily to authorities.

"Ha! A charmer, I can't understand why he sent me this bad apple. How am I supposed to do a good job with people like this?"

"Zakov!"

"Do you want me in there, Nephus?"

"Yeah, I need you. Where is Lavoutis?"

"I gave him one of those special candies and he is in "la la land" for the time being. Do you want him to come now?"

"No, he is fine where you put him."

"So what can I do for you, Nephus?"

"What do you know about Lavoutis?"

"He is one of the best when it comes to sabotage, but he has to have his implants normalized."

"Now I see why Narky sent him to me."

"Christ, if I correct his implants he'll be able to help us, but he may also get us in trouble and blow the whole thing."

"Not if he's with me all the time. I don't think he can get too far."

"If you lose him, you're dead meat."

"I know it; you don't need to remind me about that, Nephus."

"And Zakov, ask Darna to come here as soon as possible, will you?"

"Right away, Nephus."

Nephus had a plan in mind but to execute it would be difficult.

It was a lot harder to depend on other people to do their

job right and especially if you couldn't trust them. He must do a more thorough investigation of all the participants as soon as possible.

Darna was one of those girls who had expensive taste in clothes, food and wine. She was a pricey chick, and for that she needed credits. A beautiful girl in her mid-twenties, Darna was a little under two meters with slender, long legs and a figure that had all the right proportions. She had long shiny black hair, dark brown eyes, and a mouthful of beautiful teeth that looked like pearls. She was beautiful and she knew it. But that in itself wouldn't help.

She was working as a holographic technician with one of the biggest broadcasting companies and the credits she earned weren't enough for her expensive life style. That's where Nephus came in. He had the money and the looks; true he was strange and difficult and demanding at times, but that came with the male species anyway, he was just a bit weirder than the average Joe.

Darna was at work when she got the message from Zakov. He said it was important to go see Nephus as soon as possible. This must be different because he seldom called her at work. It was almost quitting time anyway, and she needed to stop by her apartment before she went to see him.

Most of the humans were getting ready for the usual four day weekend. The robots would take over from now on; in fact robots could do almost everything except detail work and final decisions. That would not change in the future no matter how much better the robots became. Darna got into her magneto and within minutes she was in her apartment. Unlike Norina's which was practical and had little décor, Darna's apartment was decorated with expensive furniture and all the latest gadgetry. She loved her surroundings and frequently had parties and friends staying overnight. Norina, on the other hand, had very few friends coming to her apartment and could hardly wait to be through with her contract and go home to her family.

Darna had had a hard week and was tired; she hoped this evening would be dinner and perhaps some fun too.

As soon as she arrived at Nephus' place, Zakov took her straight to his office. Nephus was deep in thought and barely noticed them. Zakov gently cleared his throat to get his attention, and it worked. He looked at them sharply, and then he said,

"She can stay--you go." Darna sat on the couch, looking at her holographic com, reading her messages. Finally Nephus said,

"How are you doing, sweetheart?"

"I am fine, but starving. What's up anyway?"

"Well, why don't we go to Liakos and talk about it over dinner?"

"That sounds like an excellent idea to me."

"You look beautiful tonight."

"Thanks, but I am tired."

"What's that suppose to mean?"

"It means exactly what I said, I am tired."

"I had big plans for tonight, you know?"

"Oh well, I think I'll be all right by then."

"Great, let's go." Liakos was the kind of restaurant frequented by privileged people, as well as those of the underworld.

"Are you going to have your usual?"

"Yes please." Nephus pushed the bar button and a round table about a meter in diameter came up between them. He picked up a green cup and put into it a yellow, red, and an orange cube, then he poured liquid from one of three bottles, mixed it and gave it to Darna. He fixed his own drink by using different colored cubes.

With her favorite drink in hand Darna felt relaxed, but she began to wonder what was going on with Nephus and why he was being so sweet to her. Darna was suspicious. She knew he wanted a favor but wondered what it would be. They ordered and then he came right to the point.

"Well Darna, I suppose you would like to know why I wanted to see you tonight, right?"

"Yeah, and it better be important."

"Narky has asked me to do something I have never done before. I tried to wiggle out of it but no luck. He says he needs my expertise in robotics and wants me to do the job."

"And where do I fit in all this?"

"I need you to use your charm on a guard to get him away from his post and thereby save his life."

"What do you mean save his life?"

"Well if you don't do it we will have to kill him, it's as simple as that."

"Oh dear, I don't like that at all."

"Well Darna, you know me, I don't like killing anybody, that's why I need your help."

"So you want me to seduce him?"

"Call it what you wish, all I want is to have him away for a little while."

"I suppose better seduced than dead."

"That's my girl, you can do it, and I know you can do it well."

"Who is this man you want out of the way? And why me for God's sake? Get those professional girls; they can do a far better job than I."

"I don't trust them."

"You know you're abusing our friendship, don't you?"

"Oh Darna, it's just one time and I swear I'll never ask you to do anything like this again."

"O.K. but I am scared."

"Don't be, everything is going to be all right, you'll see. Let's eat now."

"What's the rest of the story, is it a robbery?"

"Darna, you know me better than that. I am not a thief; I am a con artist and a good one too."

"Then what is it?"

"At this time the less you know, the better it's going to be for both of us."

As soon as dinner arrived, their conversation changed to more superficial matters. They stayed for the late show which Darna always loved, and they forgot the main reason they had come. After the show was over they went as always to Darna's apartment where they made love. Nephus got up early as usual and went home; Darna slept late, until afternoon.

"Christ, Zakov, how long have I been here?"

"Welcome back, Lavoutis. You slept all through the night; I guess you really got doped."

"I guess I must have. Where is Nephus?"

"Nephus is coming sometime this morning. Come and have some breakfast."

"That'll be nice, I am hungry."

"Now listen to me, Lavoutis. Nephus is going to temporarily correct your implants so you can do the job right, but from that minute on, you become my responsibility. One wrong move and you are dead, do you understand?"

"Don't worry; I am here to do the job."

"Well, let's say that I know you too well and I can't afford to trust you, O.K.?"

"O.K. man I'll behave, you'll see."

A message from Nephus projected on the middle of their table and stopped their conversation abruptly.

"Zakov, make sure Lavoutis doesn't go away before I come back."

"Nephus, Lavoutis has to report to the police in person today."

"Then go with him and make sure he is back here when he is done."

"I'll make sure of that, Nephus. Should I know where you are going?"

"I am going to see Narky; I have business to discuss with him."

"Narky, Nephus is at the door, shall I let him in?"

"Yeah, let him in." Nephus spoke first; he was calm and sure of himself.

"Narky, if you want me to do this job you have to let me in on the whole story. Who is this scientist, and why do we need to kidnap him?"

"I don't know much myself, all I know is that his name is Nick Papas and he is about to do something that some people don't want him to do. Christ, Nephus, all we have to do is: find this guy, kidnap him, and take him over to them and that's it. I know one thing for sure and that is; if we don't do this job we are out of here, we are history, you got that?"

"That important, eh?"

"That important."

"Then I have a few things I need from you, Narky."

"You name it, Nephus, and you'll have it as soon as possible, no problem."

"I want all the names of the people who are going to help me with this job, and no more surprises like the Lavoutis guy you sent me yesterday. He is a bad apple and you know it. Also I need credits, and I mean right now."

"O.K., I'll transfer fifty percent of your credits to your

account now, and you'll get the rest of them when the job is done, fair enough?"
"That's O.K."

The Abduction

I was falling into a routine and liking it too. Every morning Vrima would prepare my breakfast just as I wanted it and then she read my schedule for the day. She was programmed to be smart, quick and ready to protect me at all costs. She would drive me to the university every day and make sure that the guards were there to take over. She would come back again at the scheduled time to pick me up. Norina and I often went to have dinner at our favorite restaurant but sometimes she cooked at home and I frequently stayed overnight. Vrima also stayed overnight and talked to Ner for hours. I wondered what robots talked about.

Very often I fell into depression thinking about the life I had left behind; my family, and especially the children and Tasula my wife. Did she miss me? Did she get married again? And how long did she live? Even if she lived to be a hundred, she died four hundred and thirty years ago. And the children must have died approximately four hundred years ago. And what about their descendants? That would make it twenty-five generations to this time. I should inquire and find out if any of the Papases are around in this area; surely they must have had children somewhere along the line.

At other times I would be very busy at the university with so many new things for me to learn. The implants helped me tremendously with so much information readily available. I was given my own office in the astrophysics department. Technically I was employed by the university but in actuality I was a government employee. I worked in paleoastrophysics and specifically in the twenty-first century. I worked a lot in the NASA files and even found some of the work I had done when I was there. Those were baby steps in comparison to what they have done today, but it had to start with those small steps to arrive at this super technology. I feel proud that I was able to contribute towards that goal. I had a teacher programmed in my implants and I found myself consulting him all the time.

He was very patient with me and sometimes he would tell me stories from the old Greek philosophers. He would remind me how much they contributed to us all. Because of those implants I was an equal among equals. I was even able to speak the metric language, as they call it, and it is spoken now all over the world. My slight accent could be attributed to some of those who stubbornly spoke English even though English-speaking people had adopted the metric language three hundred years ago.

It felt good to be working again. Actually I was doing exactly the same work I did back in my office five hundred years and seven months ago. The only difference was that I was using very advanced tools. My dictations were done simply by thinking and talking to myself. My implants did the rest; spelling and checking for grammatical mistakes and finally entering into the data bank. Of course I was doing all my writing in English which was automatically translated into metric language. At quitting time Norina would come to pick me up and drive me to our usual restaurant near the campus. This had been a productive day, but I felt somewhat tired and was looking forward to Norina's company. We went directly to the restaurant. Norina wasn't her usual happy self. She seemed nervous and kept looking around.

"Norina, you don't look very happy tonight, did you have a difficult day?"

Project Anastrophe

"Oh, I am fine Nick; it's you that I am worried about."
"Me, but why?"
There wasn't time for Norina to respond. The whole thing happened with lightning speed. It started with the two guards, the human and the robot who had always been with Nick ever since he left the hospital. The two of them were sitting at their table as always keeping an eye on Nick. All of a sudden the robot guard attacked the human guard. The fight lasted long enough to get people's attention. The human guard put up a good fight but in the long run the robot was much stronger and was about to finish him up when out of nowhere Vrima appeared. She knew that the robot guard had been compromised and Nick, her master, was in great danger. She acted quickly.

Ner had programmed Vrima to be lethal in a situation like this, and lethal she was. It was astonishing to see two robots fight. The robot guard fought well but he wasn't a match for Vrima. She told the human guard,

"Go and stand by Nick and shoot to kill anyone who threatens him." Then she fell on the robot like lightning and although she was smaller, she was faster and stronger. She grabbed him by his arms and you could hear the noise their mechanisms made as Vrima tried to twist his forearms from their sockets. As they fought, lasers beamed from their foreheads. There was a metallic clicking and both of the robot's forearms were severed. His light beam kept bombarding Vrima with high intensity radiation but she was able to neutralize it. He was an older model and could not escape his fate; his head split in two and fell.

There wasn't any time to lose. Vrima turned her attention to the humans who were about to abduct Nick. She quickly stunned four of them with a high intensity light beam strong enough to put them out of commission but not to kill. But Nephus was prepared for her; he simply pushed a button on a small unit he held and Vrima was frozen on the spot. He in turn was stunned by Norina who was standing next to Nick. It was Darna who saved the day for Nephus. She quickly stunned both Norina and Nick and then with the help of two others of her group, grabbed Nick and Nephus and left before the police arrived.

Darna had followed her orders to the letter. She had approached the human guard asking for directions. She was dressed in a diaphanous shirt and looked very sexy. When she thought she was close enough, she stunned him. Then using a small unit Nephus had given her she reprogrammed the security code and left. The guard would be out of commission long enough for them to escape through the forbidden zone. They were going as fast as their magneto could go. When they approached the main gate she pushed a button on her hand-held unit and the gate opened in time for them to go through. Then it closed automatically. They kept going behind the main city on streets they were well acquainted with, and finally drove to an obscure underground warehouse.

Ner was the first one to know about the abduction through a secret coded message he had inserted in Vrima's inner noetics. He got busy right away. He already knew where she was because he was cybernetically connected with her at all times. He started to repair the damage and could see that it was an inside job for he himself had programmed her. The only other people who could possibly have entrance to Vrima's noetics would have been the security headquarters.

The first thing he did was to install a firewall and completely block headquarters. Then he temporarily deleted several of her programs and downloaded his own. Now she could function at ninety percent capacity for a while. He was doing all that, while he was driving to the site. Vrima knew her kinetic powers were slower and that she had been compromised, but she could still function well enough. There was a coded message to save Norina at all costs. Her main duty was to save Nick of course, but Nick was nowhere to be found. Norina was lying unconscious along with five others. Vrima knew one of them was a guard on her side; the other four were the ones she had put down. She quickly picked Norina up and hurried to her magneto which started as soon as she got close to it.

She headed for Norina's place and it wasn't long before her senses detected Ner behind her. He asked Vrima how Norina was doing. She answered back that she was unconscious but all her vitals were O.K. All three arrived home a short time after that. Ner laid Norina on a sofa and put a small green crystal on her forehead; it began to pulse with many different colors. Within seconds she was transported to a hospital. That was all Ner could do for his beloved mistress. Now it was up to the hospital.

Vrima was examining her own vital signs when Ner finally came back to her.

"I am grateful for all your help, Ner. The temporary programs you installed helped me immensely, but now I would like my own programs so I can find Nick."

"I have already communicated with the appropriate person at headquarters and I am waiting for clearance. I suggest that we both charge ourselves so that we are better prepared for your programming."

As soon as Darna and the other conspirators were safe at their appointed place, Darna started to administer first aid to Nephus and Nick who were both incapacitated. Transporting them to a hospital was out of the question so she called Narky for advice. He first congratulated Darna for a job well done and told her she had done the right thing to keep them at the warehouse. He said he was sending his own ambulance to pick them up. Within minutes it arrived with specialized robot medics, and took them away. After a few hours, and with the help of the robot medics, both Nephus and Nick were revived, but they had terrible headaches. Nephus drove home where Darna was anxiously waiting for him.

He was very thankful to her for helping to abduct Nick and rescuing him. The next day, after he was sure the rest of his credits were deposited into his account, he and Darna left home for an undisclosed place for a few days.

Nick woke up and found himself locked in a room alone with a huge headache. He had no idea where he was, and for the second time in this place and time he felt afraid for his life. A few minutes later a robot came in and asked him to drink some blue liquid. He assured Nick it would take away his headache which it did almost right away.

"Where am I?"

"I am afraid I can't tell you, Nick, but you are safe here."

That wasn't much encouragement for Nick. The hope of going back home was somehow disappearing with every minute that passed, and despair was setting in.

"God, what do they want from me? I have done nothing to them to be treated like this."

But then he remembered Norina. She had told him that there was security around him twenty-four/ seven and when he asked why, she had said,

"We have big plans for you."

And Norina, my dear Norina what happened to her? Did she survive? They wanted me alive for some reason. Could they have killed her and left her lying out there?

Project Anastrophe

With the headache gone and feeling reasonably well, Nick was trying to find a way out of all this.

Norina found herself in bed, with medics standing all around her. Dr. Dylos was there too. He was waiting for her to recover so he could find out what had happened to Nick. Norina's headache was finally gone and she was well enough to respond to his questions.
"How are you feeling, Norina?"
"I think I am doing well considering what I have gone through."
"Norina, I don't want to tire you, but I do want to ask you a few questions. Are you up to it?"
"Yes, of course."
"Do you remember anything at all?"
"We were having dinner when we noticed that the robot guard attacked the human guard and before long Vrima, Nick's robot, appeared and destroyed the robot and saved the human from certain death. At that moment five men appeared and tried to apprehend Nick but Vrima managed to put down four of them. The fifth one was able to deactivate her with a hand-held unit. I shot him and was about to get Nick out of there when a young woman came in with two more men and shot Nick and me. That's all I remember."
"Your story checks with what we have heard from the bystanders."
"Have you found out where Nick is?"
"No, not yet, but we are trying to get to the bottom of it. You should go home and rest a bit, we will keep you posted."
Ner came and picked Norina up. On the way home he told her how he had saved Vrima and that he was reprogramming her. He also told her that Vrima was able to re-

cord all sequences up to the minute she was de-activated. He said that it was an inside job, and that Vrima was compromised from headquarters.

Vrima was happy to see them both safe at home and she was trying to be useful but Ner told her to go and finish charging her batteries and she immediately did as she was told.

Norina was feeling much better by now but she was worried about Nick. Ner worried for Nick too, but he was doing something about it. As soon as Vrima was fully charged he started to analyze her response actuators all the way to her last cinematic actuations. He studied all the kidnappers including the young woman. They all had blocked their electronic I.D. signatures which made it extremely difficult to identify them. He was able to follow the last few sequences as they unreeled one at a time. Then he had Vrima's fast noetics work on their facial characteristics and then compared them with police records, but no luck. They had done a clean job, much to their credit. However he knew how to find them, and that was a start. Ner zeroed in on the woman's profile and he found she worked for a large media network. Her name was Darna Varnether. Now he really had something to go by.

"O.K. we got him, now what?"
"All in good time, Zita."
"Prito, bring Nick in here."
"Right away, Narky."

Prito brought Nick in and put him in a chair. Around the chair was a flashing red and yellow laser light. Nick knew he couldn't move beyond those lights. Prito moved to the right corner of the room, behind Nick, and stayed there motionless. In addition to Narky, there were seven more people.

Project Anastrophe

There was Zita Thorish, a man in his fifties. He was about 177.8 cm, well dressed with a few extra kilos to show his rich diet, a round face and balding gray hair, black eyes and a hawkish nose. Next was Vougtors Lemek a man in his sixties; 182.88cm, tall, thin with long blond hair, blue eyes, and a graying beard. Next to him was Nazara Fouruga, a woman in her thirties; well proportioned with long black hair and brown eyes. Beside her was Voha Hollanda an older woman with short graying hair, a bony face, shiny blue eyes, and arthritic fingers. The next man was Zolla Trachis, he was in his forties, 182.88 cm, tall, with dark curly hair, brown eyes and a healthy disposition and an athletic body. The last two were the Du Bois brothers, John and Jack; they were twins in their thirties, about 180.34 cm, with blond hair, blue eyes, thin, sharp facial characteristics, and a disagreeable rough disposition.

Although they were all different, they had one thing in common--they were very rich and well known in their biosphere. Narky was the first to speak, directing his questions to Nick.

"Your name is Nick Papas, is that right?"

"That's right!"

"You live in Z-Bio and you teach paleoastrophysics, is that right, Dr. Papas?"

"That's right!"

"Well, I think I know otherwise. In fact you are not from Z-Bio, nor any Bios at all, isn't that right?"

"I don't know what you are talking about, sir!"

"Dr. Papas, let me refresh your memory, and let us not waste anymore time. You have been transported somehow from the twenty-first century to our time, we know a little bit about you, but would like to know much more. Tell us why they brought you here and why they have kept you in secrecy all this time?"

"I don't think you should be asking me. You should be asking the authorities. As far as I know I was brought here by mistake."

"And who are the authorities?"

"I don't know you will have to find that out by yourselves."

"Who are Dr. Dylos and Norina?"

"I have met Dr. Dylos twice, and have no idea who he is. As for Norina, she is my friend."

"Has Dr. Dylos or Norina Anderson told you anything about sending you back home, and have they asked you to do anything for them? You must tell us the truth otherwise you will force us to get it from you in ways that would be very unpleasant for you. Do you understand, Dr. Papas?"

"I told you all I know!"

"Mr. Narky, take Dr. Papas and your robot away and make sure he is kept safe. We will ask for him when we need him."

"Ladies and gentlemen, I am sure you have seen me around, but for those who don't know me, my name is Voutros Lemek and I was invited personally by Mr. Gregory Tyron, who as you probably know, is the president of our Sentunian Club. He asked me to summon you to discuss something that is very important to all of us. You may wonder why we have kidnapped Dr. Papas, and have been asking him all these questions. The answer is simple. This man, without even knowing, it could destroy us financially along with many others like us."

"Yes, Miss Fouruga?"

"I knew scientists had been trying for hundreds of years to travel in time, but I didn't think they had already done it. But if this person was brought here to our time, we should welcome him and show him that we are civilized. We can learn from him about our past."

Project Anastrophe

"Miss Fouruga, I quite agree with you. A man who has come from the 21st century should be welcomed no less than a hero, but there are things we must do before he is sent back to his time, and the authorities are refusing to co-operate with us." First of all, let me apologize for the way Dr. Papas was treated. Mr. Narky was not authorized to talk like that. Now let me explain to all of you, why our financial well-being is at stake here."

Chapter 4

"This is one of the biggest and best hotels on Mars, don't you think, Darna?"

"Oh I love it, Nephus. How long do you think we are going to stay here?"

"How much time did you take off?"

"Ten days."

"Then we should spend most of them here because they are going to be looking for us."

"Do you think they will find us?"

"Oh yes, but I don't want to make it too easy for them."

"What are they going to do to us?"

"Don't worry; I have people in the government to help us."

Project Anastrophe

"I hope you are right, I don't want to spend time in jail."
"Relax, Darna, let's play tourists--O.K.?"

This was one of the best times to visit Mars; the wind storms had calmed down and there was clarity in the air. One could spend hours looking at the natural landscape with its red sand dunes, smooth hills, and high mountains. Here man had created many artificial oases that resembled Earth's biospheres. Anytime people came here, they saw more dwellings. One expected to see biospheres on Mars, but on Earth they didn't look good at all.
 Still wearing her diaphanous nightgown, Darna was about to have a shower, when she accidentally turned the shower head on. Cold water poured on her and she shrieked loudly enough to get Nephus' attention. The nightgown had stuck to her body, revealing her breasts and her lovely curves. Nephus went close, embraced her, and kissed her as tiny drops of water bathed their lips.
 Nephus and Darna went to the hotel's restaurant and ordered drinks and dinner making sure they used the credits Nephus had on Mars. Nephus didn't want the authorities on Earth to know where they were. From where they sat, they could see the starry Martian sky with its two moons: Phobos, nine km. high and Deimos, twenty-three km. high, obeying their eonic journeys. After dinner they stayed to see the late show which wasn't anything to be compared with their favorite one on Earth, but it was enough to make them forget their problems.
 Darna was beginning to like this life-style on Mars, but she knew it wasn't going to last forever. Sooner or later the authorities would find them and despite Nephus' reassurance she was afraid they would both end up in jail.
 "Why did I let myself get into this mess and how do I get out of it?"

Nephus made the best of any situation. This was just another little problem, nothing Narky couldn't take care of. But Darna was something else altogether. She needed to be convinced to stick with it, and to believe that everything would be all right.

Early next morning, Nephus was awakened by a call from Earth. He was told to leave the hotel immediately and go hide at # 5 Mineshaft where people would be waiting to help them.

"Darna, get up!"

"Now what?"

"We need to get out of here right away. I think they know where we are."

"And where are we going?"

"To a mineshaft."

"A mineshaft?"

"Relax; it's not as bad as it sounds."

It wasn't too long before a robot came and picked them up. They all flew in a magneto to #5 Mineshaft. There were some humans and robots waiting for them; all in their protective gear. They went into the shaft and before long Nephus and Darna were comfortable in their room having breakfast brought by a robot belonging to the company.

"Nephus, what do we do now?"

"I suppose we eat our breakfast and wait. I told you Narky would take care of us, didn't I?"

"And how long do you think we need to stay here?"

"I am sure we will be going back to Earth before long because we can hide better there."

As soon as Nourou saw Darna's name on the wanted list; he called Narky to alert him. Nourou was a very well-known chief of police in his area, and he had been on Narky's payroll for many years. In fact, he was put there by

Project Anastrophe

Narky for situations like this. In turn, Narky was on the "big boy's" payroll, and the "big boys and girls" were very much involved in the local government.

Narky called the Du Bois brothers and told them about Darna. It was their advice to move Nephus and Darna to # 5 Mine. The Du Bois owned ten of the biggest mines on Mars, and they threw their weight around on both planets. At any other time, Nourou wouldn't have a problem covering up Nick's kidnapping; but this was different. For one thing, Nick was very well known among his scientist friends. He was the only one working in paleoastrophysics. True, he was from another biosphere and was a newcomer at the University, but he was a pleasant guy and very good at what he was doing. So he was missed by many. But to the few who knew his true identity, it was an entirely different thing. His survival meant not only the survival of their biosphere, but of the entire Earth. Although Nourou didn't know the details about Nick, he could see that he was an important person and didn't want to risk losing his cover. When he called Narky to ask him what to do about this kidnapping, he was told to lay off for a while and to wait for more instructions.

Ner was hard at work trying to repair Vrima, and at the same time find Nick's whereabouts. When Vrima was restored, she began doing detective work to find Nick's abductors. Ner had a pretty good idea who the inside man was; but was surprised to discover the police department was involved too. The first one involved with compromising Vrima's noetics had to be an operator of the main computer. It was common knowledge that no one else could gain entrance to the area where the main computer was.

Ner called Dr. Dylos and told him about Nourou, the chief of police, being involved with Nick's kidnapping. Mr. Norie Sardukos, the one in charge of robot security, had most likely given Vrima's code number to Nephus, who in turn, compromised Vrima.

Dr. Dylos thanked Ner, and shortly after that summoned both Nourou and Sardukos for interrogation. It didn't take long for Dr. Dylos and his interrogators to extract the necessary information from them to find Nephus' and Darna's whereabouts. They had managed to leave their hideout only minutes before the police arrived.

"Nephus, where are we going this time?"

"Relax, Darna, we are going home, back to Earth."

"And where do you think we're going?"

"I don't know, Darna. I already told you Narky will take care of us, just relax."

Somehow Darna wasn't quite sure Narky would take care of them and was trying to think of a way out of this mess. The spaceship made an unscheduled stop on the Moon, where they changed to another of the company's spaceships bound for Earth. They landed on the company's platform, and were whisked away to a huge warehouse. There they were safe for the time being. Darna had a much needed sleep for a few hours, but was awakened by a very intense conversation coming from the next room.

"Narky, I don't want to go to another biosphere, and I am sure Darna doesn't either."

"Well, Nephus, either you are going to another biosphere, or you're going to end up in jail."

"But that wasn't our deal, Narky. You were supposed to take care of us."

"And I am; you just have to go to another biosphere for a while, until we find out who is interfering with our plan."

"Darna is not going to go for it."

"Then you know what to do with her."

"Christ, I thought it would never come to this."

"Nephus, you do it or we'll do it for you."

Project Anastrophe

"No, just let me do it my way when we're away from here."

"Oh God, they are going to kill me, Darna realized in a flash. I have to get out of here—now! But at least he is not going to do it here. I need to convince him to stay a few days longer, until I find a way out."

There was a knock on the door. Darna froze, her heart racing; she had to think quickly but the only thing she could think of was to play sleepy, and it worked. Nephus hesitantly opened the door and stepped in. He walked to her bed and gently touched her head.

"Are you awake, Darna?"

"Now I am." She acted as if she had awakened from a deep sleep.

"I am tired; let me be, what do you want from me?"

"I just need to talk with you for a little bit."

"What about?"

"It's just that we need to get going again for a while, sweetheart."

"Again--we just came here, Nephus, what's going on?"

"The police are on our heels, and Narky thinks it would be a good idea if we went to another biosphere for a while. Get your stuff together, we are going pretty soon."

"I suppose it would be a good idea to get out of here. Narky is right, but let me take a shower and freshen up a bit before we leave."

"O.k., but make it quick."

Darna knew she couldn't use her holo-phone here, but she could use her cryptic business number. A quick look at Nephus assured her he was busy talking to a hologram. So it had to be now; later it would be much more difficult. She placed a call to her manager, turned the shower on, and waited outside the stall. She knew no one would see her here. Finally after a few seconds that felt like hours, Fura, her manager, was on line smiling at her.

"Well Darna, wherever you are, you must be having a good time because we haven't heard from you at all. Enjoying your vacation? And why are you calling on this line? What's up?"

"Fura, listen to me, I'm in great danger and I need help—now! As the signal indicates, I am in a warehouse with Nephus at Northmount, and I am about to be taken away to another biosphere. We are implicated in Nick's abduction. They will kill me because I know too much."

"Oh dear, honey, don't worry, we know exactly where you are and I am going to alert the police."

"No! The police may be implicated in this. You must bypass them."

"O.k., Darna, I know what to do, and help will be on the way."

There were imprints from the holo-phone on her palm from holding it so hard; she was very nervous and she knew it. She wetted her hair, then put a towel over her head, and with another towel around her body, she stepped out and braced herself for what was to come. Nephus was still busy talking. Narky's holographic picture was in the middle of the living room sitting on a chair. Darna went straight to her room and began combing her hair. When Nephus saw Darna on her way to her room, he quickly finished talking to Narky. She could hear him coming to her room, and dropped her towel exposing her body, her breasts were still wet. Nephus knocked gently at the door and came in.

"Feel better, honey?"

"Much better, I am almost done, Nephus." He looked at her as though he was seeing her for the first time; she was truly a beautiful woman. Her long brown hair covered her erect breasts, and he could see her nipples dripping water from her hair. She walked by the window on her way to him, and her slim body reminded him of the Greek statue of Aphrodite rising from an Olympian lake. Nephus thought to himself.

"How can anyone destroy such a beautiful woman?" One look at Nephus, and Darna knew she could delay their departure for a while.

Fura had to act fast to save Darna. She called Dr. Dylos and told him about Darna and Nephus and their whereabouts. She could see that Darna was in big trouble with the law, but the fact that she called and told them where they were, had to count for something. Besides, this was going to be a juicy article worth all the trouble.

Dr. Dylos knew he couldn't trust the police; but had to act quickly before they lost their chance to capture them. He called Ner and gave him all the information needed, then called the governor and told her that the police Department had been compromised. Two of its officers had helped with Nick's kidnapping. Dr. Dylos didn't mention anything in regard to the latest information he had received from Fura. He wasn't sure he could trust the Governor either at this point. He sent a cryptic message to those involved with the plan to send Nick back to the 21st century. Dr. Dylos knew he could trust them, but said nothing over the air. He just told them they had to meet to discus an important matter.

Norina was having her usual early morning breakfast and looking at her schedule for the day; when Ner came in with the news.

"Miss Norina, I have good news for you."

"And what would that be, Ner?"

"Dr. Dylos called and said he knows where Nephus and Darna are."

"Does he know exactly where they are?"

"Not at this point, but it's a good start, don't you think?"

"Indeed it is Ner, thank you."

"You're welcome, Miss Norina. Is there anything else I can do for you?"

"Not at this time Ner, thank you."

Norina was one of the people asked to see Dr. Dylos right away. It all made sense now. She quickly finished her breakfast and was on her way to meet him at the appointed place.

"Thank you all for coming on such short notice. As you know from our previous meeting, Chief of Police Nourou, and Sardukos, the head of Robotics, have been found to be implicated in Nick's abduction and they have both been apprehended. We know now that many important people in the government are involved in this, and unfortunately, they know that we know about them. That makes it very dangerous for us. We need to be careful until we arrest them. Remember, we have the law on our side.

The reason I called you here is that I just got a call from Miss Fura who is working at the T.N.M. Media News. She said she had just had a call from Darna, telling her that she was with Nephus in a warehouse at the Du Bois Brothers Company. I don't need to tell you who they are. She said they were going to take her to another biosphere, and would kill her there because she knew too much. She also said to bypass the police and talk directly with us. Miss Fura promised she would not say anything, at least for a while. So as you can see we need to act quickly to save Miss Darna's life and capture Nephus. That, in turn, will help us find Nick."

The orders to Ner came directly from Dr. Dylos after Norina was on her way to meet him. Dr. Dylos knew that

Project Anastrophe

humans talk under duress; robots destroy themselves rather than submit to interrogations. The orders were to take Vrima and go immediately to the Du Bois Brothers' Company Warehouse #54. Darna and Nephus must not be allowed to leave the area. They must be under surveillance at all times, and must not be hurt. Help was on the way. Ner didn't have to say anything to Vrima; she was in tune with him and had registered the orders Ner had received while she was recharging. Within seconds they were in their magneto driving full speed to their destination. A few minutes later when they arrived at the warehouse, Ner reminded Vrima to set her faiser to "stun only" for humans but "use all means" for robots.

"Ner, I have located both Nephus and Darna. I believe they are in bed making love."

Ner spoke loud enough for Vrima to hear and said,

"Darna is a smart girl."

Vrima spoke likewise and said,

"Darna is a lucky girl."

They both smiled, and immediately became serious and directed their attention to the couple and to the immediate area.

Ner sent a cryptic message to Dr. Dylos. The message read,

"We have arrived at the appointed place; the fugitives are here and alone so far. Please advise. The response came quickly,

"Apprehend them if you can; otherwise wait for help."

Ner had to decide fast. Millions of digitized components performed and executed decisions in his electronic brain every split second and he decided to wait for the most opportune time. He didn't have to wait long.

Darna delayed Nephus as much as she could by making love with him, but even that could not go on forever. She was hoping that some help would have arrived by now. She got up and dressed, then gently tapped him on the shoulder and said,

"I am going to the next room to pack up."
"Make it quick, they will be here any minute now."
"I'll do my best."

On her way there she wondered, "Does he know that I am aware of what is happening? I hope not."

She opened the curtain and looked out, saw the magneto with two people in it but could not tell who they were. A better look and she recognized the robot woman Nephus had put out of commission not too long ago.

"They are here for me, this is my chance, I have to do something now before Narky and the rest of them come." She quickly locked the door, opened the window, and jumped out. Ner saw the opportunity and sprang into action.

"Vrima, go get her now!" It took but a split second and Vrima was next to Darna.

"I am Vrima, and I am here to help you get away. Don't worry, I will not harm you."

Vrima picked Darna up as though she were a child, and ran with her to the magneto.

"Good job, Vrima, now we have to catch Nephus, but I am afraid it will not be easy this time. We must act before his people come to rescue him."

"Miss Darna, is Nephus armed?"

"Yes he is. He also knows how to deactivate you, and he is very good at it."

"Don't worry, this time we are prepared for everything."

"Miss Darna, we can't leave you here alone. We have to beam you away, or sedate you, which do you prefer?"

"I would rather be sedated than beamed."

"You won't feel a thing; you will wake up in the hospital."

"Thank you, Ner."

After she had been sedated, Ner and Vrima went to the warehouse and with their x-ray eyes they could see Nephus looking for Darna. They wasted no time. They were now communicating nonverbally.

"Vrima, have you shielded yourself adequately?"

"Yes, Ner."

"I think we are now ready to apprehend Nephus."

As soon as Nephus realized the robots were in pursuit of him, he knew Darna had been taken away, and he was now fighting for his own safety. Robots were his toys; he knew how to play with them. He quickly shielded himself.

"Ner, I lost him."

"Switch to thermo-locator."

"I got him again, Ner, but he is using deactivating maneuvers."

"I know, but he can't penetrate us this time. Stun him the first chance you get."

"I am in pursuit."

Ner got a message from his magneto,

"I am detecting two magnetos, five hundred meters away, coming in my direction."

"Go into cloaking mode."

"I am now in cloaked mode."

"Stay that way until further notice."

As soon as the magneto received the order; it moved behind the nearest building and became invisible with Darna inside sound asleep. The magnetos drove close to the warehouse and Narky with two other humans, stepped out of the first magneto, and four robots out of the second. One human and one robot stayed outside guarding the building;

while Narky and the other human along with the three remaining robots, went in.

When Ner and Vrima saw they were outnumbered; both went into cloaked mode and waited for more help. Help arrived two minutes later in the form of four police magnetos and one oversized magneto carrying various kinds of weapons. Humans and robots quickly surrounded the big warehouse. There was a short battle with the human and the robot guards at the gate, the human guard was captured without much difficulty, but the robot put up a good fight for a while but eventually was destroyed. Most of the human and robot police went into the warehouse in strategic places and tried to locate the enemy. They were met by a barrage of photocides. (Photocides are made to severely damage or destroy a robot when directed from robot to robot, but when directed to humans they are not very harmful. However, when directed from human to human they can, at times, be lethal). The police engaged them immediately and there were losses on both sides, but the police force eventually captured or destroyed the enemy robots and now it became a fight between humans. Ner and Vrima decloaked and went to their magneto to wait for the battle to stop. It was now out of their hands. There was no doubt in Ner's mind that the police could handle it from now on, but they stayed to see the results.

Nephus joined Narky and the other human. Narky was surprised to see the police force there, but Nephus quickly explained to him what had happened with Darna and the two robots. They both agreed that either Darna surrendered to the robots and asked for help, or the robots apprehended her and then called the police. In any case they were in big trouble and running out of luck. They were apprehended without resistance, and were taken to the police station for interrogation.

Project Anastrophe

Darna woke up in the hospital with a robot nurse combing her hair.

"You have very nice hair, Miss Darna."

"Thank you, where am I?"

"You are in the hospital for detoxification; you were given a powerful sedative."

Darna had a slight headache but other than that she felt okay. It all started to come back to her now.

"What happened to Nephus, was he okay, had he escaped and would he really have killed me in another biosphere as he was ordered? Nephus loves me but he is a very complex man; one cannot readily take him for granted."

Her subconscious monologue was interrupted by a knock on the door. Norina came in. She was wearing a pretend smile.

"I am Norina Anderson, from the Department Of Internal Security."

"Hello, Norina, I think I remember you. We've met before under rather unpleasant circumstances. I am truly sorry."

"It was a very unpleasant experience, but I have put it behind me now. I have a few questions to ask you, and it would be to your advantage to cooperate with me."

"I will to do my best."

"Thank you, Darna."

"Do you know where Nick is being kept?"

"I don't know for sure, but he is probably somewhere with Narky, or at least Narky should know where he is."

"I see, and are you employed by Narky?"

"I am not employed by Narky or anybody. I just did a favor for Nephus, that's all."

"What kind of favor, Darna?"

"I was asked to impress the guard at the Bolza warehouse."

"Impress the guard?"

"Well, you know, be sexy; occupy him until Nephus did something with the computer."

"I see, and is Nephus your boss, friend, or both?"

"He is just my friend."

"And why did you give yourself up to the police, and turn against your friend?"

"Because I overheard someone giving him orders to kill me. They said that I knew too much."

"Do you think you know too much, Darna?"

"What I have told you is all I know--honest."

Norina went straight to her office and talked to Dr. Dylos.

"I think she is telling the truth, she is not very much involved in this conspiracy but I believe Narky is."

"I think so too, but I think she needs to be under close surveillance for her own safety, at least until we apprehend the "big boys.""

"I agree with you."

Norina drove home; she was tired and discouraged. She blamed herself for Nick's abduction.

"I could have done more to keep him safe. I let my own feelings interfere with my duty, and did not take the appropriate measures for his safety. Now poor Nick is somewhere suffering, or even dead because of me."

Narky was very cooperative with the authorities; after all this wasn't the first time he had been in trouble with the police. He was sure his bosses would get him out soon; but this time it seemed different. There were these guys he had never seen, asking questions far beyond Nick's kidnapping. This was big, and it started to worry Narky.

"Mr. Stober--is it Stober?"

"Yes, Narky Stober."

Project Anastrophe

"I see."

"Do you have Nick at your place?"

"I did for a while, but when you started to go after Nephus, they came to my place and took him away."

"And who are they?"

"I don't know."

"Were they robots or humans?"

"They were both humans and robots."

"Were they from the Du Bois Brothers Company?"

"I think they were."

"Mr. Stober, do you know the Du Bois brothers personally?"

"I saw them when they came to see Nick."

"That will be all for the time being, Mr. Stober, but we are not through with you yet."

Dr. Dylos knew he was dealing with powerful people but he also knew he had the law on his side. He had a few good friends in the judiciary system whom he could trust. Judge Stephen in the Supreme Court came to mind, along with several judges in the lower courts. If he explained the importance of this matter to them, they would understand; he was sure of that. He placed a call to John Du Bois. He didn't have to wait long.

"Dr. Dylos, this is John Du Bois, I am responding to your call. What can I do for you?"

"I won't take much of your time; I'll come right to the subject. For reasons I don't understand, I know you have abducted Dr. Nick Papas. You know this is highly illegal, and I demand that you bring him to my office right now!"

"Dr. Dylos, my orders were only to persuade Dr. Papas to come to my office to discuss a few things pertaining to his unique scientific knowledge. I would not go as far as to say he was abducted."

"Mr. Du Bois, forcing someone to come to your place

against his will, is against the law and I demand you bring Dr. Papas to my office now, or I will send the police to do so."

"You do that, Dr. Dylos, and see how far you go."

"May I remind you, Mr. Du Bois, that no one is above the law?"

"I agree with you on that, Dr. Dylos, good bye now."

Dr. Dylos could see the Du Bois brothers had much more power than he thought; perhaps the Governor was on their payroll too. This was going to take time; he placed a call to Judge Stephen.

Meanwhile, Ner had something in mind that needed Norina's attention.

"Miss Norina, may I discuss something with you regarding Nick?"

"What is it, Ner, what do you have in mind?"

"We know where Nick is kept. We have located him and we are in touch with him at all times."

"Dr. Dylos is trying to send the police, Ner, but he has problems getting permission from the Governor. I think sooner or later we'll get Nick back, it is just a matter of time."

"Miss Norina, I' m afraid they may move Nick to another Biosphere, and then it would be more difficult to find him."

"Well, do you have any ideas that might improve our predicament?"

"As a matter of fact I do, Miss Norina." Ner explained his plan in detail. It was a rather complicated plan to get Nick out of there, and it could work. Norina told Ner that she had to talk to Dr. Dylos and get permission to do such a daring thing. After all, Nick's life could easily be at risk. Ner was prepared for such an answer and said,

Project Anastrophe

"Very well, Miss Norina, I'll wait for your answer. In the meantime Vrima and I will work to become more familiar with this plan."

"I will let you know as soon as I talk to Dr. Dylos."

Nick woke up and sat on the edge of the bed, both hands covering his face--he was thinking. Was it two weeks--three weeks that he had been here? He had lost count. This could not go on too much longer. He had to do something, or someone had to do something. He opened the curtains of the small window facing a back yard. However big this building was, he must be on the lower floor. He could see a robot gardener clipping a rose bush. The clippers were part of his extended hand and they made a rhythmic noise; click, click, click. A little junco was looking down from its secure perch with its head turned sideways for a better look. The robot worked methodically. Click, click.

Nick was depressed; he had never been confined to a place like this for so long. His mind went back home. The only problem he had had with the law was from a minor traffic violation. The whole experience of being stopped by an officer, pulled to the side, and given a strong warning had been too much for him. He started thinking of his situation. Most of what was dear to him was dead. His wife and children, his parents, brothers, sisters, and friends were all covered with a five hundred year time blanket. And now this! Life had been unfair to Nick.

The door opened abruptly, three robots and a human came in. The human told him they were taking him away to another place. At that precise moment and against all odds, Nick did something he had never done before. He landed his fist on the human's face, and before anyone could react he ran through the door and closed it behind him. He kept running past the robot gardener, jumped over a hedge, and landed on a busy moving sidewalk with many people. It all happened with lightning speed. The human and the robots had not expected anything like that; it took them a while to recover and then they ran after him. Nick felt a lot safer outside among the people, but he could see the human and the robots in hot pursuit of him, not too far behind. He ran into a busy restaurant and then into a bathroom, where he stayed plotting his next move.

As this was happening, Norina got a call from Ner on her way to her office. He told her that Nick was on the move and possibly on the way to another Biosphere. Presently, however he was in the Sunset restaurant.

"Miss Norina, we must act quickly, we can be there in minutes and stop them before they go any farther. Our plan still applies."

"Ner--put your plan in effect now. In the meantime I will speak with Dr. Dylos, and I'll get back to you very soon."

"Very well, Miss Norina, the plan is on!"

Ner acted quickly. The plan called for six robot guards including himself and Vrima; they were all to meet at the Sunset restaurant. Within seconds they were on their way. Norina got in touch with Ner soon after that and said,

"Dr. Dylos concurs with us under the circumstances. You can use more guards if you need to but you must not call the police or use humans. Good luck."

"Thank you, Miss Norina; we will proceed as you command."

Ner, Vrima, and the rest of the guards arrived at the appointed place within minutes. They started executing their plan right away. They encircled the restaurant with electromagnetic neutralizers. Now any marked robots which passed through the light beam would be damaged severely.

Project Anastrophe

The marked humans would also be stunned with a temporary paralyzing effect.

"I need to do something to get the authority's attention--but what?" Nick was combing his hair, looking at the door for his pursuers; no one yet.

"That's strange, I know they have the ability to locate me, why aren't they here yet?" Nick didn't want to push his luck anymore; going out of here was out of the question. They could be waiting for him outside.

"What shall I do?" Nick finally got an idea, a little unorthodox, but it had to be done. He quickly yanked the faucet. The water spouted upwards, and soon flooded the entire bathroom area. He stood at the opposite corner waiting for things to happen. And things did happen quickly. Within minutes the robot plumbers proceeded to repair the damage, they gently asked him to leave the area.

He opened the door and looked outside; there were two robots keeping people away from the flooded area. He cautiously walked out, passed the robots and kept going down the hall and turned the corner. It didn't take long for him to be found. Two of the robots ran after him, he ran the opposite way as fast as he could only to see the two other robots and the human coming his way. The human told him to surrender and he wouldn't be harmed. Nick was at an impasse not knowing what to do next. He had no weapons to defend himself, he was about to start screaming for help.

In the meantime Ner, Vrima, and the other four robots, had entered the building and spread around. Ner was in charge, giving orders when needed. Vrima was ordered to locate Nick and get him out of there unharmed; she knew where he was at all times. It was at that precise moment Vrima appeared. She quickly marked the robots and the human with a special magnetic substance. Now they knew they couldn't leave; they had to fight it out here or surrender. Vrima jumped in front of Nick and told him to stay behind her. She started firing and they replied right away. It was three to one with laser guns spewing highly charged light beams. The people ran away from the fighting to avoid being hit. Within seconds Ner and the rest of the robot guards arrived and the fighting became even more intense.

In a few minutes it was all over. The human surrendered and the two robots were destroyed. Smoke emanated from their charred bodies. The other two robots were quickly found and destroyed. (Robots fight until victory or are destroyed.) They got out of there with Nick unscathed but two of their robots had been put out of action. They sped away before the police arrived. Ner, Vrima, and Nick drove back home. Ner called Norina and told her that they had Nick safe and sound. He also suggested Nick should not be in any place known to the police or others. Norina thought that was a good idea. She advised him to use a different magneto and go to the Museum of Fine Arts with Nick and Vrima. They should wait for her at the parking place and be prepared to fight if necessary.

"Thank you, Ner, for a well done job."

"You are welcome, Miss Norina."

Ner told Nick what Norina had said, and within minutes they were on their way. Norina and Dr. Dylos were waiting for them. Nick quickly stepped into another magneto and was about to leave when Ner said to Norina,

"Miss Norina, our plan calls for the two of you to go to an undisclosed place. Vrima and I have prepared your luggage. Have a joyful and safe trip."

Dr. Dylos told Norina once they reached their destination they should be discrete and stay out of the way. They headed for the airdrome in two magnetos--one filled with robot guards and the other with human guards following them. At the airdrome there was a private tachioplane waiting for them and they were in the air within seconds.

"Where are we going, Norina?"

"To the state of Greece, for a much deserved vacation for both of us."

"And whereabouts in the State of Greece?"

"On an Island called Skiathos--have you ever been there?"

"No, I have only been in Athens a few years ago."

"I hear it's a beautiful island, we will be living in a very small village which is out of the way."

"That sounds relaxing for a change."

"What are those planes doing next to us?"

"Oh, they want us to get to our destination safely, that's all."

"I suppose it makes sense."

It took about two hours to get to Skiathos and then another few minutes to get to Lagathy. What a change it was. The island had retained its physical beauty even though it was in a biosphere like any other place. There was quite a bit of sea water within the dome; and there was a beautiful beach that went almost all around the island. Their hotel was called Lagathio, probably named after the village. It was a two story stone building and looked very old fashioned. It had a huge oak front door, all the windows had wooden shutters and the roof had real tiles. It was built about a thousand years ago, and was a well kept building close to the beach. The only robots one could see were the cleaning staff and the gardeners. The rest of the staff were humans.

They had registered as a newly married couple, Robert and Loretta Johnson. There was a young woman at the front desk who was very accommodating. Nick had a feeling she knew who they were. They were given a large room

on the second floor with a window that opened to the beach--a beautiful view. They both had hot showers and were in their bathrobes with glasses of wine in their hands. They sat down and looked at each other with a tired, loving look. Nick said,
"There is an old Greek custom in times of happiness between two good friends. They cross their arms and drink to health like this."
"That looks like an appropriate salutation for this occasion." And with that they drank and kissed and danced across the floor, and when they got dizzy they fell down and made sweet love as never before.

Next morning they had a nice breakfast, and were the first tourists on the beach. The sun filtered through the dome preventing radiation from coming inside the biosphere--no need for sun block. They lay down to relax a bit.

"Norina, if I am not mistaken those are robots out there, aren't they?"

"You are right, Nick."

"I didn't know robots needed to sun bathe."

"They are not."

"Then what are they doing here?"

"They are our friends, they are guarding us."

"Then we are not quite alone, are we?"

"That's as alone as we want to be, Nick, besides they keep their distance and are not bothering us."

Chapter 5

It was the Governor's biggest headache so far. Nick's abduction was supposed to be an easy thing; abduct him, keep him away for few a days, get the information you need and let him go unharmed. That was the idea, but it had now become a nightmare for her. When Jim McMiness called and asked her not to interfere if there was a problem, she was a little apprehensive about it, but he was one of the big business people in town and a contributor to her last campaign. Sometimes she wondered if it was worth her time being away from her family; but she knew that was part of politics too. She knew that Dr. Dylos was a man of immense integrity, well-known in the academic world, with powerful friends too.

She decided to meet the problem head on. She called

Jim McMiness and told him that Nick's abduction was getting out of hand and if they didn't do something to stop it now, it could become a bigger problem for all of them. She also wanted to know Nick's whereabouts. Jim told her that Nick had broken out of his confinement with outside help, and he didn't know where he was.

"Do you think Dr. Dylos might know where Nick is?"

"I have a feeling he does."

"I want you to call a meeting with all the people who are involved with Nick's abduction. I am going to ask Dr. Dylos and his people to attend the meeting too."

"Do you want us to come to your office?"

"Yes, let's meet here tomorrow at 10:00 a.m."

Her next call was to Dr. Dylos.

"Dr. Dylos, this is Governor Nazer. The reason I called you is to find out how Nick is doing."

"It's strange that you should call me to find out how Nick is doing, Governor. You may have better luck asking the Du Bois Brothers."

"Dr. Dylos, let's not pretend you don't know where Nick is. We know that you helped to get him out of his confinement, and I don't blame you for doing so. This whole affair has gone too far, and I must admit perhaps I have contributed to it unknowingly."

"Governor, I quite agree with you. This affair has gone too far, but don't blame me for that. I am not prepared to make any accusations at this time, but you must know who started it all."

"Dr. Dylos, I am calling all the parties involved in this affair to a meeting, to find out the reason why this whole thing started. I would encourage you to participate in this important gathering. However I would appreciate it if you didn't say anything to anyone beyond your immediate friends. The meeting will be held tomorrow at 10:00 a.m."

Project Anastrophe

"Governor, I promise I'll be there."

Governor Mary Nazer was in charge of the meeting. There were many people from both sides. On Jim McMiness's side there were Gregory Tyron, Zita Thorish, Vougtos Lemek, Nazara Fouruga, Voha Hollanda, and the Du Bois brothers, John and Jack. On Dr. Dylos' side there were William Stephen, Judge of the Supreme Court, Peter Loveinscky, Judge of the lower court, David Furner, administrative Chief of Police, Dr. Yannis Mageris, scientist, and Dr. Hans Zimmer, scientist. The Governor started the meeting.

"Ladies and gentlemen, I want to thank you for coming here on such short notice. I know that all of you have been under intense pressure but none more than Dr. Nick Papas, who has been confined illegally in various places. I should also emphasize the fact that I was drawn unknowingly into this affair and I am sorry; I should have been more alert. We are here today to hear each other's grievances and come to the bottom of this very disturbing matter. Before I give the floor to the next speaker, I would like to ask Dr. Dylos to tell us if Dr. Papas is well."

"Nick is well and if anyone tries to go even close to him this time, they will be met with great force."

"Thank you, Dr. Dylos, you can rest assured no one is going to bother him anymore."

"Mr. McMiness, at this time I would like to give the floor to any of you who could tell us why it was necessary to abduct Dr. Papas."

"Governor, thank you for arranging this meeting. I think I speak on behalf of my group. Dr. Papas is not your average citizen or scientist working in one of our universities. He shouldn't even be with us at this time. He was brought into our time from the past, and to be more specific, from the 21st century. I understand why the government wants to keep it a secret from the people at large. At first it was only a curiosity for the few of us who knew about it. But then we heard that the government was planning to send Dr. Papas back to his time in order to make some basic changes. It was then that we realized our businesses and our lives would be affected, and we became alarmed.

To be more specific; our factories and businesses which started five hundred years ago will either change drastically, or will be completely eliminated. We consulted some of our scientist friends and asked them if that could be done. They said not only could it be done, but they are about to do it very soon. We tried to get in touch with Dr. Dylos who is in charge of the program but he said it was a government secret and he wasn't permitted to discuss it with anyone. That is why we decided to ask Dr. Papas a few questions directly. We realized this would be illegal, but under the circumstances it was the prudent thing for us to do. But at no time did we mean to harm Dr. Papas."

"Chief Furner, you may have the floor."

"Thank you, Governor."

"Mr. McMiness and all those implicated in Dr. Papas's abduction, have committed an illegal act and as such must be prosecuted by the law."

"We understand, chief, and we will take this under consideration."

"Dr. Dylos, you may have the floor."

"Thank you, Governor."

"What I am about to say is very important, and all of us must swear under oath that it will be kept secret. Otherwise it could cause unnecessary panic.

For the last year or so the radiation poisoning has reached unacceptable levels and a lot of people, especially

Project Anastrophe

the older ones, are getting irreversibly sick and most of them die. It has now reached pandemic proportions and if we don't do something to remedy this problem, eventually it will kill us all. That is the reason we did not want to share this information with anyone. I have with me two scientists who are very much involved with the problem, and are better equipped to elaborate on this complex matter. I would like to introduce Dr. Yannis Mageris, who is a doctor of chemical engineering at Western Washington University."

"Dr. Mageris, you may have the floor."

"As Dr. Dylos would attest, we have had numerous secret meetings with many scientists participating from all over the planet. There have been many suggestions from those who said that there is nothing we can do, and therefore we should start moving to Mars before it's too late. There are those who suggest solidifying all habitable areas with special chemically treated cements. That would give us three to five years until we come up with a final solution. Of course there have been many other suggestions in between, but no one has come up with a better idea. I would like to give the floor to my colleague Dr. Hans Zimmer who is in charge of cementing our biosphere."

"Ladies and Gentlemen I am sorry to be the bearer of bad news, but I can assure you we are doing all we can to slow down a total catastrophe. Many other biospheres are doing the same thing all over the planet. I am here to speak for our biosphere. For hundreds of years the radiation was in the air and that is the reason we live in biospheres. We are now able to filter the air coming into our biosphere with powerful filters and we do have clean air. The problem arises from the ground. That's where the radiation leaks now. It started leaking about ten years ago outside and inside the biospheres all over the planet. First it was in minute amounts and at the time we were able to contain it with a mixture of lead and concrete, then we came up with other combinations. But now we are trying to stop large amounts of radiation, and it's becoming difficult and expensive."

"I now would like to ask Mr. McMiness if you or any of your group would like to ask any questions, or have any statements to make."

"Madam Governor, at this time we have no questions or statements to make. We would like to hear all the speakers first."

"O. K., as you wish, Mr. McMiness."

"Dr. Dylos, do you have anyone who wishes to speak at this time?"

"Yes, Madam Governor, we have here with us the Supreme Court Judge William Stephen, who wishes to discuss the legal part of our problem."

"Your honor, it is our pleasure to have you here. Please proceed."

"It is my opinion, and perhaps the opinion of many of us, that we are at an impasse technologically speaking. We must do something to save our civilization and humanity at large. Our scientists here and elsewhere have been, and are now trying their best to fix this terrible problem, but there are other ways to approach and remedy this radiation poisoning. As you are well aware, we are trying to stop the catastrophe before it occurs by sending someone back to the twentieth century to alert and convince our forefathers about the danger that will occur in the future. If that proves to be difficult, then we will use our expertise to stop the use of weapons and nuclear plants which produce radiation. If needed, we will introduce them to alternative power and materials that are less dangerous to the planet. Our scientists are not quite there yet, and they need our cooperation if we want them to save our planet. This is pretty much what I had to say and thank you for the opportunity."

Project Anastrophe

"At this time I would like to give the opportunity to the opposing side to express their opinion on the matter. Mr. Du Bois, please go ahead."

"Thank you, Madam Governor. I appreciate all the work done by so many people in our biosphere and elsewhere for the survival of our Earth. I had a vague idea of what was going on but now we all know a lot more, thanks to all of you gentlemen. I think that I speak for all of us on this side when I say that we want to cooperate, but we also want to save our businesses and our way of life as it is now. This is what we propose and I am sure this will satisfy other business people in other biospheres.

When we eventually manage to go back in time and stop the nuclear proliferation, we should go with a list of businesses that had been using nuclear technology and have survived to our time. We should permit them to carry on with their familiar technology, but concentrate on eliminating various terrorist groups who used nuclear bombs at that time. Also, we should start a program to prevent rogue third world countries from obtaining nuclear technology. I believe if we could do that, we could prevent nuclear proliferation, save our planet from radiation, and keep our businesses in tact. We are willing to subsidize such a program."

"Anyone wishing to add to this proposal please feel free to interject. Judge Loveinscky?"

"Thank you, Madam Governor. Before I proceed with what I have to say, I would like to ask Dr. Hans Zimmer a question if I may."

"Dr. Zimmer, let us assume we have perfected the technology to send Dr. Papas, perhaps with other people, to the 20th century. Would it be something we could do readily anytime we wish?"

"Not at all, your honor, at this time we will be lucky if

we can calibrate the arrival of a person at the exact time. You see, even a split second before or after the actual time could make a difference of a few years in the arrival time. Right now we have no way of bringing the person or person back to our time."

"What you are telling us then, is that we have to do all we can in that one trip, is that right, Dr. Zimmer?"

"That is correct for the time being, yes sir."

"Ladies and gentlemen, I disagree with Mr. Du Bois' offer for the simple reason that we don't have the luxury of taking chances on the first trip. I suggest that when we manage to go there we should go without a list of names to save existing businesses. We must eliminate all nuclear plants and factories that produce nuclear energy and stop, once and for all, the radiation which was and is killing people then and now. I think this is the way we should go. Later on when we are able to improve our technology to the point where we can take chances, then we will have the luxury of accepting Mr. Du Bois' offer."

There was a lot of talk among McMiness' people, finally Mr. McMiness asked for the floor.

"Madam Governor! As we stated earlier, we understand the problem and we are eager to help in any way we can but we want to do it in a way that doesn't jeopardize our businesses. We urge the government not to act hastily on this very important matter. Give us enough time to come up with an alternative plan which would satisfy all interests."

"Dr. Dylos, do you agree with Mr. McMiness' offer?"

"We welcome any suggestions they might come up with, but I urge them to do it very soon. However we will go ahead with our plan when we are ready. To do otherwise is to jeopardize the success of our mission and that is something we will not do."

Project Anastrophe

"Yes, Mr. McMiness."

"We are very disappointed with the government's attitude, but we will do the best we can under the circumstances."

"Ladies and gentlemen, I want to thank you all for being a part of a very important meeting. It has been an educational experience for us all, and I trust that we will come up with a compromise which will take into account every party's interest. I want to make it clear that my office is available, and I will do anything I can to help you come up with the right formula to get us out of this predicament. Thank you all."

"Miss Vrima, are you fully charged?"

"Yes, Ner, my new batteries charge much sooner than the old ones."

"I need to perform an analytic check up on your noetics as soon as you are ready."

"I am ready right now, Ner."

"Do you want to be alert, or would you like to be in sleep mode?"

"I would prefer to be alert during the process, thank you."

"Very well, Miss Vrima, as you wish."

It was a feeling Vrima could not understand. She knew very well that as a robot she should not have feelings, but any time she was near Ner she felt something she could not explain. Vrima registered it as a question in her noetics and now she was hoping Ner would give her an answer. Ner too had feelings for Vrima and had spent many hours analyzing his own noetics for an answer. He had been made to have eighteen percent carbon matter, (brain matter). Could that be enough to create love in a robot's body that is eighty-two percent silicon chips and electronic components? Logically speaking it's possible, but that would mean the brain is growing and adapting far beyond its initial purpose. That explains why Vrima, with seven percent more brain matter than he, has a stronger love-like feeling. Ner finished Vrima's check up and found her in perfect condition.

"We are all done, Vrima, you may get up now."

"Thank you, Ner. If you read my noetics, you would know I had a few questions for you."

"Yes, I know Vrima, and I think we should talk about it."

"I also have these feelings, and I am sure many other robots do too. I suppose you and I have brain matter that is different from the average robot and in addition to that you have seven percent more than I have."

"But that still does not answer the kind of feelings I have when I am close to some humans and even to some robots."

"Can you describe your feelings to me?"

"When Nick was taken away, I felt a need to do something other than prepare myself for possible action to rescue Nick. It was something new, a feeling locked in a void."

"You were experiencing sadness, which is a common human feeling, but few robots have this capability. You and I, and a few other robots, are very lucky to have these feelings."

"Sometimes I feel a desire, or an attraction, to be with you."

"That is called love, but unfortunately we will never be able to fulfill this need for now."

"And what should I do when I have these feelings?"

"We should talk; that should be sufficient for the time being."

"I think I feel sad."

Project Anastrophe

It was another beautiful Grecian day; the sun was filtering through the huge dome which was part of the biosphere barely seen by the naked eye. Nick and Norina were walking on the sacred rock of the Acropolis. The restoration had been completed in the Twenty-First Century and it was still kept in good condition. Back in Nick's time the Parthenon was surrounded by scaffolding, and the restoration went on for many years. Nick and Norina walked around the temple admiring its Doric lines. It was an edifice of magnificence and splendor depicting Hellenic art and architecture which had endured through the ages.

Norina had come to the Acropolis many times in the past, but it was the first time for Nick to see it completely restored as it would have been thousands of years ago. They sat on top of a huge retaining wall overlooking the ancient city of Athens, capital of the state of Greece. It was a panoramic view. Most of the old ruins had been restored and were surrounded by huge new buildings blending the old and the new structures giving them a phantasmagoric view. They walked into the Acropolis museum looking at various statues and artifacts. There was a separate part of the museum showing the Elgin Marbles, (3) Greek sculptures of the 5th century BC, originally on the Acropolis. They were sculpted under the direction of Phidias, and were held in the British museum in London after Thomas-Bruce 7th Earl of Elgin, (1766-1841), arranged for the collection to be brought from Athens to Britain. In 2008 they were returned to the Athens museum, and Greeks were happy to have them back. Not too long after the planet Earth was federated in 2098 it was decreed that all statues and artifacts be returned to their original countries.

Norina wanted to show Nick many other beautiful places in the state of Greece, but those places were outside the biosphere and they would have to make special arrangements and wear protective gear. Norina promised she would bring him back when they had more time. They walked through the busy streets of Athens being tourists, and Norina had the best time of her life. Nick also enjoyed being with Norina and walking in the land of his forefathers. They were having lunch at one of those small restaurants close to the Acropolis when Norina got an urgent call from Dr. Dylos. She knew right away that their two week vacation was over. Dr. Dylos was giving her specific directions about coming back home.

Next day Norina and Nick were at Dr. Dylos office. He told Nick,

"We are cautiously optimistic that the scientists are close to sending you back home. They are in the last steps of calibrating a formula for the time and place of your departure. Nick, there are a few things I should tell you about your return. Norina is going to accompany you on your trip. We have purposely arranged for the two of you to arrive in the year 1938; that means that you will not see your family at this time.

We believe it will be easier for you to operate as a married couple. You will have new implants to help you make the necessary changes and also help you adapt to your new environment. We will also send Ner and Vrima along with you; we believe they will be helpful. They have both been programmed to help and protect you especially for that time. They will be living as a married couple too. You will be sent to Seattle, in Washington State, and live in different apartments. Try to blend in with the people around you in clothing and style. You will use the same name you used in Greece; Robert and Loretta Johnson. You were born and educated in England and you are both professors in astrophysics working at The University of Washington. Ner and Vrima have worked out all the details. Ner's and Vrima's

Project Anastrophe

assumed names are Roy and Mary Eastman. They were born in San Francisco, California. Roy is a mathematician; Mary is a biochemist; they are both employed at the University of Washington. They are good friends of the Johnsons. Ner and Vrima know the appointed places and times where you can communicate with us, or be evacuated in times of need.

I have just been informed the time of departure is tomorrow at precisely 11:00 a.m. metric time, you will be staying overnight in the Voyager. You have three hours to prepare yourselves for your trip. I will see you tomorrow in the Voyager before you leave. I should tell you that, although we feel certain we can place you there safely, there is always the possibility we could be wrong. In that case you could find yourselves in a different place and epoch. If that happens, I promise you that we will do all we can to bring you home safe and sound. I would also like to tell you that what you are doing is very brave and is very much appreciated by all of us."

Nick and Norina left for home. There was so much to do in such a short time. Their escort was driving behind them. Dr. Dylos wasn't taking any chances this time. They were both in a sober mood. Nick prepared their favorite drinks, and they sat down to contemplate what they were about to do. Norina was philosophical about the whole affair; she trusted the scientific team which was in charge of their expedition. Although she realized the danger they would face, she was excited to travel to the past and live in a time that she had only read about.

She tried to give courage to Nick, and make him feel better about it all, but Nick knew better. They were going to arrive at a time the Second World War was about to start. He had seen war and the destruction that comes with it. He had seen bodies coming back home in caskets. He had seen cities being destroyed and corpses lying on the streets half burned and abandoned. He wanted to go back home but not at the time the war was about to start. He knew what they were about to face and wanted to prepare her before they left. He told Norina that she was going to see humanity at its worst; it would be a humbling experience, and something that would traumatize her for life. He told her he was not proud of the people of his time. She felt sad but not discouraged. She told Nick she was prepared to go anywhere and do anything that would help to eliminate the radiation that had caused sickness and death to millions in this time.

"Nick, what we are doing is unpleasant and yes, dangerous, but it is worth doing it if it will prevent Earth from being destroyed."

"My only concern is for you, Norina. I also want to help save our planet and will do whatever is needed, so let's do what we have to do and get ready."

Ner and Vrima prepared everything they needed so Nick and Norina had very little to do. The important material for their trip was prepared by the scientific team back in the space station. They e-mailed notes to friends; Norina wrote to her brother and mother telling them she and Nick were going on a special mission, but she couldn't tell them about it at this time.

For security reasons they timed the messages to be delivered one day after they had left. Ner came into the living room and told them they were ready to go. Before long they were on their way to the Voyager with the guards right behind them all the way to the space station. As soon as they arrived all four were taken inside the Voyager. Ner and Vrima were adjusting their noetics, and checking the final lists of the things they had to do before they left. Nick and Norina were also doing a final check up before departure. All four of them gathered in the cockpit.

Project Anastrophe

Norina said,

"I suppose this is going to be our last meeting here in our time. Next time if everything goes well, we will meet in Washington State, more than five hundred years in the past. Is there anything we need to discuss?"

"Miss Norina, there is one thing we have not done yet."

"What is it, Ner?"

"We need to adjust our accents to match the West Coast states."

"I think it would be best if we programmed our implants to do so after we arrive in case we find ourselves in other states or countries."

"I quite agree with you, Miss Norina."

"And Ner, you and Vrima must humanize your speech; otherwise we will all be in trouble. Also, we must call each other by our first names."

"I understand, Norina."

"Nick, you don't have to do any adjustments, just go back to your native accent."

"I will be happy to do that, Norina."

Nick and Norina stayed late talking about their trip back in time. They were both excited. Nick was anxious to go back to his pre-birth time to see his parents and grandparents younger, and to witness great historical events a few years before his birth. Norina was hoping to see some of her relatives and learn how they had lived so many years in the past.

Ner and Vrima used their portable chargers for the first time. The chargers were embedded in their bodies and programmed to charge their batteries every night. From now on they would charge themselves horizontally, so that it was less obvious that they were robots. Their bodies were altered in a way that made it difficult, if not impossible, for them to be detected by x-rays or anything else they had back in the 20th century. Their hearts were beating at a normal pace and they had normal blood pressure. There was a hologram installed in their bodies showing human organs including a brain. In short, they could have a physical check up at any hospital in the nineteen–thirties and come out looking like two healthy human beings.

Next morning they were all up, Ner and Vrima fully charged, and Nick and Norina having had a hearty breakfast with lots of coffee. Ner and Vrima with their usual robotic attitude did everything with precision and in a logical manner. Norina and Nick were confronted by their human inadequacies: excitement, nervousness, and apprehension, but were trying to do the best they could do under the circumstances. Dr. Dylos came for a short visit and was just as nervous as they were, but he tried to be positive and told them the scientists had done all they could and now it would be up to them to do their part.

The Voyager was calibrated to misfunction again, but this time at a specific time and epoch. It was programmed to open its cargo doors at the precise nano second of the calibrated time and transfer its human and robot cargo to dry land. Norina and Nick had a final checkup, and they were found to be O.K. Then everybody, other than the four time travelers, stepped out and shortly after that the countdown started. There were a few anxious moments for the scientific team, but everything worked as expected and the Voyager was sent on its way.

Of the four of them it was Norina who worried the most. She knew things could go wrong with the Voyager and they could end up way back in the past or in the far future. Either way would be a disaster. Of course Dr. Dylos and his team would try to bring them back, but there was a strong possibility that it would not work out. There was a vibration and they felt as if they were lifted into some kind

Project Anastrophe

of a void. They started to hallucinate seeing different colors and feeling they were going to be sick. For Nick it was all "déjà vu"; he knew what was happening. Ner and Vrima put themselves into sleep mode and were not affected at all.

The change in time was instant, just as it happened with Nick, but this time they landed on a planet which wasn't damaged by radiation. They were thrown onto a knoll along with their weapons, tools and provisions. It was night as they were hoping it would be and it should be May 15 1938 in western Washington State but that would have to be confirmed tomorrow. Ner and Vrima went off their sleep mode as soon as they touched land. They quickly set up the tents, the type that would be used at that time, put mattresses in both and then all four gathered at Norina's and Nick's tent. With a gas light on top of a box which was used as a table then, they all sat around it; Vrima brought four cups with instant liquid food.

Norina was the first to speak.

"Well, it looks as if we all made it safely. I'd like to hear from each of you. How you are feeling? Nick, let's start with you."

"Oh well, this wasn't nearly as bad as the first time. I knew what to expect this time, and from what I can see we landed in a safe place. I feel O.K."

"Ner, how do you feel?"

"I feel O.K. Norina, as you know we both put ourselves on sleep mode. I ran a general check up and found myself in excellent condition."

"And how do you feel, Vrima?"

"I feel very well, Norina. I also ran a check up and found myself to be O.K."

"Well, this was a first experience for me, and I don't feel quite well, but I am sure by tomorrow I will feel much better."

"You must think I should be happy because I am home, but I am not really home. I am sixty-two years back in time, and I don't know anybody, and no one knows me. But it should be easier for me to adjust to these people."

"That's true, Nick, and we depend on you to help us adjust to them too."

"I am sure in a few weeks we will all adjust to our new life and feel at home."

"I hope so, Nick."

"Ner, remember you and Vrima are supposed to be married, so go to your tent and from now on act like a married couple."

"Yes, Norina, we are programmed to do so, and we will."

"Ner, remember for the duration of our stay here we don't own you. You are a free couple, and you can do as you please."

"Yes, thank you, Norina; we will do as you say."

"Good night, Ner."

Ner and Vrima said good night and withdrew to their tent. They lay on the same mattress. Vrima leaned over, kissed Ner, and said good night.

"Why did you do that?"

"That's what couples do, Ner."

"But it is not necessary for us to do it here, is it?"

"You never know who might be looking at us, Ner. We had better play it safe." Both Ner and Vrima went into charging mode, although Vrima did so a few minutes later. She loved being so close to Ner. Norina and Nick lay together too, but they went into discharging mode. They had another passionate night.

Ner and Vrima woke up early and went out. Their sensors detected no radiation and they found the atmosphere habitable for human and robot life, and sent a message to

Project Anastrophe

Norina's hidden receptors. Then they prepared a complete report about their status, and after a while it was ready to be presented to Norina. Nick and Norina also got up early. They were having coffee when Ner came in.

"Good morning, Nick and Norina, how do you feel today?"

"We feel great, Ner, how about you guys?"

"We have been fully charged, and are ready for the new day."

"That's great, Ner. You sound more and more like us. Make sure Vrima adopts this lingo too."

"She is doing extremely well, Norina."

"Do you have something for me, Ner?"

"Yes, Norina, here is the report Vrima and I have prepared for you. It looks as if we have landed in a habitable place for us all. We think we are in a place called The Olympic Peninsula and the sea is not too far from here."

"What do you think, Nick?"

"I know this place very well. I've been here many times, and I know how to get us out of here easily."

Nick and Norina were sitting on a grassy knoll looking down at the Peninsula. There were beautiful huge Douglas fir trees all around them. Many more than Nick had seen in his time. Most of them were first growth; many of them would be cut and replaced with second growth, smaller and not as healthy looking as these. Nick felt sad and wished he could do something to stop the logging that would start in a few years from now. He was telling Norina about that, and she commiserated with him, but reminded him that they were here to stop a worse destruction from starting. He agreed and followed her to their tent in a subdued mood. Ner and Vrima had prepared a nice steamy breakfast.

After breakfast, all four of them went outside and sat on the grassy knoll overlooking the sea. Norina couldn't believe how clear and pristine the air felt. It was so beautiful to see Earth without the biospheres. It gave her courage to stop the nuclear bombs from ever becoming a reality. Nick was also impressed with the clean air and the beauty of the country. And he was determined to do something to stop the coming menace. Norina finished writing her report. Ner and Vrima brought several samples from different places including air and water. They put them all in a special container, and after they had calibrated their exact position, they placed it in a hole and covered it with green branches. They had to do one more thing before it was taken away-- make contact with contemporary people! The hologram could be made anywhere on Earth and sent to the container but it had to be sent before the estimated time of departure. According to Ner they had six hours, fifteen minutes, and ten seconds, local time from exactly now!

They had a brief meeting in which they worked out their itinerary. They had to go to the nearest town, mingle with the people, get some papers and magazines and holograph everything including themselves to the container and send it back to the future at the exact time. Then they would rent two separate rooms and stay as long as needed before they went to Seattle. Vrima was in charge of their money. They brought fifty thousand dollars in different denominations including silver and gold coins. At the right time they were to open two separate accounts in a bank and hoped to start earning money before long.

Vrima gave them two hundred dollars in paper and coins, picked up their tents, hid them along with their weapons, and started to go downhill towards the first town. From now on Nick was in charge of their itinerary.

Nick gathered them together and told them not to say much. He was going to do most of the talking for the time being. They were carrying light backpacks with wooden

Project Anastrophe

frames to match the contemporary ones. All the rest of the material was hidden in various inconspicuous places. They were protected by electronic gear that set off a silent alarm to alert them wherever they were; but Ner and Vrima had done such a good job hiding them that none of them worried about anyone finding them.

They were walking on a well-used pathway, with Nick and Norina enjoying every step they took. Ner and Vrima were on duty at all times. They were endowed with super sensitive senses which enabled them to detect animal or human form and anything moving up and down within a kilometer's perimeter. They walked about thirty minutes when Ner said he detected two humans coming up their way about two hundred meters below. Nick said,

"Let me handle it."

They kept on going, and a few minutes later they met an elderly couple, in their sixties. They were both wearing hats with visors, were dressed loosely and had their woolen sweaters tied around their waists. They were pleasant people and when they saw them they stopped and smiled. The man said,

"My name is Scott, and this is my wife, Flora."

"I am Robert, this is my wife Loretta, and these are our friends, Roy and Mary."

"How do you do-do you come here often?"

"Not as often as we would like to."

"We love coming here; I think this is one of nature's best places to hike."

"I quite agree with you. Enjoy your hike."

"We will. Thank you."

"Well, Nick, you handled that very well, I don't think they suspected anything unusual."

"I don't think so either. They seemed to be nice people."

"Yes, and I am so glad to meet my first people in this century."

They walked another hour or so and Nick saw a big sign pointing upwards, it said, "Hurricane Ridge." Now he knew where they were. Port Angeles couldn't be too far away from here. They would be able to find a good hotel there. Ner told them they were approaching a busy place with humans and other moving things. Nick knew they were close to a road. They kept on walking; he saw another bigger sign which read, "Dungeness State Park." There were many logging trucks passing by with full loads of newly cut logs. The trucks emitted thick black smoke. The destruction of the forests had begun sooner than Nick thought.

They walked another couple of kilometers and finally came to a gas station.

The proprietor, an older man, was sitting on a chair by the wall; his hat lowered down covering his eyes, taking a late morning nap under the sun. They woke him up as they approached and he looked disapprovingly at them. He had seen many of these tourists coming to his station, using the facilities, asking for directions, and buying nothing. Nick asked him if there were a restaurant close by; he pointed down the road and said,

"Logger's Trap Eatery", bout haf mall." Nick thanked him and they kept walking.

Both Nick and Norina were tired and in need of food. Ner and Vrima were doing fine. They had turned on their solar receptors charging their batteries and were energized. Finally they came to the restaurant. It was a dusty old place with a neon Camel Cigarette sign above its main door and a Coca Cola ice chest inside. They all went in and waited to be seated. Before long a young woman pointed to a table and they sat down.

Project Anastrophe

She came back with four glasses of water and four menus. Ner said to Nick, "I detect hazardous smoke." Nick hushed him and told him that's how it was here. With almost everybody smoking, the air was indeed full of smoke, but no one seemed to be bothered by it. Norina had never been in a situation like this before, and if she had not been so hungry she wouldn't have stayed another minute. Nick was bothered by the smoke too but told Norina to get used to it; smoking in restaurants would be permitted until the late nineties.

They looked at the menus, Nick ordered bacon and eggs with hash brown potatoes and coffee. Norina couldn't understand the menu, Nick told her to try the omelet with tomatoes, green peppers and cheese; she also ordered coffee. Nick told Ner and Vrima to order the same as he and Norina had done and to eat it all. Ner and Vrima did as they were told. The room was full of people; there were many truck drivers talking loudly and the room was noisy. There were other hikers too, they were dressed pretty much like them carrying the same back- packs; Ner had done his homework well, dressing them in a contemporary fashion.

Right above their heads, there was a huge picture of President Franklin Delano Roosevelt looking down on the people with a fatherly expression. The waitresses were carrying two and three plates at a time passing by their table busily. Finally the cacophony was reduced when only two tables across the hall were occupied by loggers. One of the waitresses sat on a stool near the serving counter smoking a cigarette and looking at her nails. Another one was talking to the cook, a middle-aged man with an expanding beer belly and a dirty white apron, who was smoking a cigarette too. There were muddy prints on the floor from the logger's boots. But what caught Norina's attention most of all was a cockroach close to Nick's left foot. She pointed down to it and they all looked at it with great interest; Ner gave it its official name: "Orthopterous Insect Blatta Germanica."

The only place Norina had seen a cockroach was as a specimen many years ago in a lab. Nick was surprised to see a cockroach here in this climate. They usually live in southern climates but sometimes they arrive in boxes of vegetables from the south. Norina had had enough of this place and she was ready to go. Nick smiled at her and called the waitress. The bill came to $2.50 for all four of them. Norina had no idea of prices at all, but Nick was surprised how small the bill was. In his time they would have had to pay at least $30.00 or more; he gave the waitress three silver dollars and told her to keep the change, she was surprised to get such a big tip, but thankful nevertheless.

Nick asked the waitress if there was bus transportation to Port Angeles, and she said,

"Yes, the bus stops close to the door every half hour, and it should be here in ten minutes." They all thanked her and walked out. Ner reminded them that they had only thirty-three minutes left to send their hologram back home, and it would be prudent to send it now. He also told them that he had taken holographic data of humans and places ever since they started walking down the trail, including the restaurant a few minutes ago.

"All we need now, Norina, is to holograph ourselves and send the material back home."

"Then let's do it, and get it over with."

Ner set about three meters in front of them what appeared to be an old Kodak camera, but in actuality it was a holographic receiver and transmitter. There was a green light indicating it was in contact with the container up the hill. Ner told them it would start processing in a few seconds, and to start smiling. The green light expanded horizontally into a long thin line and then disappeared.

Project Anastrophe

"Norina, we just beamed the first material and the first hologram back to the future. In a few seconds we will know if they received it." A few seconds later there was a green star in the camera that grew larger and larger until it became the size of a dime and then it disappeared. Ner said,

"That's it, we are done. They received it."

There was a feeling of relief, and at the same time apprehension, because now they could be found by their enemy too. Ner assured them that all precautions had been taken. The material was sent in such a cryptic way that only the right people would receive it.

Chapter 6

The bus to Port Angeles came shortly after that and they were on their way. Nick asked the conductor for the price of four tickets, and again was surprised at how little he had to pay. All four sat down speechless enjoying the scenery. Last time Nick was in Port Angeles it was Greek Easter; he was in his early teens visiting his father's cousin Pappagerakis and his family. They stayed there overnight and had Easter the next day. Greek Easter is one of the biggest holidays for Greeks all over the world. His uncle Panos Pappagerakis always had friends and relatives over to his large farm house. He would roast a young lamb on the spit and there would be lots of beer, wine and retsina (a Greek wine treated with pine resin). The women would prepare the best dishes of the year. On two long tables cov-

Project Anastrophe

ered with blue and white table cloths, there would be a cornucopia of the best food the Balkan countries could offer.

In a large basket there were dyed red eggs put conspicuously in the middle of one of the tables. Before the feast began my uncle Panos and his wife Aunt Maria would pick up one egg each, then as is the tradition, Aunt Maria would hold her egg with one hand exposing one end of the egg, Uncle Panos then would hit her egg with the other end of his egg and say,

"Christos Anesti," (Christ is Risen), to which she would reply, "Alithos Anesti," (He is truly Risen). Then if he broke her egg he would have good luck for the rest of the year. The same thing would be repeated with the rest of the guests and whoever ended up with the unbroken egg would be the winner. There would be live music and dancing.

It was on that Easter day that Nick and his cousin Tasos were playing baseball out in the field, when a Greek girl called Zoe, whom he had never met before, came over and wanted to play. Tasos made it very clear he didn't want to play with girls. She left disappointed and Nick felt sorry for her. Later in the evening when they were playing soccer, (a game played by foreigners in those days), she became friendly to him when they were sitting on the grass and all of a sudden she asked him if he had kissed a girl before. He was so surprised that it took him a while to respond to her; but she gave him no time at all, she kissed him and ran away.

Norina leaned her head on Nick's shoulder and after a while she fell asleep. Vrima, sitting behind next to Ner, did the same thing. Ner didn't seem to like the idea and sent her a message telling her not to do that. She sent a message back reminding him they were a married couple now and if Norina could lean on Nick's shoulder, she could lean on his too. Ner stopped complaining and let her do as she pleased.

George Karnikis

Finally they arrived at Port Angeles. The main road was busy with "Model A" cars and even a few "Model T's." There were also horse-drawn carts along with the cars and trucks. Norina was fascinated by all this, and the slow pace of life in general. Both Ner's and Vrima's sensors and receptors were busy taking in everything. They would need to study their new environment, and adjust their lives accordingly. There was a young boy selling newspapers on the sidewalk; Nick bought one and then asked him if there were hotels nearby. The boy said there was one close to the church and pointed in that direction. They soon found the hotel called Olympia. It was an old two story red brick building with a steep roof and cedar shingles. All the trim around the windows was painted brown. They went in and registered with their new names and took different rooms. Ner had his first transaction with these humans, and was careful to use his newly acquired California accent. They got rooms next to each other, and Norina asked Ner and Vrima to come to their room in half an hour to discuss their next move. Ner and Vrima both lay in their bed and went into charging mode right away. At the same time they were analyzing all the data they had received so far, and were preparing reports for their next meeting. Norina and Nick took showers and put on some clean clothes. When Ner and Vrima came in, they decided to go to the dining room to have something to eat. Ner and Vrima had, as always, to act as though they were eating. Usually after each meal, they would make sure they cleaned their stomachs thoroughly to prevent any unwanted smells. However they were using a formula they made themselves out of proteins and vitamins for the biological portion of their bodies that needed nourishment.

They went down to the lobby. Norina was hungry and was anxious to get something to eat. She had eaten little of

Project Anastrophe

her breakfast after the cockroach incident. There were two potted palm trees and a spittoon by the door. Norina asked Nick what that cylindrical thing by the door was. But before Nick had a chance to answer, someone spat a mouthful of chewing tobacco into it and Norina got her answer first hand. She was disgusted with what she saw and Nick had to remind her; they were five hundred years back and that's how things were here and now.

They stepped into the restaurant. Norina could see this was different from where they had eaten breakfast. For one thing it was much cleaner, it had linen table cloths, not oil cloth; the waitress was clean, well-dressed and smiling and there was nice classical music coming from a speaker above their heads.

"This is much better, Nick, now if I could have something tasty to eat I would be quite happy."

The waitress came to their table and gave them the menus of the day. Norina looked at the chef's green salad and liked what she saw and ordered. The salad contained green lettuce, ground carrots, green and red peppers, with blue cheese and croutons, also some olive oil dressing that looked good. Nick ordered the same thing. Ner and Vrima had enough food for the day and just ordered coffee.

Back Home in the Future

Dr. Dylos and his scientific team were looking anxiously at the three dimensional picture unfolding in the center of the room. The Voyager with its four time-travelers had just left. There was an amorphous shape composed of many colors gyrating with tremendous speed. Every once in a while the picture would expand, and then it would decrease. It went on for a short while and then a fixed picture appeared. It began with the dimension of approximately one square half meter; and finally expanded to three square meters. In it one could see green grass and two small-sized bushes; also four people gathering boxes together, they were identified as Norina, Nick, Ner, and Vrima. The time-travel into the past was a success; there was a sign of relief on their faces. Dr. Dylos congratulated everybody in the room and asked Dr. Mageris what would happen next. Dr. Mageris told him now they had to wait for them to respond.

"Dr. Dylos, from what we see so far it appears they arrived in good health, but we are not sure exactly where and what epoch. We will know when we hear from them."

"And how long will that take?"

"It already happened hundreds of years ago so it's up to us to calibrate the right time and retrieve the information they have sent to us, and that will be a few minutes from now."

On the upper corner of the 3-D picture, there was a metric time countdown, the scientists had calibrated the exact time of the retrieval, and were now waiting anxiously for results. Finally in the center of the picture there was a square container with a bright white light on it, and then everything went black as though there was nothing there. Dr. Dylos asked in panic,

"Did we lose it?"

"Not at all. If everything went well, as we hope it did, we should have the container here any second." Before long they heard a cracking high- pitched noise; a blue and white curving line opened up and the gray container fell on the floor. The picture in the background disappeared altogether.

They all looked at it, dumfounded for a few seconds, then Dr. Mageris asked one of the robot technicians to check the box for radiation. It was clear and Dr. Mageris opened the box. In it they found many samples of various things Ner had put into it; but the most exiting moment for

Project Anastrophe

them was seeing the hologram Ner had taken of all the scenery, the restaurant, and the people including themselves. They were so glad to see the four of them looking healthy and happy, and then Dr. Mageris said,

"Look at the picture hanging above Norina's head. That is President Franklin Delano Roosevelt. That tells us the approximate time which could be from 1932 to 1945. From the sign we can see they are at the foot of Olympic National Park, the nearest town should be Port Angeles. Seattle is not too far from there. Ladies and gentlemen, I am happy to tell you that they are at the place and time we wanted them to be." Dr. Dylos again thanked them for all their efforts, and asked them to meet again tomorrow to discuss the next step of their plan. Now there were more urgent matters for him to take care of.

What Dr. Dylos had seen this morning scared him. There was another break in the ground at the Green Acres subdivision with radiation coming out at an alarming rate. So far two thousand people had been affected, and few of them were expected to survive.

All people and animals would be evacuated as soon as possible, and the crack in the ground shielded. Dr. Dylos went there as soon as he got the message from the Governor.

The crew was at the site wearing protective gear, installing a temporary shield, and ambulances were carrying people to hospitals. He was talking to the man in charge of the crew, who said,

"I have never seen anything like this before; I have a feeling it will get worse from now on." Later in the evening Dr. Dylos joined a special meeting the Governor had called to discuss the radiation problem. There were the usual scientists who had been working on it for years.

They were all shaken by the amount of radiation that

had escaped into the air and the number of people dead and injured. The Governor welcomed them and started the meeting right away.

"Ladies and Gentlemen, what happened this morning is terrible, but from what I heard from those who know more about it, it will get worse in the future. We must do something very soon to save lives."

"We are working on a plan, and if we are lucky, it will solve the radiation problem once and for all, but it will take time. Now we must do something to stop this catastrophe even temporarily; so I am ready to listen to any ideas you might have."

Many ideas were proposed, but the one Dr. Dylos liked the best was the one introduced by Dr. Ingar Nelson from the state of Sweden. It called for moving the people from the affected areas to higher ground, and then to flood the area with water. In places where this was not possible, they would cover it with special cement his company could provide. In both cases it would be only temporary; about three years at the most.

Governor Mary Nazer thanked them all and promised she would let them know in a few hours which plan they would accept; then she asked Dr. Dylos.

"Well, Dr. Dylos, do you have any preference as to which plan we should accept?"

"Governor, several of the scientists I have been working with in the last year think Dr. Ingar Nelson's plan appears, so far, to be the best we can accept under the circumstances although it comes with some dangers to the environment like most of them do."

"Could you elaborate on what dangers we are talking about?"

"In the case of flooding, the water would stay contaminated for thousands of years. As for the cement plan; al-

Project Anastrophe

though it would encapsulate the radiation, the area would be off-limits for about the same time too."

"And you think that's our best choice?"

"We do, at least for the time being."

"Then let's do it."

"We will start right away."

"Dr. Dylos, before you go I'd like to know what happened with the team we sent back in time. Have you heard from them yet?"

"Yes, we have. They have successfully landed at the appointed time and place, but I have prepared a complete report on this and you should be getting it soon."

"I should tell you that I have a lot of pressure from the business people to make changes in your arrangements. As you know, the change in nuclear energy will affect them, and they want to have a say in this."

"I know that Governor, but the survival of our planet takes priority over everything."

"As it should, but I have arranged a meeting between us and them for next week. I will let you know the exact date and time."

"That will be fine, Governor, we will be there."

Soon after Dr. Dylos left the governor's office, he got in touch with Dr. Ingar Nelson. He told him his plan had been chosen, and he could start the project right away. Dr. Dylos met with his scientific team two hours later and they discussed what had happened earlier today. They were more determined than ever to stop this killer radiation.

"According to what Dr. Ingar Nelson said, his method of shielding the affected areas would last three years at the most. This method has been used in other states and has worked so far. Does anyone of you have any questions?"

Dr. Mageris had a question.

George Karnikis

"What do we do after three years?"

"At the end of three years, the contaminated water is pumped out and moved to a large vat outside the biosphere and in the case of the cemented areas they will be excavated, moved and buried outside the biosphere too. Then we would start the process all over again, but I am hoping our team will manage to stop the radiation before it becomes more of a problem."

The scientists were busy analyzing the samples Ner had sent from the past. There was a small branch of a fir tree with a cone on it, pollen from different plants, a container of fresh water, a bag with small rocks, a cylinder filled with air, and many other small samples. Ner and Vrima had done their job well. Dr. Mageris was amazed at how clean the water and air were, and showed them to Dr. Dylos. Dr. Dylos told the team that they must have a name for their project, after all, if it worked it would abolish radiation poisoning, and save the planet and life of all living beings. It had to be an appropriate name for what they were doing. He hoped next time they met here they would have a name for it.

Dr. Dylos left the lab and drove home. It had been an extremely busy day and he was very tired. Next day when he checked his mail there was a holographic message from the whole team. Dr. Mageris smilingly uttered the project name, "PROJECT ANASTROPHE", from the Greek word for "turn things around". He said,

"After you left, we were all so determined to find the appropriate name for our project that we got busy right away, and after a couple of hours we came up with this name. We hope you like it. Dr. Dylos responded with enthusiasm, and sent them a message to let them know.

Project Anastrophe

Business versus Science

Governor Mary Nazer kept her word and called the two parties to a meeting. It wasn't something she was looking forward to. During the last week she had to talk back and forth to both parties to persuade them to compromise with something that would be acceptable to both; but to no avail. Now the dreaded day had come and she had no idea how it was going to turn out.

"Ladies and gentlemen, I would like to thank you once more for coming here today. I hope we can come to some kind of a compromise this time. I now call Mr. Jim McMiness to state the grievances on behalf of the businesses and the companies that challenge Dr. Dylos's science team. Mr. McMiness, please go ahead."

"Thank you, Governor, I can assure you that we all know how hard Dr. Dylos and his team have worked on Project Anastrophe to save our planet; and we thank them for that. Where we differ from them is in the way the new fuel and energy will be distributed to all on an equal basis. We feel that our businesses should be given priority. Otherwise it would change the status quo in our time, for all of our companies."

"Dr. Dylos, do you wish to respond?"

"Yes, Governor."

"Mr. McMiness, several of the businesses you want to help retain their status quo today, are the same ones that caused the radiation five hundred years ago. They are the ones that made and sold mini-bombs and other weapons, as well as radioactive tools and material. At that time all they cared about was the bottom line and nothing else. Now you want us to help your companies retain their monopolies once more? I am sorry, but this is one mistake we will not repeat. Our team has orders to distribute the new fuels equally to all companies. You may or may not be affected financially. We can't worry about that now. However, our team has been given orders to do all they can to make it easier for those companies to acquire part of the new fuels and energies which will be introduced at that time. I would like to emphasize the fact that this is not our priority, and if the owners of those companies try to stop our team and those who are helping them, I can assure you they will be destroyed."

"Governor, we want to make sure that our companies in the Twenty–First Century are given all the rights of purchasing the new fuels; otherwise we will be forced to send our own team back in time to make it so."

"This is very unfortunate. I was hoping that somehow our government and the business establishment would be able to come to some kind of compromise. I regret that, but when push comes to shove, I have to give priority to the success of our team out there which is trying to save our planet. Furthermore, I want to make it perfectly clear that any attempt from you, to stop or interfere with our team in any way, will be punished here and there.

My advice to you is to go along with what Dr. Dylos has proposed. Any delay caused by you may result in the destruction of our planet."

"Governor, with all due respect, we disagree; we are prepared to go it alone because we believe our plan will save our planet as well as our businesses."

The meeting ended abruptly and the business group left shortly after that. Governor Nazer was very disappointed with the negative results of the meeting; but nevertheless she was determined to stop them from interfering with the team already working on the plan back in time. She asked Dr. Dylos if there was anything he wanted her to do now that things had turned for the worst, but he said that he as-

Project Anastrophe

sumed from the beginning that they wouldn't cooperate and he had taken the appropriate measures to protect Project Anastrophe. He told her not to worry, everything was under control.

Dr. Dylos and his team left shortly after the meeting and went to their lab; there they prepared the first scheduled appointment with the team sent to the past. This time they sent the latest version of micro-weapons and special security gear. They needed extra protection from the enemy team that would be arriving near them in a short time. The cryptic message to Ner contained the words, "Red Dragon." Ner and the rest of the team knew what it meant and what to do. They quickly calibrated the time sequence and soon after that the Voyager with Dr. Narthur and a robot was on its way. They waited for the usual time lapse for the team to respond.

Jim McMiness and his group had their own meeting after they left the Governor's office. They went straight to the Sentunian club. There the discussion got pretty hot with the Du Bois brothers arguing on one hand, that the Governor was not useful to them anymore, and she had to go; on the other hand, Nazara Fouruga and Voha Hollanda argued that the Governor needed only to be persuaded to go along with them. Finally they decided to first try to persuade her to come to their side, and if that didn't work, to find or create a cause to fire her. If that didn't work either, as a last resort she had to be eliminated.

They also listened to their scientific team's plan to overpower Norina's group back in time. One of the main people they needed was Nephus, who was presently in jail.

Nephus and Narky were in the cafeteria having their usual breakfast.

"Hey, Narky, where are your friends now that we need

them; didn't they say they were going to get us out of here?"

"They will; they are not going to let us be here too long, they always come through, don't they?"

"I am beginning to wonder, Narky; we have been here three months, and I don't think I can take it anymore."

"Relax, Nephus, I am supposed to see the warden this morning, something is cooking. I'll let you know as soon as I know something—O.K.?"

"They probably want to interrogate you a little more, as usual."

"I don't think so, I think this time is different, but I'll let you know for sure."

The warden was all smiles this morning.

"Sit down, Narky; I got good news for you. You and your friend Nephus are going out today. You must have powerful friends somewhere; that's all I can say, but next time it's not going to be that easy. I am going to see to it that you rot in jail; now sign here and get the hell out of here."

Nephus was glad to be home; Zakov was glad to see him too. He told Nephus,

"Some guy by the name of Elisio Camarino called and said he had to talk to you as soon as you were out of the poky."

"Did he say why?"

"No, he just sounded urgent, he said he'd call again later on."

"O.k., now scram and if anybody calls, tell them I am not here!"

Nephus called Darna at work, but she wasn't happy to talk to him. He told her he was sorry she ended up in jail because of him, and promised her from now on they were just going to be friends. She wouldn't have to do anything for him again; then he asked her to go out to dinner. Her

Project Anastrophe

answer was a flat, "no", and she terminated their conversation abruptly. She loved Nephus and would love to go out to dinner with him but she was afraid of him. She often wondered if he would have followed Narky's orders and killed her back in that cabin. Her feeling was that he wouldn't; but why take a chance now?

"Mr. McMiness, we have everything set up for the trip back in time and we would like you to come over and see what we are doing here."

"Thank you, Dr. Dorgovich; I'll be there with the Du Bois brothers this afternoon."

"Remember this has to be kept secret."

"That's for sure, sir."

The space ship was one of the latest models, far superior to the Voyager. The scientists hired by the Du Bois brothers had done an excellent job for the trip. Everything from provisions to weapons, to the best crew they could find, were there, except Nephus. They had tried over and over again to have him join them but to no avail, he didn't want any part of it. John Du Bois wasn't used to having people not go along with his plans. He told McMiness,

"Make him a generous offer and if he denies it, tell him he goes back to jail."

"That's a good idea--I'll have Narky talk to him right away."

The call from Narky came the next day; Nephus was not happy at all.

"Hey, Narky, this isn't an offer; you are giving me an ultimatum and that's not fair."

"I know how you feel, Nephus, but this order comes from the 'big boys'. There is virtually nothing I can do for you. You have to go or you go to jail!"

"Well I have an ultimatum for the 'big boys' too. Tell them Darna comes with me or I will happily go to jail."

"I will tell them what you want, but I don't have much hope."

This time Elisio Camarino called Darna. He told her that a large credit of money would be put into the bank in her name if she would go and help Nephus on an expedition.

"I don't care for your money. The last time I helped Nephus he wanted to kill me, and I managed to get away, but still ended up in jail. Now you are asking me to go on an expedition with him? Where are we going anyway?"

"I don't know. All I know is that you go with Nephus or go back to jail."

"We'll see about that."

"You have to let me know today, or worse things could happen to you."

"Get lost before I call the police, and you find yourself in jail."

"The police huh, I wouldn't try that if I were you, sweetie."

Now Darna was scared. She couldn't even call the police. She went and talked to her boss Fura, who listened carefully and then she said,

"Darna, if I were you I'd go. I think the police are corrupt and you might indeed find yourself in jail or worse yet, dead. On the other hand you could find out more about this conspiracy, and help us expose them. In the meantime we will get in touch with the authorities we know we can trust, and get you out of there sooner than the last time. What do you think?"

"I'll give it a try, but I am scared."

"It will be O.K., you'll see."

Not long after Darna arrived home, Nephus came to her house to see her for the first time after three months in jail. Darna wasn't receptive.

Project Anastrophe

"Darna, I think we need to talk."

"Talk what?"

"You know, about you and me. I just think you shouldn't be afraid of me--that's all."

"Three months ago you tried to kill me and I shouldn't be afraid of you, come on, be real, do you think I am stupid?"

"It's true that I was asked to eliminate you in case you refused to come along with me to another biosphere, but I would never have done that, because I love you."

"Then they would have killed both of us."

"I don't think so, for the simple fact that they needed me then, and they need me now."

"And where do they want us to go anyway?"

"I can't tell you now, but I can tell you that it is going to be very unusual and exciting."

"Is it going to be dangerous?"

"Yes, it will be very dangerous, but if we make it, it will be very profitable."

"And if I say no?"

"Then it could be dangerous for you, because now you already know enough to put their plan in jeopardy."

"It looks as if I don't have a way out, do I?"

"Actually, there is a way out, just join us and chances are that we will both survive with enough credits to enjoy the rest of our lives."

Nephus and Darna went to their first meeting with the Dubois' scientific team that was preparing the trip back in time. There were three robots sitting next to them, and a man close to Nephus. The man was in his fifties with gray hair and a tall athletic body. He had blue eyes, wore a goatee, and looked very intense. The robots were two males and one female. There were two robots guarding the door. Other robots were dispersed in various key places; two of them were serving drinks to humans. There was a group of important looking people. Finally a man walked into the room and went straight to the podium. He was a tall man, about 185 cm. He was in his forties, with black eyes and black hair. He looked healthy and well kept, and had an air of command.

"Ladies and gentlemen, my name is Dr. John Dorgovich and I will be in charge of the team that is going back in time to the year 1938. Our plan must be kept secret, and for this reason I have ordered the crew of the spaceship to be sent directly to the ship after our meeting."

Then he directed his attention to the group nearest to him and said,

"You have asked me to direct this expedition to save your businesses and our planet. I am ready to do that. There will be difficult times ahead because the team that has been sent there by the government is going to resist us, but let me assure you, this crew and equipment are the best there is, and we are capable of doing the job.

Our scientists have calculated our departure at precisely 10:15 tonight metric time. The place of departure will not be revealed at this time, for obvious reasons."

There was only one question from Mr. John Du Bois,

"Dr. Dorgovich, does the government know how close we are to go back in time?"

"We have to assume they know, but we have taken all necessary precautions. Before we leave I would like to introduce you to two of our new crew members; Mr. Nephus and Miss Darna Varnether."

After his short speech everybody left except the robot guards and the crew. Then Dr. Dorgovich called the crew to a meeting and said to them,

"I have purposely kept you apart until now for security reasons; however I know each one of you very well, and I

Project Anastrophe

have selected you based on your experience pertinent to this project. Tomorrow at this time you will be living in another place and time. You will land somewhere out in the country, and you will stay there until you learn all you need to know. Then you will be given orders for your next assignment. If there are any questions you can ask me or Dr. Sam Lorkost who is sitting next to Mr. Nephus. Now I am going to let you get acquainted with each other. We will meet again after lunch."

"Nephus, you son of a bitch, you trapped me again. You could have told me they wouldn't let us out of here. I can't just disappear; what will my family, my friends, and my employer think? I can't leave like this, and what is this going back in time, are they for real?"

"Oh yes, they are for real. We are going back in time. But Darna, I didn't know they were going to keep us here so soon either."

"I don't see of what use I can be to them, why did they get me?"

"I am sorry, Darna, but I got you. You see they gave an ultimatum to me too. They said,

"'You go with us, or you go back to jail.' I didn't want to go to jail, and I sure as hell didn't want to go alone. I love you Darna, and I am prepared to go anywhere with you."

"Well I was fine without your love, and I was happy where I was; now I will be lucky to come back alive."

"Take it as an adventure, it will be an exciting experience, and you'll have a lot to write about when we come back."

"Correction--if we come back!"

Dr. Dorgovich came back right after lunch as he promised, and called the crew to a meeting.

"First of all, I want to thank you for being here. I know

that some of you are here against your will, but I chose you because you have something special to offer to this expedition. I am going to name you one by one, and tell you why you are here starting with my friend Sam Lorkost who is second in command. Should anything happen to me, he will take over this expedition. He and I are in charge of the fuel and energy change, i.e., we are going to change the atomic and carbon fuel to antimatter and electromagnetic energies.

There is a team there right now, sent by our government, which is doing the same thing. The only difference is that in the name of expediency and equality they would let everyone have access to these energies. But we are going to distribute the new energies only to those early companies that have survived to our time. They are going to fight us with everything they have, but we will do it our way and we will save our planet from radiation, and at the same time make sure our companies retain their status. This is what Sam and I are planning to do, and you are going to help us do it.

Nephus is in charge of all robotics and electronics. Darna will be our P.R. person who will take care of all living expenses, reservations, and anything that has to do with the outside world. The three robots will be given human names that will be determined later on. They are in charge of all the technical and security matters. We will land somewhere out in the country, and there we will stay for a few days to prepare ourselves before we mingle with the people of the 20th Century. As I said before, we are going to be leaving here at precisely 10:15 metric time. You are forbidden to come in contact with anybody inside or outside. You are going to be taken to a special place to relax and prepare yourselves for departure. That's all for now; I will join you later. Thank you and good luck to us all."

The room was comfortable where they were to spend

Project Anastrophe

the last few hours before departure. Darna wanted to send a message to Fura to let her know what was about to happen. But she was strip searched and they took everything she had, including her telle-unit and wallet. They told her she was going to have a different I.D. She went for a shower and then lay in bed trying to put her thoughts in order. Nephus was there studying some of the material he had been given at their last meeting.

"Feeling better, Darna?"

"No!!! I want to go back home---not back in time. I am tired and scared."

"I think you will like it once we are there."

"I can't think anything right now, just leave me alone."

The three robots had just finished charging their batteries and they gathered in the living room. They were especially made and programmed for this project. They were in charge of making the first samples of antimatter and electromagnetic energies, and they were to introduce them to the people of the 21st Century. They also had to show them how to dispose of the hazardous nuclear material properly, without endangering the environment. They were also ruthless fighting machines. They had enough power in them to annihilate a city of hundreds of thousands of people and animal life. Ner and Vrima would be against formidable enemies.

They were also programmed to be civilized, and mingle with the people of the nineteen thirties. Ner and Vrima, in comparison, were far more complex. They had the same or superior powers, but more biological matter, especially Vrima. They were psychologically, and in some cases, pathologically in tune with humans. Ner and Vrima were endowed with much more artificial intelligence. They were the best robotic science could offer at this time.

When people of the 20th Century saw the five robots

among them they would only see five simple citizens; they wouldn't have the faintest idea of the concentrated power that was in them. The three robots' identification was simply: AZM, BZM, and CZF. They were of the Z categories males and female with AZM being the leader. Their conversation would be mainly of their technical abilities and the amount of data they possessed. They would discuss war theories and battles or military engagements all through the history of mankind. A human general would envy their accumulated power and knowledge.

"Sam, are you ready for the big jump back in time?"

"I suppose I am as ready as I am going to be, although a bit apprehensive about the whole thing."

"I think it's going to work out O.K. for us. We are going to be dealing with a group of companies that are already established. All we need to do is to convince them to change to new energies. On the other hand, our opponents will have to deal with most governments in the world, as well as the companies that have the monopoly in fuel and atomic energy."

"I am afraid that Governor Nazer will eventually interfere with our project and stop us here, as well as back in time. Our opponents have unlimited help from this Government and we don't."

"I wouldn't worry about that; the Governor is going to be replaced with one of our own pretty soon. The Du Bois brothers are going to see to that; they have too much at stake to let her interfere with this project."

"I hope you are right."

Back in time

None of them had ever tried anything like this; the preparation and the time travel were awesome. The vibra-

Project Anastrophe

tion, the bright changing colors, and the feeling of being in the void of time were something they would never forget. They were dropped somewhere in the country; humans, robots, material, provisions, and weapons, all in one drop. While John and Sam were trying to find a suitable place for a temporary stay; Nephus was trying to give courage to a very scared Darna. She hadn't recovered yet from the difficulty of time travel. The robots under AZM's leadership were busy putting things in order and preparing the two tents that would be the temporary places for them to live.

The dinner had been great, and both Norina and Nick felt good; even Ner and Vrima felt relaxed. They were planning their schedule for tomorrow with Ner explaining a few technical things they had to overcome, when he stopped cold. Both Ner and Vrima were busy doing something, and that alerted Norina and Nick. Norina was about to intervene to see if Ner was compromised by someone or something, but Vrima motioned her to wait. They didn't have to wait long, Ner started to tell them the message he had received.

"We are on RED DRAGON alert. They all knew what that was. It meant that they had visitors from back home, enemy combatants with three robots and four humans.

Ner went on to say that there had been a delivery from Dr. Dylos of one robot and a human male at their temporary base up in the park. Norina was concerned for the human's condition and was anxious to get him out of there. Within minutes, Ner got a message from the robot, saying that they had found the base. They were both O.K. and waiting for orders for their next move. Norina got in touch with the human, and she recognized him. The last time she saw him was right before they left. He was one of the scientists in charge of weapons and security. His name was

George Karnikis

Dr. Neal Narthur, a man in his late sixties, with very little hair on his head. He was not in top condition, so she was surprised he had been sent here. Ner reminded her that he was the best in his field, and they must be in great danger for him to be here with an extra robot.

They went into defense mode. Nick thought they should go to Seattle sooner than planned to secure a permanent place for themselves and all the weapons and material. Norina told Dr. Narthur to stay put at the base and not to venture out anywhere until he was brought to a safer place. She also told him that she was sorry but the only way they could transport him was by beaming. He said he was prepared for that.

Now they had to find a new base and houses for all of them. Nick thought the best place for a permanent base for weapons and material would be on a small unoccupied island in the San Juan Archipelago.

They all agreed it was a good idea. But neither Norina nor Nick wanted to be beamed there. They decided to fly to Orcas or Friday Harbor, rent a small boat, and find a suitable island.

Next day Nick asked the young lady at the desk in the lobby if they could fly to either Orcas or Friday Harbor. She said they could. Norina told Ner and Vrima that this time only she and Nick would be traveling. They were to wait until they reached their destination, and then they could beam themselves to the appointed place.

Norina and Nick took their backpacks and played tourist once more. They were driven by a taxi to a small airport and flew to Orcas Island. They landed on a remote, unpaved strip of land with cows and deer nearby looking intently at them. Nick paid the pilot and asked him to come back in five hours. They walked to Eastsound, a sleepy small town, with two churches, a grocery market, a black smith shop, and a hardware store. There were a few smaller shops here and there but very few people around.

Nick went into the blacksmith shop and talked to a man who was pounding a horse shoe. He stopped and said, "You must be tourists, what can I do for ya?"

"We are looking for a place to rent a boat."

The man pointed to a gas station and told them, "You can rent one there."

At the gas station there was a woman dressed in overalls.

"Good morning, we are interested in renting one of your boats."

"Are you going fishing?"

"No, we just want to go and see some of the smaller islands."

"In that case you need to use that larger boat. It has a bigger motor and it will be just fine for what you want to do."

They followed her to a floating dock where several boats were tied up; she pointed to a wooden boat, it was large and had a huge outboard motor. The bow of the boat was covered and it was neat and clean. The woman said her name was Judy; she was sorry her husband wasn't there to tell them more about the boats.

She started the motor and explained a few things they needed to know. Then she left it running, while she went back to the office with them to fill out a form.

She said,

"It is a beautiful day. You're going to enjoy your trip."

And that was it. They took off and pretty soon they were out and away from Orcas Island in search of the appropriate small island.

Judy was right; it was a nice sunny day. Nick steered the boat, while Norina sat in the stern. She enjoyed the fresh cool air gently brushing her face with drops of salty water every now and then. Her long blond hair danced in the wind. They went around Orcas Island and visited several smaller islands in the archipelago. Finally they chose Yellow Island, between San Juan and Orcas islands. It was in the right vicinity and it was the size they wanted it to be. It was managed by the State Parks Department.

They walked on the island until they found a perfect spot; then sat down to have the lunch Vrima had prepared for them.

Norina sent a message to Ner and Vrima giving them the coordinates of their position. Within minutes they beamed themselves to the island. Ner and Vrima thought this island was a good choice and started preparations for the new base. They chose an inconspicuous place and were careful not to disturb the island's ecosystem. With a powerful laser excavator they dug a narrow tunnel that went down ten meters into the ground. There they dug a hole, 4x5x 3 meters high. The rocks and soil were reduced to ash and were scooped and thrown out to sea without much difficulty.

Into it they beamed all the weapons, equipment, material, and provisions along with the new robot. Ner gave directions to the robot instructing him to stay and guard the base until he was needed. Then they carefully covered the open pathway leaving a secret entrance. With the base secured and a robot guarding it they all felt better. Ner and Vrima beamed themselves back to the hotel. After Norina and Nick finished their lunch, they decided to walk a little more on the island. It was early in May, and there were many beautiful flowers with bees landing on them, sucking nectar and carrying pollen away. The birds were nesting and flying every which way. Norina was amazed with Nick's ability to recognize so many different birds and name them one by one. He would point at them and say,

Project Anastrophe

"Look, that's a male Varied thrush and that one over there is a Goldfinch and that one is a Fox Sparrow."

They went to the beach, found a sandy place, took off their shoes and socks and put their feet into the water. It was very cold but felt good after all the walking they had done on the island.

Shortly after that they got into the boat and headed back to Eastsound where they turned the boat in. They walked around the small town for a while and then went back to the airstrip. They arrived in time to be picked up by the pilot who was there waiting for them. They flew to Port Angeles, and the taxi driver drove them back to the hotel. Ner and Vrima were happy to see them back safe and sound. As soon as they arrived, Norina got in touch with Dr. Narthur who had been left alone after the robot and everything else had been beamed to the new base.

He was outside of the old base enjoying the last few hours of the day. He was admiring the tall fir trees, the greenery, and most of all the fresh air that was so plentiful in this time. Shortly after that a long vertical line appeared near the base indicating the coming of a holographic message.

Soon Norina's image appeared smiling at him; he smiled back and said,

"I am so glad to see you, Miss Norina."

"I am glad to see you too, Dr. Narthur, how are you feeling today?"

"I am much better."

"Are you ready to be beamed?"

"Yes, I am."

Norina's image disappeared, and the frame with its bright lights became a portal into which Dr. Narthur stepped. He was beamed into Norina's and Nick's room. He was pale, shaken, and sweaty. They put him to bed and Norina administered first aid for post travel metasomatosis.

"Have you done this before, Dr. Narthur?"

"Oh--once, a long time ago, when I was very young; then it wasn't so bad, but now at my age it's not easy."

"Just lie here for a couple of hours and you will feel better."

"I think we have a long way to go before we can travel metasomatically in safety and comfort."

"I agree with you, Dr. Narthur, I have done it twice in the past, and felt as bad as you are feeling right now."

"Dr. Papas, how nice to see you again; I feel so much better to be with the two of you."

"And we are so fortunate to have you here, Dr. Narthur."

They left him in bed and all four of them went to have dinner. Norina and Nick were starving. Ner and Vrima charged themselves as soon as they beamed back from Yellow Island and as usual they pretended to eat. They quickly started to talk about finding permanent housing. Norina said,

"We need to start looking for houses in the Seattle area. They should be in close proximity but not too close, don't you agree?"

"What do you think, Nick?"

"I think we should live outside Seattle. I believe it would be safer and quieter."

"Yes, Ner?"

"Norina, if I may interject here."

"Go ahead, Ner."

"I agree with Nick. We have to be away from the city because we need to retrofit all the houses with the appropriate safety and communication gear. We can accomplish this more easily out in the country."

"Then that's what we should do, but where?"

"Why don't we go to Kent? That's not too far from Seattle, and that's where I live, or I should say where I will live, in the future."

"Good idea, Nick, then you and I should look for our house; then help Ner and Vrima find theirs, and also find a house for Dr. Narthur. It will be easy to find a place for Dr. Narthur, he can say he is retired; but we have to declare some kind of profession, don't we?"

"That's not going to be a problem, we are in between jobs and we will pay cash. That won't be as much of a problem now as it will be in the future."

"Then we will all leave tomorrow morning at 8:00 a.m. local time."

"How about Dr. Narthur, will he be in good shape to travel?"

"I am sure he will be better by tomorrow."

The food arrived and Norina and Nick even ordered wine with their dinner. Ner and Vrima had soup and toast; it was easier to clean their stomachs afterwards. The next day bright and early they took a taxi to the bus station where they caught the Greyhound to Seattle. They rode all the way to Kingston and from there caught the ferry to Edmonds. On the other side they caught another bus to Seattle. Norina was amazed how slow the transportation system was; with her magneto she would have been in Seattle in less than ten minutes. Nick told Norina that with slower transportation they were able to see and enjoy the country; whereas with the magneto everything would look blurred. Norina agreed with Nick and said that it was beautiful country, and that she enjoyed the scenery immensely.

Ner and Vrima charged themselves while they were in the bus. They took advantage of the sunny day and used their solar receptors to fill their batteries. Nick spotted a Greek restaurant called "Athena's Cuisine"; they went in. It was a narrow place with four small tables. A man in his forties, with a thick black mustache and a heavy Greek accent, approached them and said,

"Come in, come in."

He directed them to the last free table and they all squeezed around it. Nick told Norina to order the mezedakia plate. She didn't even question what she was ordering; she was so hungry she could have eaten nails. Nick ordered souvlaky and Ner and Vrima ordered their usual salad; only this time it was Greek salad and it would take longer to clean their stomachs.

Everybody, including the Greek, was smoking. Although Norina was still disgusted with that habit; she was resigned to the fact that they weren't going to change at this time. On each long wall, there were murals depicting the Parthenon and other scenes of ancient places, gods and goddesses. The Greek man saw Nick looking at the murals and said,

"You like, yes, yes?"

Nick said,

"I like them very much, they are wonderful murals."

The food came not a minute too soon for Norina. Her plate had small portions of Greek delicacies served with warm pita bread and Greek salad for all. Nick ordered retsina wine; Norina tasted it and tried hard not to spit it out on the table.

"What is this; this is not wine is it?"

"Yes, it has a little resin in it, but it clears the wine and it's good for you."

Ner tried it and said,

"A substance used in paint thinner and other pharmaceuticals."

Norina told Ner she had heard enough and then said to Nick,

"Thank you, I think I'll have water."

Project Anastrophe

They had a wonderful lunch and then caught the bus to Kent. It was a quiet suburban area with few people and even fewer cars. In Nick's time, only sixty some years in the future, Kent would be a very busy city with thousands of people and cars going every which way. People would have to be very brave just to cross the road.

Nick liked to see his city so early in time. They went to one of the few real estate offices in town and Nick talked to a man by the name of Sam Olson. He offered them coffee and was complaining about the traffic in town. Nick wanted to tell him,

"You ain't seen nothing yet," but refrained from doing so.

Ner and Vrima were looking at the small shops, and then waited for Nick and Norina at the City Hall as they were told to do.

"Mr. Olson, we would be interested in seeing houses in Cedar Grove; do you have anything available there?"

"There are a few houses that were foreclosed by the banks and are selling at very good prices. You know people are having a hard time paying their mortgages nowadays."

"We would like to see some of them, because we have friends here from California who might be interested in buying too."

"Well, I would be delighted to show you the houses, let's go." Mr. Olson drove a new Model A car, a lot nicer than the taxi they had taken in Port Angeles.

"Are you folks from California too?"

"No, we are from England and we are going to start working at the University of Washington as visiting professors."

"I detected an accent; I just couldn't quite place it. You do know it is going to be a long drive to Seattle."

"We like it that way."

"Well then that settles it, now we just have to find a house for you and perhaps for your friends."

They drove down the main street and went by the old St. Mary's Catholic Church; only now it wasn't old. As they drove past the church Nick's heart started pounding fast. He wasn't saying anything but was looking anxiously for the house in which he would be born a few years from now. And before long there it was; a little different, but for the most part it looked as he remembered it. He contained his excitement as best he could and asked,

"Who lives in this house?"

"Oh, I sold this house last year to a Greek family called Papas. They are a very nice family and I believe they have two little boys and a little girl. Tears came to Norina's eyes as she listened. Nick felt a lump in his throat.

As they drove by, Nick recognized one of the little boys playing in the front yard as his father, Fotis. The other boy was his uncle Yorgos and the girl had to be aunt Demitra. He wanted so much to jump out and go to see them and grandfather Stelios and grandmother Meropy, who gave him sweet baklava when he used to visit her as a little boy himself.

Finally they stopped close to an old farmhouse.

Sam said this was one of the nicest places in the area, but the owners couldn't pay the bank and they went bankrupt. The crash of the stock market in October 1929 was affecting many people even today.

One thing the bank had done was to subdivide all the foreclosed lands into five and ten acre parcels and sell them with or without houses. The farmhouse was in good condition but needed some work. Norina liked it but said nothing at the time. They drove farther and saw other houses and by the end of their drive they had a pretty good idea of what they wanted. Sam drove them back to his office and reminded them that all these properties were on the basis of "first come, first served." They told him they would let him know by tomorrow, and left.

They found Ner and Vrima sitting outside the City Hall charging their batteries as the sun was sinking in the west. There were two hotels in the downtown area; they chose the one closest to them, went in and registered for the night. The hotel's name was

"Kent's Best", although Norina thought otherwise. Ner and Vrima stayed in their room and had their special liquid formula. Norina and Nick went out and found a nice restaurant and ordered dinner. Nick asked Norina what she thought of the houses they had seen so far.

"I liked the farmhouse we saw first. It's large and has a large living room which will be needed for all our equipment. It will be a good place for all of us to meet."

"I liked that house too; it's also close enough to keep an eye on my family."

"Then we should buy it; but what about the others?"

"I think the smaller house closer to town will be perfect for Dr. Narthur and the other small farmhouse out of town will be good for Ner and Vrima."

"I agree. The next thing we need to do is to open accounts in a bank in Seattle."

"Don't you think there might be a bank around here?"

"I don't think it's a good idea putting so much money in a small bank. It would look very suspicious and we need to look as normal as possible."

"We better go and tell Ner and Vrima about what we decided." Ner and Vrima were happy they were going to have a permanent house to stay in. They were eager to start securing the places because they knew the enemy was closing in. Next day Nick and Norina went to Sam's office and discussed prices for the three houses. Nick said he was authorized by the other two parties to negotiate prices and deposit down payments on their behalf. Sam showed them the prices of the three houses. The large farmhouse went for $10,000, the smaller for $9000, and the plain residence went for $7500. Nick asked Sam if the bank would come down to $9500 for the large farmhouse. Sam said these were good prices and he didn't think the bank would go any lower. Nick and Norina finally agreed and asked Sam if a $2000 down payment would be enough to secure the three houses. Sam said that it would be fine and gave Nick a receipt for $2000 in cash.

"We will come tomorrow with the other two parties and sign the papers if that's all right with you?"

"It will be just fine; could you come around 3:00 p.m. so that I will have time to prepare all the paper work?"

"That will be fine with us too."

Sam was delighted for the chance to sell three houses all at once. He gave them a receipt for the two thousand dollars and said he was sure there wouldn't be any problem with the bank.

Nick and Norina left Sam's office and went to the nearest restaurant for breakfast. Nick said.

"I can't believe how low the prices are for those three houses. In my time sixty years from now, one would have to submit $31,000 or more for a down payment on only one of these houses."

"Then why did you ask him to come down on the price of our farmhouse?"

"I wanted to look and act normal, because you always try to bring the price down on a big purchase like this."

"I am anxious to bring Dr. Narthur here for his safety

and also to have him sign the papers for the purchase of his house."

"Are you going to beam him here?"

"I would like to do that but I am afraid he wouldn't survive another beaming so soon. I think you should give him directions how to come here by bus."

"Then I had better get in touch with him very soon."

They had a quick breakfast and went back to the hotel. There Nick got in touch with Dr. Narthur and gave him directions how to go to the Bank of Commerce in Seattle where they would be waiting for him. He told Dr. Narthur that if he were to leave now he could make it on time before the bank closed. He also told him to act as normal as possible, and have ready change on hand for the buses and the ferry tickets.

Dr. Narthur felt pretty good after a full night's sleep and was ready for the big trip. He had a hearty breakfast and soon after that he was on his way to Seattle. Life was so slow here and he liked it. He had never traveled in any vehicle that drove so slowly. He was fixed at the window watching the different pace of life unfolding before his eyes. In his future time and place, life was too fast. Living in biospheres and fighting a constant battle with radiation was difficult to say the least. Living out in the open was a new and exciting experience for him. Here the air was fresh and clean without the filtration system they had to have back home in the future.

"Where did man go wrong--why couldn't they see it coming? Would it be possible to reverse all this?"

"They will soon find out, but it's worth the effort to try to save the planet Earth and humanity."

The trip was long and tiring, but he was satisfied with the experience.

He walked up the marble steps of the Seattle Bank of

Commerce. He admired its huge marble columns and its depictions of Greco-Roman scenes above the revolving doors. It looked like a Greek temple.

He met his four friends who were happy to see him arrive safe and sound.

Chapter 7

It was a beautiful early morning; the robots were preparing breakfast in the main tent for their human companions. Nephus was already up sitting on a grassy knoll looking down on thousands of conifer trees, and farther below to a sparkling sea. The scenery was magnificent and he was filling his lungs with the fresh air so abundant here. He was eager to get busy with this project. He imagined himself with Darna back home; living in a nice climate like this without radiation, under an open sky and with a lot of credits.

A squirrel, a few feet away, was chewing on an acorn looking at him suspiciously, but holding his ground. In Nephus' time and place you could only see a squirrel in a zoo. There were deer and eagles and many other animals roaming freely; a luxury their descendents would not have in the future. He went back to his tent; Darna was in bed, a sleeping beauty, unaware of his presence. He looked at her for a while and he reminded himself how fortunate he was to have her here with him. He pushed her gently on the shoulder and woke her up. She opened her eyes, looked at him and said,

"What time is it?"

"It's eight in the morning local time; do you want to have breakfast?"

"I suppose so, give me a minute to dress and I'll be out soon."

She got up and walked naked across the floor.

"What are you looking at?"

"Oh, Darna, it never ceases to amaze me how beautiful you are."

"Right now I don't feel beautiful but I do feel hungry."

"Then let's go have breakfast."

They walked into the main tent where Dr. Dorgovich and Sam Lorkost were already finishing breakfast. They sat opposite from them at the same table.

"Good morning."

"Good morning, did you guys sleep well?"

"We feel much better today, thanks."

It was Nephus who did the talking. Darna would rather sit somewhere else; much less talk to them, but she was stuck for the foreseeable future and had a job to do at least for a while. She wasn't happy at all being here to begin with. BZM robot came by and asked them if they would have breakfast now and they said,

"Yes." The breakfast wasn't much to talk about; it consisted of four sticks of different colors but they were very nutritious. They would expand in the stomach and give one the feeling that he had eaten four slices of bread. If taken in the morning, one could go on for a whole day without being hungry.

She ate her breakfast unenthusiastically and was about to get up to leave, but Dr. Dorgovich asked her to stay.

"Darna, I know you are not happy to be here, but now you are, we all are, and we need each other in order to survive. What we are about to do is very important; we are here to stop radiation before it occurs in our time. You should be proud to be a participant in such an important project."

"Dr. Dorgovich, we don't need to be here at all. There is a team sent here to do just that, and all we are going to do is make their job more difficult."

"Our way is much better because we are going to save the planet and the jobs for millions of people in our time. If we let them do it their way, we won't have some of the biggest factories which have contributed so much to comfort, luxury, and health in our time."

"All we are doing here is trying to save the monopoly and the status-quo of a few businesses, that's all. But as you said earlier we need to help each other to survive and I will do my part. My main interest is to go back home alive with the portion of my credits--that's all I care about."

"I am glad you understand that you have to do your job here and that's all that's needed."

Dr. Dorgovich went on to say that they were to meet in two hours to discuss the schedule for the next few days. Darna got up abruptly and left; Nephus followed her to their tent. He tried to talk to her.

"If you are going to blame someone it should me, I brought you here and I am sorry. I thought it would be good for both us to do this together. I didn't want to go back to jail and who knows what they would have done to you. I realize now that it was selfish for me to implicate you in all this, but I love you and want you with me. Besides, you are a reporter and when this thing is over you are going to have a hell of a story to write about. Think of the credits you are going to earn Darna--think about it."

Darna was lying in bed sobbing; Nephus sat next to her caressing her hair and telling her everything was going to be all right. Darna turned around and nestled her head on his chest. They stayed in bed for a few minutes then Darna spoke,

"I am sorry; I don't know what came over me. I acted foolishly, but I don't like these people, and I don't like being here."

"Let's go for a walk, we still have time before our meeting."

They walked to the knoll where Nephus had been earlier in the morning. Darna looked around and for the first time since they arrived here she paid attention to the country. It was truly beautiful; so many trees and the air was so clean and fresh.

"Do you feel better?"

"Yes I do, the walk helped me a lot, and it's so beautiful out here."

"I wouldn't mind staying the rest of my life. I could use the stock market, as they call it, make lots of money, be rich in a very short time, and have all the things money can buy. Wouldn't that be a good idea, Darna?"

"I like this place too but I want to go home where I belong and perhaps in a clean and safe environment."

"I was only kidding; they wouldn't let us stay here any more than we need to stay anyway."

The meeting took place in the large tent; all four humans and the three robots were there. Dr. Dorgovich started by saying,

"So far we have been lucky. We have managed to land

Project Anastrophe

here safely with all our weapons and equipment, but we can't let our guard down. The team that has preceded us is very powerful and has the help and protection of our government. We need to proceed with our project very carefully and engage in battle with them only as a last resort. Nephus, do you have a question?"

"Are we going to build our base here or are we going somewhere else?"

"We need to find a place that is infrequently visited and AZM will elaborate on this later. Darna, do you have a question?"

"Are we going to transport ourselves daily from here to town?"

"Of course not; we are going to live somewhere in town and beam material or weapons as needed."

"AZM wants to tell us his plan so let's listen to him now."

"My partners and I have found a secure area, out of the way about a kilometer from here. We are planning to build an underground base and move everything there within the day. I am going to leave BZM to guard the base. CZF and I will be coming with you whenever you are ready to go."

"Very well, thank you, AZM. Now I propose we go to Seattle proper and see if we can find suitable residences for us. But on this I am open to ideas--Sam?"

"I don't think it's a good idea to be in a big city like Seattle. I think we should be out in the country just like they have done. They have taken up residence in a small country town called Kent. I propose to find residences for us likewise but in the opposite direction, a good place would be Redmond and it isn't too far from Seattle."

"Unless someone has a better idea, let's do that. We will be leaving for Seattle tomorrow morning to open a 'checking account,' as they say here, with one of the banks.

With checks and money in hand we can do business as needed. Darna is in charge of all these matters and should you have any questions, direct them to her. Darna, do you have any questions you want to ask?"

"I don't, but I need to inform you that we all need to have new names and professions according to the plan. Here is the list I have with the changes for each one of us; memorize your new names and professions, it's very important. That's all I have to say for the time being."

"Thank you, it looks as if we are done here for the day. Go and get ready, tomorrow is going to be a very busy day."

It was another beautiful day. Nephus and Darna got up early and went and sat on their favorite knoll overlooking the forest and the sparkling sea beyond. The sun was climbing up the eastern horizon bathing nature with its young bright light. There was a harmonious sound emanating from all around them; it was something very seldom experienced at home. Darna was starting to appreciate her new environment. She knew very well this was an ecosystem on its way to destruction by governments willing to use everything at their disposal for power and greed.

The robots had done their job well; they had worked all day and most of the night making the new base and securing everything in it. AZM had given directions to BZM for guarding the base and now he and CZF were picking up the tents. Later in the morning they all gathered on the knoll where Nephus and Darna were sitting and had their last meeting before leaving. Dr. Dorgovich said,

"Our plan is to go down and find transportation to Seattle; we will have something to eat on the way." Darna asked a few questions with regard to their new names.

"I would like to hear your new names and professions one by one before we leave. Let's start with you, Nephus."

Project Anastrophe

"My new name is Gary Green, and I am an Electrician."

"Sam?"

"My new name is Frankie Gallitas, and I am a scientist."

"Dr. Dorgovich?"

"My new name is Blef Martison, and I am also a scientist."

"AZM?"

"My name is David Ampton, and I am a mechanic. BZM is not here right now; he is guarding the base but he knows his new name is Larry Cappo and he is a mechanic too."

"CZF?"

"My name is Carol Ampton, I am David's wife, and I am a housewife."

"And my new name is Susan Robinson, I am a teacher." Then Dr. Dorgovich said,

"It looks as if we all have our new names and occupations; there is nothing more to discuss here; let's go."

All four humans and two robots started down the hill following one of the more frequently used pathways leading to the main road. As they were going down they met many people coming up. Dr. Dorgovich had given them strict orders not to talk to people anymore than they had to; so other than the usual salutations they pretty much kept to themselves. After a three hour walk they came to the main road. They hadn't walked far on the road when they came to a gas station. Darna went in and talked to the lady who was manning the station, "Hi, we are on our way to Port Angeles and I wonder if there is bus service around here?"

"There is a bus on its way to Port Angeles that will stop here to get gas in about thirty minutes; this is not a bus stop but I am sure he'll let you in."

"Can we wait here?"

"Well of course, honey, make yourselves comfortable."

"Thank you very much." Darna motioned to them to come closer, and when they did she said to Dr. Dorgovich,

"The lady said we can get the bus from here when it stops to get gas, it will be arriving in about thirty minutes."

"Is this a bus stop?"

"No, but she said he'll let us in anyway."

"Ask her how long the bus takes to get to Port Angeles."

As Darna was going into the little shop she noticed the ice box by the door, she opened it and looked in. The woman came by and asked Darna if she wanted to buy ice cream.

"Yes I would, but let me ask my friends if they would like some too."

She asked them if they would like to have ice cream and they all said, "yes" except the two robots. While the woman was getting the cones, Darna asked her how long it would take to get to Port Angeles.

"You are not from around here are you?" It was one of those unexpected questions and Darna was caught unprepared, she answered as best she could,

"We are from New York and are on our way to Seattle."

"I knew you wasn't from around here, honey, I see them tourists every day in the spring and summer and once I talk to them for a few minutes I often know what state they come from. Now I forgot your question, what did you ask me, dear?"

"How long is the trip to Port Angeles?"

"Oh yeah, it takes about three hours-- here is your ice cream." She handed her the ice cream cones, and asked for twenty cents. Darna gave her a quarter and told her to keep the change. She also asked the woman the price of the

Project Anastrophe

ticket and she said, "fifty cents". Darna thanked her and they all went and sat on a long bench eating ice cream while waiting for the bus.

Darna had three dollars ready for the tickets. Before long a bus with a Greyhound painted on both of its sides stopped by the gas pump. Darna asked the driver if they could get in, and he said "yes." She tried to give him the money but he pointed to a square metal box attached to the driver's chair and she put the money in. There were many empty seats; Nephus and Darna sat together and so did the two robots. Dr Dorgovich and Sam sat in the back of the bus.

"Most of the passengers are soldiers," AZM commented to CZF electronically while at the same time appearing as though he was taking a nap.

"The soldiers are most likely on the way to report to their bases; as you know there is a war about to start in Europe and this country is taking defensive measures by beefing up its military."

"I quite agree with you, C; I wish I could take part in the coming war."

"Me too, A."

"Who knows, we may have a chance after all, C."

"I sure hope you are right, A."

Dr. Dorgovich and Sam also appeared to be taking a nap but they were both busy recalling and checking various things they had to do, using their implants. Nephus and Darna had a real honest conversation and finally he asked her,

"Darna, how do you like this place so far?"

"I like it, but I would like it better if I had something to eat right now."

Dr. Narthur was happy to see his friends.

"Dr. Narthur, how was your trip?"

"It was very educational. I am so glad you didn't beam me here, Norina. I like this slow pace of life. It gives me time to think."

"Well, we better go into the bank before it closes; you do remember your new name I hope?"

"Yes, of course."

The bank was huge and there were three lines of people, about six to seven people in each line. Some people were talking among themselves; others were waiting their turn, lost in thought. It was Friday and many were cashing their pay checks. Nick, Norina, Dr. Narthur, Ner and Vrima were in the third line with an older couple in front of them being served by the teller.

They heard a man's loud voice coming from the main door; he had a gun pointed at the crowd and said,

"Everybody on the floor, anyone who attempts to move away will be shot. Stay put, and you will be O.K."

There were two more gunmen placed strategically on each side of the people while a fourth man held an open bag and ordered the tellers to put the money in. Everybody did as they were told, including Ner and Vrima, but they were busy talking to each other in their own undetectable way. Ner said to Vrima,

"Don't use the laser gun to kill. Set the beam to stun only, send a double beam; one to the gun, the other to the body; you take the gunman on the left closer to you, and the one by the tellers. I'll take the one to the right, and the one by the door. Go!"

It was all so fast that no one knew what had happened until it was all over. Ner and Vrima moved with lighting speed. The first beams hit all four guns which became so hot the gunmen dropped them on the floor. The next four beams hit the gunmen and they too fell. Their hands, hold-

Project Anastrophe

ing the guns, were slightly burned but none of this was noticed by the people; all they saw were two persons, one man and a woman, moving fast and putting the four gunmen out of action. Ner and Vrima dragged them and set them against the wall; they all seemed to be dazed and didn't know what had hit them. They would be like that for an hour or so, easy to be apprehended by the police.

As soon as the people realized what had happened; they quickly got up and started to clap and thank Ner and Vrima for their heroism and bravery, but there were a few who wondered how they had done it. The police arrived soon after that and the four men were taken away.

Shortly after that the bank resumed its business, and one by one all the customers were helped according to their needs. The police asked Ner's and Vrima's names, they gave their cover names. The officer in charge told them,

"Some people thought you had superman's powers is that true?"

Ner's quick thinking saved them from being discovered. He said to the officer,

"We are both black belt holders in Martial Arts; we are not supposed to use our know-how on untrained people but this time we thought it was necessary to save peoples' lives."

"You did the right thing, and we thank you for that."

The bank manager heard their conversation and said,

"Thank you for helping us capture the thieves, if I were younger I would enroll in Martial Arts too."

The manager made sure they were taken care of expeditiously, and before long they had new checking accounts. He also gave them some temporary checks to use until they received their own. They had all been furnished with the appropriate I.D. cards and licenses ahead of time. Norina congratulated Ner and Vrima for a well done job, but told them they needed to be very careful as to how they used their powers. Nick said,

"I think we better go get some transportation, so we can move around easily."

Norina said,

"That would be an excellent idea, but we know very little about driving these cars, Nick."

"I am going to buy a large Buick so we can all fit in, and later I will teach you how to drive it."

It didn't take them long to find a car dealer. Nick zeroed in on a large gray Buick and the salesman was eager to help him.

"Our latest model, the nineteen-thirty-eight Buick, our best ever, and the price is good too. My name is Pete Michelson, how do you do?"

"Fine, thank you, I am Robert Johnson and this is my wife Loretta."

"Would you like to take it for a drive?"

"Yes we would, thanks." The five of them got into the car and Nick drove. It felt so heavy and strong. The last car Nick had driven was a Toyota and the difference was like day and night. He drove it around the block and when they came back Nick said,

"I like the car, how much does it cost?"

"Only $250 and that includes taxes too."

"We are new in town, and I only have temporary checks, is that all right?"

"No problem, but it has to be O.K.'d by the manager."

A quick phone call to the bank verified the check was good and after all the legalities were taken care of, they bought the car.

The next day all five of them drove to Sam's real estate office, and signed all the necessary papers. They paid with three different checks for the three houses. Sam told them that it would take a few more days to finalize the sales; but they were now the legal owners of the houses and they could do with their properties as they pleased.

They spent a few hours going from house to house making notations of the various things they needed to do to refurbish them. Ner and Vrima were more interested in securing all three houses as soon as possible. They checked and made sure there was no spying apparatus planted by the other group; then immediately installed electronic surveillance in and around the houses. Ner communicated with robot Diphus on Yellow Island and gave him the coordinates of the new houses.

While Ner was doing all this Vrima was beaming the necessary equipment and weapons into all three houses. While there was some furniture left in the houses, they needed to get more in order to make them look normal. Ner and Vrima didn't have to pretend eating any more than they had to, so when Nick, Norina, and Dr. Narthur went out to have breakfast they stayed there beaming from house to house finishing everything that needed to be done. Norina had a hard time getting used to this new transportation; what took seconds with her magneto took hours with this so called Buick car. Frequently she would know there was a car in front of them by the cloud of smoke left behind, even though she couldn't she see it.

With the houses bought and secured and a Buick to drive, Norina was anxious to get busy with their main project. But Nick reminded her that all four of them needed to learn to drive and they needed to get two more cars. Norina concurred and asked,

"What kind of cars do you have in mind, Nick?"

"I think the best choice would be a Ford for Ner and Vrima, and a Plymouth for Dr. Narthur."

"When can we buy the cars?"

George Karnikis

"I suppose we can go to Seattle and buy them today. You all know the traffic rules and regulations, you have your driver's licenses and you have driven magnetos. All you need now is to learn to drive slowly. I can give you a short course with the Buick and then familiarize you with the Ford and Plymouth."

"That sounds good to me, how about you, Dr. Narthur?"

"That sounds good to me too, let's do it."

After breakfast they drove back to the main farmhouse where they found Ner and Vrima charging their batteries and waiting for them. They used the country road for practice driving the Buick, and it didn't take long to get the idea of driving slower. In fact Ner and Vrima had run computer simulations before and drove like 'pros'. It took a little more time for Norina and Dr. Narthur but soon they were all ready and eager to get it done.

They drove to Seattle and bought the cars the same way they bought the Buick and were on their way back driving in separate cars. Norina and Dr. Narthur were a little nervous but did well. The next day Nick and Norina drove to Sears Roebuck and placed an order for new furniture to be delivered to the three houses. Norina reminded Nick of the appointment they had with the Dean of Physics at University of Washington in two hours. After a few errands and a bite to eat they arrived at U.W. on time to meet with Professor Daniel Tyler, a physicist in the Department of Fission.

Professor Tyler was a man of few words who would take his time answering a question put to him. People would often repeat themselves thinking he hadn't heard them, but he always came up with the appropriate answer. He was a Phi Beta Kappa graduate from Harvard; summa cum laude in physics. He had dark curly hair, dark brown

Project Anastrophe

eyes, he was a nice looking man in his forties, about 180 cm but he looked somewhat pale and tired.

"So you come from England? I must say you both have very impressive resumés. I see here that in addition to being well-known physicists you have both been working in Cambridge for the last five years as Exegesiologists in Radio energy and Fission; that is a new and exciting field. I see that you have been working in separate laboratories back home; I am afraid here we don't have the facilities you have there, would you mind working as a team in one laboratory?"

"Not at all, we have worked together before; it won't be a problem."

"I see no reason why we can't hire you, but you do understand your application will have to go through the board of directors; that will take a few days but we will let you know as soon as possible."

Ner and Vrima went through the same procedure and were hired as Mr. Roy and Ms. Mary Eastman, Roy as physicist/ kinesiologist and Mary as physicist/ mathematician. Norina called all of them to a meeting at their large farmhouse. She and Nick had done a good job fixing up their house with the new furniture they had received a few days earlier. Ner, Vrima, and Dr. Narthur had also received their furniture and had fixed their houses according to their needs so they were all anxious to get busy with their main project. After Norina welcomed everybody, she asked Ner to speak first.

"Last night I had a communication from Dr. Dylos urging us to start the process of nuclear conversion as soon as possible. The radiation has gotten much worse lately resulting in thousands of fatalities. According to Dr. Dylos, there is a strong possibility that Governor Nazer will be forced to resign her office prematurely under pressure from the Du

Bois brothers. That will make our task here much more difficult.

He has also given me the exact coordinates of the other group which has arrived here. Vrima, Dyphus and I know their whereabouts at all times. It is my feeling that, because of lack of time and the possible interference by a new Governor, we must act quickly."

"Thank you, Ner, we all know we have to do something soon but unfortunately we are not known here yet. We need to first start working at the University and then, as hired professors, we will be able to talk to the various people. Nick, go ahead."

"We can get in touch with the important people who make policies, all we have to do is gain an audience with them; then we can prove that we do come from the future and tell them what the problem is. We no longer have the luxury of time, and if we don't act now the other group will."

"Dr. Narthur, please go ahead."

"We know that Dr. Peter Thomas will be selected to direct the bomb project at Los Alamos; and the Trinity explosion will take place in southern New Mexico on July 16 1945, approximately seven years from now. It should be our priority to talk to him first. He is an intelligent man and it's my feeling he will believe that we come from the future. After we show him the catastrophe radiation poisoning will cause, he may change his mind and not accept the appointment. At least he would know the danger associated with nuclear weapons and nuclear power."

It was decided that Norina, Nick, and Dr. Narthur should go and talk to Dr. Thomas as soon as possible.

"O.K., Nick, how are we going to get in touch with him?"

"If am not mistaken he has a girl friend named Lisa Fillmore who is going to be his wife in the future. I propose

Project Anastrophe

we pay her a visit and eventually we might be able to meet with Peter. I don't promise much, but it's a start."

"Where does he live?"

"I don't know but Vrima is in charge of that kind of thing."

Vrima came up with most of the information they needed.

"According to my data they both worked at U.C. in Berkeley in 1938-9. In 1939 they fell in love and got married sometime in 1940. I would assume that now she knows him casually."

Vrima gave them Lisa's address and the next day the three of them flew to Berkeley California, and found her working in the biology lab.

Lisa was an attractive young woman but somewhat serious. She told them she would meet them at the cafeteria in half an hour if they could wait for her there. Norina was surprised how primitive everything looked; even Nick found a big difference in the sixty years that had elapsed from this time to his time in the future. Lisa came on time as she promised and they talked while she was having lunch. Nick and Norina introduced themselves and told her that they were both physicists from England. And they would start working as visiting professors at the University of Washington in two weeks.

"This is Dr. Frank Robertson, Professor Emeritus in physics."

"We are here to discuss an important matter that has to do with future energy and radiation; but we need to talk to both you and Dr. Thomas. So far we have been unable to locate him."

"Why me, there are so many other people much more qualified than I am, what makes you think that I can be of any help to you?"

"As you can imagine we can't discuss this matter here. Would it be possible to meet with the two of you perhaps in a restaurant and talk about it over dinner?"

"Dr. Thomas and I are casual friends and I don't see him very often but I'll see what I can do. Are you staying here in Berkeley?"

"Yes, we are staying at the Claremont Hotel and we could have dinner there if that's O.K. with you."

"That would be fine with me but I still have to talk to Dr. Thomas. I will call you at the hotel and let you know."

"Thank you very much. It's been nice meeting you and we hope to see you again soon."

Lisa wanted to see Peter and this was as good an excuse as any. She phoned him at his office and told him about the three visitors and dinner at the Claremont Hotel. He agreed to meet her at 7:00 p.m. at her house and then drive together to the hotel. Lisa called and talked to Norina and it was agreed they should all meet at 7:30 p.m. in the dining room.

Before Norina and Nick left home, Vrima supplied them with the profiles of both Lisa Fillmore and Dr. Peter Thomas. They knew about Thomas's life here and abroad; his medical history and education, and other pertinent information as well as the cause of his death from a car accident 1970. They also knew a lot about Lisa; her vital personality and her keen intelligence. They knew that she would fall in love with Peter and marry him in the near future.

Nick, who did most of the talking with Peter and Lisa, was very happy to meet both of them but especially Dr. Thomas. He had been his idol through all his professional life and now he was talking to him face to face. The conversation was turned quickly to the main subject by Dr. Thomas.

Project Anastrophe

"Dr. Johnson, what is this new energy you want to talk about?"

"In time we will talk to you about it; but first you need know who we are and why we are here at this time and place. What we are about to tell you will sound unbelievable, but it is imperative that you let us finish what we have to say before you respond. I will be quick and to the point.

All three of us come from the future, and to be exact, from the twenty-fifth century. Dr. Thomas looked at Lisa with wide open eyes and bewilderment. The same expression appeared on Lisa's face, but Nick motioned to them to let him finish.

"We wanted to talk to you especially because you, Dr. Thomas, will be one of the people who will help to develop an atomic bomb that will endanger our planet and everything that lives in it.

The so-called Trinity explosion will take place in southern New Mexico near Almagordo on July 16 1945. So seven years from now, under your direction, our planet will start to be contaminated not only by this country but by many others. The U.S. and Russia will build thousands of atomic bombs as well as hydrogen bombs which will be even more powerful.

Everybody will be living under the threat of nuclear war which could wipe out our planet in minutes. Nuclear power will be used for peaceful reasons too, but there will be accidents which will release radiation and will kill many people and animals. Dangerous radioactive byproducts of this nuclear power will be buried underground and kept there for thousands of years contaminating the earth and subterranean waters.

Terrorists will have access to smaller bombs called "Pocket-nukes." they will detonate them in large cities killing thousands of people and other life. Your own country, the U.S.A., will be the first country to use two atomic bombs in Japan; one with uranium in Hiroshima, and the other with plutonium in Nagasaki on August 6th and 9th 1945. Those bombs will kill even more men, women, and children. But why am I telling you all this? Because in the Twenty-Fifth Century the radiation will be all over the planet Earth. People will be living in biospheres to protect themselves from radiation poisoning; but at that time in the future even the biospheres will be contaminated and people will be dying by the millions. At that time anything the scientists could do would only be temporary, delaying the unavoidable destruction of the planet. We cannot change the "Prime Directive", but we cannot let our planet be destroyed either, that's why we are here. Dr. Thomas, it's too late to stop these nuclear bombs and radioactive energy from being made and used, but now that you know the danger perhaps you can help to slow and control them.

Another thing I have not mentioned yet is the oil you use for fuel in your cars and for producing electricity, to mention only two. It will be used by transportation and industry to such an extent that it will contaminate the atmosphere, and people will get sick and die. In the beginning of the Twenty-first Century the oil supply will be depleted, and there will be many wars over it. These wars will claim many young lives. But we can help you and teach you how to make and use alternative energies which are clean and safe for the ecosystem. I am not expecting you to believe who we are without some kind of proof. We will show you things that will leave no doubt in your minds that we are who we say we are. You just tell us when you are ready. It has to be just the two of you and you must not say anything to anybody else. At this time only a few selected people should know, and we will tell you who the others will be. I have said most of what I had to say, thank you for being so

Project Anastrophe

patient, now I will be happy to answer any questions you may have."

"Dr. Johnson, I don't know where to start; what you have just told us is a bit much to comprehend. I am sure I speak for Lisa when I say that perhaps the three of you have a more sinister agenda. Perhaps you want to delay us from completing the atomic bomb which will enable us to defend ourselves from unstable countries such as Germany. There are other countries experimenting with nuclear power and you will find no one in this country willing to stop the race to get the bomb first." Lisa spoke next,

"If I may interject here, Dr. Johnson, with all due respect, you have to understand that it is hard for us to believe the three of you came from the future; and that you are here to save the world. What you are telling us are stories we read in science fiction books and magazines. It's impossible for us to believe your story. I don't know about Peter, but I would like to see what you have to show us; if what you say is true, then by all means, we would like to see what we can do. What do you think, Peter?"

"I am very skeptical, but I am willing to give it a try."

"Then it's all settled. We could meet here at our hotel or at your place."

"You mean you can bring your stuff to my place?"

"Just tell us the time and place and you'll see."

"Let us meet at my place; Lisa and I will be waiting for you there tomorrow at 7:00 p.m. I live at 527 University Street here in Berkeley."

"We will be there, but as I said before, just the two of you for the time being. Please, don't say anything to anybody else."

For the rest of the evening the conversation went on to many topics. Both Dr. Thomas and Lisa were impressed with the knowledge these three people had in every subject they discussed. Nick, Dr. Narthur, and Dr. Thomas were discussing quantum theory and the possibility of measuring the frequencies and intensities of the molecular band spectrum; and how quantum mechanics, when used appropriately, could explain much about observable phenomena.

Norina and Lisa also talked science but their conversation quickly changed to more feminine topics. Norina told Lisa of her life in the future, her service as a scientist in space travel and her hopes and aspirations after she finished her service with the government. Then she spoke of her fears about the radiation poisoning that was destroying their habitat right now and killing so many people needlessly.

Lisa was starting to like Norina. She could see that she was a sincere intelligent woman; but she still had problems believing that she had come from the future and wanted to be convinced otherwise. Lisa told Norina of her life and her career as a woman scientist in a man's world. Then she moved closer to Norina and said that she loved Dr. Thomas and he didn't even know it yet. Norina had to try hard not to tell Lisa that she knew all about their affair and that they would get married soon and have children. But Norina had to adhere to the "Prime Directive" and not say anything. After three hours of eating and talking and with both Dr. Thomas and Lisa smoking, Norina had had enough and thought it was time to leave. She sent a subliminal message to Nick telling him she wanted to go. He smiled at her and said,

"Dear, I think we had better go and let these people go to bed, after all they are working people and have to get up early in the morning."

They all left soon after that. Nick and Norina went upstairs to their room and Dr. Thomas and Lisa to his place where they had another drink and talked about their new acquaintances. Lisa said,

Project Anastrophe

"I like them."

"I do too. But spies can act well, and until they can prove to me that they do indeed come from the future, which I doubt very much, I am going to think they have a different agenda. But I, like you, hope they are who they say they are."

"Maybe we will find out tomorrow."

"I sure hope so."

Peter offered her another drink but she said,

"Thank you, Peter, I had a wonderful time but now I am tired and need to go home." Then Peter did something he had never done with Lisa, he kissed her and said,

"Lisa, I think I am falling in love with you."

That came as a complete surprise to Lisa because she hadn't thought the feeling was mutual. She said,

"I think I am too." And with that they kissed and Lisa left for home.

Chapter 8

Lisa arrived early at Peter's place and brought some food for them to eat, he supplied the wine. Since they had parted the night before, they were anxious to meet again. Their friendship made them feel like new lovers, even though they had both loved other people in the past. Peter experienced something different with Lisa. For the first time he thought that he had finally found a woman with whom he could build a lifelong friendship—perhaps marriage.

He was getting tired of all those parties that lasted into the small hours of the morning. Lisa too saw Peter differently from the other men. He was sensitive, and she found that they shared many common feelings and ideas. So this time when they met again they saw one another with different eyes-they were really, truly in love.

Project Anastrophe

They had two hours to eat and talk before their visitors came. They discussed their lives and aspirations as never before. They also spoke about the visitors who were about to arrive. Lisa said,

"I am very excited about what we are going to find out about our friends; they seem to be sincere and very knowledgeable in every topic we discussed. I am beginning to believe them and hope I won't be disappointed after tonight."

"You know, Lisa, ever since we left them last night I haven't stopped thinking about them. I have thought a lot about time-travel and I don't see how it can be possible. I think perhaps it could be possible for someone to travel into the past, but how could one travel into the future when it hasn't happened yet? Anyway this whole thing seems impossible to me."

"That's why I am so excited about these people. They seem so sincere, and yet what they say is so unbelievable."

There was a knock on the door and they both blushed as they opened it.

Nick, Norina, and Dr. Narthur had talked about visiting Dr. Thomas and Lisa before they arrived. Nick thought that they should have Ner with them and then, after a while, beam Vrima to the house so that Ner had some time alone to talk with Peter and Lisa. Norina and Dr. Narthur thought they should beam both robots at the same time and talk altogether. Finally they agreed to beam Ner first and then Ner would beam Vrima. They had communicated with Ner and Vrima and told them they were about to be beamed so they knew all about the visit.

Dr. Thomas welcomed them and offered drinks which they gladly accepted. Both Peter and Lisa noticed the fact that their guests came empty handed. If they had brought something with them it had to be small enough to fit into their pockets. Dr. Thomas said,

"Thank you for the dinner; both Lisa and I had a wonderful time and we were glad to meet you." Nick said,

"The feeling is mutual."

Lisa couldn't wait any longer,

"I thought you were going to bring some kind of machinery to show us."

"Give us a few minutes and we will, but first we would like you to meet a friend of ours."

Both Peter and Lisa looked at the door thinking they were about to have someone else coming through. When nothing happened, they looked at Nick who was putting something in the middle of the floor.

It looked like a regular plate but gray in color. Soon there was a blue flame-like emanation from the center of the plate. Slowly the flame grew vertically to about two meters. It was a cool flame which looked more like an apparition than anything else. Peter and Lisa were transfixed looking at the flame and Lisa thought they were in for a good show. The flame became brighter and brighter and then a person started to be composed before their eyes. The flame stopped and a person stepped away from the plate-like object; turned around, picked it up and gave it to Nick. Then he faced Dr. Thomas and Lisa and shook hands with them.

They both offered their hands mechanically, amazed. Ner introduced himself with his new name.

"My name is Roy Eastman, how do you do?"

Dr. Thomas and Lisa stammered,

"Fine, thank you," in a mesmerized state. Then Dr. Thomas turned to Nick and said,

"How did you do that?"

"We may have our trouble with radiation, but we are a very advanced society."

Project Anastrophe

"Mr. Eastman, did you also come from the future?"

"Dr. Eastman and his wife Mary came with us a few weeks ago." The next question came from Lisa.

"How does a person feel being disassembled and reassembled in such a way; and isn't there any danger when the re- composition takes place?"

"It isn't very pleasant to be transported like that. In fact one feels very uncomfortable for a few hours, but every particle of one's body is morphed back exactly to its original shape without any problems at all. For reasons I shall explain later on, Dr. Eastman is not experiencing any discomfort at this time."

Ner didn't look ill at all; he was very pleasant and took part in the conversation in a courteous and professional manner. Norina was the next to speak.

"As Robert has already told you, our planet will be in great danger in the future; but for us the future is right now, and the planet along with every living thing is being destroyed with every minute that passes. It's very important that you believe us so that we can start the process of preventing the release of radiation before it occurs. Dr. Eastman will show you the destruction as it is happening right now in our home place and in our time."

Ner talked to them in a precise, knowledgeable way and spoke right to the point. He told them that what they were about to see would convince them beyond doubt that they came from the future and they needed their help to save the planet from complete destruction. He told them to feel free to ask any questions they might have.

Ner took something out of his pocket which looked like a large black egg, and set it on the floor. After a few seconds a white line started to materialize. It began moving from the center of the egg-like object going in a straight line horizontally to the left. It kept going for about one meter then turned up and went all around until it made a two by two square meter screen. Then from it came a twisting cloud-like shape, composed of different colors. It kept twisting very fast for a few seconds until a picture started to form and soon after that, the cloud disappeared. In its place remained a three dimensional picture of a busy city, everything looked alive.

Peter and Lisa couldn't believe their eyes; they had seen movies before but this was different. It looked so real to get all this out of something the size of an egg---this was unfamiliar technology and they were both beginning to get used to the idea that their new friends may have been telling the truth after all. As they were watching the 3-D hologram movie they were listening to Ner who was narrating what was unfolding in front of them. Soon they were overtaken by what they were watching.

First Ner showed them a busy city but it was very different from their familiar cities. There were cars flying two to three meters off the ground--- some even higher. The sidewalks were moving along with trees and people. The buildings looked very different; one in particular looked like a huge octopus standing on its eight feet. It was one hundred stories high; another one looked like a huge onion made from some kind of glass. There were few square buildings. It looked as if the buildings were made so as to catch the light from all sides.

There were trees on and off the moving sidewalks; and large flower pots in many places. The sidewalks acted as horizontal escalators with people standing or walking on them. There were many large flying ships as high as four hundred meters above the ground and cars flew in and out of the city. It looked very clean and orderly; in short, it was a city out of this world, a city to be admired.

Ner was doing a good job explaining and describing

Project Anastrophe

everything in detail, and then he showed them some places that had been affected by radiation with huge areas covered with a type of cement. All the buildings around the affected area were abandoned and there was nothing living to be seen, it was a necropolis. There were many necropolises and they were all covered with see-through domes. Then Ner zeroed in on a site as it was happening.

The ground was separating with a shrill cracking, noise accompanied by seismic movement. The people who fell in were crushed to death but the worst of all was what you couldn't see. There was a radioactive cloud emanating from the open ground so intense that thousands of people close to it died instantly. Those who were farther away suffered horrible burns all over their bodies and one could assume that most of them would die a slow and painful death a few days later.

People alive or dead would be quickly taken away by specially trained crews. The process of covering the schism would start right away; and another necropolis would be added to the grim list. Ner went on to explain that these radioactive explosions used to occur once or twice a year; but now they occurred on an average of once every month. With thousands of fatalities the planet earth would be destroyed in two to three years. Ner continued,

"Although we are an advanced technological society there is nothing we can do to save ourselves and our planet at this time."

After the projection stopped Ner picked up the little projector and put it in his pocket. Peter and Lisa were speechless. They were amazed by the technological achievements humanity had made five hundred years in the future; and at the same time they were horrified by the loss of life and the destruction that radiation had caused to the planet.

Ner asked Peter and Lisa if they had any questions.

Peter said,

"I don't understand; with all your technical and scientific capabilities you cannot stop or neutralize this radiation poisoning."

"Dr Thomas, believe me, scientists from all over the world have tried for hundred of years to do just that. So far all we have done is to temporarily stop the radiation when and where it occurs, only to have it happen again. We have now decided to prevent it before it comes to the point where it will harm us in the future. That is why we are here. As you can see, we have no other way of doing it."

Lisa was clearly shaken by all this and said,

"What do you people want us to do? We can do very little at this point."

"I think I am going to let my wife, Loretta, answer your question."

"My question to both of you is; have we convinced you that we come from the future and are you willing to help us?"

"I think Lisa and I are convinced that you are who you say you are, but I still don't know how we can help you right now."

"In time you will be able to help us. We want to stop the bomb from ever being developed, but we can't do that because we can't interfere with the "Prime Directive." But we can help you slow down the production and distribution of these nuclear weapons; as well as the radioactivity which will be used in the future.

We know the two bombs you will help to develop will be used in Japan. They will kill thousands of people and although we can't stop those bombs from being developed, we can at least educate you and your friends to the danger of nuclear power. We can help you develop new energies to substitute what you have now, and what you will have a few years from now. I am going to have Dr. Narthur talk to you about your security and ours."

Dr. Narthur stepped closer to them and said,

"We are a group of three humans and three robots; we all specialize in various things important for this mission. Our orders are to find those people who are in charge of the plans for making these weapons, and those who will be in charge in the future. Many of these people are your friends or will be your friends; that's why we start with you.

Another reason we are interested in you is because you favor the poor and middle class. We have another problem that's not related to you, but you could be in danger because of it. In addition to our group which came to your time and place, there is another group which tries to do the same thing, but in a different way. This will delay, and could jeopardize our mission. We were sent here by our government to do what we have just explained to you. The other group was sent by several private businesses which, even at this perilous time, will try to secure their monopolies at any cost.

They are four human beings and three robots. They are very powerful and determined to do it their way; they will stop at nothing in order to achieve their goal. We are also powerful and we can stop them. We work for the state and are only interested in helping humanity and our planet. We are telling you all this so that you know. We promise you and your friends that we will be on your side and will protect you from the other group.

Dr. Thomas felt ill at ease after what he had just heard. He didn't know whether he should worry about his and Lisa's safety or if he should feel secure with these people. Lisa interrupted his train of thought when she asked,

"You said that you are a group of three humans and

three robots, four of you are here, so by default one of you must be a robot, is that so?" Ner volunteered to answer Lisa's question.

"Yes, you are quite right, Lisa, one of us is indeed a robot. Can you guess who that might be?"

Both Peter and Lisa looked inquisitively at the four of them. They all looked human; they acted human, and were very intelligent. Lisa was hoping Norina would not be the one. She liked Norina and the thought of talking to a robot with her most inner thoughts was too much for her.

"Anyone but not Norina, pleaseeee she thought." Peter thought Dr. Frank Robertson might be the one; he kept to himself most of the time and never engaged in conversations unless he was asked. Finally, they both said with one voice,

"We can't guess."

Ner got them out of their predicament by saying,

"I am the robot, that's why it didn't affect me when I was beamed here a little while ago."

Now it made sense to both of them because from what they had heard, any human who gets beamed would feel uncomfortable for a few hours---but Ner? He looked so human, in fact even more so than the other. If that's true, (and from all indications it appears to be so), then he is a technological marvel to be admired. Ner went on to say that he was purchased by Dr. Loretta Johnson and he was her personal valet. He was of the latest Z models which contains eighteen percent brain matter. But for this mission he was Roy Eastman and was here as a scientist along with his temporary wife who was also a robot.

With that he took out of his pocket the egg-like object, put it on the floor, and just as before, the screen appeared and Vrima was their latest visitor. Then Ner said,

"May I introduce my wife, Dr. Mary Eastman?"

Vrima, just like Ner, was very pleasant and said,

Project Anastrophe

"I am so happy to finally meet you. I know so much about you." Then she turned to Peter and said,

"Dr. Thomas, for better or worse you will be very famous and people will know about you throughout history." Peter was awestruck by her beauty and demeanor and said,

"Are you really a robot?"

"Yes, just like my husband, I am a robot too. I was purchased by Dr. Robert Johnson and I am his secretary, but for this mission I am the wife of Dr. Eastman."

In the meantime the trip to Port Angeles was uneventful; it was dark when they arrived. They all went to the nearest restaurant and ordered dinner, but the two robots had coffee and stayed with them because they had no other place to go. Nephus and Darna sat together and said nothing to anybody. After dinner they all went to the same hotel, Olympia, just as the other group had done. They stayed for the night.

Nephus and Darna made love for the first time since they were taken to jail. Next morning after breakfast they all met in Dr. Dorgovich's room to discuss the schedule for the day. It was decided to leave today for Seattle and stay there overnight.

As usual Darna paid all the bills and purchased the various tickets in the bus as well as on the ferry to Seattle. AZM and CZF used most of their time to do somatic diorthosis, (body repair), in their cybernetics. Nephus and Darna were in love all over again and were looking forward to another busy night at the next hotel. Dr. Dorgovich and Sam were discussing and revising their plan all in complete silence with the help of their implants. Nephus and Darna were talking to each other without the help of their implants; they liked to hear themselves talking in hushed tones.

"Darna, I can see us back home with all the credits we are going to earn; living the good life for a change, and this time without the police after us. Wouldn't that be nice---what do you think?"

"You are by far too optimistic, I will be happy to go home alive and unscathed."

"But it would be great to go back to a restored environment, and be rich enough to live the rest of our lives comfortably."

"As I said before, there is a group of people doing the right thing here and with the help of our government. We are illegal here, and we'll be illegal if and when we go home. What we are doing is wrong, Nephus, and we will pay dearly for it."

"The present government is going to be changed with one friendly to us and everything will be all right, you'll see."

"I hope you are right, Nephus."

Ever since Darna was forced to come here against her own will she lived for the moment and hoped to get out alive. Nephus was a good lover and a person she could count on for protection for the time being; she leaned her head on his shoulder and tried to relax. After many hours of travel by bus and ferry they arrived in Seattle. The four humans were tired; but the robots had fully charged themselves using their solar receptors during the trip, and now they were in top shape.

They didn't even bother to go to a restaurant, but ordered dinner at the hotel and stayed for the night. The robots spent their night hours guarding their human friends. The next day they all met at the hotel's cafeteria to plot the day's schedule over breakfast. Dr. Dorgovich had each one of them report what they were planning for the day starting with Darna.

"We need to go to the bank and open checking accounts. Each one of you has enough money for three months; I hope it will be enough, but should we need more, we can get it from the base. Make sure you all register with your new names, act normal, and be polite.

After we have our temporary checks, we can go and buy cars at different times so as to not look suspicious. I have studied the kinds of cars we should have, and Buick is a good middle class car. I suggest we buy three of them. Dr. Dorgovich and Sam should drive one car, the second for Nephus and me and the third one for AZM and CZF. Follow the directions I have given you and everything will be all right. Driving simulation is a little different from the real thing, so be careful.

Buying houses is not the same as buying cars. It takes more time and money, and at the present time I don't know where we are going to settle. That will have to be decided by Sam for security reasons. That's all I have to say for the time being."

Sam had a diagram of the area where they were going to look for houses; but that would have to be done tomorrow. The robots gave their own report which had to do with security. Nephus went on to explain in detail as to the other group's whereabouts. He told them that the five of them were in a place called Berkeley in the state of California. He said,

"One of the robots is shielded and undetected presumably guarding their base, just like our robot does. At this time I am unable to find it but I am working on it. I am positive they know where we are, with the exception of our robot guarding the base."

Then it was Dr. Dorgovich's turn to talk. He said,

"We have news from home. The situation is getting worse with every day that goes by. There have been many thousands of deaths from radiation poisoning, and they want us to do something here to remedy the problem. Our order now is to go directly to the companies that have the money and power, and convince them to gradually change to energies that we are going to introduce to them.

The rules of engagement have changed too. From now on, we will search, find the enemy, and destroy it. We don't have time for niceties.

Then he turned to Nephus and said,

"Nephus, you and the robots must find their base and destroy it; also find a way to damage their robots. Remember that's the main reason you are here. If we manage to damage their robots' cybernetics, then it will be a lot easier to eliminate the humans. Is there anything else we need to discuss? Yes--Darna."

"I don't see why we have to spend time trying to find the enemy and destroy it; if they don't bother us, we won't bother them. It would seem to me that the less time spent fighting them; the more time we will have to spend on the real problem, which is stopping radiation from ever occurring in the future."

AZM spoke up.

"I agree with Dr. Dorgovich; the sooner we get rid of the enemy, the sooner we will complete our task."

"I agree with you, AZM, thank you all, now let's go do what we have to do."

They all followed Darna's directions to the letter. They went through the process of depositing money in different banks and starting new checking accounts with no problem at all. They also bought three new Buicks from different dealers and soon after that, they were driving on the freeway back to their hotel. They drove carefully and within the proper speed as they were coached by Darna.

In the last few days Seattle police had been after some thieves who had robbed several banks in the downtown area. They were looking specifically for a new stolen Buick

Project Anastrophe

that was seen close to the banks that had been broken into; so when they saw the Buick driven by AZM and CZF matching the robbers' car, the highway patrol motioned them to go to the side. AZM quickly got in touch with Darna and asked her what to do. Darna told him to do what the officer wanted him to do and to keep cool and everything would be all right.

AZM drove to the side and had his license ready at hand, but when he saw the officer pointing a gun at him, he went into defense mode. When the officer asked him to step out, AZM in turn, told the officer,

"Put your weapon down or I will be forced to eliminate you."

What happened next was very quick and final. The officer fired at AZM but the robots made a split second decision. Before the bullet left the barrel of the officer's gun, AZM's faiser instantly evaporated the officer. At the same time CZF directed her faiser at the police car and obliterated it and the other officer in it. Then AZM drove back to the road and continued driving back to the hotel.

The few drivers who were close enough to see what happened had a hard time believing what they had witnessed. What they saw was both the officer and his car burned to nothing in a split second and all that remained was a burned spot on the asphalt. Later when they told what they had seen to the police and to their friends, they didn't believe them and thought they were crazy.

When they had all arrived at the hotel, they met at Dr. Dorgovich's room to discuss what had happened on the freeway. When AZM and CZF told them of the events, Darna was very upset and said,

"You are robots---you are not supposed to kill people---that's the rule! Have you malfunctioned?"

"We have been programmed to kill humans if we find

it necessary. The order to do the alteration was given by Dr. Dorgovich. The officer shot at us; we reacted accordingly, we are not malfunctioning, we are in excellent condition."

Darna turned to Dr. Dorgovich,

"How could you do that; since when do we have robots killing humans?"

"Miss Darna, this is an extraordinary mission, it's very important that we succeed. The robots will kill humans if they have to, this is an order from my superiors--I can't do anything about it at this time. Besides, right now we need all the help we can get and if that means killing a few humans now to save millions in the future, the end justifies the means."

"It wouldn't be fair to the other group, they probably follow the rules."

"We are counting on that."

"You should never have brought me here with you, you are all evil." Darna left the room and slammed the door on her way out.

Dr. Dorgovich said to Nephus,

"We have to work as a team; we can't have Darna acting like that. Perhaps you can convince her that it would be to her advantage to behave, otherwise there might be unpleasant consequences for her."

"Dr. Dorgovich, you have to admit that altering robots to kill humans is against protocol and highly illegal."

"It wasn't my idea--I followed orders--we all follow orders."

Nephus was on his way out but he was asked to stay until they were through. Sam had prepared a report as to where they were going to buy houses and what preparations needed to be done to make them safe. He also reminded Dr. Dorgovich that Darna was an important

Project Anastrophe

component of this mission and that he needed to be more conciliatory with her.

The robots had also made a report as to what kind of weapons they were to have in the houses and who was to live where. Finally they all agreed to go tomorrow and look at real estate. It was late in the night when Nephus went back to the room. Darna was sound asleep by then and he knew better than to wake her even for making love.

Next morning Nephus, Darna, and Sam drove to the city of Redmond with Darna driving the car. It was the kind of city Sam was looking for, small but with all the conveniences of a larger city and on the other side of Seattle proper. They were shown many houses in different areas of the city. They finally found three places on the outskirts. Darna put a down payment for all three houses, and agreed to come back a few days later with the other buyers to sign the ownership papers and pay the rest of the money.

After a quick bite to eat they drove back to their hotel, but while they were driving on the freeway to Seattle they were stopped by a highway patrolman who asked Darna for her driver's license and proof of purchase of the car. This time the officer had no gun in his hand and was very polite, he asked her if she was new in this area and then let them go.

Darna was beginning to wonder if it was such a good idea buying Buick cars after all. Other than that, the day was uneventful and although they were tired; they were happy that they had accomplished what they had set out to do.

A few days later after they had signed all the necessary papers, they moved into their separate houses. The robots got busy right away securing all three residences and now they were ready for real action.

Unlike the government team who opted for employment to get close to their targets, Dr. Dorgovich decided to keep his team unemployed and they concentrated instead on going directly to the big capitalists.

His first target was Edward J Davidson, a man in his late sixties, who was a wealthy philanthropist. With his sons he owned, among other businesses, Newfound Oil Company, one of the biggest oil companies in the world.

He was a skillful man and because of that he managed to bulldoze his way in business and politics with great ease. In order to secure an appointment with any of the Davidsons one had to be important in politics, industry, art, or be very wealthy. Dr. Dorgovich sent a letter directly to the old man and in his letter he wrote that he knew of a new kind of energy that could easily replace oil as fuel; it would revolutionize the industry and transportation as we know it now.

Letters sent by plain citizens almost never reached any of the Davidsons; much less the old man, but this one had two important words; "fuel" and "new energy". The clerk who read the letter sent it to Davidson Sr. marked "Important". As soon as he read it, he agreed to meet with these two scientists, Blef Martison and Frankie Gallitas.

In the meantime he asked his secretary to get in touch with the FBI to have them check their backgrounds. The next day he received the dossiers on both men. They were retired scientists and they had both taught metallurgy at the University of Washington in Seattle at different times. Recently they had moved to Redmond, Washington. There was more private information about their personal lives that the old man didn't care to know. They were who they said they were and that was enough for him. He met them a couple of days later in his office in New York which was something he very seldom did.

"Gentlemen, what do you have that's better than oil?"

"Mr. Davidson, what we have in mind has not yet been

discovered. The science of it is still in its infancy but we know what it is and how it works. Before we show it to you, we must tell you who we are. We are going to tell you things that you will find difficult to believe and because you are a busy man we will come right to the point."

Dr. Dorgovich pulled out of his pocket an egg- like object and put it on the floor and he proceeded to do what Ner had done at Dr. Thomas' place in Berkeley.

"Mr. Davidson, what I am about to do is to transport a person here into your office within a light beam, and then I am going to let that person tell you how it's done."

Mr. Davidson was speechless looking at an expanding screen and a person morphing within and then stepping out of thin air. He stepped back with awe and fear not comprehending what had just happened.

A woman who looked like an Amazon greeted him with a smile,

"How do you do, Mr. Davidson, my name is Carol Ampton, and I was asked by Dr. Blcf Martison to come and tell you that I come from the future. I am a robot and was made in a factory that is owned by several of your descendants. Dr. Martison wanted to impress you with our capabilities; do you have any questions?"

It took a minute or two before the old man snapped out of his wonderment. He finally said,

"I have heard that this sort of thing may happen sometime in the future, but never in my wildest imaginings did I think this could be a reality in my lifetime. Who are you folks and what do you want from me?"

He kept looking at the woman with amazement and wondered if she was indeed a robot, but then he thought with these people nothing was impossible. CZF again said,

"Mr. Davidson, I think Dr. Martison is in a better position to explain our real reasons for being here."

"Yes, yes, I am anxious to know why you people are here."

Dr. Dorgovich began to tell the old man the reason they were talking to him in particular.

"Mr. Davidson, as Carol said, we come from the future, from the twenty-fifth century to be exact. Our technology is far superior to yours, but we have a big problem and we need your help, and the help of some of your friends, to fix it. Otherwise our planet will be destroyed along with every living thing in it. You can help us avoid this catastrophe by changing to different energies, and gradually stop using oil and something far more dangerous that you will be using in the near future called "nuclear energy."

This energy could be used in peaceful ways, but will also be used in weapons capable of destroying millions of people in seconds. It will be used by unscrupulous people who are thirsty for money and power. The byproduct of these nuclear bombs will be radiation poisoning. It will penetrate the air we breathe and the water we drink, and then slowly but surely it will destroy our people and our planet.

With all the superior technology we have in the future, we have no way of stopping this catastrophe and now you know why we are here and why we need your help, Mr. Davidson."

"I am very sad to hear that; but what can I do to help? Surely you don't expect me to close production of oil, even if I wanted to I couldn't do that; we depend on it for our industry and transportation. There is a war about to break out in Europe and sooner or later we are going to be involved in it too. Oil is vital to us."

"Mr. Davidson, we wouldn't want you to do anything like that now, but what we would like you to do is to make policy for the oil production to slow down and replace it

Project Anastrophe

with other fuels and energies which we will introduce to you at a later time. These new fuels and energies will be cleaner and safer, and will make your future descendants rich and powerful."

"This is another thing you keep telling me about my descendants, how do you know who my descendants are so far in the future? And how do you know this business will survive?"

"We do know who they are, and although their businesses are other than oil, they are directly connected to you and your business. In fact, they are in the cartel that sent us here because they are about to lose their lives and businesses."

"What sort of policy do you want me to make?"

"You need to specifically write in your will, that by the year 2030 they would have replaced oil and nuclear power with the new technology that we will introduce to you in time, that's all."

"And what kind of technology are you talking about?"

"I wish I could tell you now and start changing things sooner; but I have to abide by the "Prime Directive." You see, Mr. Davidson, as painful as it is, we must let certain things happen; we can't tamper too much with the "Prime Directive." Should you agree with us and do what we want you to do; we will give you an electronic device that will open in 2020 to give you time to make a gradual change. That device will give you the appropriate technical directions for the new energies."

"What if the device you are talking about, falls into the wrong hands, like our competitors or even to an enemy country like Germany?"

"The device has a self-destruct mechanism, and even if it were to be opened by anyone before the appointed time, there would be nothing in it because it is only a relay device. The information will come directly from us at that specific moment so you don't have to worry at all, Mr. Davidson."

"How can I even discuss this thing with any one; they will think that I became crazy in my old age?"

"We already made your will and signed your lawyers' name; we could have signed your name too, but we wanted you to do that of your own free will."

"Suppose I refuse to do this, what would you do?"

"We will simply go to someone else and your family will lose the opportunity to be one of the first to take advantage of the new technology."

"I would like to think about it and will let you know, Dr. Martison. I do have to discuss this at least within my family. This is too big a decision to make by myself."

"I understand but this has to be kept secret and only with your close family. This is a copy of your will, read it and let us know."

While Dr. Dorgovich and Sam were busy talking to Mr. Davidson and preparing to talk to other capitalists, Nephus, Darna, and the two robots were in Berkeley trying to find their enemies to destroy them. They had to be careful because now they were close to them and according to AZM they themselves were under constant surveillance. They were on a hill above a winding street which seemed quiet at this time of night. But according to CZF Nick, Norina, and two robots and two other humans were in a big house in the living room. It was one of the few houses with the lights on.

They approached and were preparing to break in. It was Ner who first detected the enemy and in his usual cryptic way alerted Vrima and they both went into defense mode. At the same time they were talking casually to Peter and Lisa.

Project Anastrophe

When the enemy came closer they alerted both Nick and Norina cryptically and told them to prepare for battle. Nick in turn talked to Peter and Lisa in a calm way and said,

"I am sorry to inform you that the enemy I was telling you about a little while ago is approaching your house. We need to prepare ourselves to fight them here."

Lisa reached for the phone to call the police but Norina stopped her.

"Lisa, the police are not a match for these people, they would be killed needlessly. We are the only ones who can fight them, but don't worry; you will be safe at all times."

It was at that moment Ner informed Nick that the enemy robots were in "kill mode."

"What do you mean? I thought robots didn't kill humans."

"I am sorry, Nick, but they have been altered. Norina intervened and said,

"We are not going to break protocol. Our robots will not kill humans; we will protect ourselves as best we can. In the meantime we must protect Dr. Thomas and Lisa."

They moved quickly. They first put two small units about two meters apart near Peter and Lisa. In that instant an invisible curtain went around them, a shield that would guard them from the enemy's faisers if they broke in. Next, Ner and Vrima shielded the periphery of the house and finally all four of them shielded themselves and waited.

For better or worse both Nephus and Darna were in this to the bitter end, there was no way out of this mess. They had to fight and kill or be killed and that wasn't an option. The sooner they completed their mission, the sooner they would go home. They prepared themselves for the next step; fight the enemy and win. AZM and CZF were trying to find a weak area in the shield to break in. Finally it was

Nephus who was able to gain entrance in an opening the size of a door, and both robots got in. Nephus and Darna stayed outside the shield. All Darna could do at this point was to protect herself, but Nephus was working on a hand-held device trying to break Ner's and Vrima's personal shield but he didn't have any luck.

In the meantime a battle between Titans started inside the shielded area with the four robots exchanging faiser fire. Each faiser's discharge would bathe the body with a blue super-heated cloud and if there was a tiny hole anywhere in the shield, that body would be instantly evaporated. But the shields held.

While Nephus was trying to break Ner's and Vrima's shields from outside, Dr. Narthur was busy doing the same thing from inside to the other robots. He was using one of the latest devices that he himself had helped to build. Within minutes he was able to penetrate their shields and gain entrance to their cybernetics, then he quickly managed to incapacitate them to a point that both robots tried to retreat outside the shield. Although their shields still protected them from the enemy's faisers, they could see that they were losing the battle.

Now Ner and Vrima had the upper hand and tried to take advantage of it. They quickly attached a holding beam on the enemy thereby making it impossible for them to retreat. Then Ner went close enough to them and set a small device by their feet. He was about to have them beamed and contained in his farmhouse in Kent, but both Nephus and Darna intervened with their faisers. Ner and Vrima had to set their faisers to stun mode so as not to kill humans. That put them at a disadvantage, but brought Nick, Norina and Dr. Narthur into the fight. Nephus and Darna could see they were losing the battle and the only way out now was to beam themselves away.

Project Anastrophe

Nephus was able to put the two robots into a temporary defense mode. Then using his hand-held device he was able to break the beam that was holding them captive. He ordered them to beam themselves to base, which they did right away. The battle stopped as abruptly as it had started.

There was minimal damage to the house from the faisers because they had been directed only at robots and humans. Nephus and Darna felt very lucky to escape the battle unscathed but beaming themselves home had made them very sick. Darna felt even worse than the last time. She had a big headache and she ached all over. She went directly to bed and when Dr. Dorgovich came to see how she was doing she told him,

"Leave me alone, I don't need your sympathy."

She closed the door and wouldn't even see Nephus until next morning, when he went to wake her up.

"Darna, are you up?"

"I am up now."

"How are you?"

"I still hurt all over my body, but I am somewhat better today."

"Considering what we've gone through, we are lucky-- don't you think?"

"I suppose so; how are the robots?"

"Their cybernetics have been damaged and they are still in the base repairing themselves. We are going to see Dr. Dorgovich; are you up to it?"

"I hate that S.O.B., but I suppose I need to be there, don't I?" The four humans met at 11:00 a.m. Sam asked the first question,

"How long did the robots fight before they were compromised?"

"I would say ten minutes into the fight, and then while Darna kept fighting the other robots I tried to put a 'firewall' on Dr. Narthur's device but I was unable to do it. From what I could see, they have better weapons and their robots are far superior to ours. We must upgrade our weaponry and our robots before we fight them again."

"That's for sure; they are indeed far superior to us."

Dr. Dorgovich said,

"I talked to AZM and he said they will be repaired and will be ready for engagement sometime today. I want to thank you for putting up a brave fight with the enemy, now we know their strengths and weaknesses and next time we will be better prepared to fight and defeat them." Darna could hardly wait for her turn to talk and when she spoke she was unstoppable,

"Dr. Dorgovich, this expedition was unnecessary and unwise from the beginning, but now we are here.

What I propose is to send someone to talk with them. I volunteer to speak with these people and tell them that we want to join with them for the common cause which is to save our planet and humanity. If we wait any longer there will be nothing to fight for. We can't defeat them and they can't defeat us; that's obvious--but the delay will defeat all of us if we don't stop fighting.

Can't you see what's happening here? We are the war mongers, the aggressors and all because some capitalists want to keep their status-quo and their monopolies. I say this is a good time to stop that and start all over again. Give everybody an equal share in the new energies and have a more equitable society for a change."

"The capitalistic system has served us very well and if it wasn't for this radiation problem it would have done even better. Bigger companies are able to invest huge amounts of capital and constantly renovate the industry to improve our way of life. I am happy with this system and I have my orders to do anything it takes to protect it. You may disagree

Project Anastrophe

with us, you can offer your opinions; that is your prerogative, but you will do what I say because I am in charge of this mission and have the responsibility to see it through. Do you understand, Miss Varnether?"

"Oh I understand you, Dr. Dorgovich, but your plan is foolish and will not succeed, you can be sure of that." Nephus said,

"I don't care which system survives as long as we survive and go home and I get my credits; but I fear we are not well-equipped to successfully do our job. I am of the opinion that we either destroy the enemy, or as Darna says, join them."

Sam, as always, was more conciliatory and said,

"I can't overemphasize the fact that it is necessary that we stick together on this mission. Let's stop bickering and start thinking of a way to defeat the enemy; do what we have to do here and go back home to a safe and healthy environment. That is what we must do, and the sooner the better."

Before the meeting was adjourned Dr. Dorgovich said,

"The robots will make changes to improve their safety and next time they will not be as vulnerable in battle. However, until the robots are completely repaired, we are going to lay off for a while, we can use this time to regenerate ourselves too, stay home and take it easy until further notice."

Dr. Thomas had frequent parties late into the night. The neighbors were used to occasional disturbances such as singing and laughing and many bright lights. So when the faisers started shooting back and forth they assumed that they were playing some kind of a game, although they got carried away with it, so they closed their curtains and let them have at it. Inside and around the house was quite another story though.

As soon as it was determined that it was safe, Ner deleted the safety shield and allowed Peter and Lisa out. He told them that Norina would tell them what had happened.

After Nick and Norina had examined the area outside where the battle had taken place, they determined the house had sustained little damage and were anxious to tell that to Dr. Thomas. Norina tried to explain,

"Dr Thomas, I am glad to tell you that none of us has been injured, however the enemy has sustained lots of damage and will be out of commission for a while. I am sorry we had to close you up like that but it was for your own safety, I hope you are O.K."

"We are fine, it didn't bother us a bit and I am so glad that you are O.K. too."

At that moment Nick and Vrima stepped in and Nick went directly to Peter and said,

"We have discovered that your door, part of your front wall, and several bushes have been damaged and we would like to pay for replacing them."

"Don't worry about that right now, I'll have someone give me an estimate of the damage and will let you know later."

Nick told Peter and Lisa to think about what they had talked about and to get in touch with them whenever they wanted to.

The three of them went back to the hotel, while Ner and Vrima beamed themselves back home to Kent. It had been a very busy night for all of them. The next day Nick, Norina, and Dr. Narthur flew back home. Peter and Lisa met again at the campus cafeteria and had a long talk about last night's happenings. Lisa was visibly upset and said,

"Peter, I think we have gotten into a mess and it scares me. I think our lives are in danger, shouldn't we do something about it, what do you think?"

Project Anastrophe

"I agree with you, our lives could be in danger but at this time I find it exhilarating. Think about it, Lisa, we are the first people to be visited by people who come from the twenty-fifth century, we've seen unimaginable things and we are given a chance to save our planet from a future catastrophe.

I believe that they are able to protect us from any danger. Christ, Lisa, didn't you see how quickly the robots came to my house? They can come anywhere at any time we need them, all we have to do is to press on that little device they gave us and they will come to help us should we be in any danger. By the way, do you have that device with you?"

"Yes I do, but I am still frightened. What can we do to help them anyway?"

"Well first of all, they want us not to do a few things in the future; like not using too many nuclear bombs and not using too much nuclear power even in peaceful ways. They are going to introduce us to new technologies to replace nuclear power and the oil that we use so heavily today. Don't you see they have a stake in all this as well?"

"Where do we go from here, do we tell what we know to our friends; or do we wait for them to make the next move?"

"From what I understood, we are to wait for them to pick the right people to share the secret with us."

Peter and Lisa shared a very important secret and that brought them even closer than before. Peter asked Lisa if she would like to have dinner out and then have a drink at his place. She said she would love to.

Soon after that, Nick, Norina, and Dr. Narthur, arrived back home in Washington State. Norina called everybody to her house and said,

"We have been lucky so far, last night we won the fight

and we damaged their robots, but they will repair themselves and adapt to defend themselves from our new weapons. This enemy is determined to destroy us in order to achieve their purpose; they have even altered their robots to kill humans.

We are not going to do that to our robots, but we must also adopt better ways to defend ourselves. I think Dr. Narthur is working on that, in the meantime we must be careful not to engage them in any way until we are ready." Vrima reported on the enemy's whereabouts. She said,

"They live in a town called Redmond which is on the other side of Seattle proper, and they had their first contact with Mr. Edward J Davison; he and his sons are very powerful in business and politics and they often get their way because of their wealth. They plan to meet other powerful business people as well as politicians."

"Thank you, Vrima, we also need to make more contacts and this time I am proposing to meet President Hamilton. Yes, Nick."

"That's easier said than done, you can't just go and see the President, you need to know someone close to him to arrange for an appointment, unless we send Ner or Vrima to impress him first and then arrange for us to meet with him."

"That's a good idea, Nick, let's do it, the sooner the better."

Both Ner and Vrima agreed, but Ner would be the one to go. Dr. Narthur had a long talk with Ner telling him how best to impress the President. Ner studied the floor plan of the White House and chose to beam himself into a closet near the President's office and wait until he was sure the President was alone. Hamilton liked his liquor and his doctor had asked him to cut down on it but he wouldn't hear of it. This morning he had a lot on his mind; Hitler's Germany

Project Anastrophe

and the attack on Poland for one thing, and the impending war in Europe, had kept him up all night. So when his private secretary came in with a notebook in her hand he said,

"Paula, I want my coffee strong this morning, make it double."

"But Mr. President, the doctor said no brandy in the morning."

"I know what the doctor said, but he is not dealing with a war, make it double I said."

"O.k. Mr. President, I'll go fix it."

"Yeah, fix it!"

Ner waited until Paula was through with her dictation and soon after she stepped out of the office he seized the moment and beamed himself in front of the President's desk. Then went to the door and locked it. He walked back to him with a smile on his face and said,

"Good morning, Mr. President, my name is Roy Eastman and I am a robot. I come from the future and I have something very important to tell you. Please don't call for help; hear me out first."

The President's first thought was Paula was right. I should stop drinking in the morning, now I am hallucinating, I can't do that in my position, I have to see the doctor. He was about to ring for Paula and again Ner pleaded with him to hear him out. Then the President looked at Ner hesitantly and said,

"Put your hand on the desk, I want to touch it."

"Certainly, Mr. President." Ner went close to the desk and put his hand on it. The President quickly touched Ner's hand and held it for few seconds. He looked at him intently then he said,

"My God, I think you are indeed who you say you are; what do you want from me?"

"As I said, I have something important to tell you, but

first ask Paula not to disturb us for ten minutes." The President pushed the button on the intercom and said,
"Paula, are you there?"
"Yes, Mr. President."
"I don't want to be disturbed by anyone until I say so."
"Yes, Mr. President, of course. Are you all right?"
"Yes, I am fine."
"Now then, Mr. Eastman, what is it that you want to tell me that is so important?"
"Mr. President, I, along with two more robots, and three humans, came here from the future to stop a catastrophe that is taking place right now in the twenty-fifth century. It all starts here in this country; you are going to build two atomic bombs and explode them over Japan. From then on the radiation released from these two bombs and other more powerful ones built by you and other countries, will eventually destroy our planet and kill all living things on it.

I am only here to persuade you that we do come from the future and have seen what is happening. The three humans are far more qualified to talk with you about this problem and I would like to arrange a time for you to meet them at your convenience. My human friends asked me to tell you that you should have Dr. Peter Thomas with you; he is going to be one of those in charge of the atomic program."

"I haven't been convinced that you are a robot, you look so human to me, Mr. Eastman."

"Mr. President, please take another look at my hand. I am going to lift part of the skin on my forearm and expose part of my artificial makeup---as you can see I don't have flesh, veins, or blood. My body is built mostly from silicon although it contains some carbon too. My thinking process is done through artificial intelligence, I am not a human like you, I am a robot, now do you believe me?"

"I suppose I do. I am willing to see your fiends two days

Project Anastrophe

from now at 10:00a.m. right here in my office. In addition to Dr. Thomas I am going to have with me General Michael Sheldon, he is in charge of this project also and I value his opinion."

"It is important that no other people should know about this at this time, Mr. President."

"I don't think I can discuss this sort of thing with too many people anyway, Mr. Eastman."

Ner beamed himself out of the President's office. President Hamilton looked at the way Ner disappeared and if there had been any doubt in his mind, it was quickly forgotten. Ner told the rest of the group about his meeting with the President, and about the appointment he had made for two days from now. He also told them that in addition to Dr. Thomas, the President would have General Michael Sheldon with him.

President Hamilton worked fast. Right after Ner left, he summoned General Sheldon to his office and had an undisturbed meeting with him. He told him about his meeting with the robot and how he had appeared and disappeared; about the bombs, the radiation, and the destruction of the planet more than five hundred years hence. He also told him about the appointment with three people from the future which was scheduled two days from now.

General Sheldon couldn't believe what the President was telling him; he thought that the alcohol had finally damaged the President's brain and wondered if he was fit to lead the country anymore. But he didn't dare say anything at this time. Finally the President said,

"Mike, I want you to call Dr. Thomas, the two of you must come to see me here at my office on Thursday at 10:00a.m. I don't want you to say anything to anybody of what you heard here, this is an order and I expect you to follow it to the letter, do you understand?"

"Yes, Mr. President, you may rest assured I will say nothing of it to anyone."

"You are a good man, Mike, now you may think that I've gone crazy, and I wouldn't blame you, but I know what I am talking about and when you listen to these people you will see that I am right. Now go and get Dr. Thomas."

The President went on with the rest of the day, kept all of his appointments and said nothing to anybody about his two early meetings.

Chapter 9

Two days later on Thursday at 10:00 a.m. they all met in the President's office. Paula had been told to keep 10:00 a.m. to 12:00 noon free from any calls or visits. The four of them had a pretty good idea as to how the meeting was heading, but General Sheldon was at a loss and didn't know what to expect. Two days ago the President had acted as though he were crazy and although he kept his word and said nothing to anyone, he was nervous and anxious to find out if the President was right. President Hamilton spoke first and said,

"Two days ago I was visited by a robot; actually he beamed himself out of thin air into my office. For a moment I thought I was hallucinating, but he proved to me, without any doubt, that he was indeed a robot.

He said that he and some other robots and humans were here to prevent our planet, and all living things, from being obliterated sometime in the twenty–fifth century.

Now I assume that the three of you must be the three humans from the future--is that right?" Nick spoke first,

"Mr. President, my name is Robert Johnson, this is my wife Loretta, and this is Dr. Frank Robertson. We know how busy you are, and we thank you for having us here in your office on such short notice.

We have already met with Dr. Thomas, that's why we insisted that he should be with you today. We know a lot from history books about General Sheldon and we are glad to see him here too. I would like to show you first how desperate the people are where we come from before we go any further."

Nick put the egg-like device on the floor and just as before, showed them in three dimensions the destruction the radiation was causing to human life and property. But this time it had the latest news from home with more tragedies that surprised even Dr. Thomas. He also showed them the main city and how technologically advanced they were.

After the projection of the tragedies both the President and General Sheldon were determined to do what they could to avoid such a catastrophe. The President said,

"Mr. Johnson, you have convinced us that you are here from the future although it's beyond me how you could do that. We are very sorry that your people have to suffer so much because of something we are about to do; but what is it that you want us to do to avoid such a calamity?"

Now it was Dr. Narthur who spoke.

"Mr. President, as you can see, with all our technology there is very little we can do to stop this radiation poisoning from killing us; that's why we are here in a last attempt to have you help us. You and several other countries that are

Project Anastrophe

going to build these bombs can help us by realizing how dangerous they are, and initiate a program to stop producing them and their byproducts.

In turn we will introduce you to new fuels and energies that are more productive and less dangerous to the environment."

"How can we stop proliferation of something we don't even know how to build yet?"

"But you will build thousands of them and several of them will be used. You will use uranium and plutonium in weapons, as well as for peaceful purposes. You will invent other substances that will be just as lethal when used in large quantities.

After many years of using these materials they will seep into the ground, the seas, the rivers, lakes and air. They will contaminate everything with radiation and people in the future will resort to living in biospheres to protect themselves, but even that eventually will fail.

Mr. President, I wish we could stop all that right now before it starts, but we have to let the "Prime Directive" prevail for now. Later we can control this menace and stop it. All you need to do is to let us help you."

"Dr. Robertson, we want to help you but there is a war going on in Europe and it's about to get bigger. There is a maniac in Germany called Hitler and he is working feverishly to build atomic bombs. From what I hear, his scientists are very close to building the first one. We don't want to build these terrible weapons, but we have to defend our country and the free world.

As long as we can protect our country with whatever weapons we can build, and that includes atomic bombs, we will be happy to help you in any way we can."

"That's all we want from you, Mr. President, your cooperation. We will do the rest." Norina was the next to speak.

George Karnikis

"Mr. President, there are a few other things that need to be mentioned so that you have a clear picture of what's happening here. My husband and I are physicists and so is Dr. Robertson and two of our three robots. We will be working as visiting professors at the University of Washington in Seattle except for Dr. Robertson who is now retired, but he will help us in many technical matters. We will always be available to protect you should you need our help.

At this point I would like to mention the fact that we don't want to be known as the people from the future, it has to be kept secret for obvious reasons. So far, you are the only people who know about us, and that brings me to another important point. There is another group of four humans and three robots who have also come from the future. They want to do much the same thing we want to do, with one big difference. We have been sent by our government; they have been sent by private corporations.

Our orders are to set a program where all the new energies and fuels will be distributed equally to all existing companies which want to participate in a prescribed future time. The others will select only a few large companies, thereby maintaining their monopolies in the future. They have already contacted the Davidson family and are planning to bypass your government and go directly to those chosen companies.

They are very powerful and will try anything to accomplish their goal. We are within the law; they are here illegally. Even at this dangerous time their priorities are to maintain their monopolies, the rest is secondary. Mr. President, as I said, they are powerful and they may even interfere with your government, but we have already taken protective measures to prevent that, and our government is ready to help us." The President sounded alarmed, he said,

Project Anastrophe

"You mean to tell me that my country and my government are going to be interfered with by this group?"

"That is a possibility, Mr. President, but as I said, we have taken preventative measures and you are secure with us here."

"We will try to help you, but my country takes priority right now and although we appreciate your help, we are in a position to take care of ourselves." He was quite upset and was about to terminate the meeting abruptly, when Dr. Thomas intervened and said,

"Mr. President, if I may interject here."

"Yes of course, Dr. Thomas."

"I have seen the power these humans and robots have, and believe me we cannot match them, no one can, except these people here. I have seen them fighting the other group and they are superior to them. If I were you I would be happy to have them on my side and let them protect me."

"Dr. Thomas, how do you know so much about these people?"

"I was one of the first to be visited by them, and I have seen first hand how they fight. It was only a few days ago when these people were visiting me and my girlfriend Lisa at my house to tell us what they told you, Mr. President. It was at that time the other group attacked them. They have powerful guns called 'faisers' that can vaporize anything they hit but they can also protect themselves in an invisible cocoon. These people fight differently from the way we do. Dr. Robertson was able to incapacitate their robots with a handheld device and those robots escaped by beaming themselves away along with their human companions.

We don't have the weapons or the 'know-how' to fight these people. They can only fight among themselves. We can only take sides and if I had my 'rathers' I would side with this group right here because they represent the law and the others, anarchy."

General Sheldon had listened all this time and said nothing, but when he heard about the technology these people possessed, and about the faiser guns, his interest was piqued to the point he could hardly wait to intervene, and when he got a chance he did so by saying,

"If you people really want to help us, you could give us some of your weapons and we could defend ourselves. With these weapons we can also defeat Hitler."

"Unfortunately we can't do that, General Sheldon, because the "Prime Directive" forbids us to intervene in your time. Anything we do now affects the future. If we were to give you our weapons, most likely the future would change for the worst, but we promise to protect you from the other group should they decide to harm you in any way."

"And yet you are here to do just that by depriving us from having the atomic weapons, aren't you?"

"We are doing that, only as a last resort, to save humanity from complete catastrophe; to do nothing is not an option in this case."

The President interrupted and said,

"Dr. Robertson, what do you want us to do?"

"Mr. President, we have prepared a program that you must follow to the letter in order to avoid the destruction of our planet in your future and our present. In the program there are perimeters that tell you how far you can go with nuclear bombs and nuclear power plants, as well as their byproducts such as spent plutonium and other heavy metals.

In the 21st century, around 2030, we will introduce you to the new energies and from then on, simultaneously you will be decontaminating the ecosystem by using them. If you do as we say, everything will be all right and our planet will be saved. There is one thing we demand and that is that the new energies must be available to all who want to produce them. We will not have monopolies in the future.

The other group will do all it can to make it so that only a few selected companies will have the right to produce it. You and the other governments in the future must not allow that to happen. If you do, we will intervene and destroy those companies, be it here or anywhere in your world, this is our only demand from you, Mr. President."

"How are we going to enforce such a policy, and how can we tell the Germans, the Russians, and other countries to adhere to this plan?"

"We will go and talk to them, just as we talked to you, they will also have to follow the same policy."

"What if the other group of yours convinces the other countries to go a different way?"

"That does not concern you or the other future governments. That other group is here illegally and we will never allow it to interfere with our plan, you can rest assured of that, Mr. President."

"What do we have to do now, Dr. Robertson?"

"Nothing, Mr. President, except to be vigilant and to adhere to the policy we have talked about."

"And where is this policy?"

"It has already been introduced and is part of your government's strategic policy."

"My God, can you do that?"

"Yes, Mr. President, we can do that and more. It's our policy too, and it's our survival. We have to leave now and remember, do not say anything about our meeting; just follow the program. Part of it is already in your schedule today."

After Nick, Norina, and Dr. Narthur left, the President asked General Sheldon and Dr. Thomas to come and see him tomorrow morning at 10:00a.m. to go over this new policy and come up with some kind of a plan.

The President thought of what had transpired a while ago and tried to put his thoughts in order. He could fight a war with Germany and with any contemporary enemy, but how could he fight an enemy that came from five hundred years in the future? Dr. Thomas is right, we can't. The wise thing to do is to rely on the group that was sent here by that future government. Only they can fight them.

He was looking at the daily schedule Paula had prepared for him and there was a meeting with a representative of King Ibn Saud of Saudi Arabia about protecting the Royal Family for easy access to their oil. There was a reference in parentheses, "Important: see 'Project Anastrophe.' " He called his secretary,

"Paula, come in, I need to talk to you."

"Yes, Mr. President, I am coming right away."

"Paula, what is this 'Project Anastrophe'? I have never seen it before."

"It's something you have approved and signed recently, sir."

"I have?"

"Yes sir, it has yesterday's date on it and it is stamped as 'top secret'."

"I want to see what it is, bring it here."

"I can't do that, sir; you have to go to some place called Y-O-40. And I don't know where that is."

"Thank you, Paula, I know where it is, I'll go right away." The President was puzzled as to why such a simple meeting with a representative of the Saudi Royal Family would be considered 'top secret'.

He got up and headed for the Y-O-40 area. When he approached it he was met by two marine guards; he was taken to the door and they stayed outside guarding it all the

Project Anastrophe

time he was in. The room was a special vault constructed of heavy sheets of metal. It was bigger and much stronger than the average bank vault and very few knew the combination. If anyone of these people were to quit or die, including the President, the combination to the lock would be changed. He zeroed in on the Saudi Royal Family files and soon enough found the file he was looking for. He opened it, and there in front of his eyes he found what he wanted.

There was a file containing many pages explaining how to deal with this new kingdom; it was all typed, dated, and signed by the Secretary of State George Preston and President James Hamilton himself---it really bore his signature. And then it all made sense; didn't Dr. Robertson say that part of the new policy that was formulated by them would appear on my schedule today?

"I do hope these guys are our friends because there is no way to fight them."

He went on to read the portion of the policy that had to do with today's meeting; they were to arrange a meeting with the Patriarch King Ibn Saud, one of many that would follow in the near future. The more he read the more he could see the significance of this policy and how this country would dependent for its oil on this newly created Arab country.

Dr. Thomas and General Sheldon met with the President next day and talked about the predicament they were in and what they could do about it. The President asked General Sheldon if he had anything to say.

"Mr. President, I think we should get in touch with the other group and see what they have to say, after all their policy doesn't differ much from this group. They want to go to the private sector, so what's wrong with that, we have a free enterprise system here.

They want to make the new energy and fuel available to a selected group and a few other countries, there is really nothing wrong with that. The fact that five hundred years from now there is going to be a monopoly on this energy and fuel by a few surviving companies, doesn't affect us at all, on the contrary several of these companies would be good contributors to future governments, isn't that the way we operate now?"

"General Sheldon, from what I see here, they have the ability to control the existing oil right now; they can make our life easy or give us hell, it's up to them. I have here in front of me part of the policy they have made for us, it tells me in detail what to do and say to the representative of King Saud who I am going to meet an hour from now. There is a master policy which tells us what to do for the next five hundred and sixty years, these people have seen the future and are here to correct it.

I am sure they have or will visit other countries and do the same thing with them. We have to be careful with which of these two groups we affiliate because they can do things to us which are beyond our control. Dr. Thomas, I would like to hear what you have to say on this subject."

"Mr. President, we shouldn't have any problem with which of these two groups to choose to affiliate with. One was sent here legally by a government which is ready to help us with every step on the way and the only demand they have is to make future energy and fuel available to everyone; as opposed to the other group which was sent here illegally to represent several monopolies who want to retain the status-quo.

It seems to me their government is determined to punish these companies. They may even arrest the other group and then we will be on their bad side. I see no benefit whatsoever to see them, much less side with them. I say

Project Anastrophe

stay with the group we already know, and let them deal with the other group as they are quite capable of doing."

"Thank you both very much, you may go now, I will call you when I need you. I don't want you to say anything to anyone at this time, this is an order!"

The robots Dave Ampton, Carol Ampton, and Larry Cappo were hard at work repairing and reinforcing themselves for the next fight. This time they were equipped with the latest weapons which had just arrived from back home. They were more than eager to engage the enemy. They ran a final test and found themselves in perfect condition. Dave asked to talk with Dr. Dorgovich.

"Dr. Dorgovich, I am here to report that all robots including myself are in top shape and ready for the next battle."

"That's wonderful, Dave, tomorrow at 11:00 a.m. sharp we are all going to meet at my place to discuss our next move, so be here with your robots."

"Yes, sir, we will be here at the exact time."

They all met promptly, and Dr. Dorgovich spoke first, as usual,

"Dave has told me that he and the rest of the robots are now through with all the necessary repairs and have enhanced themselves with newly-arrived parts and weaponry from home and are now ready for the next fight. I trust the humans in our team have recuperated from our last engagement and are ready for what comes next." Dr. Dorgovich went on to discuss what he and Sam Lorkost had been planning all this time and asked Sam to elaborate.

"As Dr. Dorgovich has said, we are now ready for anything that might come our way, and like last time, we are going to initiate a surprise attack. We have located the base where they keep their powerful weapons, and from what we have found, it's guarded by one robot on a small island not too far away from here.

Our plan is to attack and destroy both the robot and the base. If we can accomplish that, we can eliminate the rest of the robots and humans more easily.

We are going to attack during the night just in case there are any islanders around. Dave will explain the plan to us in detail so that we know exactly what to do."

Dave projected a 3-D picture of the plan which contained Yellow Island for the benefit of the humans, and then went on explaining how to execute the plan. The day and time of the attack would be announced later. Nephus and Darna went back to their room with Darna anticipating more trouble this time, and perhaps the possibility of never returning home.

"Nephus, what are our chances of surviving the next fight?"

"I would say this time we are in better shape than we were before, and I feel we have a chance to destroy them, and finally go home and forget this episode ever happened."

"I hope you are right, but I think the other guys are just as prepared, and we are in for a perilous engagement."

"If we surprise them, we'll have the upper hand."

"I sure hope you are right, Nephus; I am very scared. Let's go out and have breakfast at that nice German Restaurant. I love their cuisine."

"I can't, I have to do some preparatory work for our next engagement."

"O.K., have it your way, I am going out alone."

A smiling young woman brought Darna a cup of hot coffee.

"What will you have today, Hon?"

"Just the usual, thanks."

Project Anastrophe

"Sure thing."

Across from her table was a huge mirror which covered most of the wall;

Darna looked critically at her reflection, she thought she looked tired. She could see that coming here had taken a toll on her, and this coming engagement with the so-called enemy could be dangerous--even fatal.

"I have to get out of this--but how? I can't just go and mingle with the people at large; both groups know where I am at all times, and I can't go back home alone."

Then it dawned on her; the idea came out of the blue, or perhaps desperation, she thought of it over and over and became obsessed with it.

"Hon, here is your breakfast, some more coffee?"

"Yes please, thank you." She finished her breakfast and felt good, and then she thought of her idea again only this time it became a plan--a plan of survival.

Darna wasn't about to let Dr. Dorgovich risk her life---and for what? To maintain the status-quo of those capitalists back home? No way! She had to fight back and this plan was her only way back home. Now that she could do something about her predicament she felt much better. She wasn't going to say anything to anyone yet, not even Nephus, although she would like to help him to get out of here. But he enjoyed what he was doing, and he believed that he would go back home safe and sound with lots of credits.

"Poor Nephus, I love you but I can't help you this time, you have to take your chances."

She left a good tip for the waitress and stepped out. It was a wet autumn day, cool rain fell on her face, and she felt reinvigorated.

As she walked home her plan started to unfold again in her mind. First she had to wait to hear the day and time they were going to attack; then she would get in touch with Norina and bargain with her. She would demand that they send her back home. There she would expose the group sent illegally back in time by the Du Bois brothers. Her thinking was that even if they refused to send her back home, at least she wouldn't have to fight anybody.

When she arrived home Nephus was still at work organizing his portion of the plan of attack. When he finally came out of his office he looked tired but satisfied. He boasted that he had found a way to neutralize any of the enemy robots in three moves at the most and that the fight wouldn't last long. Darna had heard this kind of boasting from Nephus the last time they attacked Norina's group, only to have their robots almost destroyed. If they hadn't managed to beam themselves at the last moment they would have been captured and their expedition would have come to an early end.

She acted natural and told him she could hardly wait to have this expedition finished, go home, and forget all about it. Nephus said,

"This time we will go home with lots of credits and live the good life."

Her answer was,

"Sure, Nephus, keep on dreaming." She was sure no one knew of her plan and she was determined to keep it that way. When Nephus asked her to come and see what he was doing, she was more than eager to oblige and show that she was part of the team.

However, she had to admit that he was truly the best in his line of work; no wonder they had brought him here. Nephus was showing her the schematic diagrams of the enemy robots, and how he was going to neutralize them with just three specific hits on his handheld unit. Darna said,

Project Anastrophe

"Wouldn't they have a way to protect themselves from such interventions as the one you have designed?"

"No, they wouldn't know what hit them. I know their schematics by heart and the program I have designed will compromise their noetics analyzers in a split second."

"How about the humans, wouldn't they fight back?"

"Yes but without their robots they will be overcome by us in a very short time; besides we now have orders to shoot to kill. Believe me, the whole battle won't last more than ten minutes and then we are done. The rest of what we have to do here will not take more than a month and then we go home rich Darna, rich!"

"But I though we had strict orders never to kill humans."

"We now have orders to do just that."

"That is insane--insane!"

"It may be, but it would be more insane to be captured and sent to jail for life."

If Darna had any hesitation about going ahead with her plan before, she didn't have any now. She didn't want any part of this fight and the sooner she left these evil people, the better she was going to feel. The next day they were asked to meet at Dr. Dorgovich's place. He had even given access to the guard robot for this particular meeting; this was big--so it must be the pre-attack meeting.

This time it was Dave, the robot, who talked first,

"I was given permission to attack by Dr. Dorgovich. We are now in far better shape for battle than we were the last time. Nephus has not only devised an ingenious way to neutralize the enemy robots, but he has made us virtually impenetrable by the enemy.

However, as good as we are, our enemy could be just as lethal so it's very important that we have the element of surprise on our side. That, combined with our superiority will be the ticket to the final destruction of the enemy, and a quick victory for us."

"Thank you, Dave, I couldn't have said it better myself. Humans and robots--this is it--the time has come once and for all to destroy our enemy. With them out of the way, we can concentrate on the real reason why we are here. It is important to eradicate radiation and save humanity and our planet, but we are going to do it our way. Our way is the free and capitalistic system, practiced and defended by free people like us. Their socialistic system will send us back to the bad anachronistic days and we are not going to allow that. So, friends, the sooner we get rid of them, the sooner we go home. It's as simple as that. Now listen carefully. On Wednesday at 8:00 p.m. we are going to attack simultaneously at their base on Yellow Island, and at Norina's and Nick's place. We know at that time they are going to have their usual meeting.

We are going to send our three robots to their base on Yellow Island; we humans are going to drive as close as possible to the house and wait. As soon as we verify that they are all in there, I am going to give the order to our robots to attack. We figure it will take at least one minute for their two robots to beam themselves and assist their guard robot at the base. Timing is important, we have sixty seconds of surprise time and we believe within that time our robots will destroy the guard robot and the base, then they will engage their robots either here or there depending on how soon they arrive.

As soon as their robots leave, we humans will attack humans and this time we have orders from our superiors to kill. If all goes well, as I believe it will, we will be victorious. If anyone has any questions this is the time to ask them—yes, Darna."

"Is it not against the law for robots to kill humans?"

Project Anastrophe

"Under normal circumstances yes, but now we are in a different time and place and that law doesn't apply here, so our order is, 'shoot to kill'."

There were no more questions and the meeting ended abruptly. Nephus was very excited and was glad to finally have a date and time for the attack. Darna, on the other hand, was very apprehensive. She could see that everybody was excited and figured that it must be a "male thing."

Now she had to act quickly if her plan had any chance to succeed. But there was one thing bothering her; what if they were to change the date and time? Would there be another chance for her to alert the others? She decided to take it one step at a time-- come what may. She had three days within which to act and thought tonight would be a good time to put her plan into effect. Nephus and Darna were at their favorite restaurant enjoying home-cooked food and drinking good wine.

As part of her plan Darna looked exceptionally beautiful tonight. Nephus too, looked more relaxed having all this preparatory work for the attack behind him now. He was talkative and felt closer to Darna than he had felt for a long time.

"You look so beautiful, you make me feel proud. Darna, I really do love you."

Nephus saw two pearl-like tear drops running down her cheeks and quickly asked,

"What's the problem, why are you crying, is it anything I said?"

"I don't think you would understand. It's hard to explain the pain I have in my heart, so let's just forget it and let me be."

"I would really like to understand you if I could, just try me."

"You really want to know what's bothering me, Nephus?"

"Yes, I do."

"I have this feeling that I don't have long to live. I know you think that we are going to win this coming battle but I think otherwise, and I would feel a lot better going into this if I could send a message to my mother to tell her how much I love her and miss her. You know I left home saying nothing to anyone."

"That could be very difficult, because for one thing, the robot guard is the only relay between us and home and he answers only to Dr. Dorgovich."

"Nephus, you are smart enough, you can bypass the robot. Please do it for me pleaseee?"

"Darna, you are asking me to do something so difficult it's almost impossible, but I'll try because I don't want to see you feeling unhappy."

"Thank you, Nephus, I have no doubt that you can do it, you made me feel so much better, thank you."

Darna seemed to be so happy and Nephus didn't want to disappoint her. Bypassing the robot would be difficult but he knew he could do it; after all it was only a robot. They had a nice time being out together, they even went to a bar to watch the late show just for old time's sake. After the show they went home and Darna was extra amorous.

Nephus was an "early bird," he would be the first one up to make the coffee. Then an hour or sometimes two hours later, Darna would walk into their little kitchen not quite awake and it would take a couple of cups of coffee for her to really be herself. By then Nephus would be out and about.

This morning however it was different; Nephus had gotten up very early, took his coffee into his office, and worked there for hours. When Darna walked into the kitchen he wasn't there.

Project Anastrophe

He finally appeared and with a broad smile he said,

"I did it, but we don't have much time, you need to send your message right away. Can you do it now?"

"Yes, of course."

"As soon as you have sent it, you must delete it, otherwise the robot will trace your message and we will both be in trouble."

"I understand."

Darna didn't waste any time, she had already rehearsed the message she was going to send. She addressed it to her mother and after she sent it, she made sure to delete it. Nephus came in after she was done to see that the page was deleted properly and he was satisfied. Then he turned around and said,

"Are you happy now, Darna?"

"Very much so, thank you, Nephus." Then she hugged him and gave him a sweet kiss and this time she meant it.

The message found Flavia in her studio; she used it more often lately on account of her daughter's disappearance. It was the only place she could forget her pain; she was working endlessly painting, some times late into the small hours. Her robot, Nerios, brought the message to her; he said it was urgent to read it now. She asked him to project it and he obediently did so.

She saw her daughter smiling at her, and her heart started pounding uncontrollably,

"Dear God--Darna is alive.

"Mother, I am sorry for leaving so abruptly, and not letting you know where I have been all this time, but there is a good reason for this. All I can tell you now is that I am well, and hope to see you soon.

Please take this message to my manager Fura, at work;

it's very important she only sees this message. My life depends on it. I love you and hope to see you soon."

The message was written in some cryptic language Flavia couldn't understand. She quickly sent a message of her own to Fura asking her to come to see her in person at her house. She said she had something important to tell her.

Fura was just as anxious to know about Darna. The last time she heard from her she was on her way to talk to some officials at the Du Bois brother's company. She had been apprehensive about going there but Fura encouraged her. She told her it was a hot story and would be worth her effort. After Darna's disappearance she worried and had felt guilty ever since. She hoped Flavia would have some news about Darna. Before long Fura was reading Darna's message and when she was done, she was visibly disturbed.

"Well, what's she saying, is she all right?"

"She is fine right now, but I have to help her and I need to go."

"But what's she saying--I need to know, I worry about her."

"All I can tell you is what she told you; she is O.K. for now. I can't tell you what she is saying to me, it's 'top secret'. I promise to keep you posted if there is any change, now I have to go. Please don't say anything to anyone and especially to the police; your daughter's and other's lives are at stake."

Fura could see Flavia was worried about her daughter's well being, but she couldn't risk revealing the rest of the message to her. As she was driving back to her office the message unfolded once more in her mind,

"It is imperative that you reveal the plot to Dr. Dylos about the surprise attack on the government team, and tell him I want to be taken out of here and sent back home according to my directions.

Project Anastrophe

The attack is scheduled to commence precisely at 8:00 a.m. on Wednesday our time; please see details. Dr. Dylos must see this message as soon as possible. Our survival depends on your quick response, thank you and I hope to see you soon, Darna."

When she arrived at her office Fura got in touch with Dr. Dylos and told him she needed to see him right away; she had important information concerning something called "Project Anastrophe." Dr. Dylos was used to being bothered by the media and had given strict orders to his staff that unless there was something very important, he wanted nothing to do with it. But one of the staff named Lozinei saw the name "Project Anastrophe" in Fura's message and knew that this was important enough for Dr. Dylos to see it.

Dr. Dylos went to Fura's office and had a long discussion about the message. He pleaded with her not to say anything about it and she, in turn, promised to say nothing for the time being. Dr. Dylos knew he had to act quickly if he was to foil a surprise attack by the enemy on his team out there. He quickly summoned his staff.

"Friends, I have received a very disturbing message from a person called Darna. She is a member of the enemy team sent back in time by the Du Bois brothers. I was not pleased with their behavior, but at the time I thought as long as they kept to themselves, we were confident our team could accomplish what it was sent there to do with no problems at all.

Apparently Darna was taken there against her will, and wants our help to get out. In her message she also mentions the fact that her team is preparing a surprise attack to destroy our team. As I said before, as long as they kept to themselves I didn't mind them being there, but we can't allow them to destroy our team. They are scheduled to attack simultaneously at our base, our robots, and our human team on Wednesday at 8:00 p.m. their time. We need to respond quickly, so I am open to ideas."

There were many suggestions about how to respond; from sending more weapons, robots, and even more humans as soon as possible to alert their team right away. But there was a question from a senior staff member that was discussed in great detail. He said,

"What if she is part of the plan to confuse them by giving them a certain day and time and then attacking at another time?"

Dr. Dylos answered emphatically by saying,

"I have discussed the sincerity of the message with Miss Fura, her boss, and she said she believes Darna is telling the truth and I quite agree with her."

They finally agreed that all they had to do was to alert their team about the surprise attack right away, and if enemy humans attacked them with fully charged guns, to respond likewise. The message was sent to Ner.

Chapter 10

Back in Time

The Northwest Autumn was coming to an end; the foliage turning to yellow and gold and the ground covered here and there with fallen leaves. On the horizon one could see huge clouds passing by and the sun playing hide and seek between clouds. As the morning progressed, the wind strengthened causing the branches of a nearby fir tree to move rhythmically. Cold drops of rain streamed down Norina's kitchen window.

She was eating her breakfast, watching the change in the weather. Back home the weather was totally controlled; rain came when it was needed and even the sunshine was controlled by an artificial blanket of fog. She liked these unpredictable changes in weather and an ecosystem that hadn't yet been destroyed by human experiments.

Had they come too late; could they still save the planet? She was going to try; the alternative was unacceptable. A vibration and a flashing red light in her otherwise regular wristwatch let her know that Ner had something important to tell her. She pushed a small button on the side of her watch and waited for him to come. In a few seconds he materialized in the center of the kitchen.

"This better be important, Ner."

"It is indeed very important, Norina."

"Well?"

"I just got a message from Dr. Dylos; he said we are in extreme danger from the enemy team. I have more to say but I think it's important that the rest of our team should hear it too."

"I will summon them."

Within minutes everybody was there except the guard robot. Nick and Dr. Narthur each took a cup of coffee and sat on the couch. Norina sat next to Nick and Vrima was there too. Ner started by saying,

"I am going to be brief because we don't have much time. A few minutes ago I received a cryptic message from Dr. Dylos so I am sure the message is from him. In it he says that Darna sent a message to him through some trusted people, and told him that her team is about to launch a surprise attack on us this coming Wednesday at 8:00 p.m. As you all know, that's the time of our next meeting. It looks as if they are doing a good job spying on us.

They are going to attack simultaneously here and at our base. According to Darna, Nephus has worked out a program to destroy all three of us robots. They have also received new material for their robots and have made themselves much more powerful than we are. The humans have received orders to set their guns to kill humans. With a surprise attack, they have good reason to believe that they can overpower us.

Now what can we do to protect ourselves? I have already given orders to our robot guard at Yellow Island to be on high alert. It makes no difference how powerful they are, they have already lost the element of surprise and now it would take hours to overpower just one robot, never mind the sixty seconds they are counting on. That gives us time to prepare; but as I say, we need to start preparing right away.

Another thing they want us to do is to remove Darna from where she is now, to our side and then send her home. She said that during the first few minutes of any engagement between us and them, she will remain unshielded so that she can be taken by us. We should be careful not to harm her before we beam her over to our side. Also we have been given orders to shoot to kill humans of the enemy team only; this is my report for now."

Norina said,

"Ner has explained Dr. Dylos' message; now it's up to us to come up with a good defensive plan. Dr. Narthur, I assign this job to you. We must all get busy--especially Ner, Vrima, and our guard robot, to be on par with the other robots. We will meet here again tonight to compare notes and make adjustments to our plan. That's all I have to say for the time being; unless there are other questions."

Ner and Vrima left right away, but Nick asked Dr. Narthur to stay for breakfast which he gladly accepted. Over breakfast the three humans talked some more about the upcoming battle. Nick worried the enemy might have heard what had been said earlier here and be compromised. But Dr. Narthur told him that they are constantly protected by a blanket of electronic gear. Nick said to Dr. Narthur,

"What if we were to attack at an earlier time and surprise them?"

"You know, Nick, that may not be a bad idea. They are, after all, on a surprise attack mode--not a defensive one. If we attack them they will not be as well prepared."

Norina thought that was a good idea too. She called Ner and Vrima back and told them what they had decided, and asked them to switch their plan from defensive to offensive. They all put their best efforts to come up with an offensive plan which would secure a victory.

Ner programmed himself as did Vrima and Dyphus, the guard robot, to initiate an offensive of their own and make themselves just as lethal as the enemy and even more. Dr. Narthur was also busy plotting the attack meticulously. He made cloaking virtually impenetrable by reprogramming their handheld devices. He also changed the rules of engagement; set all the faisers to kill. Dr. Narthur knew that Nephus was a skilful opponent, and in this case, one of the worst enemies. But war scenarios, weapons, and all the gadgetry that goes with it were his forte; he wasn't going to allow anyone to beat him at his own game.

He worked tirelessly on the plan from its genesis to its completion and he was satisfied that if the plan were properly executed, it would annihilate the enemy and bring victory to them. Norina proved to be a perfect leader for the occasion. She supervised everything like a general; conducting frequent meetings and comparing notes with humans and robots. Nick was an astrophysicist and didn't contribute much to the effort. All he could do was to psyche himself to be as ready as possible for what was to come.

On Tuesday morning the humans and robots met at Norina's place for the last time and agreed to put the plan into effect on Wednesday night at precisely 7:45 p.m. 15

Project Anastrophe

minutes before the enemy attack. The plan called for two phases but it was drastically different from the enemy's. Dyphus would initiate the attack by hitting the enemy base. The second phase would commence when they were altogether minutes before the enemy started their own attack.

"High Noon"

Both teams worked feverishly to ready themselves for the final battle; both had high hopes to outdo one another and the time of reckoning was almost here. Norina, Nick, Dr. Narthur, Ner and Vrima, were all at their posts. This time Dr. Narthur was in charge of the whole operation. Everyone was wearing their invisible panoply specially devised by Dr. Narthur for this occasion.

A hundred kilometers to the North on Yellow Island, Dyphus was tuned for this battle; his cybernetic mind was executing thousands of decisions in split seconds. He was programmed to defend or attack at anytime. He was capable of destroying cities in a moment; his armament was awesome but his might was concentrated on this one battle and he was ready.

For this occasion Dr. Dorgovich was second in command; Sam and Nephus were in charge of the surprise attack and they were not to be underestimated. Nephus' ingenuity in robotics, noetics, algorithmics, ergonoematics and cybernetics was unmatched. On the other hand Dr. Sam Lorkost was the other powerful contributor to this team. He was familiar with all the new weapons and the gadgetry that went along with them.

He had taught polemic strategies in many universities, although no war had been waged in the last three hundred years. Nevertheless the art of war and weapon production was kept up; a policy not expected to change anytime soon. Sam designed the plan down to the smallest detail and there was no doubt in his mind that this plan was one of his best and was going to work.

AZM, BZM, and CZF were the robots created just for this expedition; they were pure lethal power ready to be directed to any battle. Their power was equal to, and in some cases, more than the other team's robots. The only thing they lacked was organic matter in their brain cells like Vrima and Ner had. Their cybernetics were made mostly from silicon and in some cases it made them more dangerous.

They arrived in Kent. Dr. Dorgovich, Sam, Nephus, and Darna were in one car; AZM and CZF in the other. BZM was guarding the base as usual. As soon as they got onto the county road they turned off their lights, and drove on until they could see the lights of Norina's and Nick's house. They stopped about two hundred meters from it; the time was 7:30 p.m. They scanned the house to see if everybody was there. There were three humans and two robots; they were all there--so far so good.

The house was not shielded; it was wide open, they had no idea what was about to happen to them, all systems checked. At 7: 45 both cars approached the house within meters and stopped. Humans and robots communicated for the last time and prepared for the attack which was to start at Dr. Dorgovich's signal at exactly 8:00 p.m.

At 7:45 Dyphus received a simple communication from Dr. Narthur that changed him into an instant war machine. T h e b a t t l e w a s o n. Four small missiles cloaked in a blanket of invisibility, and completely noiseless, left the Yellow Island base. They traveled like ghosts with unimaginable speed and within seconds penetrated the hard rock walls of the enemy's cave base like a hot knife cuts through

Project Anastrophe

butter. Once they gained entrance things happened all at once. First, all the triggering mechanism apparatus including those in BZM were compromised, then the shield that protected all the weapons was deleted. Next a large bubble was thrown over BZM which quickly engulfed and immobilized him; several explosions in succession pulverized and burned everything inside.

What was left was a blanket of non-radioactive ashes. BZM received an alert of the incoming missiles a second or so before his base was struck--enough time for him to retaliate. He released all twelve missiles and directed them to the enemy base; he also sent a coded message to AZM before he was compromised.

The missiles reached their destination in seconds; nothing could stop them from delivering their lethal cargo. They all fell on target causing a huge crater and pulverizing everything. At the same time they shook the small island and the rest of the archipelago like a strong earthquake. Within minutes huge waves covered the crater with sea water. On the neighboring islands people got out of their houses lest the "earthquake" bury them alive. There was no doubt in their minds that they had been hit by an earthquake.

BZM's message reached AZM, Sam, and Dr. Dorgovich at the same time. Sam knew right away that their surprise attack had been foiled and quickly ordered everybody to go into defensive mode. He sized up the situation and felt that although their surprise attack had been compromised, both sides had suffered heavy losses and he could still overcome the enemy with his defensive plan. His group had practiced enough to know how to react: defend, regroup, attack.

Dr. Narthur received a message from Dyphus too. It read:

"First phase executed, switched to phase two; enemy retaliated with extreme force." Dr. Narthur nervously bit his lower lip and gave the order to attack. If people were to look at this place a minute before the attack, they would have seen a farmhouse out in the field, and would think nothing about it. But a minute later, things changed drastically.

A bright light surrounded the whole area, and rainbow-like volleys flew back and forth. People would think that the newcomers had some kind of celebration; although a bit eccentric for this time of year. As soon as the order to attack was given, the house was covered by a protective shield; both humans and robots were shielded too.

Ner and Vrima stepped in front of the humans and unleashed a barrage of killer salvoes at the enemy. Nick and Norina had their faisers ready to go and waited for the next move while Dr. Narthur used his handheld unit and conducted the whole operation with mathematical accuracy. There were two invisible shielded walls, one on each side of the combatants. Dr. Narthur was in charge of one wall; he would open it, and faisers would discharge and it would quickly close again. If the wall didn't close soon enough, the enemy had an opportunity to incinerate everything inside.

The same lethal game was played on the other side of the wall, with Sam holding the other unit. It was a fight fought with the latest weapons the twenty–fifth century could offer and two theoretical generals putting their expertise into practice. Breaking an opening in the enemy's wall was possible on either side and that depended squarely on Dr. Narthur or Sam and how quickly they could close the gap before the enemy could gain entrance.

Unlike Sam, who's only aim was to destroy his enemy, Dr. Narthur had a big problem and that was to curtail any operation until he rescued Darna. But that proved to be a bigger problem.

Project Anastrophe

As though Darna could read his mind, she took advantage of an opening near her and as soon as AZM stopped shooting, she stepped out completely unprotected by her shield, threw her faiser away and waited to be beamed by the enemy. It was a daring move on her part and could have cost her life, but there was no other way. Darna's move surprised both Dr. Narthur and Sam but since Dr. Narthur was trying to get Darna out of there anyway, he took advantage of the opportunity and quickly beamed her to his side of the wall. He shielded her and moved her into the house where she would remain incapacitated until victory or defeat.

Now Sam knew what had happened; it was Darna who foiled their surprise attack and the old dictum came to mind,

"One spy equals thousands of soldiers and materiel"-- too late now to do anything about it. Now Dr. Narthur was free to fight on an equal basis with the enemy.

Whether you are beamed a few meters or thousands of kilometers away, it makes no difference to your body; it still goes through the process of reconstitution and it's a course of action the human body hasn't yet adjusted to; it's painful and it takes many days to recover. Darna found herself in an invisible cocoon but she was happy to be away from the war zone. Fighting was not her thing; she would rather argue than fight, that's why she was a reporter in the first place. She had a splitting headache and her whole body hurt; this was the third time she had been beamed and it had taken a toll on her.

She felt guilty about not taking Nephus with her, but how could she? He was so fixed in doing his programming, she knew he would never let go. Besides he liked what he was doing and was in it for the credits too. Poor Nephus, he could be killed. Darna realized that she wasn't out of the woods either. If they won the battle, Dr. Dorgovich would kill her right on the spot for being a traitor. She decided she had done all she could have done, and now it was out of her hands. Finally exhaustion overtook her mind and body and she fell into a deep sleep.

The battle went on for a few more minutes; both groups fought heroically using every technique they could employ. They used mini-concussion bombs, constricting bombs, aposynthesizers, and kenoptotique bombs too. Nephus tried to neutralize Ner and Vrima and at times succeeded but only for seconds and never both at the same time; consequently one always protected the other. Dr. Narthur also tried many times to penetrate the enemy robots and kill them, but they were impenetrable.

Finally a synchronized attack initiated by Dr. Narthur broke the impasse. Ner and Vrima kept pounding AZM and CZF while Nick and Norina armed their faisers with bio-searchers with Sam's and Dr. Dorgovich's signatures. After many tries Dr. Narthur managed to momentarily weaken Sam's and Dr. Dorgovich's protective shields. Nick and Norina both fired at the same time and the killer searchers found their targets. Both Sam and Dr. Dorgovich were instantly incinerated; AZM and CZF quickly went in front of Nephus and protected him with their massive bodies.

Meanwhile Nephus was also trying desperately to break the enemy's shielded wall and finally he brought it down. Now the enemy was totally exposed and this time his robots had a clear shot. Dr. Narthur quickly matched Nephus' charge and brought down their shielded wall too. That was his last contribution to the battle, a coordinated attack from both AZM and CZF hit his protective shield and it was shattered, vaporizing him instantly.

Now a titanic fight began with humans and robots in an open and unprotected environment. Nick and Norina im-

Project Anastrophe

mediately doubled the strength of their shields and braced for a possible early death. AZM and CZF changed tactics, now they became ballistic only to be followed by Ner and Vrima. There began a chase resembling F-16's engaged in a dog fight; all four robots diving up and down and shooting at each other at supersonic speed.

There were three humans left on the ground, two against one. Nephus, protected in his shielded cocoon, put up a good fight, but eventually a coordinated barrage from Nick and Norina broke his shield. It wasn't a fully charged shot; there was no need for more human killing. Nephus was injured enough to put him out of commission for a few days. He was put into a new shield and brought into the house unconscious. They lifted their faisers and searched for the enemy robots, but the four robots were so intermingled, that it was hard for them to distinguish foe from friend, but they kept an eye on the battle.

Vrima, being the latest robot-issue, was better equipped and managed to shoot down AZM in a complicated dogfight. CZF put up an heroic fight, but in the end Vrima and Ner shot her down too. Both enemy robots fell near Nick and Norina, disintegrating upon contact with the ground. The battle was over--but at what cost? Their beloved Dr. Narthur gone, two other human beings dead needlessly, and Nephus wounded.

As bad as they felt, they also felt lucky; it could easily have been the other way around. Soon Ner and Vrima landed near Nick and Norina and quickly cleaned the remaining debris. The battle had lasted less than fifteen minutes but to Nick and Norina it felt like hours. With the bright lights and the noise gone everything came back to normal. The rain which had stopped for a while had started again and everybody, humans and robots, were happy to have the fight over, and even happier to be safe inside the house.

George Karnikis

Norina made some fresh coffee and they were about to sit down and relax, when Vrima approached Nick and Norina and told them that she detected a convoy of cars coming their way. They immediately made the house look like they had had some kind of celebration and acted as though they were busy cleaning the place and putting things in order. They watched the cars come close to the house and waited for whatever was going to happen next.

They didn't have to wait long--a knock on the door told them someone wanted their attention. Nick opened the door. A sheriff and deputy were standing outside.

"Good evening, I am Dave Smithson and I am the sheriff around here; this is my deputy John Travis. We couldn't help but see all those fireworks and wondered what was going on here."

It had been decided that Nick would be the appropriate person to handle these people.

"Sheriff--deputy--I am Robert Johnson and this is my wife Loretta and our friends Roy and Mary Eastman, won't you please come in out of the rain?"

Both officers stepped in and removed their wet hats.

"Thank you."

"Coffee?"

"No thanks."

"I can explain why we used some fireworks. We are members of the 'Aristotelian Order of Freedom in Philosophy.' In the old days, many years back, our members used to carry lighted torches through the town, to celebrate the day of birth of this great philosopher; now we have simplified that by using fireworks."

"I accept your explanation, Mr. Johnson, but do you have a permit for using fireworks?"

"Oh I am sorry, Sheriff, but we were not aware that we needed a permit out here in the country."

Project Anastrophe

"Yes sir, Mr. Johnson, even out here you need a permit. Next time make sure you have one and perhaps you'll let us and all those people out there know, so that we can all enjoy the show."

"We'll do that, and next time we'll make sure you are here too."

"We'll be on our way--sorry for bothering you folks."

"Not at all, Sheriff."

Norina, Nick, Ner and Vrima stayed long into the night and talked about their day and especially their fight with the enemy group. They were all happy that the battle had turned in their favor, but sad that they lost their good friend Dr. Narthur. Norina brought up the subject of their prisoners.

"Well, O.K., we won the battle now we have a lot to do with our two prisoners, and then we need to work out a plan for the immediate future and what follows. Ner said,

"The first thing we have to do is to send the prisoners back home; but in order to do that, we have to communicate our status to the base, and have them send a new ship with more weaponry and other materiel to replenish what we have used so far." Norina was next with a question.

"Why do we need a new ship, what's wrong with the one we have now?"

"We want to make sure we always have a ship here, if we send the prisoners with our only ship and something goes wrong; then we would be stuck here. Remember the Voyager is not coming back; we now have our own ship. As soon as the new one arrives we will send the prisoners with the old ship along with the crew from the new one."

"Good idea, Ner, in the meantime we have to see to it that both Darna and Nephus are taken care of." Vrima said,

"Darna is already up and feeling much better, she is

happy that we won the battle, but she is anxious to go back home; she also wants to talk to Nephus."

Nick asked how Nephus was doing.

"He took quite a beating in his shielded cocoon; he lost a lot of blood, but has been given a synthetic transfusion. He is not in good enough shape to talk to anyone."

"Then see to it that she doesn't go anywhere near him."

"I'll make sure of that, Nick."

Norina asked Ner about the status of their base on Yellow Island.

"The last message Dyphus sent to Dr. Narthur was that he had switched to phase two, and that the enemy attacked with superior power. He must have sustained heavy damage and cannot communicate, but since he had time to go to phase two, it shouldn't be very bad."

"What is phase two?"

"It is to move to another area in case of heavy attack, to avoid full catastrophe."

"And was there another area to move to?"

"Yes, we had dug another cave on the other side of the island as part of our pre-attack preparatory work."

Finally Ner said that his and Vrima's batteries were down to their minimum level and they had to go home to recharge. Nick and Norina went to bed and the robots went home but they agreed to meet again tomorrow morning.

Next morning before their scheduled meeting with Norina and Nick, Ner and Vrima beamed themselves to the Yellow Island base to have a closer look at it and the condition of Dyphus. They found the base completely destroyed and covered with sea water as they thought it would be. They walked to the new base and entered.

Dyphus was in a charging mode and did not react to their intrusion. That wasn't a good sign, a look around verified the fact that this base had sustained damage too. Fortu-

Project Anastrophe

nately it wasn't great, but the base looked as if it had been struck by an earthquake. Vrima ran an analysis on Dyphus and downloaded his memory into hers, and then she turned to Ner and said,

"Dyphus is on repair mode and is fifty-five per cent done."

"Then let's help him finish up." They both tapped into his cybernetics and within a few minutes he was repaired, and acted as though he had been awakened from deep sleep.

Dyphus recognized his friends and was glad to have them there. He didn't need to bring them up to date, Vrima had forwarded his memory to Ner and all three knew what had happened there. Dyphus began to put things in order and Ner and Vrima beamed themselves to Norina's and Nick's house in time for their meeting.

Vrima surprised everybody when she poured a cup of coffee and sat next to Ner who said,

"You don't need coffee--you are a robot--remember?"

"Yes, I know, Ner, I just have the feeling to act like our human friends."

Nick and Norina smiled and said that they liked the gesture. Darna came in and helped herself to a cup of coffee and joined the meeting; she looked tired but beautiful as always.

Norina welcomed her and said,

"Darna, we all thank you for letting us know in advance that your group was going to attack us; it made all the difference in the world."

"I hope you reciprocate and send me back home. I don't want to be here anymore than I have to."

Ner interjected and said,

"We are sending you home along with Nephus as soon as the ship arrives."

"And how long is that going to take?"

"Three or four days--as long as it takes for Nephus to be ready for the ride."

"Well, if I am going to stay here that long, I need to have my belongings from the other house."

Vrima said she was going to those houses later today and would send her stuff along with other necessary things. Darna ate some breakfast and then excused herself and went back to her room where she slept most of the day.

Ner said,

"This morning Vrima and I visited the new base and found it pretty shaken up but O.K. for the most part. We also found Dyphus in repair mode so we helped him finish the process and now he is cleaning house. Last night as soon as we got home, we sent a report to Anastrophe One and told them that we had eliminated the enemy. We also reported our mutual loses and put in a request for a new ship so that we can send the prisoners back home.

This morning we received a communiqué from Dr. Dylos congratulating us on our victory. He said the ship and materiel would be arriving at the new base in four days, he also said Nephus must be kept in his cell at all times until they arrive there and Darna must be kept safe because she is our principal witness." Norina said,

"We are going to relax and take it easy this weekend but on Monday I am going to talk to my class about the dangers of bombs and radiation poisoning. Whenever you have a chance you must talk about it too."

Saturday morning turned out to be nice and sunny. Nick asked Norina if she would like to drive to town and make it an "out and about" day. She thought it would be a great idea.

Vrima beamed herself to Nephus' and Darna's house and spent lots of time downloading as well as destroying

Project Anastrophe

information. She found their personal belongings and beamed them home, then visited the other two houses and downloaded all important data and secured it in her memory data base. Of all the data she analyzed, Nephus' was by far the most important and dangerous information she collected. No wonder Dr. Dylos wants him locked up in his cell at all times--for a human, he is a genius.

Ner was at home keeping an eye on both Darna and Nephus; he didn't worry much about Darna but Nephus had the potential to be very dangerous, especially to robots. As a precaution he and Vrima were always shielded in his presence. Nick and Norina were in the village walking on the sidewalk when the Papas family walked by, Nick knew who they were right away. He kept looking at them until they disappeared into the grocery market. Norina noticed him staring and said,

"What is it that you are looking at, Nick?"

"Remember when we drove by a house with two kids playing in front of it?"

"Oh, the Papas' house?"

"Yes, the Papas family just walked by and went into that grocery market, they are, or will be, my family."

"I think we should go in there and introduce ourselves, what do you think?"

"I couldn't do that, Norina; they wouldn't understand who we really are."

"We don't need to tell them who we really are, Nick, we'll just tell them we live close by and we are introducing ourselves to them, it is a neighborly thing to do."

"I suppose you are right, Norina."

"Well of course I am right, let's go."

It didn't take them too long to find the Papas family. The market was one of those "Mom and Pop" stores. Both children were trying to behave, the girl was holding the little boy from his left hand but he wanted to break loose and run away, their brother George wasn't there for some reason. The parents were busy talking to a young man wearing a white apron who was eager to help them.

The father was dressed in a brown suit, brown fedora, gray overcoat, and Florsheim shoes. The mother wore a dark blue dress, laced black shoes with Cuban heels, a heavy gray coat with a fur collar and a modest black hat. The girl had a fluffy white bow in her hair and was wearing "Mary Jane's", a plaid wool skirt and white sweater. The little boy had a beanie and was dressed in short pants, sturdy brown oxfords and a heavy knit sweater.

Norina commented on how neatly they were dressed and Nick looked at them and couldn't believe how young they were. Sixty years from now they would all know who he was, but now he was a stranger to them. Nick approached the parents and said,

"Hello, my name is Robert Johnson and this is my wife Loretta, we bought the farmhouse down the road and I believe that makes us neighbors."

The man spoke with a Greek accent and said,

"I am Stelios Papas, and this is my wife Meropy. Did you do the fire works?"

"Yes, we did. I hope we didn't disturb you with all that noise." Nick shook hands with Mrs. Papas; her young hands were soft and warm. The last time he saw her, she was an old woman complaining about her arthritis; she was such a beautiful woman and he felt so lucky to see her back in her youth.

She was very courteous and her English was much better than her husband's; she spoke with very little accent and perfect grammar. His grandmother, Meropy Artemidu, had come from a rich and well-known family in Athens Greece; she had gone to Athens University and earned a diploma in

Project Anastrophe

philosophy and political science. She met Stelios there where he had earned a diploma in civil engineering. They fell in love, got married and settled down in Athens for what they thought would be a busy and happy life; but that changed abruptly when the German army was about to invade Greece.

After Greece defeated the Italian army on her northern borders, it was time for those Greeks who could afford it, to leave Greece. Many people did just that, Meropy's parents gave them money and told them to take their family and go to America to meet their relatives who were established there. And that's how the Papas' found themselves in America, a young family in a new country, starting their life all over again.

They were intelligent, well-educated and had enough money to help them adapt to their new country. Their diplomas would not help them here, but they had enough money to go into their own business. At the time Nick was talking to them they hadn't decided what business they were going to do. Eventually they would buy this little store and devote all their lives to it. By the time Fotis was a grown man with his own family; this little store will be a huge super market. But that would be later on when Kent became a larger city.

Now Nick was here at the very beginning of the Papas family. Demitra brought little Fotis to her parents and was relieved not to have to care for him. Nick turned to the children,

"Hi. We live close to your house and my name is Robert, what are your names?"

"My name is Demitra."

"My name is Fotis."

I was looking at my father at age three and my aunt at age four. I asked Fotis if he liked his new place. He didn't understand me and looked up at his sister questioningly. Demitra spoke to him in Greek, and I understood every word she said, his answer was "Ochi" which was an emphatic "No." While Norina was talking to Meropy, I talked to Stelios. Everything he said about the war in Greece I had heard many times when I was growing up, but I acted as though I was hearing these stories for the first time.

Norina thought Meropy was a very intelligent woman and had good command of the English language. She spoke mostly of world affairs, women's rights, and civil liberties. In Norina's time and place women never talked about these subjects. I had an urge to hug my grandfather Stelios and tell him, "Papou, I am your grandson Nick, you took me fishing at the lake many times and sometimes to Orcas Island. We went to so many baseball and basketball games--remember?"

But how could I do such a thing--he would think I was crazy. My Yaya, Meropy made the best baklava in town, and sweet koulurakia. Any time I would visit with my parents, she would say,

"Come, come, Nikolakimou see what I have for you." She would give me homemade sweets. My mother would say,

"Yaya, you will ruin his teeth."
I forced myself to behave and act as the new neighbor in town. When we were through talking, all four of us looking like contemporaries, Demitra, my aunt to be and little Fotis, my father to be, held hands as they walked out of the store and simply said,
"Good bye, hope to see you soon."
Nick and Norina walked the opposite way. Nick was in deep thought when Norina whispered,
"Are you all right, Nick?"

Project Anastrophe

"Yes, I am O.K." They went to their usual little restaurant and ordered lunch.

Under Vrima's care Nephus was getting better every day, he even started walking a bit around the house. When he found out that he and Darna were the only survivors, he was sad but he was especially angry with Darna. His body was getting better but mentally he felt awful; there was no hope for him anymore, his life was ruined. He knew when he went back home he would be punished. Most likely he would be sent to jail, this time perhaps somewhere on Mars, and be left there for the rest of his life.
He thought to himself,
"What's the use of living? I wish I were dead."
Ner received a message from Dyphus, it read,
"Ship with new weapons and materiel has arrived." Ner beamed himself to the base for a close look and was satisfied with what he saw. The ship was new and up-to-date, and all the crew were robots. He especially liked the new weapons and he was sure the humans would appreciate the new food supplies and medicine.

Ner and Dyphus supervised the robot crew to unload the cargo, and told them to wait for two passengers to take back home. He quickly beamed himself to his house and told Vrima all about the ship and its cargo. Then he communicated with Nick and Norina and told them the ship was here and he was about to take Nephus and Darna to the base. Norina was concerned that Nephus and Darna were not strong enough to be beamed to the base. But Ner assured her they would be O.K.

Nephus was put once again into his shielded cocoon; he wasn't very happy about that, but Ner told him that's the way it was going to be and to stop complaining. Darna didn't like the fact that she was going to be beamed again, but she didn't complain. At the base, Ner gave strict orders to the crew that these two humans must be kept apart at all times, and that they should be extra vigilant with the male human for their own security.

The robot crew and the two humans moved into the old ship and waited for the order to go. Both Nephus and Darna were very tired from the last beamed trip and were hardly aware of what was happening in the ship. Closed in his cocoon, Nephus was no more his vital self; he would not be a problem to anyone. Darna quickly fell asleep and dreamed that she was floating in a rainbow and was trying to go to Nephus who was sitting at the end of it extending his hand to her and urging her to grab it. She was trying hard but just as she approached him, she was pushed away by a strong wind and then she had to start all over again.

Chapter 11

Darna was awakened by a robot nurse. She looked around and realized that she was home.

"How long have I been here?"

"This is your third day in the hospital, Miss Darna. You were in bad shape when you arrived, how do you feel now?"

"I feel much better now that I am home."

"You have a visitor; do you feel strong enough for company?"

"It depends who the visitor is."

"I think you will be pleasantly surprised."

The visitor was her mother, Flavia, who hugged and squeezed her with motherly love. They both cried, but this time because they were happy.

George Karnikis

Darna felt good being back at work, she felt reborn, with a new lease on life. The last few months, living five hundred years in the past, had been a nightmare that would stay with her for the rest of her life. She had come so close to dying that life had now taken on an entirely different meaning. The one good thing she brought back from the past was the feeling of being in an open environment, an environment that was clean, unspoiled and without radiation poisoning.

Darna knew she had to do all she could to save this planet. A 3-D call came from Dr. Dylos; he appeared on her desk and said,

"Darna, I need to talk to you personally as soon as you feel better. I can't say too much on an open line, I hope to see you soon."

Darna sent a message saying she would come right away. She jumped into her magneto and left for his office.

"Nice to see you, Darna, you look so much better than the last time I saw you."

"Thank you, Dr. Dylos, how can I help you?"

"The Du Bois brothers are at it again, trying to send another team back in time to stop Project Anastrophe, and this time they might be successful if we don't stop them. We thought we should let you know that we are going to put you under witness protection right away. We have reason to believe they may harm you. Tomorrow we are going to request an injunction to close part of their company, and apprehend several people connected with their attack on our team back in time.

We have prepared a nice place for you which is under surveillance at all times, and we believe that you will be safe there. You can still go to work and live your life as you do now; you will just have a few more guards to keep an eye on you--that's all."

Project Anastrophe

"I am more than happy to help you in anyway I can, Dr. Dylos, however I have a request and that has to do with Nephus.

I realize that you are planning to punish Nephus for participating with that other team, but what you should know is that he was also forced to join them or be killed. If he hadn't helped me send that message to you, things could have gone very badly for your team back there. I would like you to be somewhat lenient with him during his trial."

"He is a very dangerous man but we will try to be fair with him--that's all I can promise at this time."

Next day, as expected, Darna was the main witness for the prosecution against the Du Bois brothers and others. The evidence against them and the rest of the conspirators was overwhelming. The judge found them guilty of conspiracy against the Government and guilty of murder. This time their power and money didn't help them. Even Governor Nazer, who tried so hard to help them in the past, was now against them.

The punishment was swift. The Government confiscated and ran their companies temporarily, and put all the conspirators in jail. It was a good thing the judge acted quickly, because the conspirators' second expedition to be sent "Back in Time" was only days away. The judge made an exception for Nephus who was in the hospital at that time; his trial was to be held soon after he was released.

Darna finally got to do what she had always wanted to do---report. She had a long discussion with her boss Fura,

"How does it feel to report on your own trial, Darna?"

"I love it--but I have so much to write I don't know where to start."

"I would start from the time you were abducted, that's a good place, don't you think?"

"That's pretty much what I was thinking, Fura."

There were rumors about an expedition into the past with some kind of time machine, but rumors come and go and people forget. So when Darna's article came out, it hit the whole planet like an A-bomb. The story had everything: conspiracy, murder, love, abduction, police and government participation with underground characters. The most important of all was the fact that the scientists were finally working on a way to save the planet Earth from radiation poisoning. It was the juiciest story in many years and Darna became a celebrity overnight. She was asked to visit many biospheres all over the planet and even on Mars.

"Fura, I just want to report, I am a journalist, and this is too much for me."

"Darna, this is the best thing that has happened to you, me, and our company. Take advantage of it. Things like this don't happen everyday; besides you worked hard for it and almost lost your life."

Darna began to get used to her new life. All of a sudden her 3-D projections were in many living rooms. She became rich and famous and was recognized anywhere she went; she was asked to act in movies too. Nephus eventually had his day in court. Although he was one of the brains of the conspirators the judge took under consideration the fact that he was taken there by force and sentenced him to one year in jail; and with good behavior he could get out even sooner.

The dream of coming back home rich and famous and living the rest of his life with Darna had fizzled out the minute she betrayed them. Now she was rich and famous, while he was rotting in jail--and to think he had helped her send that message. Nephus was furious, jealous, and resentful, but he still loved her more than anything.

Project Anastrophe

Back in Time

Norina mentioned to her students, for the first time, the possibility of radiation poisoning as a by-product of an atomic bomb. There were many questions; one student asked,

"How can you be so sure of that when we don't even have the bomb yet?"

Norina felt like saying,

"Because I have seen first hand the destruction it has caused."

But she thought better and said,

"Based on preliminary work done by many scientists in other countries, especially in Germany; when a nuclear explosion occurs as a result of the rapid release of energy from an uncontrolled nuclear reaction, the driving force may be nuclear fission, nuclear fusion or a multistage cascading combination of the two. Atmospheric nuclear explosions are associated with "mushroom clouds" although they can also occur with large chemical explosions." She went on to explain that it was possible to have an air burst nuclear explosion without these clouds. Nuclear explosions produce large amounts of radiation and radioactive debris. If radioactive debris was released into the air it could travel into residential areas and make people sick and possibly kill them. That was why we should be extremely careful how we handle such a dangerous weapon.

Up to this point the A-Bomb was considered the weapon of choice and the panacea for all. Both Germany and the U.S.A. were working hard at it, and whoever got the bomb first would have the upper hand. So the race was on and no amount of money was spared by either country. This was indeed the first time anyone spoke ill of this project--it was downright unpatriotic.

Norina had to be very careful with every word she said, but she managed to convey the unpleasant side of this wonderful weapon. As time went on Nick, Ner, and Vrima showed their students the good and bad sides of the A-bomb. Little by little, through articles in the papers and radio news, the truth of the bomb came out in the open. The "Project Anastrophe" had started--although with baby steps. As the time went on people would start to question their representatives about the wisdom of using weapons of such destructive power.

On the cold day of September 1, 1939, the Germans invaded Poland, and the world went to war for the second time in 27 years. Germany, expansionist in its aims, had simply invaded another country so soon after the "War to end all wars." Nations and their leaders had allowed another conflict to threaten the planet.

This war would last six years, involve more than two hundred countries, and cause millions of people to suffer. It would cost 58 million lives, and material damage of approximately 3 billion dollars. It affected the lives of three quarters of the world's population and influenced all the world's inhabitants.

Within months of the German move into Poland much of Europe had been occupied by the Blitzkrieg technique of the Third Reich's military power.

When the Battle of Britain was at its height and Hitler was planning to invade England, the English people were fearful but determined. England had already suffered heavy damage and many deaths. The people said the war in Europe had started and the Germans were to be blamed.

Norina called Ner and Vrima to her place and talked into the small hours about their next move. It was decided that they should go to Europe. Norina suggested that now

Project Anastrophe

was the appropriate time for them to make changes that would affect the progress of the elimination of nuclear weapons. It would be best to go to Germany and make sure they didn't develop the bomb. Norina suggested they should all give notice to the University for a leave- of-absence due to the war in Europe.

With so many young people joining the service for the war effort, the universities all over the country had fewer students; their request for leave-of-absence was easily granted to them. They decided that this time they should all beam themselves to Lausanne in Switzerland which was a neutral country. From there they could go to various countries in Europe as needed. They beamed themselves during the night so that they wouldn't be seen, and landed in a park. Now it was up to Nick to arrange for a hotel and other necessities.

They walked from the park to the nearest main road and Nick stopped a taxi. He spoke to the driver in English, and asked him to take them to The Royal Savoy Hotel. Within minutes they were registering. Ner and Vrima registered as Americans; Nick and Norina as British. Their reason for visiting was "business."

Norina and Nick went to bed right away, while Ner and Vrima went into charging mode. It took most of the next day for Nick and Norina to feel well enough to go to the restaurant and have something to eat. Ner and Vrima were already hard at work making plans for the next move. Germany was the first country they were scheduled to visit. Beaming themselves there was out of the question; Nick and Norina had had enough of that for the time being.

Now they had to have a legitimate reason for being there. Their predicament was--should they be there as citizens or foreign nationals? Finally after a lot of thinking and with every detail worked out, they decided to be German citizens with Bavarian accents. Their implants would easily handle the German vocabulary but Nick and Norina had to work a little bit on their accents.

Ner and Vrima had no problem at all. They could pick up any language and speak like natives. Everything was innate for them. The German linguist in their implants had a good sense of humor. In addition to the proper Bavarian accent he taught them many slang words and the colloquial speech. He also taught them several Bavarian beer drinking songs, important holidays, the basic history of Germany and German people, and the German National Anthem.

Nick and Norina used this time of learning to have some needed relaxation and while the robots were doing all the preparatory work for going to Germany, they spent that time going around and just being tourists. They went back to the park where they had landed the night before. It was cold but they were well dressed for their outing. They caught a taxi and went downtown, walked around and looked at the shops; they found a nice restaurant and had dinner.

From their vantage point by the window they could see people going about their business as though nothing had happened. Life looked surprisingly normal. Every once in a while someone would stop and look at the news papers that were hanging outside the kiosk. Most had the headline, "IT'S WAR." Nick held Norina's hand and said,

"I hope you're prepared for this war; it will be one of the worst in human history."

"As part of my education I have studied wars from the Peloponnesian war in Greece in 441 B.C. to the Chinese war that took place in 2037. I believe that was the last full scale war that was fought with nuclear weapons and brought radiation poisoning to our planet."

"It's much worse to see the blood and gore live, than to

Project Anastrophe

read about it in an historical text, and this is what you going to see this time, Norina, so brace yourself, it's going to be ugly."

Ner and Vrima had obtained, or in some cases, made all the necessary German documents including passports--they were ready to go. Their plan was to go through Austria and enter Germany through Salzburg into Munich. They were to stay for a while to polish their Bavarian accents; then go north to Hanover and Hamburg where most of the experiments for nuclear weapons were taking place. They had a nice train trip through beautiful country; in the higher elevations there was already a blanket of fresh snow.

They all had dinner together, this time Ner and Vrima ate like everybody else. Vrima had the best time pretending to be human, Ner was more pragmatic, he only ate when he had to, and this was one of those times. Nick and Norina enjoyed their dinner and bought some of the best wine to go with it. They went through Austria without problems but at Salzburg they had to go through German customs and immigration. They were taken aside and asked where they had been and if they had visited France or England. The authorities went through all their belongings and asked them to write down, in detail, all the places they had visited and all their business transactions.

Both Nick and Norina spoke well; they had memorized their German names so they felt like they had had them forever. The immigration officer asked Nick if he remembered the day he graduated and who were his best friends at that time. That was something he had never learned and he was heading for disaster, but the German professor in his implants quickly gave him the day and the names and Nick provided all the right answers. The officers said,

"Willkommen Zuruck zu ihren fatheland."

They answered back,

"Vielen dank." And stepped out of there. Now they had all the necessary documents to go anywhere in Germany and they started planning right away. They found a taxi and asked the driver to take them to the Kempinski Hotel. He took another look at them because that Hotel was one of the most expensive in town.

Upon arrival, Nick gave the driver a generous tip and they proceeded to register at the front desk. The young woman at the desk was helpful and Nick, Norina, Ner and Vrima registered as couples. As they were about to be shown their rooms, a person who was standing at the other end of the desk, moved closer and said,

"Eine minute bitte. May I see your passports?"

He looked at them suspiciously and asked many more questions than the immigration officers had asked at the border.

"So much for going to an expensive hotel to avoid being checked," Nick thought to himself.

The young man who helped them with their baggage and opened the doors for them said,

"Gestapo, they never trust anybody."

Nick gave the man another generous tip at the door. Ner suggested that from now on anything important should be discussed subliminally through their implants for greater security. They agreed to meet tomorrow morning at the restaurant and discuss the schedule for the day.

Nick and Norina had showers and made love until the early hours. Ner and Vrima assumed that they were going to be seen and charged themselves in a very inconspicuous way. Next day they all met at the restaurant and ordered breakfast including Ner and Vrima. Ner told them it would be wise for Vrima and him to beam themselves to Hanover and for Nick and Norina to go by train.

"We will arrange the hotel reservations for all of us and

Project Anastrophe

also do some preliminary work to find the team that works on the bomb; we'll come and meet you at the railway station when you arrive."

Back to the Future

Dr. Dylos asked the Anastrophe team to meet once more in the laboratory's office to discuss the worsening environment and to do something to alleviate the death and destruction that was occurring daily. He welcomed everybody, and told them briefly what was happening and that they had to do something soon. He said that about one hundred thousand people were dying from radiation poisoning every day in the state of America alone, and at that rate humanity would not last very long. Then he asked Dr. Thamion to explain how changes done now by our team in the Twentieth Century would affect us, and how long it would take for things to get better here in our time and place.

"First of all, at the time they are in now, no atomic bomb has been made and there is no radiation in the atmosphere, so there is nothing for them to correct yet. In order for them to minimize or eliminate the radiation poisoning, they must jump in time once more and this time immediately after the first bomb explosion or very close to it. But that will not solve our problem here. We will still have the problem although perhaps a little less. For the radiation to go away completely they must change the "Prime Directive" from the beginning and that's what they are doing now."

"Dr. Thamion, we are now at a point of extreme danger; if we can't do something to slow this menace, it will be too late for them to save us."

"Technically speaking even if all of us were to die,

when they accomplish their mission, we will all be saved. We will know nothing about this catastrophe; we will not even know that we died simply because they changed the "Prime Directive" in a way that radiation poisoning never reached a dangerous level. However there is a problem and that is, if we die first, there will be no one to bring them home and they will be lost in time and space."

"Is there anything we can do to rectify this before it happens?"

"At this time very little, you see we were hoping things would not deteriorate so soon. Now we have to change plans once more."

"Do you have anything specific in mind?"

"There are two things we can do, one is to move our lab into a specially built spaceship to house the lab staff and their immediate families; then calibrate the time sequence to the present time. When the full catastrophe occurs and life is abolished on Earth we will be in a position to bring our people from the Twentieth Century back home to a changed planet. No one will know that anything happened to our planet except us and our team back there.

The second one is to move our team six years ahead in time to August 6 and 9, 1945 to the time the bombs were exploded in Hiroshima and Nagasaki; also prevent the bigger one scheduled to fall on Tokyo September 2, 1945. We can direct our team to stop the next two bombs, one from the USA to the Soviet Union, and one from the Soviet Union to the U.S.A. That would delay the effect the radiation has on us now by approximately one year. One year ago the radiation was bad, but not as bad as it is now, and that would give our team more time to do the job right. It needs to be understood that anytime you change the "Prime Directive" you don't know how it is going to affect us in our time."

Project Anastrophe

"Dr. Thamion, could you give us the worst scenario of how a change in the "Prime Directive" could affect us?"

"The best way to do that is by giving you an example. Dr. Dylos, you are the one who started this program called Project Anastrophe--before that you spent most of your life finding people and material that delayed the progress of this radiation, thereby saving millions of people from sickness and death.

Now let's suppose some of your ancestors were living at precisely the time and place we are about to change, and let's suppose again that some of your direct family were in a car going on a picnic trip as they used to do then, and suppose a military truck on its way to the base preparing the Tokyo bomb, hit your relatives and killed them all. You would not have been around at this time, there would be no Project Anastrophe, and many millions would be dead because you would not have been around to save them. That's just one person, how about all the other people that didn't make it because of that change? That's why we do not interfere with the "Prime Directive" unless we really, really, have to."

"Dr. Thamion, you have given us a good reason as to why we shouldn't change the "Prime Directive," but now we are about to do just that, because as you say we really have to. Now I would like anyone of you to think hard and tell me which of these two plans we should choose, or do you have any better ideas?"

There were many who chose the first plan, still others chose the second, but there was a young woman, a new staffer, Dr. Jain Stapleton, who had a third idea. She said,

"Why don't we combine both plans--that way we don't take chances?" Dr. Dylos thought it was a good idea, but asked Dr. Thamion again what he thought of it.

"I think it's a good compromise, but we still run a

chance of having people missing when we come back to our changed Earth."

"Dr. Thamion, I suppose that's a chance we have to take if it will help to postpone this tragedy and give time to our team to do the job right."

And so it was decided to send an urgent message back in time to their team with all the necessary directions, asking them to proceed as soon as possible. The staff started preparing the ship for them and their families. They were very discreet about what they were doing and only at the last possible hour told their families they were going on a business trip. Dr. Dylos asked Darna to come to his office once more, and told her that it was part of her security program to be kept at an undisclosed place for some time in the near future. She could bring two people with her.

"Where and how long this time, Dr. Dylos?"

"I can't tell you that, Darna. All I can tell you is that your life will be in extreme danger if you stay where you are now."

"O.K., there are two people I want to come with me---my mother and Nephus."

"You may bring your mother; Nephus is out of the question."

"Why? Nephus has completed his time in jail and has been an exemplary citizen ever since."

"Nephus is a very dangerous person and cannot be with you where you are going."

"Then I am not going anywhere."

"If you refuse our offer, then you forfeit your right to be protected, is that what you want?"

"I have to think about it."

"O.K., but I need to know by tonight."

Dr. Dylos liked Darna a lot. She was a gutsy and indomitable woman. She was known very well by all the

Project Anastrophe

people that were to come on board; she could join and be a valuable addition to his staff. However Nephus was a rebel; had lived most of his life with the underworld and could easily cause trouble on this expedition. On the other hand he was a very intelligent man; he was the best when it came to robotics and electronics. He could be a great asset. Dr. Dylos had to think about that and think hard. His staff was working on refurbishing one of the biggest spaceships they had found; they were changing it into a floating hotel for over a thousand people of all ages plus hundreds of robots, material, equipment, and weapons. It was a daunting undertaking but they were confident they could do it on time.

Darna found Nephus in his office; she hadn't talked to him since he got out of jail and she wondered how he was going to react after what she had done to him. She had to tell him about her departure, and perhaps convince him to go with her if that could be arranged. In all this time, ever since they came back, and he ended up in jail, he had only talked to her and seen her in 3-D visits but never in person. His first reaction upon seeing her was both hate and love, he loved this woman with an inexplicable pathos, but it was because of her that he had ended up broke and in jail.

His life had taken a turn for the worse; he had barely enough credits in his account and was under constant surveillance by the police. In some ways he was to be blamed too, after all, she hadn't wanted to go with him on that failed expedition. He had demanded that his bosses let her go with him or he wouldn't go anywhere. Seeing her coming into his office with that smile, Nephus stopped feeling miserable momentarily and he felt genuinely happy.

She sat in her usual seat. He looked tired and haggard; he had lost weight and one could see the last few months in jail had taken its toll on him.

"Hi, Darna, you didn't come as hologram, so it must be important."

"I have a proposition for you."

"Ha, I haven't had a proposition from you in a long time, it really must be important."

"It--my bodyguards have informed me that for my own safety, I have to go to an undisclosed place for a while longer. This time they gave me a choice of having two people with me, my mother is coming, would you like to come along too?"

"Darna, you know me, I'll go to the end of the world with you, but as part of my parole I am under twenty-four-seven surveillance by the police and they will not let me go anywhere until I am done."

"Suppose I manage to gain your release---would you go?"

"I know you are now rich and famous, but even you couldn't get me out of here, but if you could, I am all yours."

"Then it's settled, I'll let you know as soon as I find out."

"How would you like to go to our favorite restaurant and have dinner tonight?"

"I have a better idea. Why don't we go to my new house and have dinner there? My new robot is one of the best chefs in town."

"That sounds great; I would like to see your new house anyway."

The house was more lavish than he had expected, and the robot did an excellent job with their dinner. Nephus stayed overnight and they made love for the first time since they had come back from their failed expedition. Darna was happy. Fame and money were good to a certain point, but the last few months had been hectic and she was looking forward to going somewhere just to get away from it all for a while. If Nephus could come along, it would be even better.

It was a gigantic spaceship, the biggest cargo ship they could find, and it had been made into a passenger ship for a long voyage. They didn't know how long they had to stay away before they came back to the present time, presumably to an undamaged Earth. Dr. Dylos met again with Dr. Thamion and wanted to be brought up-to date with the refurbishing of the ship.
"We are finishing a few details, and should be ready for embarkation within two days. Do you have a precise date for departure?"
"After we have everybody on board, we'll let you know."

Two days later everything was done according to plan; all five hundred robots of every design were already onboard including the security guards. They had provisions, necessary material for most needs, and all kinds of equipment and weapons. The spaceship was ready to go---all it needed was the people. Dr. Dylos had to think very hard about bringing Nephus onboard, but both the jail warden and Darna had told him repeatedly that Nephus was a changed man and would be all right for a government appointment. He could also be trusted with people, so when Darna called to find out if Nephus could come with her, Dr. Dylos hesitantly said it would be all right for him to go but he had to behave or he would be back in jail.
All those chosen to come onboard, except the staff, had no idea they were going into a spaceship. All they had been told was that they were going to a hotel where they were

going to be given special instructions for emergency evacuation to safer grounds. They would live in the hotel for a few days and then they would go home. The people finally did come--all 1022: mostly young couples, children of the Project Anastrophe staff, parents, and close relatives. Most were women and children but there were also a few older people in their seventies and eighties. There were a few cats and dogs and other small animals that came along with the young families.

The first day was busy with people checking in and being given their rooms in what they thought was a hotel. They were directed through a hallway and into the spaceship which was made to look as if it were part of the hotel. Next day there were more speeches about survival and other related subjects. The second night, late into the early hours, when everyone was onboard and most of them asleep, some people heard noises somewhere in the hotel. They assumed it was the hotel robot staff cleaning, but in actuality it was the crew of the spaceship Anastrophe readying the ship for departure.

Darna, her mother, and Nephus had checked into the hotel, and had been given two rooms; one for Darna's mother Mrs. Flavia Varnether, and the other room for the two of them. Just like everybody else they were told to stay in the hotel at all times and attend the various Emergency Evacuation seminars. Darna and Nephus didn't attend any of the seminars, instead, they spent their time going in and out of the hotel buying things with Darna's credits and spending their time entertaining themselves and making love in their room.

It was Nephus who sat up in bed wondering what was happening, only to be followed by Darna. What they were feeling was familiar to both of them.

Project Anastrophe

"Darna, do you think what I think?"

"Yes, I think we are traveling in time again."

"But why, what's the purpose of it? Do you think we are being sent back in time?"

"God, I hope not, but I think we are going to find out soon."

They both jumped out off bed, dressed and opened the door to go out. They were promptly stopped by a robot guard. They could see down the hall where more people were trying to get out. Nephus asked the guard what was happening and why couldn't they go out? The guard said,

"I don't know, but I have orders to keep everybody in their rooms until morning." Next day the people were allowed to go out as they pleased. They were told that they would be given answers to their questions within the day.

Nephus and Darna asked to see the manager and to their surprise, they were allowed to go into his office and talk to him personally. They didn't have to wait long; a side door opened and again to their surprise, Dr. Dylos and Dr. Thamion stepped in. Dr. Dylos said,

"Good morning, Darna--Nephus, how are you this morning?"

Darna answered as politely as she could under the circumstances,

"We are O.K., but we would feel a lot better if you would tell us what's going on here. Are we in a spaceship, and are we traveling in time?"

"The answer is yes to both of your questions and if you allow me, I will explain the reason as well as I can.

You, of all people, know that we have sent a team back in time to make changes in order to save our planet from radiation poisoning. What you don't know, is that one hundred thousand people are dying from radiation poisoning every day in the state of America. Approximately the same ratio exists in other states on our planet, and according to our scientists the number is going to double, and triple, in the very near future. At this rate humanity is not going to survive for long.

Our prognosis is that the atmosphere in every biosphere will get extremely toxic and eventually it will kill every living thing in all biospheres all over the planet within seven to eight weeks. We have sent orders to our team back in time to make some quick changes to slow the production and use of atomic bombs, which will minimize the mortality rate in our time. Eventually they will be able to reduce the production of nuclear bombs to a safe level and prevent the destruction of our planet.

Our scientists tell us that whenever the "Prime Directive" is changed, one cannot predict what changes will occur in the future. This is the reason why we decided to move the lab staff, their families, and other chosen people away in space and time. Our aim is to save a part of our civilization: people, culture, material, and technology. In case something goes drastically wrong, we could bring our team back from the past. That is the reason the two of you are here. We hope that you will understand and help us in our difficult experiment."

"Did we move to the past or future--and how far in time?"

"We moved one year back in time, so that if for any reason we have to go back home to our biosphere, it would not have changed too much."

"Why not move five years or more, when it wasn't as dangerous?"

"Again that would interfere with the "Prime Directive", and we want to come back to a life that hasn't been altered much."

The spaceship Anastrophe with its micro-cosmos,

Project Anastrophe

moved close to the dark side of the moon, an area that wasn't visited frequently by cargo ships. They stayed there in limbo, waiting for the right time to go back to a changed, but safer home.

Chapter 12

Back in Time

It was while they were eating breakfast and discussing the day's schedule, that Ner went into complete silence. Nick and Norina knew he was in communication with the base back home. They were anxious to know what kind of message he was getting this time. They didn't have to wait long. Ner looked them straight in the eye and spoke subliminally. Their conversation lasted only a few minutes but they all had a vivid picture of what was happening at home. The number of people dying every day was inconceivable, and it was getting worse with every passing hour; they had to act quickly.

Ner suggested they should go out to the park where

Project Anastrophe

they could talk freely. Before long they were sitting on a bench; it was a nice sunny day and there were a few other people walking on the pathways. Two young mothers were pushing carts with their young babies in them. Ner said,

"Perhaps it would be best if Vrima and I were to beam ourselves to Hanover, find their lab and sabotage the area so that we can delay their plans for building the bomb at least for a while. Then we can all beam ourselves back to Yellow Island and travel to the year 1946 in time to stop the other three atomic bombs from exploding." Nick said,

"It would be better if we were all there to help." But Norina agreed with Ner and said to Nick,

"Ner is right; we can't beam ourselves two more times and then travel to 1946. We would be like corpses and wouldn't be able to help anybody."

It was agreed; Nick and Norina would wait at their hotel until Ner and Vrima had accomplished their mission. Then they could all beam themselves to the base at Yellow Island and there they would decide when to travel to the future.

They all went back to their rooms, and soon after that Ner and Vrima beamed themselves to Hanover. Nick and Norina spoke to each other subliminally and mostly in metric language. Nick reassured Norina that the Germans would never understand that language and they wouldn't have enough time to decipher it, no matter how smart they were. Norina was very upset with all the people dying back at home. Thinking of her parents and her brother she couldn't stop herself from crying. Nick empathized with her; he knew how she was feeling, it wasn't that long since he had felt like that for his own family.

"Norina, if this is any consolation to you, you should know that if we are successful with our mission we will stop all these deaths before they occur."

"I know that; but there is a strong possibility that by changing the "Prime Directive", our friends and relatives may not be in existence. If they are, they could be different, and at the very least they may not know who we are. To me that would be worse than if they were dead."

"I suppose you are right, but that is a chance we have to take in order to save the people who are there now."

"Yes of course I know that, I am sorry Nick, I suppose I am not much help to you, am I?"

"Your reaction is normal, Norina, but I think the minute we start doing something about it; you will feel much better."

Ner and Vrima chose a quiet place out of the way to re-morph themselves; then they slowly mingled with the people. Their internal maps showed them the way to the lab. Their special sensor could discriminate any unnecessary chemicals and alloys; they could detect the smallest particles of isotopes connected with radiation, and all in nano seconds.

"Ner, I located the lab."

"I knew you would, Vrima, your sensors are so much newer and faster."

"Now listen carefully. At the end of the hallway right after you pass the door to the lab, there is a bathroom; that's where we are going to land, and let's hope there is no one in there."

"I understand. I am going first."

Fortunately the bathroom was empty and Vrima had no problem re-morphing in there. Soon Ner appeared too; he communicated with Vrima subliminally and said,

"Let's go in cloaked mode and keep in touch at all times."

They walked into the lab unseen and were not bothered.

Project Anastrophe

They stood in a corner out of the way and watched the scientists at work. They couldn't help but admire them. They were methodic, precise and diligent. Ner and Vrima were witnessing the fathers of the atomic bomb at work. Vrima was impressed and she told Ner,

"They are at least one year ahead of the Americans and at this rate they will be the first to have the bomb."

"Then I think we are not a minute too soon to stop them, let's initiate our plan right now."

At exactly 12:00 noon all the scientists took off their gloves and protective gear and went out for lunch. Ner and Vrima knew Germans were always punctual. At the same time four guards, two on each side of the door, stayed there until the scientists would came back, at exactly 12:30 p.m. Ner and Vrima got busy right away. If the guards saw things moving every once in a while, they would simply think they had had a little more beer than usual last night, and would say nothing to anyone.

Vrima and Ner located the area where the Deuterium-Hydrogen Isotopes were kept. Next they found Uranium 235 and 233, and Plutonium 239. They gathered all the notes they could find. The last thing Ner did was to place explosives in various areas in the lab and he timed them to go off ten minutes later. Ner and Vrima walked away from the building still in cloaked mode and were clear of it behind a parked truck about five hundred meters away. Then the explosives went off. Doors and windows as well as human bodies were thrown every which way; the explosions were powerful enough to break the glass on windows and doors as far as one thousand meters away.

Ner and Vrima knew their job here was done; the Germans would never recover on time to use the bomb anywhere. Ner sent a message to Norina and Nick telling them the plan had been successfully executed and they were beaming themselves back to base at Yellow Island. Nick and Norina were happy with the news and before long they also beamed themselves back to the base.

It felt good to be in friendly territory again but it took a couple of days for Nick and Norina to get together with all three robots. They held the meeting in the spaceship where they had been living for the last two days. The ship was kept at the base for extra security; it was in excellent condition and ready to go at anytime. The base guard robot, Dyphus said,

"I have prepared a list of what you are going to need for your time-travel; there are enough provisions for two humans for one year, also enough material, organic and inorganic, for two robots for an indefinite time. I have repaired all the damage caused by the missile attack; finally I have an urgent hologram from Dr. Dylos for Miss Norina."

Norina, who was conducting the meeting as always, asked Dyphus to project the hologram. Soon Dr. Dylos' hologram was projected on the middle of the table; he looked tired but very determined and addressed Norina.

"Norina, I am sure by now Ner has given you our bad news here. From my last communication with Dyphus you were preparing to beam yourselves back to base. I am hoping you are there now. This is our status; we have gathered one thousand and twenty-two people of all ages, five hundred robots, and enough provisions, material, equipment, and weapons to last us at least one year. We have refurbished the biggest cargo spaceship we could find, and have time-traveled one year into the past. We have moved our ship to the dark side of the moon, and are anxiously waiting for you to make the necessary changes according to the plan.

We send frequent probes to Earth to check conditions. I am sorry to inform you that things are getting progressively

Project Anastrophe

worse and they are now approaching the final stages of destruction. We realize you will need our help for time-travel and we will arrange it for you as soon as you tell us you are ready to go. We are working on material and software to make it possible for you to travel in time without our help; but that will be in the near future. We wish you good luck. The planet and all the remaining living beings depend on you."

Nick and Norina were shaken by the latest news; even Ner and Vrima were visibly disturbed. They were all anxious to start right away. Ner gave a quick report of what he was doing and then excused himself and left to start preparations for the jump into time. Vrima gave her report.

"I have made all the necessary preparations for the duration we are going to stay there. We are going to land in Washington D.C. and this time we will talk to John Paterson, the President of United States of America. We are going to persuade him not to explode the third bomb over Tokyo, or, a year later, a bomb of the same size in Moscow. After that we must go to Russia to persuade Chairman Stanoff, who is the dictator over all the Soviet Union, not to bomb Washington D.C. in the U.S.A. with an even larger bomb. Once we are there, I will take care of the money and the place we are going to stay temporarily. That's all I have to report."

Vrima spent a lot of time studying the bombings that took place in different countries, from Hiroshima and Nagasaki in Japan, to the ones used during the last nuclear war between the U.S.A. and China. In the case of the so-called "cold war" between the U.S.A. and the Soviet Union which lasted over sixty years, there was a build up in nuclear weapons and preparation for a nuclear war that never happened.

Both countries realized an exchange with nuclear

weapons would be mutually destructive; instead the nuclear bombs were used as a deterrent. But those first years in the forties were very dangerous and anything could have happened. Although both countries lacked ballistic capabilities; they had placed nuclear bombs in each other's countries in strategic places like Moscow and Washington D.C. Those were the bombs they had to stop before they went off. Ner announced to Nick and Norina that he had done all the preparatory work, and had gotten clearance from the Anastrophe One for the lift off.

Norina and Nick situated themselves as well as they could in their ship and with Ner and Vrima piloting, they jumped into the future, and specifically to September 2, 1945. They landed outside Washington D.C. in a wooded area, cloaked the ship and stayed inside overnight. The next day turned out to be a bright sunny day. Ner and Vrima got up early and looked around to make sure the ship had landed in a safe area--they were satisfied. Nick and Norina got up with another huge headache. It took a while to adjust to their new timing, but they were happy to have made the jump into the future with no other problems.

They all had breakfast and made plans for the day. It was agreed that Ner would appear in the President's office this morning, and convince President Paterson he needed to see Nick and Norina to talk about the bombs. Vrima would stay to guard the ship. Vrima had supplied Ner with all the necessary information which included the President's schedule. Ner waited a few minutes for the President to settle down and have a few sips of coffee; then he appeared right in front of his desk.

President Paterson reacted just as President Hamilton had, wondering if he were hallucinating. Ner told him not to be afraid, and that there was a good explanation for this apparition. Ner proceeded to explain to the President the

Project Anastrophe

reason he had come, and that he and his friends were here to ask him to cancel the atomic bomb program. All this time President Paterson listened very intently but said nothing, finally he managed to find his voice,

"I don't know how you managed to come in here like that, but you are trespassing and I am going to call the guards to arrest you."

"Mr. President, there is another thing you should know about me and my friends; we come from the future and to be exact, from the Twenty-Fifth Century. It is very important you listen to me before you call anybody."

"That's it, young man, I have had enough of this nonsense; I am calling the guards." President Paterson pushed the button for help and waited. Ner stood there very calmly and with a gentle smile he said,

"Mr. President, no one is going to come in here, I have made sure of that. I am not here to harm you; I just want you to see my friends who want to tell you about the dangerous time our planet is entering and about the atomic weapons you are about to use. As I said, we come from the future and we have seen the destruction these bombs and their byproducts have done to our planet."

"What is your name, young man?"

"My name is Roy Eastman and I am a robot."

"Mr. Eastman, I think this has gone too far, at least state the true purpose of your intrusion here and have done with it. Quit acting foolishly, I am the President of this country, and I am not going to have anymore of your gibberish."

"Mr. President, please allow me to prove to you that I am who I say I am."

Ner first made himself disappear and then quickly appeared again. Then he pulled part of his sleeve up, and showed the President all the electronics crammed into a small area on his forearm. Different colors: red, green, and yellow, traveled up and down in miniscule tubes which crossed each other like freeways. Next he pulled a chair close to the President's desk and said,

"Mr. President, six years ago I had the same conversation with President Hamilton. Back at that time we set a policy as to how to handle these atomic bombs before they were even made. The policy is held as "Top Secret" and you can find it with this number. I should tell you that few people have this privilege and you are one of them."

The number read Y-0-40.

"What's this number?"

"You go down to the vault and ask the guards to show you the Y section and you will find it. Read the first paragraph and you will know what to do after that. I will be waiting for you there."

The President started to believe the intruder, but he wanted to see this policy first so he could be one hundred percent sure. The guards showed the President the Y section and went back to resume guarding the door. Paterson walked in the dimly lit corridor. He had heard of this secret place before, but even as Vice-President he wasn't allowed to come here.

He walked down the corridor and followed it for another fifteen meters until it turned to the right and there Ner was waiting for him. Ner pointed to the number on the safe deposit box. The President entered the number into the combination lock, opened the heavy steel door, pulled out a gray metal box and opened that too; then he pulled out a book. Its title was: PROJECT ANASTROPHE TOP SECRET. He opened it and read the first paragraph just as Ner had asked him to do. After he was done, he put everything back into the heavy locker that closed automatically; turn back to Ner and said,

Project Anastrophe

"Mr. Eastman, I believe you; what do you want me to do?"

"I would like you to set an appointment as soon as possible, with Mr. Robert and Mrs. Loretta Johnson, they will tell you what needs to be done, Mr. President."

"They can have my first appointment at 11:00 a.m.; I will arrange it with my secretary."

"Thank you, Mr. President. They will be here on time."

Ner beamed himself back to the ship; President Paterson walked back to his office with his head bowed, deep in his thoughts.

Ner told Norina and Nick they had an appointment with the President at 11:00 this morning. They wasted no time, and before long they were outside the President's office. His secretary personally ushered them into the office. She went out and closed the door behind her. President Paterson smiled and shook hands with them, then pointed to two chairs close to his desk and said,

"Please sit down---would you like something to drink?"

"No thank you, Mr. President. My name is Robert Johnson and this is my wife Loretta."

"Nice to meet you both, please sit down. I am surprised you didn't appear out of thin air like your friend Mr. Eastman."

"We can do that too, Mr. President, but it is very hard on us; we do it only in emergencies. Our friend, Mr. Eastman, can do it with great ease because he is a robot."

"Yes, yes, he proved that to me--without a doubt he is a robot. So how can I help you?"

"Mr. President, you probably know what the Project Anastrophe plan is by now, and you also know that we have come to visit the White House in the past, and will, in all probability, visit it again in the future. We come only to guide you in times of emergency and this is one of those times. You are about to drop another atomic bomb over Tokyo, and we are here to ask you not to do that; in fact we don't want you to drop the next bomb over Moscow either."

"Mr. Johnson, you came here with a long wish-list. Now according to this so-called "Project Anastrophe" plan, which I haven't yet read in detail, but rest assured, I will. I am supposed to cooperate with you. I have to run a country too; we are at war with Japan and the atomic bombs are the most powerful tools I can use to win this war---and you want me not to use them? As far as I know we don't have another bomb to drop over Moscow."

Now it was Norina's turn; she was polite but firm,

"Mr. President, five hundred years from now in your time, which is now in my time, there are millions of people dying every day and humanity is in the last stages of being obliterated. The planet will be dead for millions of years because of radiation emanating from these atomic bombs and many others to be built in your future.

We are here first to slow the production of these killer bombs and eventually stop them once and for all. Part of the slowing process is stopping these two bombs from being dropped over Japan and Moscow and a third one that will go off here in your city from the Russians."

"Are you telling me the Russians have the bomb and are going to hit us here in Washington D.C.?

"They don't have the bomb yet, but by the time you hit them, they will."

"The Russians are years behind us in missile technology, we have the best air force in the world; they couldn't be ready by next year, could they?"

"They wouldn't have to, Mr. President, both the Unite States and the Soviet Union will hide atomic bombs in each other's capitals; it will be the American bomb that will go

Project Anastrophe

off first in Moscow, and a few minutes later the Russian bomb will go off in Washington D.C. There will be hundreds of thousands of people dead right away and millions of people very sick from radiation poisoning."

"What do you want me to do now?"

"Stop the third bomb destined for Tokyo. You don't need to kill more people needlessly; Japan will surrender. Do not hit Russia with the bomb if you don't want to be hit by them."

"What if they hit us anyway?"

"They will not; we will go and talk to them. They also have to abide by the "Project Anastrophe plan."

"I will call an emergency meeting in the Situation Room and have a talk with the Chief of Staff and his Generals and Admirals; but I need you there because there are a lot of hot heads in that group."

"We will be there, Mr. President, but this has to be kept secret from the people at large."

"People from the future visiting us? I don't think I have to try hard to keep that a secret, I hardly believe it myself, and I am talking to you right now.

It was a pantheon of Generals and Admirals, the main players in the Second World War, all crowded into one place. No one knew why they were there, but they had had to leave their posts quickly to gather in the Situation Room. They were all sitting around the table with their shiny medals of honor except the Secretary of War, the only civilian. There were five top generals, and two admirals. When President Paterson entered the room all the brass stood up and saluted their Commander-in- Chief.

He asked them to sit down and said,

"Well, gentlemen, you must think there is something important to ask you to come here on such short notice---well there is! We are not going to bomb Tokyo with another atomic bomb. I haven't gone out of my mind, there is a very good reason for it, but I am not the best man to talk about it. In a few minutes we are going to have some very important visitors to tell you why I changed mind."

The generals and admirals looked at each other questioningly; even the Secretary of War was caught unprepared. Those few minutes felt like hours to the Brass, some of them looked mechanically at their watches. The President was quite calm looking at his staff, pushing his glasses up on his nose and smiling at them.

If they were looking at the door for the visitors they were in for a big surprise. It was Ner who beamed himself first, then Vrima. Their entrance was spectacular. The Brass saw a cloud of sparkling colors in the shape of a huge top turning at extreme speed; then gradually morphing into a human shape. They were all caught by surprise and had no time to react. Ner and Vrima walked to the President and Ner said,

"Mr. President, this is my wife Mary."

"Nice to meet you, Mary."

Then Ner turned to the generals and admirals and said.

"Gentlemen, my name is Roy Eastman--my wife and I are both robots. We have come here from the Twenty-fifth Century on a mission to save humanity and our planet from complete destruction; my friends who will be arriving in a few minutes will talk about it in detail."

After the first surprise, the generals became more at ease with the robots and were asking the President questions about them. But the President said,

"Gentlemen, now hold your horses, the next visitors will be far more qualified to answer your questions."

There was a knock on the door and the president's secretary came in and asked him if he was ready for the Johnsons.

"Send them in---send them in---we are ready for them."

Project Anastrophe

Nick and Norina stepped in and were surprised to see so many generals and admirals in one room. This time President Paterson introduced the new visitors to his staff.

"Gentlemen, these are the Johnsons. They also come from the future, but they are not robots, they are humans like us. Before I ask them to talk to you, I should tell you that I was just as surprised as you, when Mr. Eastman, the robot, came unannounced into my office. Believe me, it took a lot of persuasion to convince me to accept him for who he said he was, and I am sure after you hear what they have to say, you will too. Now I give you Mr. Johnson."

"Gentlemen, it must be difficult for you to believe what is unfolding in front of your eyes. After all, robots and time-travel come to you in cartoons and Sci Fi books at this time; but to us in the Twenty –Fifth Century robots are indispensable, although time–travel is a new technology for us. Before I go any further I would like to give you the opportunity to ask me any questions you might have." I one of the generals spoke up,

"I do have a question for you. Did we win the war with the Japs--- I mean the Japanese?"

"Japan will surrender after Hiroshima and Nagasaki, that's part of the reason we are here. We want to stop you from dropping the next atomic bomb over Tokyo; there is no reason to kill more people." Another general said,

"I think the robots, if that's what they are, have performed admirably. You say you come from the future and you want us to stop the next bomb that's scheduled to be dropped over Tokyo; we are not ready to accept your explanation, and I am sure that I speak for all of us here. But even if you were from the future, it wouldn't mean much to us here. Japan started the war and we are simply defending ourselves. You say Japan will surrender, I don't know that we are ready to believe you on that. With the third bomb over Tokyo we feel sure we will have the final victory. I don't think it's wise for us to stop now." Next was an admiral,

"I agree with the General, but I would like to hear more of what you have to say before I am ready to express my full opinion on this subject." The rest of the generals and admirals let it be known that they wanted to hear more before they offered their opinions.

Nick continued to tell them how the radiation poisoning would affect future generations because of all the atomic bombs, and even worse, the hydrogen bombs that were going to be built in the future. He told them that in the year 2037 there would be war between the U.S.A. and China; it would be fought with bombs that were a thousand times more powerful than the ones they were using today and millions of people would die. Even though the countries of the world would decide never to use nuclear bombs again, the radiation poisoning would be around for thousands of years.

People would continue to die by the millions and finally, hundreds of years from now, people would resort to living in biospheres. Life would go on like that and eventually they would protect themselves so that only thousands of people would be dying from radiation poisoning. People would live and prosper for another two hundred years, during which technology, culture, and health would reach the highest level in human history. But towards the end of the Twenty-fifth Century people would be hit by radiation poisoning again; this time through small cracks in the ground inside the biospheres.

For decades they would close those cracks as best they could and the people would be cured of radiation poisoning, but then eventually the cracks would get larger and larger requiring more time and resources. People, again,

Project Anastrophe

would be dying by the thousands, and in the Twenty-Fifth Century, by the millions.

"Gentlemen, right now the planet has reached its final stage of destruction and a few weeks from now it will be all over for every living thing and the planet as a whole. Our technology, as great as it sounds, was unable to fix the problem. Before we even reached the state we are in now, we decided we had one last option left to us, and that was to go back to your time and convince you to stop building these bombs.

We are especially anxious to stop the nuclear war that will commence in the year 2037 between the U.S.A. and China. That's why we have introduced a policy called 'Project Anastrophe', meaning 'turning back', to stop radiation poisoning on our planet.

"Now Mary will project in three dimensional pictures the best and worst of our times so you have a clear understanding of the grave danger our planet is going through in the year Twenty-Five Hundred."

Vrima placed the small square unit on the floor, and soon it began to project three dimensional pictures in the center of the room. It started with an overview of the biosphere and at the same time there was a very strange melody emanating from the unit. The biosphere looked like a huge mountain. There were thousands of people dressed in space suits working on it like little ants on a watermelon. Inside, the city looked enormous; it resembled New York City.

There were what appeared to be cars on the roads but most of them were flying very close to the ground. As the camera came closer one could see a vibrant city with thousands of people walking on moving sidewalks, the buildings looked very different, some of them looked like huge octopi one to two hundred floors high, others were in the shape of onions, countless stories high, made mostly of glass. There were many other buildings of all shapes spreading horizontally and vertically, but few square buildings.

The city looked orderly and clean, there were many small sized trees mingled with the buildings, and a lot of green grass and different colored flowers. In short the city looked very advanced in technology, landscaping, and culture. And then the scenery changed abruptly. One could see people dressed in protective gear working in groups on large cracks in the ground; ambulance-like vehicles went in all directions, the surrounding buildings looked abandoned, the trees, grass, flowers and other vegetation were brown, dry, and dead.

There was a gray cloud-like fog hanging a few feet above the ground, the city looked dead.

Now Norina started talking to the generals, "Gentlemen, I hope after what you have heard and seen, you don't have anymore doubts as to our authenticity.

We will let you have your say in a minute, but let me repeat, we are who we say we are, we are here from the future to save our planet from complete annihilation and as you see, we are running out of time. We desperately need your help now within the day, not tomorrow, not next week not next month. Let me clarify something important to you; every hour that passes here, is years that already have passed in the future, therefore anything we do today, is already done in the future, so if we stop the bomb from going off over Tokyo today it has already happened in the future and millions of people will not have died needlessly. Now we will be happy to answer any questions you may have."

President Paterson was the next to speak, he said,

"Gentlemen, I don't know about you, but I tend to believe these people here. Now let me tell you another thing,

Project Anastrophe

they have told me that only a few months from now, we are going to explode an atomic bomb in the heart of Moscow and blow most of the city to smithereens; here is the other side of it, they in turn, are going to hit us here in Washington D.C. with an atomic bomb of equal destructive power. Gentlemen, these people come from the future and have seen it all; if we are to believe them we have to act quickly or we risk having our own Armageddon right here in our city. As they say,

"The buck stops here with me; but Gentlemen, I could use your honest opinion at this important time." The Secretary of War spoke directly to the President and said,

"Mr. President, it shouldn't be difficult for us to decide if we should bomb Tokyo. It comes down to believing these people or not; if we believe them, then we do as they say, if not, we do what we think is right, there is no half pregnant here." President Paterson asked Norina,

"Let me ask you, Mrs. Johnson, if we do not follow your advice and explode the bomb or bombs what would you do?"

"We have to follow the "Prime Directive" as much as possible, and that is to have you make the changes by your own will. If the alternative is the continuation of using these bombs which will result in destroying the planet, and all its living things, then the "Prime Directive" is irrelevant---we will stop the bombs."

"Can you do that?"

"Yes, Mr. President, if we have to, we will do it."

"Gentlemen, here is your answer." A general stood up, pointed his finger at Norina and said,

"We will fight you with all we have!"

President Paterson responded in a fatherly manner,

"Sit down, General, you don't know what you are up against."

"Mr. Johnson, did you say that this Project Anastrophe will be enforced by all countries participating in this war?"

"Yes, Mr. President, we will see to it that they abide by all the requirements of Project Anastrophe."

"I assume you will do the same thing with us."

"Yes, Mr. President."

"I would like very much to give you an answer right now, but we are a democratic country and I must consult with several important members of both parties before I respond to you; how can I get in touch with you?"

"You won't have to, Mr. President; we will be available to you at all times. All you have to do is ask for us, and one or all of us will be here."

"I see. Then on behalf of my generals and admirals I want to thank you for your heroic efforts and I promise that I will ask for you as soon as I have something to share with you."

"Thank you, Mr. President, and all of you gentlemen who made the effort to come to this important meeting."

Ner and Vrima left the same way they came in; Nick and Norina went out through the door. There was a quiet moment and all eyes fell on the President, then one of the Admirals said,

"Mr. President, it looks as if they have all the cards and there is very little we can do at this point."

"It looks like that, Admiral, but I for one, don't see them as enemies, I believe they are telling us the truth. Now Gentlemen, I know you are anxious to go back to your posts, after all, we are still fighting a war, but I need you for the next meeting scheduled for 4:00 p.m. After that you can leave. Now I would like you to go have lunch and we will meet again in the war room. I don't need to tell you how important it is to keep this a secret. No one must know about this, especially the press."

Project Anastrophe

They all had lunch at the White House as special guests, but after lunch some of them went out and of course the Press was waiting for them. They knew all the Brass were here for something big and they wanted to know about it. One of the reporters asked a general if any more atomic bombs were going to fall on Japan. The general answered for most of the Brass when he said.

"Gentlemen, we are at war and it wouldn't be wise for me to give you that kind of information, but there is one thing I can tell you, and that is; we are winning the war."

Ner and Vrima went into the spaceship and put themselves in charge mode right away; their batteries were dangerously low. Nick and Norina went to a nice restaurant to recharge; they noticed many senators and congressmen were there too.

Norina looked tired and she sounded impatient.

"What's the matter, Norina?"

"I am afraid we are not moving fast enough to stop the suffering and dying back home, Nick."

"What if they decide to postpone voting for another day to stop the next bomb from falling over Tokyo?"

"Then we'll have to tell them to decide tomorrow or we will do it for them."

"I hope it doesn't come to that, I don't want to put pressure on them."

Norina felt much better after talking to Nick and having something to eat. They walked for a while looking at the various shops. It was a cool day and it helped clear their minds for the next meeting. They knew that sooner or later the President would call upon them to impress people coming to that meeting.

They arrived in the war room ahead of time; only Ner was there with them. Vrima stayed to guard the ship, but was prepared to beam herself to the war room if she was needed. The three of them were cloaked and out of the way in the farthest corner of the room, waiting for the meeting to start. They could see and hear everything, but could not be seen or heard by others.

The meeting started in earnest; all the generals and admirals were there plus eight more senators from both parties. Also present were General Sheldon and nuclear physicist, Peter Thomas.

"Gentlemen, welcome to this important meeting. Before I go any further I would like to welcome the Senators and also General Sheldon and Dr. Thomas, who happened to be in town. I don't need to tell you who they are, you all know them very well. The generals and the admirals were fortunate to have been here in the morning and to have seen our visitors in person. As for the rest of you who were not here, I am told that my staff has brought you up to date with what transpired this morning. As you know, they want us to stop exploding atomic bombs starting with the one we are about to explode over Tokyo.

Now I am fixing to go along with their request for obvious reasons, but I would like to give you a chance to express your opinions on the subject." A senator stood up and said,

"Mr. President, I know you pretty much have made up your mind to stop the atomic bomb program, but wouldn't it be wise, on our part, to check those other countries that are building these very same bombs and see that they conform to this so- called Project Anastrophe?"

"In the first place, they don't stop us from building those bombs; it has something to do with the "Prime Directive." I guess they just don't want us to explode them. Now about checking those other countries, I am sure these people are far better qualified than we are, to do just that."

Most of the senators from both parties were against

stopping the bomb destined to go off over Tokyo. They said,

"We have spent lots of money and effort to build these bombs and now that they are ready they want us to stop using them? We feel we should use them not only in Japan, but also in Russia; by doing so we will stop them from building their own bombs. If we only have the bombs, there will be no reason for us to use them. That would stop the so - called radiation poisoning and win the war at the same time."

It was a strong argument and the President had a hard time convincing them otherwise, but he tried,

"Senators, I am afraid my staff didn't do a good job of convincing you to stop thinking that way; didn't you see the pictures, didn't you hear what these people told us, didn't you hear that our planet, with all its living things, is heading towards annihilation? These people come from the future and have seen it all---your policy didn't work." Another senator spoke for the Republicans,

"Mr. President, with all due respect, sir, we disagree with you. We feel our idea makes a lot of sense, you see, we don't even believe these people are telling us the truth when they say they travel in time."

"I wish they were here. No doubt they would do a better job convincing you, Gentlemen."

Seconds after the President uttered those words, a melodic chime was heard in the room and everybody's attention turned towards the corner from which the chime was emanating. There were rainbow colors positioned vertically, and right behind them, a light blue cloud-like blanket covered the corner. It opened like a theater curtain and out stepped Norina, Nick, and Ner. It looked as if they had come out of thin air. Everyone looked at them in awe and trepidation; then the three of them walked closer to the President and Norina said,

George Karnikis

"Gentlemen, it looks as if we haven't convinced you yet. I dread what I have to show you next, I was hoping I wouldn't have to do that, but I see it is necessary, so there won't be any doubt whatsoever.

When you drop an atomic bomb on a populated city there are consequences beyond the afflicted people of this time; the results of these explosions are cumulative in radiation for the people living in the future. What you are about to see is a very small example of what is happening now in our time and place."

Ner walked to the center of the room and again placed the little square unit on the floor. Then just as before, it started to project a large city, only this time it looked familiar to everybody in the room. They saw onion domes, Red Square and the Kremlin wall with its towers. The weather was clear and people were going about their business. Mothers were pushing baby buggies in the park and women were sweeping the streets; the city was vibrant and busy, everything was projected three dimensionally and looked so real one felt as if he could walk into the city.

Then everything changed dramatically. There was a huge crater right in the middle of the square, and all around the crater and for kilometers beyond, the terrain was flattened and incinerated. Flames and smoke rose as if a stream of lava had flooded the whole area. Farther away thousands of buildings were half standing up, others were intact, but doors and windows had been blown away and people of every age lay scattered on the ground. Some were burned beyond recognition, and others were decapitated or dismembered. The pictures were unfolding in front of their eyes. They saw more people out in the country vomiting, looking dazed and confused while, those who could walk, were walking as if they were zombies.

The projection continued but this time, in addition to a

Project Anastrophe

huge crater and the devastated area close to it, there were buildings recognizable by everybody in the room. This time the dismembered bodies littering the streets were Americans and the tragedy unfolding in front of them was their own country---then the projection stopped. For a few seconds there was dead silence in the room; then the President said,

"I don't know about you, gentlemen, but I feel sick to my stomach and I am not going to allow this carnage to take place." Norina said,

"Gentlemen, may I remind you that what you have seen today is but a small sample of what will be later in the year 2037 when you will be engaged in a nuclear war with China. That war will send humankind hundreds of years back; with only a small number of people surviving. Some will live in biospheres for hundreds of years, only to be destroyed again, and this time for good.

Stopping these bombs is only the beginning. We will show you how to save our planet before we lose it, but you have to follow Project Anastrophe to the letter. Eventually we will introduce you to new kinds of energies to replace the destructive fuels you are using now, including nuclear plants for electricity. Those future energies will be much safer and eventually our planet will have a clean and safe environment where we can all live a prosperous and healthy life in our different times.

It was agreed by all that no other atomic bombs would be exploded over Tokyo or any other country by this government. The only reason they would continue to build more bombs would be for defense.

They all left except General Sheldon and Peter Thomas as well as Nick, Norina and Ner, whom the President had asked to stay behind. He first spoke to Dr. Thomas,

"Peter, I know you are not the FBI's best friend and I

know there are many others who would like you to just go away. Now there have been times I had doubts about you too. You see, Peter, this country is scared to death of the Soviet Union and Communism; you know that, and being a communist sympathizer doesn't help your case either. But let me make something perfectly clear--- I, unlike the others, never doubted your patriotism and I appreciate your ingenuity and the service you have given.

I know now, that our visitors have visited you in the past and have greatly influenced you against building and using nuclear bombs after the first two you helped to build. But we only recently found that out from our visitors. I will rectify that by reappointing you the director of the Nuclear Program which will give you direct access to all future projects." But Norina disagreed and said,

"Mr. President, we have already changed the "Prime Directive" a lot and changing it any more would not be a good idea. Dr. Thomas must fulfill his destiny and stay where he is now; things will change for the best, despite all the obstacles he will face in the future."

Dr. Thomas responded to the President by saying,

"Thank you, Mr. President. The fact that you believe in me means a lot to me. There will be no more bombs exploded in the immediate future. If the Project Anastrophe plan works as intended there will be no future wars with these terrible weapons of mass destruction."

With their latest task successfully accomplished, they traveled back in time once more. They had to do more in the year 1939 to effectively put Project Anastrophe on track. They landed at the Yellow Island base. Dyphus was there to help them park the space ship and unload. It would take a few days for Nick and Norina to bounce back and be themselves again.

Project Anastrophe

Back to the Future

The first drone was calibrated to get outside Zita Biosphere one week after they had left. It made a few reconnaissance flights, checked for further deterioration of the landscape, and found more craters and higher amounts of radiation poisoning. Then it entered the biosphere itself and what it found was difficult to observe. The 3-D pictures were coming steadily into Dr. Dylos' office.

Dr. Thamion and the rest of the crew were watching intently. The incoming pictures were horrendous; but most of the infrastructure held together and the emergency evacuation procedures were followed to the letter. Hospitals and other emergency centers appeared to be filled to capacity, and only ambulances and medical personnel could be seen on the streets. But no matter how heroically people were trying to keep things in order, one could see the end wasn't too far away.

They sent more drones to other biospheres with the same results; people were suffering all over the world, and it appeared that they were doomed to perish. It was a sobering experience to see humanity dying in such a short time. Darna and Nephus were looking at the incoming 3-D pictures and Darna was sick to her stomach. Finally after the transmission stopped, she was the first one to talk.

"Isn't there something we can do, Dr. Dylos?"

"I am afraid not, Darna, there is very little we can do on this side. The only people who can save our planet now are Nick, Norina, and the robots back in time."

"Well if they wait any longer, there may not be anything living left to save; couldn't we send a message and ask them to hurry up?"

"We are preparing to do just that at the appointed time which will be three hours from now."

George Karnikis

Back to the Past

After a few days of rest, both Nick and Norina felt regenerated and ready for their next project. Ner and Vrima also made the necessary repairs on themselves and were fully charged.

Ner requested a meeting with Norina, Nick, Vrima and Dyphus as soon as possible. In a short time they were all gathered in the spaceship's meeting room.

"Friends, I just received an urgent message from Dr. Dylos." He then projected Dr. Dylos' image in the middle of the room.

"My dear friends, I hope you are all well and have received this message. What you are about to see will make you understand its urgency."

The 3-D pictures unfolded in slow sequences. Norina wept seeing the losing, but heroic effort of her people back home in Z-Biosphere.

The robots, lacking human emotions for the most part, were registering data in their cybernetic files. Vrima looked at Norina and wished she could cry but managed to sniffle a little bit. Before the message finished, Dr. Dylos reappeared and pleaded with them to hurry and do something before everything perished. After the message was over, everybody was sober. Ner said,

"We all know, that as bad as it looks now, none of it will happen if we accomplish our mission." Norina reacted harshly.

"Yes, we all know that Ner, but people are suffering and dying right now and it's tearing me apart."

"I am sorry, Miss Norina."

Norina asked Vrima to read their schedule starting from today.

"Today or tomorrow we are supposed to visit Chairman

Project Anastrophe

Stanoff in Moscow, and then England, France, India, China, North Korea, Iran, Syria and Israel. Other countries are of minimal importance at this time."

"Then we will start with Russia first; we will leave today." Nick asked Ner a question,

"From what I see from the message we got, they only have hours before they are completely destroyed. We need at least weeks or months before we accomplish our goal--or am I wrong?"

"It may take even more time than that, Nick, but remember our present time compresses to seconds and minutes in their time, so even if we are delayed here a bit, it will not change their situation that much."

Ner sent a message to Dr. Dylos telling him that his message had been received and that they should see changes for the better in a few minutes. Ner also asked for the latest time-travel converter to be sent as soon as possible. They decided to wait for it before they left. Nick and Norina went by boat to Friday Harbor and from there they caught a plane to Seattle. Ner and Vrima would come home to the farm next day with the new spaceship, Anastrophe Two.

It was early afternoon when they arrived; everything looked fine in the house, no one had disturbed it. They went to town and had lunch and on the way back they visited Nick's grandparents and parents.

Again Nick felt the impulse to say who he really was, but he realized that would have been too much for them to understand. They were very hospitable people but that wasn't a surprise to Nick; he knew his family very well. His grandfather asked him where they had been all this time, and Nick said they were in Europe for business. The grandfather wanted to know how the war was shaping up in Europe and Nick told him the Germans had the upper hand for the time being, but England, France and Russia were building up their defenses as fast as they could. The grandfather said,

"Greece can fight the Italians and win, but they will lose to the Germans; they just don't have the army or enough weapons to fight them, you know?"

"Greece will not be left alone. Sooner or later the allies will help her."

"I sure hope so, Mr. Johnson."

They were invited to dinner, but Nick and Norina gently declined. They said,

"We have to go home and prepare for another trip to Asia this time, thank you but we will accept a 'rain check' for another time." Both grandfather and grandmother were confused with the 'rain check' phrase. Nick explained to them that it was an American expression, meaning they accept their invitation for another time. They were happy to hear that and wished them a safe trip to Asia.

They said their goodbyes and were walking towards the gate when they saw the two children playing. Again Nick felt sentimental seeing his father as a little boy and his aunt as a little girl. The boy was holding a paper plane above his head; running with it, imitating the roar of the engine with his voice going up and down, 'Brrrr.' Norina talked to the little girl and said,

"Hi Demitra, I like your doll; does she have a name?"

"Yes, her name is Elleny, and I like her too."

They drove home and after dinner they went to bed early; tomorrow promised to be a busy day.

The Time-Travel Converter arrived next day and Ner couldn't have been happier. It was an amazing piece of technology. Ner said to Vrima,

"Now we can calibrate our own time-travel independently from home base and go anywhere at will."

"That will save us a lot of time, won't it Ner?"

Project Anastrophe

"Yes of course, Vrima, we are now quite independent from Anastrophe One." Ner and Vrima put all the necessary provisions, parts, and weapons into the ship. They gave orders to Dyphus and they were off.

They landed outside Nick's and Norina's farmhouse early in the morning in cloaked mode. Nick and Norina were having breakfast when Ner and Vrima came in. Ner told them of the changes they had made on their ship and that they were now independent from Anastrophe One. They had also installed new technology. Humans could now beam themselves away without ill effects, just like the robots did. Norina was very excited and said,

"Well this is the best news I've heard in a long time." Nick was happy too, because that meant no more headaches and going through days of recovering from each beamed trip.

They decided to leave for England right way and landed in the country in cloaked mode; then beamed themselves into a train station. From there they took a taxi and told the driver to go to the Parliament. Both Nick and Norina felt well and just as Ner had said, beaming themselves here hadn't affected them at all. They all went to a restaurant and had some lunch, Ner and Vrima just had tea for obvious reasons. Now they had to decide how to approach the Prime Minister and deliver the Anastrophe plan to him. They decided to go about it the same way as before. Ner and Vrima would beam themselves into the Prime Minister's office and wait in cloaked mode; Nick and Norina would visit with him the usual way. But how could one visit with him especially in time of war? That's where Vrima came in. Her idea was for Nick and Norina to go in with a "top secret" letter written by President Hamilton himself. She would write the letter and it would look as though he had written it.

George Karnikis

Nick went to one of the phone booths, and used the special number that went directly to the President. He was in bed at the time, but Nick told him who he was and what he had done in order to meet with Prime Minister Derecton. Once the President realized he was speaking to Robert Johnson, he gave his consent without any hesitation. Vrima wrote the note that said,

"Charles, you need to listen to Robert and Loretta Johnson, they have a very important message for you and for your country," she signed it as "Ed."

Nick and Norina went straight to the receptionist, said who they were, and asked to see the Prime Minister. They said they had a letter from President Hamilton and it had to be delivered personally. The receptionist, an austere young woman, said,

"Please wait here." She went away for a few minutes; then came back with two officers who escorted them to the Prime Minister's office. All four of them went in and the officers stayed, keeping a close eye on them.

Nick and Norina introduced themselves as Robert and Loretta Johnson and handed the Prime Minister the letter. He said,

"Please be seated." He left and went to the next room, after a few minutes he came back with the letter opened. He asked the two officers to leave and said,

"I just had a chat with the President. What's so important that you had to come all the way here to see me?" This time Norina said,

"Mr. Prime Minister, we know you are a busy man and we won't take too much of your time." Then she told him who they really were and that they came here to save the planet from future catastrophe. As was expected, he was taken by surprise and said,

"Do you expect me to believe all this gibberish? I am

Project Anastrophe

fighting a war here and have no time for this nonsense, now leave me alone!"

Then the usual chime sounded, and Ner and Vrima appeared from behind the multicolored electronic curtain. They introduced themselves as Roy and Mary Eastman. Ner said to Charles Derecton,

"Mr. Prime Minister, I hope we didn't scare you, but we do come from the future; we are from a society that's more technologically advanced than yours. We are not humans; we are robots. He opened his chest and showed him all his electronic apparatus.

If you wish, you can ask me or my wife any questions, but Mr. and Mrs. Johnson are real humans and it would be wiser to talk with them."

"Now I see why Edward sent you here. I shouldn't doubt him, he is an honest man. But I still have a hard time believing you come from the future; my fear is that you could be German spies." Then Nick said,

"Mr. Prime Minister, if you give us a few minutes we can tell you why we are here and I promise that you won't have any doubts about our authenticity at all."

"Well, go on then, I am a busy man you know."

Nick went on telling the Prime Minister all he had said to other heads of state and then he spoke about the Project Anastrophe plan. The Prime Minister said,

"Where is this Project Anastrophe you are talking about?"

"You already have it, sir, and your next meeting has a lot to do with this plan."

"I have it? Well where is it?"

Nick gave him a certain number and letters, a code only he and a few others in his government knew. Mr. Derecton wasn't surprised any more. He told them to wait a few minutes and when he came back he said,

"I believe you, but I have two questions for you. Is Germany obligated by the same rules---and which country won the war?"

"I can answer the first question. Yes, Germany obeys the same rules, but the 'Prime Directive' does not allow us to answer the second question."

"That's too bad, because that would help us a lot, but I understand."

They left the same way they had arrived and beamed themselves back to the ship. The next day Vrima told Norina that it was imperative to visit China before any other country; it would take much more time to find Wu Ming.

"We must talk to him before he becomes Chairman Wu, and we need to find him on The Long March."

"Then let's do it and get it over with."

"It's not that easy. I can't calibrate the exact time of Wu's whereabouts in The Long March in the time converter. The best and fastest way to do it is to visit a friend of one of Wu's associates, Anna Smith. We can find her best friend who is in the state of America, in California. Her name is Aino Taylor and she lived in a town called Ojai from 1938 to 1997."

Since Ner didn't have to be too accurate, anywhere between the forties and fifties would be all right. If Ner could get a letter from Mrs. Taylor sent to her from her friend Anna Smith, who was a reporter in China at the time, then he could calibrate the time converter to within months of Wu's whereabouts.

They arrived in Ojai in the year 1941. That was close enough for Norina; they landed out in the country away from people in cloaked mode. As it turned out, Aino Taylor's house was in Meiner's Oaks, a small community within walking distance. Outside the house was a little girl around 5 or 6 years old playing near a playhouse. Norina approached the girl and said,

"Hi, what's your name?"

"My name is Ingrid Taylor."

"We are looking for Aino Taylor; do you know if she is here?"

"This is my play house and I have all my dolls in it; do you want to see them?"

"I would like to see your dolls later. Is Mrs. Taylor your mother?"

"Yes."

"Is she in the house?"

"Yes."

Norina knocked at the door, a gray-haired woman opened it.

"I am Loretta Johnson and this is my husband Robert, are you Aino Taylor?"

"No, I am Elviira Haanpaa and I am her mother, come in, I'll get her for you."

They didn't have to wait long, a beautiful young woman in her late twenties with light blonde hair and light blue eyes, appeared in the hallway.

"Are you Aino Taylor?"

"Yes I am, can I help you?" Nick said.

"We are reporters for the New York Daily, and if you don't mind we would like to ask you a few questions about a reporter and friend of ours, Anna Smith. We have not heard of her whereabouts for sometime now. The last time we heard from her she was in Shanghai, China. She had talked to us in the past about you and we know you are good friends."

"Well come in, come in, and sit down. Would you like a cup of tea?"

"That would be nice, thank you."

"So what would you like to know?"

"Anything you can tell us would be helpful towards finding her, Mrs. Taylor."

"I don't think that I have the liberty to tell much about her. If you are friends and coworkers as you say you are, then you probably know as much or more than I." Then Norina said,

"Mrs. Taylor, if you could tell us where she was the last time she communicated with you, that would suffice. Did you get a letter from her recently?"

"Yes I did, about two weeks ago, but I don't think it is right to give it to you or to anybody."

"Mrs. Taylor, all we need is the day it was postmarked and the place it was sent from, that's all we need to know."

"I suppose I could give you that much information, if that would help you find her."

"It would help us a lot, Mrs. Taylor."

On their way out, they saw a young man talking to little Ingrid. He looked surprised to see them coming out of the house; he appeared to be in his late twenties, with dark brown hair and brown eyes, the little girl was pulling him from his trousers saying,

"Daddy, Daddy, come and see my dolls." Nick introduced himself,

"We just had a nice visit with Aino Taylor and Elviira Haanpaa, you must be the father of little Ingrid."

"Yes, my name is John Taylor."

"We promised Ingrid we would see her dolls too, may we?"

"Yes, of course, she will be thrilled; she likes to show her dolls to anybody who comes by."

They all looked at Ingrid's dolls and she proceeded to name each, one by one. Norina commented to Mr. Taylor how sweet and smart his little Ingrid was.

They said their goodbyes and they were off. With Mrs.

Project Anastrophe

Smith's last date and place, Ner could now calibrate their arrival close to where they needed to land, and before long they were on their way. They landed in Anhui, China in the year 1941. Nick and Norina were dressed as Europeans of those years. They tried to make contact with Anna Smith. Ner stayed in the ship but Vrima went with them and did all the interpreting. Vrima picked up one of the local newspapers and they went to the address where it had been printed; there they found an old man working on an old printing press.

Vrima spoke to him in perfect Chinese and he was surprised that a foreigner could speak his language so fluently. She asked him if he knew where they could find Anna Smith and he directed her to the army headquarters. They hired two rickshaws and were taken to a run-down hotel. When Vrima asked for Anna Smith, the hotel man asked them to sit down on an old couch and disappeared. He came back with her ten minutes later.

She was surprised to see three foreigners in such a small, out-of-the-way place. Norina, Nick, and Vrima introduced themselves and said they were here to meet Wu Ming, and would she help them find him? She told them Wu was a very busy man and he wasn't here anyway. She suggested the only man who was in a position to help them was a man named Pang Du, who was a leader of the Red Army, and a good friend of hers.

She asked them why they wanted to see him, and Nick told her they had a proposition for him involving money for the cause. Anna's hair was cut short; she was dressed in an army uniform and looked stern. She chose her words carefully,

"If you want to help the cause, as you said, with money, I am sure Pang Du will arrange for you to meet Wu. Do you have a place to stay for tonight?"

Norina said they didn't.

"Well in that case you can stay here and have dinner with us; Commander Pang will be here too."

The five of them had dinner in the hotel's dining room. The main course consisted of dog served with fresh vegetables, salad and rice wine followed by dessert. Commander Pang raised his glass and said, "To victory."

All four of them raised their glasses. Then he said, "This is a young dog butchered this morning and prepared by the best cook in town."

Anna looked at them for their reaction. Vrima communicated subliminally with Norina and Nick and told them to say they liked it and that it tasted good. Then Commander Pang asked Nick,

"Why do you want to see Commander Wu?"

"We want to discuss with him the possibility of giving him money to purchase rifles."

"Why do you want to do that?"

"Because we believe in your cause and would like to help you."

"Well, anyone who wants to help us in any way is our friend. I will arrange for you to see Commander Wu Ming; but he is in another town and you will have to travel a few hours by truck. Mrs. Smith will travel with you."

They stayed late into the night discussing the war and how Communism would save the world from the capitalists and imperialism. Next day, early in the morning, all four of them got into an open truck driven by a soldier. Anna kept to herself, looking at the country as they drove by. Norina tried to engage her in conversation but she said few words. Then Norina told her that they had met Aino Taylor and her family in Ojai. The mention of Aino Taylor's name got Anna's attention right away. Norina continued talking about the Taylors and what nice people they were.

Project Anastrophe

"How did you get to know the Taylors?"

"We had to find you to get us to Wu Ming and we knew Aino was a good friend of yours. She only gave us the place and date of your last letter. We told her we were reporters like you and wanted to find you."

"Are you reporters or spies?"

"We are neither but we are friends and want to help the Chinese cause and the whole world."

"How are you going to help the whole world by giving Commander Wu money for rifles?"

"That is a matter we would like discuss with him."

"So you have another reason for wanting to see Commander Wu?"

"Yes we do."

"May I ask what it is?"

"We can't say much at this time, but you will find out soon."

"The fact that you are giving money to buy rifles will be important to him. But helping the whole world would be irrelevant to Commander Wu right now."

They arrived at Anching late in the night and were taken to a private residence. Even in the dark they could see it was a well-kept house, large enough for all four of them to stay overnight. Nick and Norina were given their own private room, and so was Vrima. Anna told them a soldier would knock at their door at 8:00 a.m. for breakfast.

The soldier driver took Anna somewhere into town. In their room Nick and Norina found food on a large tray. There was fruit, cheese, bread, and two bowls of cold vegetable soup. They ate and soon after that went to bed. Vrima didn't touch any of the food but went into charging mode right a way.

Next morning, just as Anna had said, there was a knock on their door but that wasn't necessary, they were both up and ready; so was Vrima. They were driven a few miles out into the country in another open truck. Anna wasn't with them, but they found her waiting for them in an army barrack. She walked with them a few meters to a well-guarded house and took them directly to Commander Wu's office. When she knocked at the door a soldier opened it from inside.

She spoke a few Chinese words and then she turned and talked to Nick and Norina.

She said,

"Commander Wu will talk to you through an interpreter, and she pointed to a young soldier who smiled at them and said,

"Welcome."

Vrima responded by speaking in perfect Chinese and said, "That will not be necessary; I can do all the interpreting. However we need Anna Smith to stay here."

Both Wu, Anna, and the Chinese soldier interpreter were surprised by Vrima's fluent Chinese. Commander Wu asked Vrima,

"Where did you learn to speak Chinese so well?"

"It's a long story, Commander Wu. I will be happy to tell you after Robert Johnson speaks to you."

Commander Wu pointed at Nick and said,

"Go ahead, speak."

"Commander Wu, my name is Robert Johnson and this is my wife Loretta. We came here for two reasons; one is to give you money which will help to liberate your country from tyranny, and the other is to save our planet from complete destruction."

Vrima interpreted what Nick said and Wu responded by saying,

"I will be glad to have your money, but how can I help to save the planet when I can't even help my own country right now?"

Project Anastrophe

Vrima quickly interpreted again, this time in English to Nick and Norina.

"Commander Wu, what we are about to tell you right now, is of great importance and it needs to be kept secret. You must have only people you can trust to hold a secret."

Wu gestured to his interpreter to come closer and talked to him in a low tone. The interpreter left the room quickly and within a few minutes two older men appeared and sat next to Wu; the two guards kept their position in the room with their eyes fixed on the foreigners at all times. Then Wu gestured to Nick and said,

"Now you can speak."

"Commander Wu Ming, what I am about to tell you will be difficult for you to believe; but I can assure you that by the time I am through, you won't have any doubt whatsoever. Please let me finish before asking any questions." Wu Nodded to Nick and said,

"Talk."

"The three of us have come from the future, and to be exact, from the year 2500 A.D. My wife and I are humans but our interpreter is a robot, that's the reason she speaks Chinese so well; she speaks other languages fluently too. We are here on a mission to save our planet from complete catastrophe. Your country and America will be the biggest participants in our earth's destruction. First we must prove our authenticity to you. We promised to give you money and we will give you 200,000 English pounds and $400,000 in American currency.

Now I am going to call one of our robots to bring the money to you."

They were all riveted by what he was saying, and as Nick had told them in the beginning, they had a hard time believing him.

Ner was listening from kilometers away in the spaceship and when he heard his cue word, he sprang into action. He beamed himself, with the money, which was in a black handbag, into the center of the room. They were all in awe. The two guards pointed their rifles at Ner as he was materializing, but Wu gestured to them to put their guns down which they did.

Ner smiled at Wu and said in Chinese, "Commander Wu Ming, my name is Roy Eastman. I am a robot just like my partner, the interpreter. I brought the money we promised you." Wu asked one of the two old men to get the bag; he did so and then proceeded to open it, took out some of the money, and showed it to Wu who asked him to take all the money from the bag and put it on the table. Then he asked the old man to bring him one bundle of each currency and he examined it closely for authenticity. After he was satisfied, he gave it back and asked him to put the money back into the bag. Then he said to Nick,

"I don't know who or what you are, but I thank you for the money, it will go a long way towards helping us with our struggle. But I still have a difficult time believing what I see in front of my eyes. If you are who you say you are, you are so powerful--- how can we help you?"

"Commander Wu, I see that I haven't convinced you yet, therefore I am going to take you on a trip to the future. Prepare yourself for what you are going to see. It will be good but also very sad." Ner placed the little unit on the center of the floor and from it emerged bright colors---then China appeared in all its glory. It was a changed China to Wu and his contemporaries in the room. Cities, buildings, and people---indeed the whole country looked different. Ner zeroed in on the city of Beijing. Everything appeared three dimensional, and it was a splendid city of mythical proportions, very different from how it was in 1941. There were many high-rise buildings, new parks, different cars

Project Anastrophe

speeding on long freeways, and glass elevators. Trains traveled above the ground with unimaginable speed and well-dressed people dined in restaurants. They looked healthy and happy.

China was a very prosperous and powerful country indeed. Nick asked Ner to stop the projection for a few minutes and said to Wu, "Commander Wu, what you see now is China on July 30th, 2037. Now you are going to see what happened to China on that day----as well as to America and the rest of the world."

Then Nick asked Ner to start again. The projector showed first a park with young children playing near a zoo and parents nearby talking while keeping a watchful eye on the children. Then something hit the park with tremendous force. What followed after that was horrible. The park, with everything in it, was instantaneously incinerated and what was left there were remains of burnt buildings. A once vibrant city had become a necropolis.

Far away from the bombed cities, properties and people survived, only to be affected by radiation poisoning. They would finally die a slow and painful death. Now Ner switched to California in America, to what used to be San Francisco and Los Angeles, and farther north to Oregon and Washington states. Almost every large city of every state including New York had been destroyed the same way. A chain reaction started in every country that had nuclear bombs-- destroying them.

Ner was telling Wu that the planet Earth would be destroyed to the extent that most countries would have to start all over again. After hundreds of years, those who survived would live in biospheres and would be safe for a long time. They would never use nuclear bombs or energy again. Their civilization and technology would become better than that which was destroyed hundreds of years earlier. Eventually radiation poisoning would start to come out of the ground within the biospheres, and it would take buildings and people into huge "sink holes." Then radiation poisoning would seep through the ground and slowly, but surely, kill them by the thousands, and then by the millions. Ner was speaking in perfect Chinese, then he stopped the projector and Nick spoke to Commander Wu and said,

"Commander Wu, this is the reason we are here today, to save our planet from this madness."

"What do you want us to do, Mr. Johnson?"

"All you have to do is follow directions. Everything has been done for you; we have a plan called Project Anastrophe and it has been given to every nation that will have these nuclear weapons in the future and that includes your country."

"Where is this Project Anastrophe plan that you are talking about?"

"We have gone into the future and have deposited the plan in a secret place to be found by the appropriate government. If they follow the directions we have given them, the nuclear exchange will never happen and our planet will be saved. The reason we came to see you is because you will be the first Chairman of China and you must have part of that plan with you now, so that every Chairman in the future will follow it to the letter."

Then Nick gave part of the plan to the future Chairman Wu Ming. He opened it and looked inside, it was written in Chinese and it started from today's date. Then Wu asked Nick if he could tell him more about the future, when he would be Chairman of China. Nick said,

"I am sorry Commander Wu, but I can't interfere with the "Prime Directive" which dictates that we should not tell people anymore than we have to about the future."

Project Anastrophe

They said their good byes, but before they left, Norina told Anna,

"I can tell you this, Anna, you will be regarded as a hero by the Chinese people and you will be buried among the heroes of this country." This time the four of them beamed themselves to their ship, leaving the people in the room in awe.

In the next few days they visited all the countries on the list; some of them were not nations yet, but they talked to the future leaders of those countries-to-be. When they finally turned back to the base, Nick and Norina were very tired; even Ner and Vrima had to regenerate. Ner sent a message to headquarters right away saying, that the mission had been accomplished, and they were ready for new orders.

Chapter 13

Back to the Future

They were all waiting anxiously for Ner's message; it arrived a few minutes later. Darna was holding her cup of coffee while Ner's face morphed slowly at the center of the table. He uttered the words, "Mission accomplished," in his usual man-robotic way.

There was a moment's silence and then everybody cheered. Dr. Dylos was overcome by emotion. He had to clear his throat a few times but finally got the courage to talk.

"Ladies and Gentlemen, we did it--I can't find words to thank you and especially Norina, Nick, Ner and Vrima who

Project Anastrophe

did a superb job under the most difficult circumstances. We have saved our planet.

Now we have to find out what kind of civilization we have down there, but whatever we find, there should not be radiation poisoning anymore.

A few minutes later they sent another probe and waited anxiously for its report. This time the probe was cloaked and in a few seconds there was a view they had anticipated but had never seen before. There were no biospheres anywhere to be seen. There were trees and other plants just as they had them in the biospheres, but now they were out in the open and there were many different animals that had been thought to be extinct. Dr. Dylos said,

"This is all we can do with the probe; we need to go down in person to find out how much of a change we have created. But one thing is for sure, we have saved our planet.

The meeting was over for now; they were to meet again tomorrow to discuss their next move, they all left happy but apprehensive. Darna saw her mother on her way to the cabin and felt so lucky to have brought her here in time to be with her.

"Where are you going, Mother?"

"Where else, to my studio, how is everything with you, darling?"

"I will tell you later, Mother, now I am tired."

Nephus was tired too, but mostly apprehensive about what they were going to find down there. They walked to the cafeteria and had something to eat. Darna was talkative but Nephus wasn't saying much.

"What's your problem----we saved Earth, mission accomplished, you should be happy----what's eating you?"

"You brought your mother, you have what remains of your family, but I have no family here at all."

"Just be happy I brought you here, you could have been down there as a nonentity."

After a few minutes she got up and left. Nephus stayed there contemplating his next move. Next morning they all met again in Dr. Dylos' office. He welcomed them and said,

"The mission is not quite accomplished until we go down there and find out how much of a change we have created. I propose a team of scientists and sociologists visit the planet in all major capitals and cities, and report back to us as soon as possible." They all agreed; Nephus and Darna were part of the team that left a few hours later.

They landed in a park in cloaked mode; most of them stayed in the ship, but a group of ten including Nephus and Darna spread out in the city and agreed to be in contact at all times, and meet in the ship tonight. What they found was beyond their expectations.

In the beginning of the 21st century around 2010 people of the Earth used small atomic weapons. They were first used by the super powers but later by smaller countries too. There were many reasons given for using nuclear weapons; the super powers insisted on retaining their monopoly to keep them from spreading to rogue countries. That worked well for several years, but then they started using them to control and bully smaller countries. That worked for a while but smaller countries eventually used those same weapons for their own protection.

After a few years of using nuclear weapons, even though they were very small, they started to contaminate the atmosphere to the point that people were getting sick and dying at an alarming rate. The initial use of nuclear weapons by the super powers to control the rogue countries didn't work. It resulted in the world being unsafe and pol-

Project Anastrophe

luted. Finally in 2015 A.D. the United Nations Committee, after pressure from citizens from every country of the world, managed to stop using nuclear weapons, and started to use new non-polluting energies. This was part of the Project Anastrophe plan. In a few decades the atmosphere began to get cleaner. At the same time people became afraid of science altogether. That resulted in only a few scientific breakthroughs.

Many different religions became powerful claming that Evolution was wrong, and science was the work of the devil. Science was replaced by the theory of "Intelligent Design" in most of the world. Science and the theory of Evolution gradually came to an end, and all major religions took over with some of them becoming despotic like they were in the Middle-Ages. It was only at the end of the 24th century that people started to teach and use science again, but by the 25th century Earth had advanced very little.

This was the world the Anastrophe One team found when they went back home. The first thing Nephus did was to go back to his parent's neighborhood, but what he found was an entirely different world; there wasn't even a neighborhood. It was now a corn field with crows and other birds flying around and pecking at the corn. Disappointed, he beamed himself back to where Darna was. He told her what he found and she said,

"I am not surprised; the only other thing you could do now is to use D.N.A. You may or may not find your parents and even if you do, they won't know who you are. Why don't you accept your fate like most of us have?"

"You do have your mother with you, many others have their entire families with them on board--I have nothing."

"I also lost my brother and other relatives, so have many others, we knew there was a strong possibility we wouldn't find our loved ones. The sooner you accept your fate the better you are going to feel. Besides there are other important things to do in a very short time, so let's get going."

One thing they noticed was how many churches, cathedrals, synagogues, mosques, temples and small chapels were around. Many of them were works of art. The pace of life was slower, and the atmosphere was clean, but people didn't look healthy. They looked malnourished and poorly dressed; they were unfriendly and bad mannered. The police were everywhere as though they were expecting trouble. There was a feeling of uneasiness and people spoke different languages. The transportation was mostly electric but they were using anti-matter as supplementary energy; there were many factories, but no smoke any where to be seen. That was in sharp contrast to their anachronistic society. Obviously they had adopted Project Anastrophe in many ways but in other ways they had remained behind; they had become an anachronistic society.

The group beamed to different countries and found inadequacies in the distribution of the wealth. The most unfortunate thing they found was that there were wars, mostly between religious factions.

At the end of the day they went back to their ship. They were happy they had found a clean environment with clean industry; although not very advanced in technology. The social structure was chaotic and theocratic. They witnessed an episode of police killing a group of ragged protesters who were complaining about the shortage of food. The police shot them indiscriminately. It appeared to be a common occurrence in most countries.

They flew back to the mother ship, and were scheduled to meet in the morning to discuss their next move. Darna woke up early and on her way to the cafeteria she stopped to see her mother. Flavia was up too.

"Darna, you are early this morning, what's going on?"

Project Anastrophe

"I am going to an early meeting and I thought of having breakfast before I go there. Mother, I have some bad news for both of us."

"Oh dear--now what?"

"Yesterday a group of us went down to earth to check and see if it would be safe for us to go back home. I am happy to tell you that we have no more radiation poisoning and Earth is, for the most part, clean and habitable. But our intervention with the "Prime Directive" has changed life as we knew it. Everything is changed, Mother, from people to buildings to social structure; it's a different world down there. Our city, our neighborhood, our home, and Mark are no more."

"What to you mean, Mark is no more, where is he?"

"He is not there, and even if we could find him he wouldn't look like Mark, in fact none of us here could find our relatives as we knew them; they have all changed and some of them may not have been born. That's what happens when one interferes with the "Prime Directive.""

Flavia burst into tears but didn't utter one word. She walked to the next room and closed the door behind her.

"Mother, I am sorry. He was my brother too."

"Leave me alone, just let me be."

Darna had a quick cup of coffee and started to go, when behind her she heard Nephus trying to get her attention.

"I am busy; I have a meeting to attend."

"Cool down, Darna, you can grace me with your presence for a few minutes; I am going there too. We still have another half hour before we are expected to be there."

"I have some preparatory work to do, what do you want?"

"I am sorry for my behavior yesterday. I was upset

with what I found, or I should say, what I didn't find down there."

"So was I. I lost a brother too, but I am not a cry baby."

Darna left leaving Nephus lonely and heartbroken. He didn't like this place at all; it reminded him of his jail time. If it wasn't for Darna he would beam himself down there and use his wits and be something; there must be underworld people there, they are humans after all, aren't they? His heart hardened, his mind blurred, he started to curse,

"To hell with you, to hell with all of you, I am getting out of here."

The meeting took place soon after he arrived. This was an open meeting for everybody to attend. Dr. Dylos was determined to keep the democratic system going even here.

"Thank you for coming, this is an important meeting and what we say and do here will affect the rest of our lives. This meeting is broadcast live all over the ship, so that everyone is aware of what we are about to decide today.

Yesterday we sent a team of scientists and sociologists down to Earth to find out if our efforts have produced the desired effect which was to stop the radiation poisoning and save our people and our planet. I am happy to report to you that Earth is saved, and so is every other living thing. That was our intent and we accomplished it, however, now everything is different down there. The buildings, the cities, and the people, even though they look like us, are different.

The change we made back in the 21st century has drastically altered the way people live now and the way we were accustomed to living before we left our planet. The worst of it is that our friends and relatives are not there anymore. Their D.N.A. might match ours, but they look and act differently from us. Folks, in a nut shell, we are very much on our own."

Project Anastrophe

He went on to say that they were planning to send four more probes, one for each future century in order to find a century in which people lived closer to their current standard of living. Most of the people in the hall agreed with Dr. Dylos, but there were a few who wanted to go down now and assimilate with them. The fact that the people on Earth were religious and dictatorial didn't bother them at all.

One of the most outspoken was Nephus. He said,

"It is our right to choose our own destiny and we want to go now." Dr. Dylos said,

"It is against the "Prime Directive" to assimilate with these people. Their technology and social structures are very different from ours. We need to find a society that is comparable to our own and we will do that by checking into their future as they progress. We are a civilized and democratic society and we will adhere to these rules."

With the exception of a few people, the majority agreed with Dr. Dylos and the meeting was over. It was agreed to meet again after they had sent the four probes into the future, and had gained enough information to decide whether or not they should go down to Earth and settle there for good.

There were about twenty people who disagreed with the rest of the crowd, but Nephus knew there were more who could be persuaded otherwise. He made it his business to get in touch with them and manipulate them just like old times.

Back to the Past

Norina and Nick decided to beam themselves back to the farm to wait for Dr. Dylos's orders. In the meantime Ner and Vrima made preparations to vacate the base, remove all weapons and prepare for the trip back home.

They neutralized some of the weapons at the base, but kept some on board the ship. Everything that was not needed at the base was destroyed by a powerful bomb minutes after they left. The explosion caused several houses on the islands to shake a bit, but the islanders assumed it was another tremor of the recent earthquake and after a few hours went back into their houses and soon forgot it ever happened.

The tremor moved a huge body of water into the cave-like base and a few minutes later it was covered. There were no remains of the base at Yellow Island. Ner, Vrima, and the guard robot Dyphus, all flew to Nick's and Norina's farmhouse in the country and kept the ship cloaked at all times. Ner and Vrima went into the house, Dyphus stayed in, guarding the ship.

Norina and Nick were having breakfast when they arrived. Vrima helped herself to a cup of coffee, imitating Norina as best she could. Ner reported to Norina everything they had done at the base on Yellow Island in the San Juan archipelago. Norina said to him,

"So we are ready to go as soon as we get the order from Dr. Dylos---right?"

"Right as you said, Norina."

A few minutes later, Ner and Vrima left and went to their house to take care of things they needed to do before leaving. They also went to Dr. Narthur's, collected all his electronic gear and beamed it, along with theirs, to the ship. Then they beamed themselves to the ship. Before they left, Nick and Norina took care of one last thing. They went to a law firm and wrote a will leaving their house and Ner's and Vrima's, to the Papas family in case they didn't returned from the War Zone. They also presented a letter signed by Dr. Narthur directing the lawyer to do likewise with his house.

Project Anastrophe

Norina was a little nervous this morning and Nick didn't fail to notice,

"What's the matter, Norina, are you sad because we are about to go home?"

"I am feeling sad because of what I have to tell you, Nick."

"What is it, Norina?"

"I have orders to take you back to your time and home when this is all over. The problem is that Ner, even with the latest technology he received, can't deliver you to the precise moment in time. There may be a variation of ten to twenty years. I know how much you want to go home to your family, Nick, and that makes me feel sad."

Nick had forgotten all about his epoch, his family, and relatives. He had been so busy lately and his mind had zeroed in on saving humanity, and the planet. Now they had done it. Norina was sobbing openly not trying to hold back her tears. She knew Nick had to go back to his family and she had to go back to her time and to her people.

Meeting Nick was nothing but a fluke in time-space, an accident---one in a billion. Nick thought of his family, he wanted so much to be with them. This time he would appreciate every possible moment. He had done all he could to save the planet; now he could live the rest of his life knowing that the Earth and all its living things had a chance to live without the threat of nuclear annihilation.

Yes, he wanted to go back home and ten years before or after would not make much of a difference; he would adapt to the change whatever it might be. Nick was busy so much with his inner thoughts, that he only now noticed Norina crying.

"Norina, why are you crying---what's the matter?"

"Oh you wouldn't understand and I would be too ashamed to tell you how I feel."

"Is there something I said or did? If I did, I am truly sorry. Norina, you know how much I love you and I would do anything for you. Tell me what's bothering you."

"There is nothing you or I can do, Nick, to make me feel better; I am sorry I acted like this. I must be tired, that's all. We must try to get you as close to your epoch as possible, and send you back to your family." Nick moved closer to Norina, hugged her and kissed the top of her head.

"Thank you Norina, how can I ever forget you?" Norina nestled her head into Nick's warm chest and managed to stop another wave of sobbing, but she sniffled quietly.

Next day they all met at Nick's and Norina's house. Ner was very businesslike; he told them how he had calibrated their course down to the smallest detail, but he made it very clear that there was always the possibility of landing ten years before or after the appointed moment of arrival. Norina was now eager to have this done and put it behind her as soon as possible. She looked tired with a permanent stamp of sadness on her face. Vrima sensed Norina's feeling for Nick and empathized as much as a robot could. Norina said to Ner, "Let's do it today; how long will it take you to get ready to go?"

"About an hour, Norina."

"Then let's do it."

The trip took only seconds. The ship landed outside the city in cloaked mode. Ner told Nick that they landed in the year 2012 A.D.

"I am sorry Nick, we missed the moment of your departure by twelve years, but that's the best I could do." Norina said,

"Nick, you can go alone or one of us could come along to make sure you make contact with your family. Would you like one of us to go with you?"

"I would love it if you came," he said to Norina. Vrima

Project Anastrophe

had prepared the appropriate clothing, along with cash and credit cards.

They beamed themselves to Kent where they walked for an hour or so, looking at the various shops and buildings. Nick was surprised how much it had changed in the last twelve years; there were many more cars and the traffic was awful. But Norina liked the vibrancy and vitality of the city. She was so glad they had saved it. They finally took a taxi to Nick's father's supermarket; it was busier than he had ever seen it. His beard, mustache, and dark glasses did a good job to cover his true identity from any friends or relatives, but he didn't see any one he knew---even the staff was different.

Nick wasn't sure that it belonged to his father anymore but the Agora Market name was still there; it appeared to be one of many other chain stores--a far cry from the small "Mom and Pop" market of the forties. They took another taxi to his house and as they approached, Norina felt nervous and tears spilled down her cheeks.

Nick was apprehensive and excited. Twelve years had passed and the children would be grownup by now. Takis would be nineteen, Sophia seventeen, and little Julie fifteen. He was the lost father and husband, Odysseus, coming back to his island, to his Penelope---only this was for real.

The neighborhood had changed; there were more houses, and the quiet suburban area was now full of traffic. They asked the driver to park across the street and wait, but as Nick was about to step out he said,

"Norina, you go and ask for Nick Papas and see what reaction you get from Tasoula; then I'll come out too."

"Nick, this is not a nice thing to ask me to do but if it will make it easier for you, I'll try."

Norina crossed the busy road to Nick's house and

knocked at the door. Nick was close enough to see everything clearly from across the street. A man opened the door with a young child right behind him,

"My name is Loretta Johnson from the Department of Social Security. We are updating our records on missing people, and I would like to ask Mrs. Papas a few questions about her missing husband, Nick Papas."

"Tasoula is now married to me; my name is Vagelis Garvaniotis." Then he said to the little girl,

"Maria, go ask your mother to come down, tell her there is a lady who wants to talk to her."

Little Maria ran up the stairs calling her mother, "Mom—"

"What is it? I am coming."

"Is she your daughter? She is beautiful."

"Yes she is, we also have an older boy, and he is at school."

Tasoula came down to the front door. She was in her late forties with curly graying hair. A lovely Mediterranean-looking woman; she was still slim. She spoke with an air of confidence and her vocabulary indicated she was highly educated. Mr. Garvaniotis excused himself, took little Maria by the hand and went inside. When Norina mentioned Nick's name, Tasoula was taken aback and she started to cry. Norina tried to hold back her tears.

"How long has Nick been missing, Mrs. Garvaniotis?"

"It must be twelve years now."

"What do you think happened to him?"

"I would say he drowned; there is no other explanation."

"It would appear to be so; are the older children living with you?"

"Only Julie, she is now in high school; Takis and

Project Anastrophe

Sophia are both in college, they have all missed their father a great deal."

"How are his parents and grandparents dealing with Nick's disappearance?"

"It was very hard for all of us at the time, but now both parents and grandparents have passed away---God bless them."

"Mrs. Garvaniotis, you have been very cooperative, thank you very much."

Tasoula went inside the house and closed the door behind her. Nick had been able to hear everything. The twelve years hadn't changed her much; she still looked beautiful. The passing of both his parents and grandparents saddened him, but he was glad to hear of his children doing well with their education. Nick was thinking about his predicament and his heart ached. Slowly but surely he came to understand that there wasn't a place for him in their lives.

He hadn't been husband or father to his family for the last twelve years, and now Tasoula, his lovely wife, was married to someone else. He had missed the opportunity to spend time with his children and now they were all grown up. With his parents and grandparents gone it would be hard for him to live there anymore. Would they believe that he had been taken away all this time by a UFO? How would he explain his youthful appearance; he would be an anomaly to them and to himself. No-- there was no place for him in this time and place. His life had been snatched away from him and from them that early March morning twelve years ago.

He wiped his tears just as Norina came into the taxi, and he asked the driver to take them to the park by the museum. A few minutes later they were sitting on the grass by a small pond. Norina asked Nick,

"What have you decided to do, Nick?"

"Everybody has aged by twelve years and I have not changed at all, how am I to explain that to them?"

"I am sure Vrima could work on you and make you look older to match your contemporaries."

"My family as I knew it, is gone, I have no parents or wife; my children have grown up without me---there is no life for me here. I don't belong here anymore---let's go back to the ship."

"Are you sure you want to do that, Nick? You know it is very difficult to recalibrate the time sequence to bring you back, once we go."

"I know that very well, let's do it."

They beamed themselves back to the ship. Ner and Vrima were surprised to see Nick, but Vrima was glad to have her master back close to her. Now the question was where to go and wait for new orders. Ner suggested going back in time to a remote place to wait. Nick had a better idea,

"Let's go to an island in Greece, there are three thousand islands there, we should be able to find one out of the way."

"We can't be too much out of the way, we need provisions for the two of you, we robots will be O.K. for a long time."

They moved back in time to ancient Greece, to the year 445 B.C. They landed on a small island called Scorpios, in the Ionian Sea, where they found a cave and parked the ship in cloaked mode. They landed in a time when the Athenian Empire was going through major changes.

The Empire which was maintained through threat of force, had begun to lose its power lately. When Megara and a neighboring state, Boeotia, revolted from the alliance,

Project Anastrophe

Athens no longer had a buffer zone between it and the Peloponnesian states allied with Sparta. In 445 B.C., Pericles, a strong leader in Athens at the time, averted disaster by making a fifty-year peace with Sparta. Both sides got what they wanted. Athens gave up political power over most states on the Greek mainland; in return, Sparta recognized Athens as a legitimate political institution. With that agreement the Athenian Empire, which had been gradually forming, was now official. (4)

Both Nick and Norina were excited to be in the time and place of such an important event in western civilization. They stayed in the ship for a couple of days for them to recover and for the robots to regenerate. Norina felt guilty for having Nick all to herself but happy at the same time. After all, he had been the one to make the decision and come back to the ship with her.

Nick also felt guilty, but he was relieved with his decision to leave what remained of his family. He found comfort being with Norina. The night before they made passionate love and for the first time they felt like husband and wife. They abandoned their pretend name, Johnson, and adopted his name, Papas. To make it more official, they asked Ner to marry them.

It was a beautiful sunny morning when all five of them, the three robots, Ner, Vrima, Dyphus, and Nick and Norina gathered on the sandy beach. Ner asked Norina and Nick to step forward and said,

"By the powers vested in me by the Zita biosphere I hereby pronounce you, Nick Papas married to Norina Anderson. By this union you are to be her husband, and you, Norina Anderson, are likewise married to Nick Papas, and from now on you are to be his wife.

From this day you are registered in the Zita Biosphere's

archives as Nick and Norina Papas and you are to be husband and wife until one of you or both wishes to terminate this union."

Vrima was very sentimental and she wanted so much to be able to cry and show Nick and Norina how much she loved them--she even managed to sniffle a little bit. This feeling was something new to Vrima and she wondered if love might be her next feeling. That would be the most wonderful human feeling of all. Ner finished the ceremony by saying,

"I suppose now would be the most appropriate time for the newly married couple to kiss." Nick and Norina hugged each other and kissed for a long time while all the robots clapped in unison.

Nick and Norina walked on the clean white sand of Scorpios holding hands, facing the young sun on the horizon. The next day Vrima had everything ready for them; a white tunic for Nick and an off-white gown for Norina with a yellow kerchief to put over her head. She also gave them enough drachmas in silver and gold coins. Ner and Vrima dressed likewise, and with enough money all four beamed to the Agora in the center of Athens.

It was a very busy town with many people walking around wearing white tunics, others wore long embroidered blouses. Some sold their crafts; others carried vegetables in baskets on their backs. Two men talked animatedly as they leaned on the columns of the Agora.

A man pulled an ox by its harness; powerful muscles bulged, it sweated as it carried its heavy cargo of marble. The wheels made a rhythmic clatter on the cobble stones. Temples and statues were painted in bright colors and there were children running with their mothers close by. A group of men were listening to a bearded man on a platform. It

Project Anastrophe

was Socrates who spoke eloquently pointing at times to the parliament and uttering accusatory epithets about the authorities.

Ner went to the man who was pulling the ox and helped him. He pulled with such strength that the man looked at him and said,
"You must be a God; for only Gods have such power."
Ner smiled and went away. Vrima had adjusted their implants with the ability to speak the ancient Greek tongue. Ner and Vrima bought lots of vegetables, grains, fresh and dry fruits, and meats. Because of the large quantities Ner and Vrima bought, they said they were preparing food for a wedding party.

Nick and Norina broke away and followed a narrow road to the residential area; they gazed at the Parthenon, one of humanity's splendors, and above it the blue Attic sky untouched by the pollution that was to come in the future. They both knew this peaceful time would not last for long. But thanks to Pericles, the first democratically elected leader, it would last for fifty years. The Athenians would use this time to keep Pheidias, Iktinos, and Kallikrates busy building temples and statues that would last for thousands of years. In that short time poetry, academics, theater, and architecture would reach the zenith of civilized society and it would be called, "The Golden Age of Athens."

It would be the start of western culture and its democracy would be spread throughout the world and would be adopted by many countries thousands of years from now.

They walked up to the temple of Athena, the Parthenon. It was new, and was painted blue and red. Inside the temple stood a fourteen meter statue of Promachos Goddess Athena covered with 24 karat gold and ivory.

They asked permission from the high priest and went into the temple to see the statue. It was magnificent; the sunlight filtering through the columns bathed the whole body with the gold reflecting the sun into thousands of brilliant little stars.

Norina and Nick felt fortunate to see the temple and the statue as it had existed; they were both in awe. They stepped out into the bright mid-day sun, sat under a pine tree, and enjoyed its shade.

Ner and Vrima put all their shopping behind a wall and waited until there were no people around, then they beamed the goods back to the ship. Dyphus would know what to do with it. They walked up the hill and there they found Nick and Norina close to the temple sitting under the pine tree. Ner said to them,

"We finished our shopping and have sent it back to the ship."

Nick said,

"Sit down, Ner-- you too, Vrima, and when it gets a little quieter we will all beam back to the ship."

Back to the Future

After many long discussions with his staff, Dr. Dylos decided to send five different probes to future times, one for each century. The first probe from the 26th century showed that Earth was advancing in science and culture but theocracy still had the upper hand in making major decisions. Earth now was divided into four sections; China was in charge of most of the Far East countries; America in charge of North and South America. Israel and all the Arab countries including Africa had finally established peace among themselves and governed their countries as one country. The fourth section was Europe which included West, East, North and South, including Russia.

The second probe from the 27th century came back with

Project Anastrophe

information of a more advanced Earth as was expected. But in 2647 there must have been a devastating war. Although without nuclear weapons, it was just as destructive and forced them to partially unite for better protection. By the end of the 27th century Earth had been divided into two huge powers: all North and South America and the Far East including Australia on one side, and all Europe, the Middle East and Africa on the other side. They had established a temporary peace accord, but both sides were spending huge amounts of money for newer weapons which suited an oligarchy of powerful people on both sides. It deprived the majority of people of a better life.

The third probe from the 28th century was more to their liking. Now the whole world was united. They had one representative government. The standard of living was much better, people looked healthier and happier and the technology and culture almost matched their own. There was a lot of talk in the ship that this would be the best century for them to finally go back home.

Still many others wanted to check two more centuries so as to be better informed. They sent another probe to the 29th century; the data they got was both good and bad. Good, because the people of the Earth still did not use nuclear weapons, they were now far advanced in technology and culture but they were sure they could easily catch up with them without any difficulty.

The bad part of it was that they now had a new enemy, an enemy from another planet far away. Now the people of the Earth were united and eager to help in anyway they could to save their planet. This time the enemy was more powerful than they were. Now for the first time in all these years they were preparing to use nuclear weapons to defend themselves against an enemy with much superior weaponry.

George Karnikis

They eagerly sent the last probe to the 30th century. They wanted to find out how the people of Earth had overcome the challenge of a powerful enemy. What they found made them very sad. They found an Earth still at war with the same enemy, very weak and barely holding the enemy at bay. They could see that it was only a matter of time before it was all over. Dr. Dylos invited anyone who was able to come to the meeting and many people came.

This time Nephus was organized. He had a group of two hundred people with him and they all spoke with one voice.

Dr. Dylos spoke first we are gathered here to discuss a very important subject, and that is our survival and our planet's survival. Yes, you heard me right, the survival of our planet. The 28th century would be perfect for us. In some things they are ahead of us but in other ways, a little behind, but that will not be a problem---we can adjust. The problem comes later in the 29th century when an alien species will attack our planet and Earth will revert to using nuclear weapons again.

We sent another probe, this time to the 30th century, and found Earth's environment very polluted; people were weak and about to collapse, and the aliens were ready to take over the planet. Since the humans on Earth were surprised, they missed valuable time getting prepared. We know ahead of time what's going to happen to them and we can do something now to help them in the future. I don't know how we can help them at this time, but we have hundreds of years on our side to do something.

Now we need to decide. Do we go to the 28th century and settle with them and have our future generations suffer the consequences along with the rest; or do we find the future enemy, and do something to delay them, thereby giving time to the humans to prepare? Maybe we could find a way

Project Anastrophe

to stop them before they had a chance to attack Earth. We are going to settle this matter by vote right now. Those who want to postpone going to Earth now and save the planet from the aliens, raise your hands."

Most people raised their hands. Then Dr. Dylos again asked,

"Those of you, who want to go and settle in the 28th century on Earth, raise your hands now."

All two hundred of Nephus's people raised their hands. It was obvious the majority of people wanted to postpone for now. Dr. Dylos again said to all those gathered,

"It seems to me that it is our destiny to help save our planet. We will let you know in the near future how we can best help."

The conspirators

Nephus and his closest conspirators, about ten of them, went to the cafeteria. Nephus was quick and to the point.

"We are not going to go along with their plan, are we? We must devise our own----a plan that will work for us. Now this is what I propose, listen carefully. We are going to take over the ship and go where we want. If we go to an earlier century we could use our technology and know-how to build a better life for us. We will be rich and powerful, we can eventually take over the planet. Who can stop us? On the other hand, if we go to the 28th century, we will be the underdog and will live a mediocre life at best. I have a plan and if we use it soon, we can compromise all the guard robots. Dr. Dylos and his staff will be taken over by the same guard robots which will be answering to us. We must act quickly before they know what hit them, what do you say?"

Threvous said,

"How about the aliens? According to the last probe's data they are going to take over our planet. Dr. Dylos says they are going to come up with some kind of a plan to save it; we have nothing."

"We don't have a plan now, but we will have hundreds of years to prepare later on. Remember we will take over the whole planet and we will call the shots, surely we can come up with a good defense plan. What to you say?"

Varcous, another of the conspirators, said,

"How about the rest of our people; how do we convince them to go along with our plan?"

"They already disagree with Dr. Dylos, they'll trust us, we don't have to tell them what we are doing right away-- they'll find out when we are all done."

Several of them thought the plan was very daring but eventually they all agreed to go ahead with it. Nephus spoke again and said,

"We mustn't tell anybody of this plan, not even your wives and children or your best friends. Tomorrow all of us will meet in my room and I will show you how the plan is going to be executed. Be there at 8:00 a.m. and we will take it from there. They all left with hope, but with fear and trepidation too.

The next morning they met at Nephus's room. He showed them the schematics; it was an ingenious plan. He pointed out how he would penetrate the robots' cybernetics and program them to switch allegiance to their group. He went on to say,

"From that point on we will arrest Dr. Dylos and his staff, and put them under house arrest. I can assure you; no one will be harmed it will be a very clean operation. After we take over the ship we will simply announce to all people that the ship is now under new staff, and we will let them know of our plan to save our planet as soon as possible.

Project Anastrophe

Later we will decide where we go and that will be it, friends---as simple as that.

For reasons of secrecy and security I will let you know a few minutes before the plan goes into effect so that we all are part of the operation."

The meeting was over shortly after that, and they all went back to their duties with orders to say nothing to anyone. Dr. Dylos had another meeting with his staff. This time they were to discuss how best to help save the planet Earth, as well as their own people. Dr. Thamion had two ideas; one was to move to Mars and establish a base and then build a colony and from there try to help Earth. His second idea was to find out who the alien enemy was, go to its planet and if possible, stop it there before it came to Earth, but that would take technology they didn't have at this time.

Dr. Lozinei suggested building a colony on the Moon and building the technology needed to either fight the enemy on Earth or go to its planet wherever it might be or perhaps to come up with a more appropriate plan in the future.

Dr. Dylos said,

"We know one thing for sure and that is that we can't stay in this ship for too long, therefore I propose to build a temporary colony on the Moon and later we can decide our final destination." They all thought that was a good idea and decided to build and stay on the Moon for the time being.

Darna hadn't heard from Nephus since their last argument, and she liked it that way. Nephus had changed for the worst lately and she didn't want anything to do with him. She had her mother and other friends to associate with and didn't miss him at all. She was on her way to the office when she noticed a little girl crying on the children's play-

ground. The teacher was busy with some other children at the time and wasn't paying attention. Darna sat down by her and asked,
"Why are you crying, are you hurt?"
"No-o-o."
"Then why are you crying?"
"Be c a u s e."
"What's your name?"
"Loucra."
"My name is Darna and I don't like to see you feeling sad, is there something I can do to help you?"
"I don't want my Daddy to die."
"Why do you think your daddy is going to die?"
"The robots are going to kill him."
"Why are the robots going to kill your daddy?"
"My daddy said he and his friends are going to take over the ship and the robots are going to kill him and I don't want my daddy to die."
"Well I am going to tell those robots to never, ever, harm your daddy; would that make you feel better?"
"Yes."

Darna was alarmed by what she had heard from little Loucra.
"Was that a little girl's fantasy, or did she overhear her parents talking about a real takeover of the ship?" There were a lot of unhappy people at their last meeting and this was something Nephus could do----certainly he was capable. She went straight to Dr. Dylos' office and asked to talk with him. He was surprised to see her coming to see him so early.
"This must be important, or you wouldn't have come to see me this early, Darna."

Project Anastrophe

"I am not sure, Dr. Dylos, but if what I heard is true then you had better do something about it."

"Well let's hear it, Darna, what's going on?"

Darna told Dr. Dylos what little Loucra had told her and then she said,

"Dr. Dylos, as I said, it could be a little girl's fantasy, but what if it is true?"

"Do you think Nephus could pull off something like that?"

"Nephus is a very capable man, if that is what he has in mind, he can do it; I have no doubt about it."

"Thank you, Darna; I will bring it up to my staff in our next meeting."

"I wouldn't wait that long. I know Nephus well and if he has something in his mind, he will not waste time doing it."

"Don't worry, Darna, I'll get on it right a way."

Dr. Dylos wasn't about to have a special staff meeting based on a little girl's fantasy, but he did something that would be crucial in the very near future. He prepared a hologram addressed to Ner and placed it in a private line, one that he only knew. He would have to cancel it after a certain time had elapsed or it would go on its own.

Chapter 14

Nephus was ready to go; he had asked his conspirators to gather at his place.

"Friends, the time has come. Today is the day Dr. Dylos and his staff are meeting. They are all going to be in one place and it is the opportunity I have been waiting for. I have finally gained access to the main computer that controls the guard robots and have changed the code of obedience. All I have to do now is to put it into effect."

Nephus proceeded to push a few keys on his hand-held unit and said,

"If my plan has worked, the chief robot guard will be knocking on my door any time now."

Sure enough, a few minutes later there was a knock on

Project Anastrophe

the door and the chief guard Phylios reported to Nephus. It was amazing, the change was complete. He said,

"Master Nephus, I understand that from now on I am to report specifically to you. What do you wish me to do?"

"I want you to place your robot guards at all crucial intersections and also place ten guards in the meeting hall and wait for my orders."

"Yes, Master Nephus, it will be done as you say." Then Nephus said to his conspirators,

"Gentlemen, now all we have to do is give the order----are you ready?" They all said,

"Yes we are." Nephus gave the order to Phylios.

"Phylios, I want you to apprehend Dr. Dylos and all his staff and put them under house arrest; we are taking over the ship. If there is any opposition from anybody, I want them arrested and put in jail until further notice."

"Yes sir, Master Nephus, it will be done as you say."

"Ladies and gentlemen, before I hear anything about building the colony, I would like to discuss something very disturbing Darna told me a few days ago. She said that some dissatisfied people are planning to take over the ship. Now I can't be sure whether this is true or not but I have placed all guards on high alert. If anyone knows anything about this, now is the time to discuss it."

There was no one from the staff who said anything. But the door opened and ten guards came in and placed themselves right behind the staff around the table. Then Phylios went to Dr. Dylos and said,

"Dr. Dylos, you and all your staff are to be put under house arrest until further notice by order of my master Nephus."

"I am in charge of this ship and I am ordering you to arrest Nephus and bring him right here."

"I am sorry, Dr. Dylos, but I can't do that."

At that moment Nephus and his conspirators came into the room. Nephus walked up to Dr. Dylos and said,

"It's too late, Dr. Dylos, we have taken over the ship; do as Phylios says and you won't be harmed."

"Why didn't you come and discuss your grievances with us? Was it necessary for you to take over the ship?"

"We have other plans for this ship and its people which I don't care to discuss with you at this time. Phylios, take them away!"

"Yes sir, Master Nephus." The guards did as they were told; Nephus's plan had succeeded. Now they were in charge of the ship. Nephus turned to his conspirators and said,

"Gentlemen, we have done it; now go home and relax. Tomorrow we will meet here to discuss our next plan, thank you for your trust and your cooperation, I'll see you tomorrow."

Darna wasn't surprised at the takeover of the ship by Nephus and his close conspirators, but she was surprised by Dr. Dylos's lack of action on her warning. He had had ample time to beef up his guards and keep an eye on Nephus and his associates. Obviously he didn't take her warning seriously and now the deed was done.

Darna knew Nephus too well, he was going to govern as a dictator; democracy was dead. The question was whether he was going to be a good tyrant or a bad one; that remained to be seen. Darna kept a low profile and tried to stay away from Nephus.

Nephus kept an important secret from his comrades; he knew the takeover wasn't complete although it appeared to be. Although he had broken the main code inside the robots' cybernetics and changed their noetics to report to him, he knew that there was a built-in mechanism in every robot

Project Anastrophe

to correct itself sometime in the future and change allegiance back to its first master.

Nephus's interference in the robots' noetics would be treated just as humans fight a disease, they would cure themselves in due time.

There were two things he could do, one was to work with each robot's cybernetics and reprogram it. That would take too much time considering the number of robots he had to work with. He knew he could only convert about ten percent of them before the others became his enemies.

The second one was both easy and difficult; Dr. Dylos had the master code, if he could extract it from him, it would take seconds to place the new code in the robots' cybernetics and the takeover would be accomplished. He would have complete power over robots and humans.

He started reprogramming the robots right away. The first one, chief Phylios, took two days; he was hoping to reduce that to one per day and that would be pushing it.

Nephus didn't waste any time meeting Dr. Dylos, he had him brought to his office early the next day.

"Dr. Dylos, you know why I brought you here, don't you?"

"I know, but you will be wasting your time, because there is no way I will give you the master code, no matter what you do to me."

"Now Dr. Dylos, there are good ways to get the code from you and there bad ways. I don't want to harm you, but one way or another I have to have this code, so cooperate with me and I promise you that you will live the rest of your life in peace and comfort. Otherwise I will torture you to an agonizing death until I get it---you choose---it's up to you."

"I will die before you get that code from me, but you won't last long either, you will perish too."

"Take him away, Phylios, you know what to do with him!"

"Yes sir, master Nephus, I will do as you say."

Two guards took Dr. Dylos away. Nephus was sad but it had to be done that way, he had to have the code or as Dr. Dylos had said; he wouldn't last long. Dr. Dylos was prepared for that too. He knew Nephus would come for the code sooner or later. Dr. Dylos was an honest man, he had worked hard the last few years to save the planet. For the most part he had accomplished that, although with some changes that affected the people on the planet and his people in the ship. But he had done the best he could do under the circumstances and he wasn't about to give Planet Earth to Nephus on a platter and have him ruin all he had accomplished.

There was only one thing he could do, and he had to do it now. It would be difficult for Norina and her crew to fight and win with all the guards on Nephus's side, but he had to deprive Nephus from having the code. The little lump on his forearm was still there. All he had to do was to apply some pressure on it and it would be over in seconds; there was enough venom in there to kill a bull--he pressed.

Nephus was preparing to make an announcement to proclaim that he was the new governor of the ship, when his 3D-comlink got his attention.

"What's up, Phylios?"

"Master Nephus, Dr. Dylos just killed himself."

"Are you sure he is dead?"

"Yes sir, Master Nephus, I detected a heavy dose of hydrocyanic acid in his blood, he is extremely dead."

"Take him away; I don't want his death to be known right now."

"Yes sir, I will do as you say."

Nephus knew Dr. Dylos would not give his code eas-

Project Anastrophe

ily, but didn't expect him to kill himself. Now he would never have the code. It would be more difficult for him to retain his authority on the ship. He had to find a way to speed up the reprogramming of the robot guards before they revolted. So far he had converted fifteen of them. He needed at least fifty on his side, then he could put the one hundred remaining out of commission until he felt more secure. He could reprogram the rest of them one at a time. Yes that's what he must do.

He called his staff to a meeting and told them what had happened,

"Gentlemen, with Dr. Dylos's death we have lost the chance to use his code for a quick conversion of the robot guards. So far I have converted only fifteen--it's a time-consuming process and I need human guards ready to replace the robots when the time comes." Varcous, his first lieutenant, asked the question everybody in the room was thinking,

"We already have all the robots on our side why do we need to reprogram them?"

"There is one thing I didn't tell you Gentlemen, all robots have some kind of recovery mechanism, which, after a while, deletes any new inserted codes, and then reverts back to their original. When they realize they have been altered they will turn against us and the robots I have converted. That's why I am anxious to reprogram as many robots as possible. I would like to have at least fifty converted before that happens; that's why I need human guards ready to take over in case I am not ready."

"Even if we were to find enough human guards we will never be able to fight the hundred remaining guards; we are no match for them."

"I can put the remaining robots out of commission until I am ready to reprogram them one at a time."

"Then what's the problem?"

"The problem is policing all the people who are going to be against us, that's why we need humans for the time being."

Varcous and the rest of the conspirators promised to find and train able-bodied men and women, and report back in a week's time.

Nephus had missed Darna since their last argument in the cafeteria. He hoped now that he had taken over the ship, she would be more interested in coming to talk to him, but that hadn't happened yet. Finally he decided to go and find her at her place. She was there with her mother. Two of his robot guards stayed outside the door, he went in and sat on the couch and said,

"In the last few days I have been trying to get in touch with you, and you have avoided me--why?"

"You dare come into my place and ask me why I don't want to see you after what you have done?"

"Darna, there are a lot of people who are sick and tired of hiding in this ship and want to go home, do you realize that? We can save Earth by living on Earth, we have four hundred years to spread the word to these people; prepare and arm Earth before the aliens come. Why in hell do we need to go and find them in their home world? Even if we finally decide to go there, it will take hundreds of years. We and many generations in the future will spend our lives as vagabonds, on a futile journey. Is that how you want to spend the rest of your life?"

"That's what you think, but the Earth is no longer as we knew it. There are different people down there, they are now a theocratic society, their culture is different from ours; their technology is stagnant and anachronistic. But we know in time they will change. What we need to do is to

Project Anastrophe

stop the aliens before they come and destroy our planet. The best way to do that is not to go back to Earth, but to go to the aliens' home world and stop them there or at least arm Earth with the same weapons.

In the 29th century these alien beings are going to be superior to humans with weapons of mass destruction which humans will not be able to match. We have been in the future and have seen Earth losing its battle to the aliens. We need to go to their homeland, copy their weapons and arm Earth or stop them there before they come to Earth.

Your way will make you and your friends rich and powerful but you will never convince the Earth people to build these kinds of weapons; that's why we need to go there."

"I am now in charge of this ship, and I am going to do it my way."

"Well Nephus, count me out!"

"We'll see about that."

"What do you mean by that?"

"Never mind, Darna."

Nephus left Darna's place in anger and disbelief. He went straight to his office and made an official holographic announcement.

"Ladies and gentlemen, my name is Nephus Northmount and I am now in charge of the Anastrophe One. We are making preparations to move back to Earth." He then asked all available guards to be stationed in strategic places and keep an eye on people who might want to cause trouble.

Most people were dumbfounded by what they heard. Even those who were willing to go back home were amazed to hear that they were on their way; but many of those who voted with Dr. Dylos not to go at this time, were enraged with this new governor called Nephus. Many of them wanted to know what had happened to Dr. Dylos, and wanted to see him, but were stopped by the guards. That made them even more anxious and determined.

Finally there was another announcement; this time by chief guard Phylios,

"There is going to be a curfew starting in thirty metric minutes, those who do not obey the curfew will be arrested. Governor Nephus will talk with you tomorrow morning at 11:00 metric time. At that time you may ask questions about Dr. Dylos."

Most people left right away, and the rest of them were gone well before the curfew went into effect and all hallways were quiet. Nephus was thinking to himself,

"That was a close call, but I still have to come up with some kind of an explanation about his death. They'll never believe me when I tell them he killed himself."

Next day the room was packed with people; those who wanted to go back home and those who wanted to stay. The majority wanted to see Dr. Dylos. The first to speak was Varcous, he said,

"Many of you want to know what happened to Dr. Dylos. I am afraid he won't be around today, the guards told us he is dead; he took his own life."

A shout of anger erupted from the crowd, many blamed Nephus and the rest of the officials for his murder, others chanted "m u r d e r e s," "m u r d e r e s." Some people got out of control and the guards had to move them out of the hall. Finally Nephus got up and began to speak, but the people wouldn't let up. They told him they didn't recognize him as the new Governor.

"We had no reasons to kill Dr. Dylos, he killed himself for reasons I will never know. There are some of us who do not wish to go on a wild chase for the aliens. We believe we can build the necessary weapons on Earth to fight them

Project Anastrophe

when they come four hundred years from now. We believe this is the best time for us to go back to Earth. We are technologically advanced in all areas and, in time, we will take over the whole planet and establish our own system. Once this happens, Earth will be ready for the enemy when it arrives.

    We tried to reason with the previous administration but they wouldn't even listen to us. That's why we took over the ship. We will try our best to show you that we can be trusted to do the job well."

    After the speech Nephus and the rest of the conspirators left, leaving most of the crowd very unhappy but unable to do anything about it.

Chapter 15

It was one of those hot Athenian days and Nick and Norina were happy to be under the pine tree protected from the sun's bright glare. Nick was resting his back against the tree; while Norina rested her head on Nick's lap. But Ner and Vrima were sitting in the sun charging their batteries. One could hear the cicadas singing their seventeen year song. It was at that moment that Ner received Dr. Dylos' message. He and Vrima were talking about the capacity of their batteries when they both froze. Nick and Norina knew they were getting some kind of message; probably from Dyphus at the ship, but that must have been a long message because they remained frozen for a long time.

Finally Ner addressed Norina and Nick with their proper names. He said,

Project Anastrophe

"Miss Norina, Dr. Papas, we must beam to the ship right now; I have important news for you." Norina and Nick looked at each other wondering what kind of news Ner had for them that had changed his personality like that.

They chose a moment when people were not around and beamed themselves back to the ship. Dyphus was aware of what the news was all about and had the ship ready to go. They all gathered in the main room and Ner said,

"I have a holographic message from Dr. Dylos that you must see, and after that I will explain the protocol." Dyphus projected the message and Dr. Dylos's familiar face appeared and spoke directly to Norina,

"My Dear Norina, I wish I had more pleasant news for you and your crew, but Darna brought some very disturbing news and I must follow protocol. Ner will explain to you. Nephus and a number of his friends are preparing to take over the ship. If they succeed we will all be compromised, and as you know, I have the master code that keeps the guard robots in check. If Nephus and his conspirators take hold of this code, he will have complete control of the ship. I send this message as a precautionary measure. If he doesn't succeed, I will delete it, but if this message has reached you, that means that I have been compromised and protocol directs me to eliminate myself for the safety of the code. Therefore by default you are in charge of this ship, good luck."

Dyphus took the unit away and Ner got up and said,

"Miss Norina, I, as well as Vrima and Dyphus pledge allegiance to you. We will protect you until we are destroyed or cease to exist. I have opened all the codes sent to me by Dr. Dylos but the last one is the master code which only you can open. Once you open it, it will register automatically in your implant as well as in your mind.

Please open it right away by using your personal code number."

Norina sent her code number subliminally to the unit Ner held in his hand. The master code was transmitted subliminally to her implant and mind. It was an easy code to remember it read, "*38*", and now with Dr. Dylos dead she was the only one who knew it. All three robots shook hands with Norina and then saluted her. Then Nick shook hands with her and kissed her and said,

"I don't need to tell you that I am also one hundred percent on your side."

After a long minute of silence Norina said,

"I want to thank you all for your love and devotion. If Anastrophe One had not been compromised, I know many of its fine crew who would be far more qualified than I; but I can see Dr. Dylos' logic. I am the only human native of Z-biosphere and by default I am the last in line to have the code. Now I need your help to liberate the ship and our people in it."

Ner told Norina that she had to pick a new chief guard robot on a temporary basis until the chief guard had been liberated and was fully functional. Norina suggested he should assume that duty, but Ner said,

"Thank you, Miss Norina but I can function better as an adviser. I suggest Vrima is better equipped for this kind of duty. She is a newer model and will make a better chief of guards." Norina asked Vrima to step forward and said,

"I hereby name you, Vrima, the new robot chief of guards on a temporary basis until the chief guard is restored."

Vrima saluted Norina and Nick, and then in turn Ner and Dyphus saluted Vrima and offered their allegiance to her as the new chief of guards. Norina asked Ner to tell them the status of the Anastrophe One, and he said,

Project Anastrophe

"Dr. Dylos has sent me the present position of Anastrophe One; it is parked on the dark side of Earth's Moon. I have transmitted all the pertinent information to chief Vrima and she is now in a better position to explain the status of Anastrophe."

Vrima said,

"Now that Nephus has been deprived of having the master code, he will try to reprogram as many robots as he can. I would presume that chief guard Phylios has already been reprogrammed; therefore he is to be considered, for the time being, our archenemy. Nephus will try to reprogram the rest of the guards, one hundred and fifty of them, one at a time, which will delay him. I have estimated that by the time we are in a position to take action against him, he will have reprogrammed ten percent of the guards or fifteen of them including chief Phylios; therefore it's very important to attack as soon as possible." Nick said,

"I thought he had already taken over all the guards and the ship."

"He has, but all robots, including us here, have a defense mechanism that restores our allegiance to whoever has the master code; in this case, Miss Norina. When they are restored they will choose, among themselves, the most qualified robot to be their chief. There will be a war between the restored robots and those that have been reprogrammed."

"Then why don't we wait until most of the robots are restored and have them fight it out? Surely they can easily win over the fifteen reprogrammed robots."

"That would be an ideal way to defeat Nephus, Dr. Papas, but there are humans who will fight against our robots and robots don't like to fight humans. Nephus is an ingenious person and he can devise a way to speed up the conversion or even overcome the Master Code. He is a dangerous man and we must attack him as soon as possible." Norina asked Vrima,

"Have you devised a plan of action against Nephus?"

"As a matter of fact I have."

"Let's hear it."

"Our aim is to get to the master computer; once we are there, Miss Norina, as our new Governor, will be able to transmit the order to the unchanged robots to switch allegiance to her and then to me as the new chief of guards. Then we will fight the rest of the robots and the humans involved."

"And how are we going to gain entrance to the ship now that he has all robots and at least a portion of humans on his side? He must have the ship under strict surveillance."

"We will blind part of the electronic surveillance, attach a pod over that area, open a manhole and follow the diagram I have made. Dyphus will stay behind long enough to close the hole, and dispose off the pod. Then proceed as per plan. I am positive that we will not have any contact until we are close to our target. We will fight our way to the computer room, and give time to Governor Norina to enter the order into the computer. Once that's done the conversion will be instant, and I will be in command of the unchanged robots.

From then on it will be a matter of minutes before we defeat them." Vrima explained in detail what each one of them had to do and transmitted the appropriate schematics to their implants then she said,

"Governor, we are ready for your order to go."

Norina asked Dyphus if the ship was ready for the trip and Dyphus answered in the affirmative, then she gave the order, "Let's go." It took some time for Ner to calibrate the place and time of arrival, enough time for all of them to prepare for the attack on the Anastrophe One.

Project Anastrophe

Nick and Norina kissed and wished good luck to each other. Then they stepped into their e-Vac suits. The jump to the future was instant. Ner piloted his ship close to the mother ship in cloaked mode. Then Dyphus attached the pod onto the appointed area and quickly punched the manhole; they all lowered themselves into the ship. While Dyphus was closing the hole, Norina and Nick got out of their e-Vac suits and joined Ner and Vrima; they followed their plan to the letter.

It was nighttime and most people were asleep. Dyphus soon caught up with them and all five arrived at section D and loaded their faisers to "maim" for humans and "destroy" for robots. From now on they would have to fight their way to the computer room. Nick thought a quick prayer to St. Nicholas, the protector of seamen and spacemen in Greek culture. Then Vrima signaled them to go. What happened in the first few minutes was a perfect surprise attack designed by Vrima and executed by all five of them.

The battle started as soon as they were discovered, the alarm went off for the humans. The robots sensed the intruders right away and their faisers started spewing fire at them. The intruders returned fire in earnest but Vrima had entered a nasty virus into their faisers, one that would cause the enemy robots to slow their response time as soon as they were hit. They only slowed by milliseconds but that was enough for Vrima's group to quickly get the upper hand.

There were five faisers against ten and the number was increasing by the second. Nick and Vrima were on one side; Ner and Dyphus on the other, back to back, they formed a safe pathway for Norina to reach the computer room. Nick and Vrima went in with Norina protecting her all the way. They fought humans and robots as they were beamed into the computer room. For a while Ner and Dyphus kept the enemy at bay; but then Dyphus was hit mortally, and Ner was left alone fighting against the multitude of enemy guards. It was only a matter of seconds before he too would be overcome.

In the meantime, as Norina approached the computer there were two humans in her way; she blasted one, and the other was hit by Nick who was right behind her. She quickly entered the code into the computer and soon after that, things started to happen. Ner was overwhelmed and knew he had only seconds before he was taken down too; but then most of the robot guards froze. Ner's faiser was hot to touch but now he was fighting two humans and three robots. He quickly incapacitated the humans but most of the robots now turned against the three robots still answering to Nephus which kept on fighting--so Ner was saved. He knew most of the guards were now on his side and didn't stop them from going into the room.

Vrima was recognized by most of the robot guards as their chief. They all looked around and found the few remaining reprogrammed robots that were guarding Nephus's office.

Nephus was awakened by Phylios's holographic message,

"Master Nephus, we are being attacked and the enemy is very close to the computer room. We are trying to stop them but it's a matter of time before they gain entrance to the room. Once they are in, Miss Norina, who now has the code, will enter it into the main computer. When that happens, all the temporarily reprogrammed guards will change allegiance to her. What do you want us to do?"

"Come with all the converted guards outside of my room. How long can your guards keep the enemy away from me?"

Project Anastrophe

"I have all my fourteen guards intact, we can fight them for thirty to forty minutes before we are destroyed."

"We are going to be leaving the ship. Fight defensively, I need you and as many guards as possible to come with me. Be prepared to beam away at a moment's notice."

"Yes sir, Master Nephus."

Nephus called all his conspirators and alerted them to what was happening. He told them they had only thirty to forty minutes to leave the ship or they would all be captured. He said to Varcous,

"Pull all your human guards away from fighting and prepare the two shuttle ships for a long trip. Fill them with as many families as you can find who are sympathetic to our cause; and report to me no later than twenty-five minutes from now." Then he called Phylios and said,

"On your way to the shuttles I want you to bring with you Miss Darna and her mother whether they want to come or not. How are you doing out there?"

"So far we are O.K. but that will change very soon."

"In twenty minutes from now beam all your guards into the two shuttles."

"Yes sir, master Nephus, I will do as you say."

Nephus beamed himself into the larger shuttle along with all the necessary things he could carry, and soon after that Varcous called from the other shuttle,

"We have filled both ships with people as you requested and we are ready to go."

"Good job, Varcous, you are in charge of the ship. As soon as the guards arrive, wait for my order and then take the shuttle away following these coordinates, that's where we are going to meet, good luck."

"Good luck to you too, Nephus."

Phylios divided his guards in equal numbers for both

ships. He beamed himself to Darna's room and without even asking her, beamed her to the larger ship. He did the same with her mother, and he beamed himself there as well. Phylios immediately reported to Nephus.
"Master Nephus, we are ready to go."
"Good job, Phylios, standby for my orders."
Nephus gave the final instructions to both the shuttles and they were off.

During the battle Phylios knew that the only way he could save his robot guards from certain destruction was by fighting defensively; he did something no robot guards had done before. He used humans as shields to protect his guards. Vrima wasn't surprised with Phylios's polemic tactics but this was breaking robot protocol. "Robots must always protect humans under their charge."
Vrima could see that Nephus had tampered with Phylios's noetics, which was highly forbidden, but she also knew Nephus had no moral guidelines.
The humans in front of the guards were mostly women and children, and she gave strict orders to her guards not to shoot, unless they were absolutely sure they were shooting at the guards. After she suffered a few losses she ordered her guards to go into defensive tactics. She was sorry to see the enemy robot guards beam away, but she was glad not to have to shoot the enemy through the humans.

Nick and Norina were relieved to have taken the ship back but sad to have found Dr. Dylos and other important people dead. Norina called a meeting with what was left of Dr. Dylos's government. The first thing on her agenda was what to do with Nephus and all the people he had taken with him. She asked Ner to give her a list of the people and robot guards who were missing. Ner told her fifteen guards and

Project Anastrophe

one hundred and ninety one humans of all ages, including Nephus and Darna, were gone.

He also told her that ten men had been killed, and thirty people of all ages injured. There were seventeen destroyed robot guards and nine damaged including Dyphus. Norina was sad about Dyphus but hoped he could be repaired. She asked Dr. Lozinei, who specialized in spaceship engineering, to comment on the two shuttles that had been taken away and how far they could travel in space.

"The shuttles are built for interplanetary voyages for people and cargo; they can go into hyperdrive speed but not for long distances. However they can be modified to go farther."

"Where do you think they might have gone?"

"They have a lot of people and they are going to need adequate food provisions and material, so I would venture to say they have gone to Earth."

"Then why can't we detect their signature anywhere?"

"This puzzles me too, because it's very hard to hide or delete the signatures of so many people and so much machinery. Nephus must be a very smart man."

"He is, but we can't let him stay on Earth with so many people, it's against our "Prime Directive." We must capture them and bring them back here as soon as we can."

"We can do that, but first we have to find their signatures."

"Dr. Lozinei, can you work on it?"

"Yes, Miss Norina, we will let you know as soon as possible."

Norina discussed the status of the ship and the importance of restructuring the government and of having the democratic system reestablished. She said,

"I would like to express my sorrow for those who lost their lives on both sides. I hope that we will eventually find the other people and bring them back to our ship. Now I have to show you the message I received from Dr. Dylos before I go any further."

Ner, as usual, placed the unit in the center of the floor and this time Dr. Dylos' life-sized 3-D image appeared in the middle of the room. All the people saw and heard his message except the code numbers. Then Norina said again,

"As you can see, Dr. Dylos entrusted me with the ship's security code; he also wanted me to take over Anastrophe One once we liberated it. But now I have to follow protocol and ask for your vote of confidence." She asked Ner to explain the modus operandi. Ner went on to describe how it's done and what procedures to follow. He ended by saying,

"If Miss Norina does not receive the required sixty-five percent of the vote of confidence you will have to elect another person as your next Governor. You may start voting now."

There was a lot of hushed talk around and finally the leader, whom the people had chosen to announce the results, got up and said,

"Miss Norina, the people of Anastrophe One have given you one hundred percent of their votes."

Then Ner stepped forward and said,

"Miss Norina, the people of Anastrophe One have chosen you to be their next Governor. I must now inform you that the law requires you to choose your Vice-Governor. I must also inform you that you may not choose a robot under any circumstances. If you find it difficult to choose one now, you may choose a friend or relative you trust, but he or she must be voted in by the people."

"I wish to nominate my husband, Nick Papas, for Vice Governor. He has risked his life many times to save our planet and now again to save Anastrophe One. I know that

Project Anastrophe

in my absence he would execute the duties of Governor as well as I would."

Ner explained how they had to go about choosing a Vice-Governor and the people voted to elect Nick Papas. But this time some people had second thoughts about electing a close relative. Nevertheless Nick got eighty percent of their votes and he was now Norina's second-in-command. She couldn't have been happier.

In the next few days there would be more meetings to elect cabinet members for her new government. But for now the meeting was adjourned.

Chapter 16

The two shuttles were on their way to the coordinates they had been given, and it didn't take long for those in charge to realize that they were going to the planet Earth. Both shuttles landed, in cloaked mode, in Northern California near a wooded area close to what used to be Golden Gate Park.

Nephus gave the guards special electronic devices which were placed in and around the two shuttles. He told them that these units would cover their presence here on Earth, at least for a while, from Anastrophe One.

All guards were put on high alert security mode and people settled down to rest for the day. Tomorrow promised to be a busy day indeed.

Project Anastrophe

Next day Nephus called his closest associates to meet him in his office. He asked Varcous to report on the status of the two ships.

"How are we doing with our necessary supplies in food and other material?"

"The supplies kept for each shuttle are for fifty people for one month at the most. We have one hundred people and eight robot guards on the shuttle you command and ninety-one people and seven robot guards on the one I command. On both shuttles we have one hundred and ninety-one people of all ages and fifteen robots. We also have a few animals that I have not counted yet. Depending how long we are going to be here, we are going to need more food and other material."

"We cannot stay here too long; sooner or later we are going to be discovered by Anastrophe and we are not in a position to fight them and win. We need to retrofit the shuttles for a long trip. We must go to another planet far enough in the galaxy so they won't find us. Later we will see what we can do. I propose to get enough food provisions and material; then go to a place out of the way and do all the required retrofitting for the long journey deep into the galaxy."

"We have with us Dr. Philip Zenon, Dr. Thomas Nerios, and Dr. James Lafkoscky; all three specialize in space ship engineering. We also have Dr. Joan Greenferos, who is an institutional dietician and nutrition specialist, and Dr. Liana Vanderburgh who is a sociologist."

"I suppose we need to ask you gentlemen to tell us what is entailed in retrofitting the two shuttles." Dr. Zenon responded,

"First we have to update and reprogram our nanotechnology to rebuild these two shuttles; then we will know what kind of material we need to have with us and where we can get it. We need to design the ships for a long journey into deep space."

Dr. Nerios elaborated on the design of the ships,
"We have to incorporate the two ships into one, with an artificial sun and a heliotropic garden to supply us with vegetables and adequate oxygen. It will take far less time to rebuild the two shuttles into one bigger ship than to work on them separately; also it will give us more space in the middle."

Dr. James Lafkoscky spoke about the need to enlarge the ship.

"Having so many people in a small space on such a long voyage will be very difficult to say the least. We need to enlarge the size of the ship to about half the size of the Anastrophe One." Nephus said,

"We will do whatever it takes to do the job. The only question I have is; where do we find all the material we need, Dr. Lafkoscky?"

"We have already located enough raw material to satisfy our Nanos for a long time."

"And how about other provisions such as food and water?" Dr. Joan Greenferos answered that question saying,

"Again all we need is enough raw material. The Nanos will micro size it into its basic elements which will last for many generations. As for water, we will get enough and then re-circulate it. Also as we go on we will find M-type planets to replenish our raw material as needed."

"Dr. Vanderburgh, do you have anything else to contribute to all this?"

"We need to have some kind of political structure to maintain order in the ship."

"This matter is too complicated to deal with at this time. We will work on it once we are on our way; in the meantime I am in charge of these two ships and my guards

Project Anastrophe

and I will keep things in order. Thank you all. I will let you know when it's safe for us to go out."

That didn't go well with Dr. Vanderburgh, but at this point there was not much she could do.

Darna told Phylios that she and her mother didn't wish to go with them wherever they were going and she reached for her faiser, but Phylios quickly beamed her and her mother to Nephus's shuttle. Darna and her mother found themselves among many other people who had been beamed, like them, into the shuttle. The move was unexpected for most of them and they were trying to find out what had happened and where they were going. Minutes later Nephus's voice was heard simultaneously on both shuttles,

"Ladies and gentlemen, a short time ago we were attacked by Anastrophe Two. It was a surprise attack and they were able to compromise our defenses and take over Anastrophe One. Our only course of action was to abandon ship with as many people on our shuttles as possible; we are now on our way to Earth."

The message stopped as abruptly as it had started. Darna was furious with Nephus.

"Son of a bitch, you are not going to get away with this." Her mother looked tired and disoriented.

"Come on, Mother, let's go to the lobby where everybody seems to be gathering." The situation there was chaotic. Children were crying and people murmured in fear and confusion. Finally some people who seemed to represent the authorities came in and said,

"Those of you who have young children and those with older people come closer and state your names."

Darna waited patiently until most people had moved forward, then she followed with her mother. The people in charge were allocating rooms for the needy. When Darna said who they were, there was a little hushed talk between the two officials, then a young woman said,

"Please follow me." They followed her; finally she stopped at the end of the hallway, opened a door and said,

"This is going to be your place for the time being."

The room was almost as nice as the one Darna had in Anastrophe One, and she realized that Nephus had something to do with it. It had all the comforts one would need. She helped her mother to bed and then she sat down with a cup of coffee to gather her thoughts.

By the time they landed on Earth, people on both shuttles had a temporary place to stay, and were anxious to know what would happen next. Nephus let the people and the crew settle down for a while, always making sure they were not detected by Anastrophe One or the people on Earth.

On the third day, he called his close associates and several chosen scientists to a meeting. He started by asking Varcous to report on the status of the two shuttles.

"We have enough food and water for everybody for two weeks. The living quarters are a little tight, but people think this is only temporary and they will be moving out to live permanently on Earth, so they are not complaining at this time."

"I wish we could live on Earth, but as long as we have Anastrophe One after us, we have to get away to a place where they can't find us. Then after they go away, as they are planning to, we will come back to Earth. In the meantime we need to get the necessary material for a larger spaceship, and enough food and water for our long trip. But for now, let the people think we are planning to stay on Earth until we finish the repairs on the ship."

The rest of the scientists submitted their lists for the

Project Anastrophe

material needed for the construction of the new ship, and it was decided they should go and get it the next day.

Dr. Zenon suggested a team should be sent to Brazil to find a suitable site in the Amazon forest, and beam everything there. After that both shuttles should fly there too. Everybody thought that was a good idea, and it was decided to leave early next morning.

They located various kinds of groceries in warehouses in San Leandro city, and building materials for the ship in warehouses in Oakland and Richmond cities. They found vegetable outside of Salinas city.

Next morning four different groups left the two shuttles; they were protected by electronic umbrellas devised by Nephus to conceal them from Anastrophe One. One group was beamed to the Amazon in Brazil, where they found an area well camouflaged by high trees with no humans around. They veiled that area with a special electronic blanket, making it completely undetectable from Anastrophe One.

The other three groups beamed to their designated areas and found what they needed. Everything was beamed away undetected, even though there were many people in the warehouses working the nightshift. When all the material had been beamed to the chosen site, Nephus gave the order for the two shuttles to go there too.

There was a huge pile of groceries and other material. Many of the people working the nightshift would have to answer for all those stolen goods.

The first thing the crew did was to build a high fence with a huge electronic canopy above it. This made them invisible from their archenemy. People were now able to step outside the shuttles as long as they stayed within the fence. With enough raw materials the Nanos got busy building temporary housing for everybody according to their needs, then they began putting the two shuttles together. Other Nanos worked on converting all the fresh food down to its basic components, and then reconstituted and micro-sized it to different forms, which would enable it to last for long periods of time. Then all the food was packaged in different sized boxes and put into a warehouse. There was enough food to feed an army for many years.

It had taken them two weeks to build the housing and once they moved all the people into their temporary quarters, the work on the shuttles started right away.

In another two weeks, with billions of Nanos working day and night, the spaceship was built to both Dr. Zenon's and Dr. Nerios's satisfaction. There were frequent forays into the woods by both humans and robots, bringing fresh food for the small community.

The departure day was approaching and Nephus was getting very uneasy; he needed Darna's company so much. With Darna by his side, life would be a lot easier. He missed the old days and the nice times they spent together, but he didn't want to push his luck and go to see her. He knew she was mad at him; and she would never forgive him for abducting her and her mother. But he also knew Darna would never have gone with him on her own initiative. He loved her so much, and he couldn't possibly go anywhere without her. Perhaps in time she would come around and forgive him and they could be lovers once more.

Darna and her mother were treated very well; even in the temporary housing they were given a spacious room with all the comforts, but they would have been a lot happier in Anastrophe One. She believed in what Dr. Dylos was doing. Earth needed help, and the best way was to confront the alien enemy before they came to Earth. They needed weapons to match the aliens', and most scientists

Project Anastrophe

knew that they could not accomplish that on Earth, no matter how much time they had. They traveled to the future and saw how advanced in weaponry the aliens were, and even with all the human bravery, the humans were losing the battle. It was only a matter of time before Earth was taken over by the aliens.

Nephus was power-hungry, an egomaniac, and his way would not succeed, no matter how much he or generations in the future would try. For better or worse Project Anastrophe had changed the course Earth was taking. There was a slower pace now and the lack of nuclear weapons, although it saved them in the first place, also made them more vulnerable to a future alien enemy.

People would make nuclear weapons again to fight the aliens, but it would be too little and too late, and by using nuclear weapons they would contaminate Earth once more, even if they won the war.

The aliens used massive destructive power without destroying the environment; they were an older civilization and had learned their lesson earlier, or perhaps they were looking for a cleaner homeland. Either way Earth was for the humans and Dr. Dylos had the right plan to save it. Now he was dead, but whoever was in charge, sooner or later would pursue and find them. Darna was sure of that, but she couldn't understand why it had taken so long.

Nephus called for a community gathering and tried, as best he could, to explain their predicament. He said,

"I would like to inform you that we have been forced to change plans to stay on Earth for now. The Anastrophe One is after us, and at this time we are not in a position of strength to fight them and win. We think it would be wise for us to move away from here to another planet, and wait until they leave from the Moon on their scheduled trip to the alien planet.

This will take weeks, perhaps months. After they leave, they will never bother us in our lifetime and perhaps many of our generations in the future.

We have managed to hide our whereabouts so far, and I am sure we can do that for the foreseeable future if we get away from here. Otherwise, it will be a matter of time before they find us and then we will be forced to go with them.

Our plan is to find an M-type planet and wait there until they leave; then we can come back and stay home on Earth where we belong."

There were many questions from the floor about their ability to fly into deep space and find an M-type planet. Some asked if they had enough food and fuel for such an endeavor, however the scientists sounded very encouraging. They told them they had built a spaceship capable of taking them anywhere in the galaxy. Not only did they have enough food for the duration, but they would be able to find more food and other fuel and material out there.

The only strong objection came from Darna. She said,

"We are wasting our time and their time. Sooner or later they will find us and we will go with them. What we are doing is unethical; we should be trying to help people on Earth, not take advantage of them with our superior technology and know-how." She stressed the fact that Anastrophe One would never let them stay here and would even destroy them rather than let them interfere with the status-quo. There were a few people beginning to have second thoughts and they asked difficult questions making Nephus nervous.

The last few days the little community had been living in the spaceship in their permanent quarters. The Nanos had been dismembering their temporary dwellings in the forest and converting them into basic material which was put in special storerooms to be used again. Everything was left as it had been found; the only thing still remaining was the pro-

Project Anastrophe

tective canopy. Finally it too was removed and the spaceship with all its occupants took off in a shroud of secrecy.

The first few minutes were "nail-biting" for the crew on the bridge, but Nephus had devised a special cloaking mode which kept the ship undetected by Anastrophe One. After they had passed the dangerous area they all felt relaxed. "Dyplopherus", with its shiny outer shell, thrust into the dark lonely space seeking an M-type planet on which to hide.

It was a beautiful and spacious vessel, cleverly built to host and maintain a small community with all the comforts of a city. The artificial solarium in the middle of the craft provided the much needed space for a huge garden which would supply them with food and oxygen. A park next to the garden offered room for children to play and for grownups to walk about. The artificial gravity was especially made to give one the feeling of living on Earth. All the cabins were built large enough to fulfill every need. Even Darna admired what they had done with the newly built spaceship. She and her mother were given spacious quarters and had no reason to complain.

There was a new generation of specially built androids to maintain the ship inside and out. As Darna and her mother sat in the park enjoying the sunshine from high above at the apex of the solarium, they could see the androids busily planting the new crop of vegetables. Everything looked and felt so organized and she was beginning to think perhaps Nephus could pull it off, at least with the first phase of his plan. But she knew somewhere out there the scouts of Anastrophe One were looking for them. There was no doubt in her mind about that.

As soon as he felt they were out of the dangerous area, Nephus asked for a general report on the status of "Dyplopherus".

Chapter 17

Nick and Norina had a much needed rest from the latest battle and the election procedure which resulted in Norina's election as Governor and Nick's as Vice Governor. The last few hours had taken a toll on both of them. In their room Norina began to sob uncontrollably. Nick became alarmed with her behavior and asked,
"What's the matter?"
"I have never seen so many people die in battle. How could Nephus program his robots to kill humans? I can still see the terror on their faces."
"Nephus has no respect for human life; he is a desperate man and will do anything to save his skin and achieve his goal, whatever it may be. He is a dangerous man and we must capture him before he harms anymore people."

Project Anastrophe

Nick held Norina's face in both hands, kissed her and said,

"Take heart, Norina, you are now the Governor of this small community; you have a big job ahead of you and you must show them what a good leader you are. The people are tired and discouraged and they will be looking to you for guidance and purpose in their lives. You can't afford to lose heart at this important juncture."

"I suppose you are right, Nick. I must be strong; you are always there when I need you, thank you."

Vrima gave orders to her guard robots and humans to move all the wounded to the hospital and those salvageable robots to the recovery shop. The unsalvageable robots were taken to the scrap pile; the dead humans to the mortuary.

Vrima was in her element, she was doing what she was made to do. She was a soldier warrior, and tactician. She was omnipresent and methodic. Ner knew he would never be like her. She was made of the right stuff--he had chosen well.

But like Norina, Vrima needed Ner for crucial programming and advice; he would always be the only other robot she could trust. Ner and Vrima, whenever it was possible, would go and charge their depleted batteries together. That was their equivalent of candle light and wine, and if there was love in her cybernetics she was in love with Ner.

Next day Norina met with her new government.

"I would like to welcome you all. This Government was formed under rather unusual circumstances due to the fact that our beloved Dr. Dylos took his own life to protect the code entrusted to him. I can assure you that I will protect that code with my life too. Right from the start we are confronted with two important situations; one is to apprehend Nephus and his conspirators and bring them to justice, the other is to continue building the Anastrophe for the big voyage to the alien planet according to the plan voted and passed by Dr. Dylos's Government.

I think it's important to start with finding the two shuttles, and for that I would like to ask chief Vrima to bring us up-to date."

"As soon as they left, I sent my guards after them but we were unable to find their signatures. I am afraid Nephus has used a very ingenious scrambling device to make them and their shuttles undetectable. They must have gone to Earth for supplies and that's where we are concentrating all our efforts for now."

"We must not allow Nephus and his group to settle on Earth under any circumstances; keep looking until you find them."

"Governor Norina, I am positive that sooner or later we will unscramble their signature and find them. They cannot stay on Earth for too long.

Next Norina turned her attention to several of the scientists who were present and asked them how they were progressing with the building of the Anastrophe One spaceship. They said they had been able to find material on the moon but needed more from Mars and Earth to complete their project.

It was agreed that anything else needed from Earth would be taken from different states so that it wouldn't be noticed right away. They spent a few more hours discussing other matters having to do with the well-being of the people; then adjourned for the day. As they were stepping out, Nick said to Norina,

"I was proud of you, Norina. You acted like a "pro" on this first day."

Project Anastrophe

"I don't know if I was a "pro" or not but I felt that we accomplished a lot. What worries me is Nephus and his gang; we can't leave here until we find them."

"Don't let that worry you, I am sure Vrima and Ner will find a way to get them very soon."

"I hope you are right, Nick."

They walked to the cafeteria to have something to eat, and were met with friendly smiles. Norina was even more determined to be a good leader for the people.

For the last forty days, drones sent by Vrima had been combing the planet Earth with no luck in finding the whereabouts of the two shuttles and the people in them. But today the scrambling changed to a faster broadcast and a higher pitch indicating wherever they were, they were moving---then it stopped broadcasting.

Vrima knew they had left Earth but didn't know where they had gone at this time. It didn't take her team long to analyze the time and the place of change. They zeroed in on that particular spot which took them to The Brazilian Amazon. After they thoroughly combed that area, they discovered the shuttles had been there all the time.

After a closer examination, coupled with analysis of fresh excavations of nearby areas, they deduced that not only were they hiding there, they were also building their ships.

Vrima requested an urgent meeting with Norina and Nick. They met at Norina's office and Vrima said,

"I have good and bad news about the shuttles and the people. The good news is that we found out where they had been hiding all this time; they were in the Brazilian Amazon. The bad news is they have left Earth and are traveling somewhere into deep space, perhaps to find a more suitable place to hide."

"What are you prepared to do, Vrima?"

George Karnikis

"Just as we are planning to gather the appropriate material for building Anastrophe One, so have they already done. They took what they needed from some industrial places on Earth and they also got enough food, I am sure of that.

Our understanding is that they have rebuilt their shuttles or perhaps built them into one, for better control and speed needed out in space. They are either going to some place to wait for us to leave and then come back to Earth, or they now have the capability to travel far enough into space and find an M-type planet and settle there.

We are going to find them wherever they go, but we must either upgrade our search shuttles or wait until we have re-built the Anastrophe One and then go after them. Either way we will find them, they can't get away from us."

Norina told the community,

"Chief Vrima has informed me that she has located the place where Nephus and his group had being hiding all this time; but I am going to let her tell you the particulars of her findings."

Vrima went on to tell them the same story she had told Norina and Nick. There were a few questions and answers between Vrima and members of the government as well as the scientists. Then Norina said,

"As you can see, Nephus has outsmarted us once more. The question is, how long will we play this "cat and mouse" game? Chief Vrima is telling us we need to upgrade our search shuttles or go after them with the Anastrophe One when it is finished being rebuilt. What I would like to know is; which is the most appropriate way to go about it?"

Dr. Ingous Vlasik, the engineer in charge of rebuilding Anastrophe One, readily gave an answer to Norina,

Project Anastrophe

"Governor, it would be a waste of time and material to upgrade the shuttles; it would be more to the point to go after them when we've finished the Anastrophe One."

"Please correct me if I am wrong, but it seems to me it will take weeks or months to finish building the Anastrophe One and with the speed they are traveling we will never catch up with them."

"Our warp drive will be far superior to theirs and once we trace their signature we will find them within minutes."

Vrima interjected,

"Governor, I agree with Dr. Vlasik. Once we know where they are, time and speed will be on our side."

Dr. Vlasik, along with others in charged of the expedition, submitted lists of various materials needed for the completion of the upgrade and preparation for the long voyage. Several teams were formed to go and find them on the moon, Earth, and the nearby planet, Mars.

There was no need for temporary housing on the Moon; there was ample space in Anastrophe One and especially after so many had left with Nephus. People would be moved around all during the rebuilding of the vessel, but it would be far better than building on the surface of the Moon.

However it was necessary to build a shop on the surface of the Moon and materials were brought in. There were huge components built in there and then attached to the main ship. With every new attachment Anastrophe began to look like a large city. Finally after two months of continuous work the Nanos and humans completed the job.

The new Anastrophe was ten times bigger than the first one and now looked more like a small biosphere than a spaceship. But it was a spaceship capable of flying through the galaxy and beyond. It was equipped with the latest weapons, including nuclear bombs, and now that they were away from Earth, they wouldn't hesitate to use them if they had to. The cabins had all the comforts. They now had a parliament, a city hall, parks, gardens, and a solarium that was ten times bigger than the one on Dyplopherus.

The shape of the new Anastrophe One looked nothing like the first one. It now looked like a huge saucer designed especially for long warp drive jumps. After being tossed and moved around so many times, the people were happy to live in such luxurious quarters.

For the last two months Nick and Norina, whenever they could, would be dressed in overalls and would go around the ship talking to the people and being part of the community. They mingled with the workers and were available to anyone who needed them. They were well liked by all and that made them feel happy and useful.

The next day, Dr. Vlasik found Norina in one of her usual working sessions. He told her officially that the Anastrophe One and Two were ready for their separate voyages. Norina asked him to stay and participate in the coming session because she thought he would be needed. At the meeting Nick said,

"Before we leave for the aliens' planet, we need to have certain things from them. In order to get those things we need to go to the thirtieth century at the time the aliens are attacking Earth. From the last drone we sent, we learned the aliens have come from the center of our own Galaxy. We don't know precisely where their planet is. We cannot get that kind of information from a drone.

There are two things we must have from them; information as to where their planet is, and several of their powerful weapons.

We know we can't reproduce their weapons here on Earth because we don't have the kind of materials they have used. We are unable to find these materials on the

Project Anastrophe

neighboring planets, and have no alternative but to go to their planet.

I am going to be in charge of this expedition but I am going to let chief Vrima explain our trip into the future."

Vrima projected a few pictures of the aliens' ships, and then she said,

"We have rebuilt our Anastrophe Two into a powerful warship, just for this purpose. But as you can see, the aliens have more and better ships, so we are not in a position to fight them; we can at best defend ourselves. What we want to do is to get into their data base and retrieve as much information as we can. Our scientists have devised a program which can do that with ease from within the safety of our ship. The next thing we need to do will be much harder; we have to actually steal several of their weapons.

We have a plan for that too. All we have to do is to survive our expedition and come back with the weapons and enough information about their home world. We must be ready to defend ourselves the minute we jump into the future because we might appear right in the midst of their fire exchange.

Another thing that may work against us is the fact that we are not going to be known by either the Earth people or the aliens so it is possible that we might be hit by both of them.

I have enough robot fighters, but I need human volunteers and I have no doubt that we will have a full crew by the time we are ready to leave."

Nick spoke again to the legislators and the scientists and asked them if they had any questions. Nick and Vrima answered a few of the questions which came from the floor and then Governor Norina thanked everybody and especially those who had helped with the rebuilding of both ships. She then wished good luck to those who were about to jump into the future and brought the meeting to an end.

On the way back to their place Norina said to Nick,

"I believe this trip to the future is going to be one of the most dangerous you have made so far, Nick, and I am terrified that you may not make it back safely. I don't think I can carry on without you, so please, be careful and come back to me--do you hear me?"

"Don't worry, we are going to be extremely careful and will be back safe and sound, I promise you that."

Nick managed to get enough volunteers eager to sacrifice their lives for the cause, and when the time came to leave, the whole community gathered to wish them good luck and a speedy and safe return.

Vrima had prepared everybody for battle engagement and when Nick asked her if she was ready she said,

"We are as ready as we can be."

Then Nick gave the order and within seconds they jumped to the thirtieth century.

They arrived at nighttime and immediately went into cloaked mode. Evidently both humans and aliens were in cloaked mode too, but one could see the terrific beating Earth had sustained. There were fires in many places. But humans were fighting back. Every once in a while one could see explosions in space. Nick asked Vrima,

"Have we been detected yet?"

"I don't think so, but I am sure they know there is something close to them and they are trying to find out what it is. So far we are confusing both sides because we flip in and out in time sequence from past to future in different locations. We have a very small window of opportunity to do what we need to do. I am sure that sooner or later they are going to discover our mode of cloaking and we will be attacked possibly by both sides---we must hurry!"

Project Anastrophe

"How large is the enemy fleet?"

Vrima asked one of the crew to show Nick the enemy fleet on a screen. Although they were under cloaked mode, Nick could see the forms of many huge ships, hundreds of times bigger than their Anastrophe One, with thousands of small ships flying in and out from them, in infrared color forms. It was an immense concentration of power, one which Earth could not possibly defeat.

Earth was fighting a defensive war but it was a losing battle. Occasionally they inflicted great damage on the enemy but it slowed them only temporarily.

To their horror, the crew of Anastrophe Two quickly discovered the humans were using nuclear weapons in space; it was one of them that hit one of the mother ships inflicting major damage, but the damage on Earth appeared to be far greater.

Vrima told Nick,

"The Nanos are ready to go. We wait for your order."

Without hesitation Nick said,

"Let them loose and brace yourselves for attack!"

Two clouds of Nanos were released to two different destinations. The "katascopic",(spy agents), traced one of the incoming alien fighter ships and imbedded themselves in its outer skin then quickly neutralized themselves temporarily to pass the possible filtration check up. Once they had gained entrance into the mother ship, millions of them dispersed in singular entities all through the ship gathering information. Within minutes they went out the same way they had come in, and quickly found their way back to Anastrophe Two where they deposited themselves in a special decontamination unit.

The other cloud of Nanos was especially programmed to identify and retrieve missiles and bombs from their destructive mission to Earth. Once they attached themselves to the outer skin of the missiles and bombs, they drilled themselves inside and disarmed them. They caused the weapons to make a loop close to Earth, then drove horizontally and up again towards Anastrophe Two where they were held in a safe place for later examination.

Many of the aliens' ships containing nanos were destroyed by missiles from Earth, but the Nanos always dislodged on time and went back to the ship where they were promptly decontaminated. Once they had enough of the aliens' missiles and bombs, the chase and retrieval were over.

The first attack on them came from the aliens who now identified them as an enemy ship, and attacked with all their might. As though that wasn't enough, there were missiles directed at them by humans from Earth, as well. For a moment Nick thought it was all over, but their ship proved to be a technological marvel. Its shield held during those crucial first minutes which gave them enough time to maneuver out of that time zone and into the past. Although they managed to escape the humans, the aliens quickly adapted to their strategy and followed them in time-travel too.

Nick pushed his ship into many space-time epochs only to be followed persistently by the aliens.
Nick looked for Vrima but she was nowhere to be found. Now that he most needed her, she wasn't there. He had to make a quick decision; if he took the ship back to the time and place where the Anastrophe One was, he was sure that between the two of them they could destroy the aliens; but then there would be other aliens after them and that would put both ships in grave danger.

There were fifteen superior ships after them, and it was only a matter of time now before he would lose his ship crew. But Nick wasn't going down without a fight. He turned his ship around, said a quick prayer to St Nicolas, the

Project Anastrophe

protector of travelers, and thought of all his loved ones. Then he gave the order to shoot back at the enemy. The guards obeyed and there started a fight against impossible odds.

The aliens were caught by surprise when his ship turned around and started firing. They lost two of their ships but quickly reformed, and now all thirteen of them were coming at him.

There was one thing left for him to do. There would be one more missile fired from the Anastrophe Two; a powerful nuclear bomb would explode between the Anastrophe and the aliens and they would all be vaporized, but the Anastrophe One would survive with all its people to try again---this time without him and his crew.

Nick was about to push the button when Vrima shouted,

"Stop---there is another way."

"It better be quick because we won't last more than a few minutes."

"That's all we need---a few minutes and we will save our ship."

"I am putting the ship on automatic self-destruct in five minutes."

"That will be enough, Commander."

Nick ordered the bomb's time recalibrated to five minutes delay, but this time he put it on an automatic self-destruct mode, and for the next few minutes started a "cat and mouse" chase. Nick had one of the best navigators in his implant advising him how best to evade the enemy.

He jumped from epoch to epoch, releasing awesome power behind him, but the aliens were just as determined to destroy him. In any dimensional sequence in which he appeared they would be right behind him and would hit him with superior weaponry. He only managed to be a split second ahead of the aliens using evasive maneuvering.

He had caused great damage to some of the alien's ships, but he also sustained damage to his own ship resulting in the death of several of the humans. Many of his robots were completely destroyed. Now the ship's shield was down to thirty percent, leaving it unprotected for the most part.

A few minutes earlier Vrima realized that the only way to survive the alien's attack was to use Nephus' cloaking device and she went to see Dr. Ingous Vlasik. A week before they left for this expedition, Vrima asked to find out what kind of cloaking Nephus had used to avoid being detected for so long. She gave him the forensic results of several items they had left in the jungle of the Amazon.

The two Anastrophes were finished and now Dr. Vlasik was able to work on it right away. He was fascinated by what he found. The more he worked on the forensic results the more interesting it became. This Nephus person was unquestionably a genius, too bad he is not working for us---what a waste.

Nephus had devised an entirely different mode of cloaking, one that had never been done before; no wonder they couldn't be found anywhere. He had actually changed the photons into metaphotons thereby altering the basic molecularity of light. This resulted momentarily in a void of space encompassing his spaceship or an area in which he wanted to hide. It was the perfect cloaking mode.

Dr. Vlasik now knew the concept of it, but only in theory. He still had to build the mechanism to make this a reality. When he was asked to join Nick's crew he took this project with him and hoped he'd have enough time to work on it. But he had a long way to go before it could be done. He was in his shop when Vrima burst through the door and said,

Project Anastrophe

"Dr. Vlasik, how far along are you in completing that new cloaking device?"

"It will take a while before it's done---why?

"Because unless we find a better way to escape, the aliens will destroy us in a very short time. There are fifteen enemy ships after us and so far anything we have tried on them has failed. Is there anything you can do to hide us from them?"

"How much longer can you fight them?"

"No more than fifteen minutes if we are lucky, after that, we will have to follow protocol and destroy our ship along with all the enemy ships."

"I will try to find a way, but you are not giving me enough time for such a project. I will require your help."

Dr. Vlasik was an ingenious man in his own right, but he had never found himself in a situation like this. He knew he had to find a short cut to make this project work at least temporarily, but to do that in fifteen minutes was asking too much, but he had to try; there was no other way out. He asked Vrima to work on some difficult equations and she was more than ready to oblige. Her bionic brain came up with the answers within seconds. He then asked his crew to make certain implements and they started right away. Now if Vrima's answers to his equations were right there was a possibility to create a temporary disturbance in space and time using Nephus's theory of metaphotons. He quickly applied his theory, and then asked Vrima to go up to the bridge and prepare the ship to go into warp drive on his mark, which would be in about five minutes.

Nick tried heroically to keep his ship from being destroyed, it was being battered on all sides and those five minutes felt like eons. Vrima had informed him about being prepared to jump to warp drive and he was about to push the button to destruction or the button to warp drive, the situation was worsening by the second. Finally Vrima said, "Commander, go to warp drive now!"

In a split second, time stopped and all things went into slow motion, everything morphed into elongated objects including human bodies. It was a long moment in a void, and then, everything came back to order; all the electronic apparatus started to function again and although people felt like zombies for the first few seconds, they quickly recovered.

When the crew looked outside they could only see a polychrome light, one moment shooting every which way; another moment rolling like huge light waves.

They were ready to resume the fight if needed or go into self-destruct mode. All eyes and instruments were combing the area around them. Before the latest jump, anytime the Anastrophe Two would make an evasive maneuver, seconds later the aliens would be right behind them; this time they could not be seen anywhere. It appeared that whatever Dr. Vlasik had done, had worked, but that didn't satisfy Vrima. She said to Nick,

"Commander, we need to be absolutely sure that the aliens have lost us, I propose to send several drones to investigate the area."

"I agree with you Chief Vrima, make it so."

Four drones were immediately sent to thoroughly scout the area, but found no signature of the alien's vessels. Nick breathed more easily and for the first time he thought perhaps they might make it home after all. Vrima also thought they had successfully escaped and were out of danger but she suggested, as a precautionary measure, that they should go back home using different epochs in time for extra security.

Nick calibrated three different arrival times consecutively through 29th, 27th, 26th, centuries and finally back

Project Anastrophe

home to the 25th century. During the four different arrivals they did not see the aliens and they felt quite sure they now were safe.

As soon as they arrived home, Dr. Vlasik uncloaked the Anastrophe Two, and the community was happy to have them back although they could see the ship was badly damaged. They knew they had to expect fatalities and many wounded.

Vrima handed Nick a list of the losses they had suffered and he was surprised they didn't have more dead and wounded. They had lost three young men and one young woman. Eleven men and seven women were wounded; some of them in pretty bad shape, but their biggest loss was in robots. Seventeen had been completely destroyed and thirty needed to be repaired. Nick knew it would be very hard to tell the parents of the dead about the loss of their loved ones, when he had only sustained bruises and scratches. But as sad as he felt, he thought it could have been a lot worse.

The Anastrophe Two was taken inside the mother ship where the wounded were treated at the hospital and the dead were taken to the mortuary. The ship would have to undergo extensive repairs.

Governor Norina grieved for all the losses they had suffered but she also told them how happy she was to have them back home. Norina was careful not to show any emotion when she welcomed them. But after Nick was released from the hospital and they went into their quarters she hugged him and said,

"I am so glad you are back. Vrima gave me a report of what happened to you out there and when I saw how damaged the ship was I thought the worst---how are you feeling?"

"I feel much better now that I am here but there were times I thought I would never see you again. If it wasn't for Dr. Vlasik and his incredible cloaking device we would all have gone."

"In a way we should also be thankful to Nephus for his invention."

"That's true, but it also makes him all the more dangerous."

Nick felt lucky to be home, close to Norina. The last few hours had been especially difficult for him. He had never shouldered such responsibility. The dead and wounded and the loss of robots were going through his mind when Norina took his hand, held it tight in her hand and walked with him to their bedroom, there he lost himself for the night in the arms of his beloved Norina.

In the last two weeks the whole community had been preparing for the long voyage. Because of their experience with the aliens, they had now armed Anastrophe One to resemble a floating fortress. Dr. Vlasik and his staff worked around the clock checking all the data and the weapons they had taken from the alien ships. They were well on their way to discover their technology and copy it.

They made changes to their weaponry by incorporating the alien technology and their weapons were now more powerful. But they were unable to copy the alien weapons for lack of material. They also had difficulty in deciphering their language; but finally after many days of hard work they broke the code. It was amazing what a treasure they found.

The aliens were an old and very advanced species, a humanoid genus, one that had many things in common with the humans on Earth. They were bipedal and decadactilous, (ten digits), they breathed oxygen, had pale yellow skin, two

Project Anastrophe

light brown eyes, two large pointed ears, and almost no nose except for two large holes above their very small mouths. They had unusually long necks, with unproportionally large heads, and were about one and one half meters tall. They were far advanced from the humans of the thirtieth century in literature and technology.

Governor Norina set a special investigating committee to find relevant information before the voyage started. Within a week they were able to find specifically where the alien planet was. They came from a planet called Voursa in the Pleiades cluster named "The Seven Sisters" by the ancient Greeks. The Pleiades are identified as M45, Mell 22 14 degrees Northwest of Aldebaran and around the magnitude 4.1 star Merope 23 Tauris. Voursa is about the size of Earth and in statistical terms is as follows: its Troposphere, (0km-13 km.) Ozone Layer, (13 km -24km)

Stratosphere, (23km-48km. Mesosphere, (48km – 70 km.) Thermosphere, (74 km – 145km.) the solid Voursa biosphere is composed of water, organic substances, skeletal matter, and plants and animals.

Its Hydrosphere is fresh salt and sulfuric water. Some snow, mostly fresh water, but in some areas mixed with sulfur. Voursa's internal crust is composed of silicate, rocks, granite and basalt. Its mantel is composed of ferromagnesian rocks. The Core is composed of iron, nickel, mostly liquid on the upper part and solid on the lower part. Its outer Core is 2700km -4985km below Voursa's surface and it's approximately 2% of Voursa's total mass.

Now they knew where the alien's planet was, and it was amazing how closely it resembled the planet Earth, but it was too far for this community to reach it in only one generation.

Dr. Vlasik requested a meeting in the parliament to discuss all the information they had retrieved from the alien's ship, as well as their weapons and what they had done so far with them.

It was a full house with many people participating. Nick started the meeting by saying,

"Dr. Vlasik and his scientific team, as well as the group appointed by the Governor, requested a meeting to discuss their plans for our voyage to the alien planet. Dr. Vlasik, you have the floor, please go ahead, sir."

"Thank you, Mr. Vice Governor, as you know I have already discussed my plans with you and the Governor, but I am also required by law to discuss them in an open meeting.

In the last two weeks my staff and I have been working to gain knowledge about the aliens before we leave. We have learned enough to have a pretty good idea about them. It doesn't surprise me that they chose our planet from millions of others; the reason is clear, it's because our planet resembles theirs. I won't tire you with technical data which we have already given to the Governor and her staff. But what I would like to tell you is that the aliens can easily live on our planet, and we on theirs, with some minor adjustments.

We don't know exactly why they needed our planet at the time they arrived, but they must have had a good reason because they came from a far away planet deep in space, and to be exact, from the constellation of Pleiades. It could be that their planet was destroyed, or that they had overpopulated their home planet and were looking for a suitable new home like ours.

Whatever their reason might be, we cannot allow them to take Earth from us under any circumstances. As I said, we do know a little bit about their world and we are learning more everyday. We are making adjustments but we could do all that on our way to their planet.

Project Anastrophe

You may have guessed by now that our voyage is going to be a long one. But let me tell you how long it's going to be before we leave so that you have a clear understanding. We have plotted a very complicated course that will take us to the alien planet. At this time, and with the means we presently have, it will take us two hundred years or ten generations of our little community to go one way and perhaps the same time to come back, unless we find other ways to accelerate our speed in the future.

We will not be able to travel in our ship for more than fifty years, so our next vessel will not be another spaceship; it will have to be a good sized meteorite on which we can live and travel. We can do that by propelling and navigating it just as we do with Anastrophe One. Although we will have better gravity than we now have on the ship, it will not be like Earth. In time the future generations will adjust to their new gravitational pull.

It will not be a dull or boring life for us in our spaceship or on the meteorite. We are a civilized society and we will continue to be so wherever we go. We will visit new worlds and we will learn as we go on. Our Voyage will be an important legacy not only for generations of our small community but for Earth too.

Our main goal is to save Earth, and we hope our descendants will be able to do that by returning to Earth in time to destroy the alien enemy and finally settle on our beloved planet."

It was a powerful speech Dr. Vlasik gave to the small community that early morning, one that would be remembered for many years to come. The next one to speak was Governor Norina. She said,

"Thank you, Dr. Vlasik; no one could have said it any better. At this time I would like to ask all of you if you have any questions for Dr. Vlasik."

There were a few questions from the floor but no one challenged Dr. Vlasik's wisdom. However there was one person who asked an important question. He said,

"Why couldn't we find an M-type planet and live on it until we have learned more of the aliens. We may find that we don't have to travel to the alien's homeland after all. With the knowledge we acquire from them we might be able to copy their weapons far sooner."

But that was quickly dismissed when another scientist said that it could be accomplished on board the ship.

There were a few other questions, but in the end when Governor Norina asked them if they were all of the same mind to go ahead with the voyage, they all agreed that it was the right thing to do under the circumstances. Governor Norina called the meeting to an end and they all left feeling skeptical but comfortable with their decision.

Chapter 18

Everything that needed to be done before the historic take-off had been accomplished. All the debris and the temporary shop on the Moon had been cleared away. Nothing was left to show that this area was ever occupied by humans. Inside the new Anastrophe, everything was secured for the big blast and the lift-off that would follow.

Finally Governor Norina gave the order for the take-off, and a roar was heard by all; huge flames shot from the jet engines around the perimeter of the vessel and then Anastrophe One lifted up and away into deep space.

Norina and Nick were on the bridge during the launch, and were amazed with all the newly installed electronic gadgets which flashed and beamed continually. The staff, mainly humans, were understandably excited with the whole operation and when the ship lifted and flew into dark, starry space, all on the bridge were elated that everything had gone well.

Norina and Nick thanked them for the good job they had done on rebuilding the Anastrophe One and they were especially thankful to Dr. Vlasik for his resourcefulness and ingenuity. Then they drank champagne, and wished themselves good luck in their new and difficult endeavor.

Many of the people in the community were happy to be on their way, but sad because they knew they would never see their beloved Earth again. They watched the blue and white ball disappear slowly from view in the cold darkness of space.

Nick thought of a poem he had read back in the twenty-first century by some unknown poet, and recited it to Norina.

"Cocooned in the bridge, instruments buzz, numerals flicker.
Earth's latest fruit of knowledge floats into uncharted territory.
Space: dark, cold, empty, unfriendly.
Stars, planets, bright beacons of curiosity.
Anybody there?"

"Wow, this poem certainly expresses our feelings right now, doesn't it, Nick?"

"It sure does, and to think, whoever that person was, he is long gone." They walked away from the bridge and went to the bar and ordered a couple of drinks. They were both sentimental; Norina's eyes brimmed with tears. They sat in a semi-dark area of the bar sipping their drinks and for a few minutes remained quiet, then Norina said,

"We are leaving our world, never to see it again." Nick replied,

Project Anastrophe

"Our world changed the minute Project Anastrophe went into effect. Our relatives, friends, and our whole world disappeared; only to be replaced by one completely strange to us. In a way that should make it easier for us to break away from it."

"But it doesn't. This is our planet Earth we have left and we will never see it again."

"We have each other, and many good people with us, we can start a new life and make the best of it."

"I suppose you are right, Nick, I am sorry I am so sentimental." Nick put his arm around her and pulled her close. They stayed like that for a while talking about future plans.

Next day Norina got her usual reports from the staff. She was told that the ship was functioning well and that they were on their way to find Nephus and the rest of his people.

Vrima, who was the last to leave, explained to Norina her plan for capturing Nephus. She said they knew where he and his crew were, and that it would take at least two weeks to catch up with them. Vrima also told Norina that Nephus had rebuilt his ship into a powerful fighting force and would not give up easily. But she had no doubt in her mind that she would capture his ship. She warned Norina that there might be fatalities on their side because of the fact that Nephus had programmed his robots to kill humans.

Norina was very concerned about having more fatalities but she could see that it was unavoidable. Another day came and went and her new life was beginning to be a routine with a busy schedule in the office and daily walks in the park with Nick. The artificial sun from the top of the solarium was comforting to them.

She had been brought up in a huge biosphere back home on Earth for most of her life, so this ship was just another smaller version of it and it was easy to adapt to. To Nick the change came a little harder; after all, his background was the antithesis of Norina's. He had lived in an open, clean environment on earth, but he had lived in the biosphere only a few months. He was accustomed to drastic changes; after all he had been forcibly scooped away from a normal twenty-first century life and brought to the twenty-fifth century, losing his family and his way of living in split seconds. So even before this latest change, he was already a changed man. But as long as he had Norina on his side, life was bearable and worth living.

During the last two weeks Vrima had been busy preparing for an attack on Nephus' ship. Two days ago they had spotted a shiny pea-sized object, and by all indications they were looking at Nephus' ship, but the fear of an alien ship in the area was always on Vrima's mind.

She went to the war room where both Norina and Nick were participating, along with all the war specialists. Vrima told them what they had discovered and most of them thought it had to be Nephus' ship but there was a possibility of an alien ship too.

Ner suggested they should be prepared for the aliens as the primary target and secondarily for Nephus' ship. By now Dr. Vlasik and his staff had devised special portable units which they were using now to detect the foreign object.

Soon they were sure they were looking at a ship made of Earthly material, and there wasn't any doubt that it was Nephus's ship. That didn't make it any easier for Vrima and the rest of the fighting force, for while they had to adhere to the rules of war, Nephus had programmed his robots to kill humans.

Vrima knew she had to hit them with surgical accuracy. Her orders were very clear,

Project Anastrophe

"If possible, there will be no human fatalities on Nephus' ship."

They were approaching a dangerous area, and they could see the enemy vessel was taking defensive maneuvers.

Meanwhile on Dyplopherus they all felt sure they had gotten away from the Anastrophe One, thanks mainly to Nephus's ingenious cloaking devices that had blinded the enemy. Nephus was in a good mood; he welcomed all and said,

"I told you we were going to make it, didn't I?" He continued to tell them that what they were doing was the right thing and that it wouldn't be too long before they found a suitable planet for temporary living. After the enemy had passed them, they could go back to Earth, take it over, and live the rest of their lives in power and wealth.

"I haven't forgotten the aliens either. As soon as we take over Earth and are established there, we are going to start building our defenses in preparation for their coming in the thirtieth century. My friends, we can have it all and still save our planet Earth from the aliens."

There were more shouts of approval from all, indicating they totally agreed with him. Finally he asked for a general report about the status of the ship, and he got a very positive one from all departments. He told them to keep up the good work and they agreed to meet again at the usual time, unless there was a need to meet sooner.

Nephus should have been happy with everything going so well, but he wasn't. There was an empty spot in his heart that made him ache; he wouldn't be happy until he had Darna next to him. He loved her, and wanted her, but didn't want to push too hard; he wanted her to come to him on her own initiative.

Darna and her mother lived in a large, luxurious section

in the ship close to the officials who managed the newly rebuilt Dyplopherus. But it was very hard for Darna's mother Flavia to endure all these recent changes. She was a retiree and before the "Change" she had been doing what she had always wanted to do--paint. Her husband had passed away a few years earlier, and her son Mark and daughter Darna, both unmarried, were her only contacts in her sunset years. It was a big blow to her secure life when Darna disappeared for so long. But the loss of her son Mark during the "Change" was too much for her to bear; she became ill and fragile when she was brought into the ship and had a hard time adapting to her new life. She became progressively sicker with every passing day. These last few days she even refused to go on her usual walk with Darna; she wouldn't take nourishment and finally died peacefully in Darna's arms.

With her mother's passing, Darna was very lonely. Her mother was the last thread to her previous life. During the funeral she felt heartbroken. Nephus went out of his way to help Darna; he arranged for her mother's funeral and was there with her in her grief at a time when she most needed someone to lean on. Darna discovered the better side of Nephus, he was humane and kind, caring and loving, and she appreciated that.

Since that day Nephus and Darna had become closer again. Darna moved in with him, and a new and loving relationship blossomed between the two of them. As time went on Darna got used to her new life in the ship with Nephus, but she knew this wasn't going to last long despite Nephus's reassurances. So she wasn't surprised when she was told Anastrophe One had caught up with them and was practically on their tail.

They were all in a state of frenetic preparation. The

Project Anastrophe

children and older people were taken to a safe place and robot and human guards took the necessary measures for Anastrophe's inevitable attack. Nephus was in the war room next to the bridge, looking tired, but nevertheless giving orders to his staff and acting as commander-in-chief during this whole operation.

It wasn't long before the battle started with missiles hitting the protective shield, and with every barrage the shield was weakened. Soon it was reduced to sixty percent, and it was getting worse.

Nephus knew Anastrophe One would have had to be rebuilt to go on such a long voyage but this was a huge ship and had no resemblance to the Anastrophe One he had left a few weeks ago. This was a kind of force he could not fight, and Dyplopherus' shield would not hold for long. He knew he couldn't penetrate the Anastrophe's shield with anything he had, so he ordered them to go to plan "B" which called for hiding among meteorites and bringing the enemy into the narrows. A bigger ship would have a harder time maneuvering around them than a smaller ship like his.

It had worked in the past with the Greeks in the narrows of Salamis; with the English in the English Channel; and with the Gabra battle, before the confederation of Earth. He ordered the Dyplopherus to go to a group of meteorites two light years away and then jumped into warp drive. Norina and Nick were both in the war room with Vrima. They were all amazed with the transformation of the two shuttles into one huge ship, able to withstand the kind of force Anastrophe had been delivering for the last half hour. Vrima had expected to have taken the ship by now.

They had both miscalculated each other's capabilities. Vrima suggested also going to their plan "B" which was to send a powerful beam immobilizing Dyplopherus, and then sending shuttle ships with enough robot and manpower to break in and take over the ship and its crew. But before she finished explaining her idea, the Dyplopherus disappeared from their view. Anastrophe One matched its speed and jumped, only to stop abruptly to avoid crashing into millions of large and small meteorites; some of them hundreds of meters in diameter.

There was no way Norina would put the Anastrophe One close to those boulders. She looked at Vrima and the rest of the human crew for the next move. Vrima suggested sending shuttles with enough guards as per plan "B" and they all agreed that would be safer. Anastrophe One would bombard the Dyplopherus from a safe distance. Norina told them to go ahead but to be careful not to kill or injure humans if at all possible. In minutes three shuttles with robots and human guards left the ship towards Dyplopherus.

It was easy to navigate Dyplopherus around the larger monoliths but it was very hard keeping away from the smaller ones. It was one of those small ones that hit the war room. It punched a hole on the starboard side, and several humans and robots were vacuumed out into space. The blow also injured many humans. The androids quickly started to close the hole, while medics administered first aid to the wounded.

Three humans and four robots were gone and there were many more injured. Most of the injured were treated and released to go back to their assigned posts but there were six seriously wounded who were taken to the intensive care unit. Of those six, Nephus was in the worst shape and there were doctors working on him. Darna was next to him holding his hand.

From Anastrophe One Norina and the rest of the staff in the war room saw what had happened to Dyplopherus and ordered the three shuttles to hide behind the closest meteorite and wait for new orders. There were a few minutes of "cease fire" while guards from both sides waited for new orders.

Chief Phylios was given orders not to shoot unless the enemy resumed firing. In the trauma center, despite all efforts to save his life, Nephus was slipping away. At the last moment he pulled Darna close to him and whispered the security code. He said,

"Your name is the security code. Save the ship, I love you." Nephus died right after he uttered those words.

Darna put her cheek on his and stayed there for few minutes while tears came down her face. Then she got up and went to the main control room, and entered the security code. At that precise minute all robot guards everywhere in the ship transferred their allegiance to her. All the officers who were present quickly realized what had happened and accepted her leadership. She sent a message to Norina and asked to talk to her on Anastrophe One.

Norina acknowledged her offer and ordered her guards to wait for new orders. Before Darna and her top officers beamed themselves over to Anastrophe One, she gave strict orders to robots and human guards to stay put until she gave them new orders; then she and her top five officers beamed away. They landed on the visitor's platform with many guards around. Norina and Nick were there to welcome them. The two parties walked to the war room and closed the doors. Norina and Darna sat across from each other with Norina at the head of the table and Darna at the foot; the other officers occupied the other sides of the table.

Norina welcomed them again and said,

"I am sorry to see that Dyplopherus was hit by a meteorite. You could have surrendered and spared your ship and crew; but it was brave of you to go in there."

"We lost some of our human and robot guards but our androids are fixing the gash as we are speaking."

There they were--two beautiful women--Norina with golden hair and blue eyes, and Darna with black hair and black eyes. They looked seriously at one another. They were both here as leaders representing their people because of two deadly events which had taken their leader's lives. Norina began again, this time punctuating every word she said,
"I was hoping to talk to Nephus as well, why isn't he here?"
"Nephus is dead. I am now in command; shall we proceed?" Norina and her officers were caught by surprise. She thought perhaps Nephus was playing one of his sinister games again, sending Darna to represent him. Nephus dead? That changes the whole equation; they are in more trouble than Norina thought.
"We are sorry to hear that Nephus is dead, we believed he was a dangerous man but we were hoping to change his mind and have him with us. He was a very clever man. What can we do for you now, Darna?"
"I loved Nephus, but I never agreed with his policies, however I know what the people in my ship want, and I am here to discuss their wishes and perhaps put an end to all these killings."
"We are listening."
"Although I realize we should not go back to Earth at this time, we don't wish to go to the alien's planet either. We don't believe much can be accomplished by going there. I am sure my people would be satisfied if we could stay on an M-Type planet and use our know-how to build the weapons. Once we are ready, then we could go back home, fortify Earth, and wait for the aliens to come."

Project Anastrophe

At this time the officers on both sides talked among themselves and then passed their thoughts via their implants to their leaders. Norina said,

"My staff and I have thought of such a scenario but unfortunately it won't work. According to our scientists we will not be able to find the kind of material we need on earth. Even if we were to look on the neighboring planets it's doubtful we could find what we need. We couldn't fight them and win. Even by comparing the human's and the alien's technologies of the thirtieth century, the aliens are far ahead.

We need to go to their planet or the neighboring planets, to find the material we need; spy on them, get as much information as we can get, then go back to Earth to fortify it. Then we can fight the aliens on an equal footing."

"I am sure your scientists have told you the time it will require for us to go to their planet, and unless you are able to use a "worm-hole" or something similar as a conduit, it will take two hundred years to go there and the same to come back. We could do it in less than half the time by doing it our way, and I am not convinced that we humans cannot build the same powerful weapons using local material anyway."

There was more talk between the two sides again exchanging ideas among themselves and after they had transmitted their thoughts to their leaders, Norina resumed talking to Darna.

"I wish we had a faster way to go to our destination but we don't. This is what we have in mind should you wish to join us. We travel with Anastrophe One until we find a good-sized meteorite. According to our estimations it will take at least fifty years of travel until we come to a place where this would be possible. While we are still living in our ship, we will build our new home on the meteorite. It will be a home for us and for all the generations to come.

We have the technology to propel it the same way we propel Anastrophe One, it would be even bigger than the biosphere that we were accustomed to on Earth. The only difference would be a lighter gravitational pull, but in time we would correct that too. We will use that meteorite for going both ways, unless future generations can come up with a better idea. According to our scientists you won't be able to find an M-Type planet in this area and you would probably have to travel about the same distance as we to find a suitable place for human life. It would make more sense for you to join us."

"As I said before, I agree with you about not going to Earth at this time. It would not be fair to the people of Earth if we were to impose our way of living and take advantage of them with our superior technology. Therefore I am going to give my people a choice of either going to the alien planet with you or going with you until we find a planet of our choice and stay there until Earth has advanced to the same level. At that time we will offer them better weapons to prepare them for the aliens. We have traveled to the future and know the 28th century is the appropriate time for us to go back."

"We are not going to allow you to go sooner than we go. If you choose to go to another planet, you will have to wait for us to come back. Then, we will all go back to Earth at the same time, that's the only demand we have of you."

There was more talk among the officers, then Darna said,

"We will go back and talk to our people. This time they will have to decide which way they want to go; should they decide to go to another planet, there must be a

Project Anastrophe

treaty amended in your constitution giving us the right to leave Anastrophe One, once we find an M-type planet.

We will prepare a list of other demands and should you agree, we will sign a peace treaty and live together for the duration. We will try to be reasonable with our demands, but should you deny going along with them, there will be war with all its consequences. As you know, you can't get us out of there as easily as you think. We will fight you and it will be a costly and prolonged war for both of us."

"We don't want war either but if your demands are unreasonable, we will fight you and in the end you will lose. So for the sake of both our people, I hope we achieve peace."

They agreed on a forty metric hour ceasefire; then they all shook hands and Darna and her officers beamed back to the Dyplopherus.

The androids had repaired the gash, all guards were manning their posts, and the ship was poised for battle. Darna told chief Phylios there was now a forty metric hour cease-fire between the two ships, but they must be ready to resume fighting on her orders. She told the same thing to her lieutenant, Mr. Varcous, and told him to gather all the people in the war room.

Within thirty minutes or so, there was a crowd anxiously waiting for Darna. Shortly after that she and her officers came in. She started by saying,

"You have heard that we lost our leader, Nephus. We also lost three human guards, four robot guards, and we have many injured. I am now in command of this ship and it is my responsibility to see to it that we stop this killing. We can fight a prolonged war and lose more of our people and robots but in the long run we are not a match for Anastrophe One. I therefore started negotiations with Governor Norina for surrendering, provided they accept our demands.

George Karnikis

I want to do it in a democratic way and have all of you participate in this process. I suggest we prepare a list of our demands and if they don't meet them, we will have no alternative but to fight. We may not win, but we are in a position to inflict a lot of damage on their ship, of that I am sure. I am also sure they don't want war either, and they will try their best to accept our demands provided we are reasonable.

We have arranged a forty metric hour ceasefire so we can start our deliberations without fear of war.

They have offered us two options; one is to go with them to the alien planet." There was a lot of murmuring within the crowd with many were visibly disturbed. Darna continued,

"Please hear me out! They want us to live with them as one community with all the rights and privileges they have. The second option they proposed is; we go with them until we find an M-Type planet, then we move to that planet, colonize it, and live there until they come back from the alien planet. Then those who wish to go back to Earth will join them and go back together.

There are no habitable planets in this area, and we will not be able to find any until we reach the Bachda Zone which will take at least fifty years; but we were prepared for such a journey anyway. We have demanded that our requests be part of the Anastrophe's constitution so there will be no doubt when the time comes for us to leave. We have prepared and are sending you the list right now. Go through it thoroughly and check your preferences and be reasonable, for our lives depend on the decisions you are about to make."

There was a lot of commotion on the floor. People were talking animatedly and after they had read the list that was sent to them via their implants, they finally voted.

Project Anastrophe

After an hour or so all had replied and the votes were tallied. Darna appeared on the platform and announced the results. The people had overwhelmingly chosen to surrender Dyplopherus and live on another planet. They also voted on various issues regarding their stay on the Anastrophe One on the long voyage to their next planet. Darna was satisfied with their decision and told them so, she said,

"Dear friends, the outcome of your vote is even better than I hoped; now I have something to bargain with. In the next few hours we will make the results of your vote official and we will negotiate with Governor Norina. Should there be any changes, you will be asked to vote again and when everything is done you will be asked again to ratify the new amendment to the constitution.

Now go back to your quarters and try to relax; there will be no war until the forty hours are up. But let's hope for permanent peace."

Norina and her staff were anxiously waiting for the results of the vote from Dyplopherus. She knew a war between the two people would be very costly in lives and material no matter who won. She would try any reasonable way to avoid it. She was glad to be dealing with Darna and not Nephus. Darna was a more trustworthy person, but she also knew Darna would try hard to achieve the best for her people.

The voting results were in Norina's hands and she distributed them to the rest of the staff. No one had any objections except for Ner. He said,

"Governor Norina, I have gone thoroughly through the list and haven't found anything about the reprogramming of their robot guards. They should not come in here as they are."

"We have prepared a list of our own requirements for them, let this be one more."

Requests from both sides were analyzed and accepted, then in a special election held by both peoples simultaneously; the amendment was ratified and became part of the main constitution. Thanks to Norina and Darna the Dyplopherus became part of the Anastrophe's fleet and Darna's people, including Darna herself, were now together with the rest of Anastrophe's people as one large community.

Nephus's guards were reprogrammed as they had been before; however they had first allegiance to Darna as part of the constitution's checks and balances. Darna was given substantial powers as long as she was elected by her own people and acted as an opposition party in the parliament. They had finally achieved permanent peace and lived once more as one community.

Chapter 19

With the addition of the Dyplopherus and its robot guards and androids, Anastrophe was an even stronger ship ready for its long voyage. She was now on her way to the Gumaras area in the outskirts of the home solar system where they hoped to find a large enough meteorite to make their next home base for many generations to come. But first they had to find an M-type planet for those who didn't wish to go for the long run.

There was a reunification and a welcome party. People were happy to be drinking together rather than killing each other. The dancing and merriment went on for many hours. Darna and her ex-officers, together with Norina's government, were participating in the happy event.

It was strange; but both Norina and Darna were uneasy

with food and drink. In fact they could hardly wait to leave the party. Nick was alarmed by Norina's discomfort and asked her if she was all right. She said she was tired--that's all--but she knew better. She had been feeling like this for a few days now and wondered if it was indeed what she thought it was. She pushed the thought away from her mind.

Darna also felt uneasy. Nothing tasted good; she had lost her appetite and all she wanted was to go to bed. She had to force herself to attend and be part of such an important event.

Both women learned to live with their pregnancies and be good leaders at the same time. Another thing Norina and Darna had in common was that both were expecting fraternal twins.

Darna missed Nephus; she needed him now more than any other time to help bring up their children. But her political duties kept her busy and less lonely all through her pregnancy. She was elected as the main opposition leader in the parliament and although she disagreed with Norina on some of the issues, she liked Norina as a person and a friend.

They were now traveling deep into space, a piece of Earth from the twenty-fifth century, an advanced society in technology and culture, lost in uncharted space; carrying the torch of Earth's civilization. They were determined to save Earth from a future alien enemy by going to their home planet; compromise or destroy their superior weaponry before the aliens arrived on Mother-Earth.

Dr. Vlasik and his staff now devoted all their energy to the alien's weapons. They got acquainted with their advanced technology and learned more each day. Other groups were studying the alien's culture and learning about the enemy's history and everyday life. Many human generations would study them and when they finally reached the

Project Anastrophe

alien's home planet, humans would know everything that was needed to be known. Nick and his brave crew had stolen all available data from the alien ships as well as several of their powerful weapons.

As the time went on Norina and Darna gave birth to their fraternal twins and all four of them were beautiful and healthy. Norina and Nick named their son Nikitas and their daughter Thora. Darna named her boy Damien and her daughter Chloe All the community celebrated the birth of their leaders' children and there were festivities that went on for many days.

The people had fallen into a routine, living a life different from that of Earth but in many ways very much the same. They celebrated the same holidays and many attended services in different places of worship. Some practiced polytheism but most were agnostic. As in any free society there were differences among the people that kept both human and robot guards busy. But for the most part they lived a peaceful and very satisfactory life considering they were locked in a spaceship going on a long voyage.

Back on Earth Mr. Varcous had been a producer in a large multi-media corporation so he and Darna had a lot in common. Many times in the past they had seen each other on a professional basis, so it was natural for them to have a close relationship. He was older than Darna by ten years but he was a good man and in many ways resembled Nephus. Varcous didn't have the excessive intelligence Nephus had, but was smart enough to succeed in his own way. He was an honest man and the only reason he had joined Nephus was because he didn't want to leave Earth. As time went on Darna and Varcous established a more permanent relationship.

The twins were the darlings of the whole community. All four of them were taken to schools and play grounds with children of their own age and they were loved by all and treated like royalty. The good relationship between people and government went a long way to create a stable symbiosis in the community.

Eighteen years had passed since Anastrophe had left the Moon's surface; it had been traveling in dark space without encountering any land mass. It looked as though Anastrophe wasn't moving at all; but it was moving faster than when it started after Dr. Vlasik and his staff enhanced the main engines with newly acquired alien technology. They were still decades away from their destination.

Anastrophe One had changed too. It had now become one third larger to accommodate the increased population. This was the new generation, one that had not seen land, except in libraries and schools. They would never see Earth in their lives; for them, it was a mythical land of their progenitors. Anastrophe One was homeland for them and their lives had been adjusted to live and enjoy life within these metal walls. They looked more hybrid than their parents and one could see all the races in them. They were nice looking and very healthy. However their life styles were different from their parents, they differed in the way they dressed and the way they expressed themselves. They had a very independent attitude.
    They would frequently walk nude in the corridors to the embarrassment of their parents and elders, that's why the elders resorted to going to churches; it had worked in the past---it could work for them too. Their different attitudes and life styles didn't make them less responsible in their duties. They excelled and sometimes surpassed their

Project Anastrophe

elders in their studies and work; they were exemplary citizens.

They were trained to be good warriors in case they needed to defend their ship, but most of all they were trained to be good pilots. Many times they flew their newly built fighter ships out into dark space; learned to navigate long distances away from the mother ship and to come back safe and sound. Dyplopherus was taken out many times for scouting the nearby areas and it was a big honor for the young trainees to go on long training trips on Dyplopherus.

Nikitas was eighteen years old, an attractive young man. He looked a bit like his father but resembled mostly his mother with his blue eyes and golden curly hair; he was tall, strong and serious. He was already a good pilot and a good navigator but his parents wanted him to go into politics and perhaps one day be the Governor of Anastrophe. Chloe, also eighteen, was a beautiful young girl. She looked more like her father, Nephus, but she had her mother's black hair and black eyes. She was tall and lean like her mother Darna but she had inherited Nephus's intelligence without his eccentricity and egomaniacal behavior. She shared her mother's opinions on most subjects.

It was on one of those Dyplopherus trips, as young trainees, that the two of them were able to exchange their most inner feelings. This time they were grown-ups and not the children they had been when they played together. There were times in the past when their parents were enemies, but Chloe and Nikitas were very much in love.

Chloe, without exception, was the smartest student in the ship. She did well in everything she endeavored to do; but science was her best subject and she was allowed to visit Dr. Vlasik's lab whenever she chose. He was happy to help her because he could see in her the promise of a very useful scientist.

George Karnikis

Nikitas and Chloe were both on the bridge on duty, philosophizing about life, when the monitors showed a faint light a few thousand miles ahead. It appeared to be a planet although every indication pointed to a non-M-Type planet. Still it was very exciting; this would be the first time this new generation would see real land.

The information had already been transmitted to the superiors. Nomarchos, the captain in charge, arrived along with his first officers. The officers who were off duty came too. This was a very exciting moment---a break in their routine. On Anastrophe, high officials from the Government went to the bridge. Norina, who was now the first president since they had changed to a parliamentary system; Darna, Prime Minister, and Nick who had been in charge of the fighting fleet for several years now, watched along with other government officials as the information came in Dyplopherus. The planet looked like a moving soccer ball on a huge screen as the computers moved it around and examined it. It had a very unfriendly environment for human habitation and they knew that from the beginning, but it had important minerals which they needed.

It was one of the academy's rules; those who first found the planet would be the first ones to visit it, unless they declined, and Nikitas and Chloe weren't about to do that. They were enthusiastic and ready to go.

The planet was now getting bigger by the hour and details of its properties were pouring out of the instruments. An expedition to the surface of the planet was put together. A group of twelve men and women were readied to go on one of the newly built shuttles. It was a shuttle especially made for expeditions like this; Nikitas and Chloe were in charge. Nine of the crew would descend onto the surface, including themselves; three would remain to command the shuttle.

Project Anastrophe

They were all excited as they were about to exit. There were many goodbyes and people wished them good luck, but both Norina and Darna were very nervous seeing their children going away on an unknown mission. If Nick felt the same way, he didn't show it.

They flew into the dark void traveling to the shiny planet below them. They came as close as they could, avoiding the planet's gravitational pull, then they embarked in two space capsules and descended to different sides of the planet.

Nikitas was in one of the capsules and Chloe in the other; they landed about ten thousand kilometers apart checking for different minerals. The planet was frozen with many meters of ice at both poles. Most of the tests had already been done by the shuttle's crew. The ice was H2O, water, but there were other minerals mixed in it which would be filtered later in the ship. Then both Nikitas and Chloe gave permission for the androids to be beamed down for excavating the minerals from below the ice.

There were ten androids with the machinery and they went right to work. They started by cutting chunks of ice and beamed them up to the shuttle. Farther down, and away from the icy poles, they gathered different kinds of minerals. In the meantime both capsules traveled to other areas of the planet. In areas where there was no ice the ground was hard and frozen. There was no oxygen in the atmosphere and no light.

After both capsules flew extensively over the frozen planet they landed by the androids who were finishing up and they were about to beam to the shuttle when an earthquake to shook the ground. The Androids were able to beam to safer areas right away but humans couldn't do that in an unfiltered environment; they had to physically move away, and then quickly get into their capsules. Nikitas' capsule lifted up and was hovering a few meters above the ground waiting for Chloe's capsule to lift so they could both go back to the shuttle. At the last moment the ground cracked and split causing a huge crevasse into which the capsule fell with all four occupants trapped inside.

They had fallen on a ledge ten meters down and hung there precariously. Another smaller earthquake shook the ground again bringing the capsule dangerously close to the chasm. Nikitas' capsule still hovered above ground, and he tried frantically to get in touch with Chloe's crew. Finally her voice came in on the intercom. She said,

"We are a little bruised but O.K."

"Chloe, listen to me carefully; you are very close to a crevasse that goes hundreds of meters down. Stay put where you are and make sure you don't move; we are trying to find a way to get you up. Do you understand me?"

"Yes, we will stay put and wait for help."

"Help will come soon."

The Anastrophe crew had been watching the expedition ever since it had left the ship. Everywhere they went cameras projected every move; now they were witnessing the drama as it was unfolding in front of their eyes. Norina was holding Darna's hand giving her courage, while the rest of them were holding their breath; people were on the verge of tears.

Nikitas and his crew quickly worked out a plan to save their comrades; they ordered the ten androids to assemble on both sides of the crevasse and direct their powerful magnets at the capsule to stabilize it. Then Nikitas asked Chloe to carefully check and give him a report on the capsule's ability to fly. She said,

"It appears that most of the instruments are inoperable; if we can move in there, perhaps we can start repairing them."

Project Anastrophe

"Stay put where you are, we have another plan in mind."

What happened next was a cooperative rescue between the androids and Nikitas's capsule. While the androids kept the capsule from falling, Nikitas directed a magnetic beam onto it thereby getting a good hold on it. Then he started to lift it little by little with the androids lifting at the same time. When it was up, they rested it on solid ground. Then he quickly lowered his capsule beside Chloe's, attached to the emergency door and opened it. They helped the other crew get in, and abandoned the destroyed capsule. Then they all flew back to the shuttle.

The androids followed by beaming back. When they were all secured in the shuttle, there was a sense of relief everywhere in the Anastrophe and people were anxious to have the shuttle and its crew back without delay. Next day robots and androids went back and retrieved the damaged capsule.

Now they were traveling in an area where they found more non-M-type planets and there were more expeditions, by young and old, but they were mostly of a scientific nature. Damien and Thora were also good pilots and excellent navigators but had different interests from their siblings. Damien was a born leader and he wanted to go into politics like his mother. He was in broadcasting and wrote editorials that had to do with politics and everyday life in the small community. A handsome, well-spoken young man, a good combination of his parents, he was very intelligent in his own way but didn't share any of his father's interests.

Thora loved her father. Ever since she was a little girl she thought her father was special because of the way he had been brought to the twenty-fifth century. She would ask him to tell her stories about "The Old Times" when people had so many wars and they were so simple. When they spoke many languages and drove vehicles called automobiles which used carbon-based fuel. They didn't even have implants. Nick always found time to talk to her.

As a young girl she liked to hear the stories of her parents' traveling in the past, living through, wars and helping to save Earth from radiation poisoning. Thora became a linguist, an anthropologist and a philosopher. She read many electronic books in different languages. One of her favorite books was Homer's Iliad and Odyssey which she read in ancient Greek. She also read Plato's Republic and other philosophers such as John Milton, Montaigne, Thoreau, and others. She loved gardening and even as a little girl she used to go and watch the android gardeners working in the community gardens. Thora loved teaching and she hoped to teach philosophy in the future.

Thora and Damien would talk for hours about social mores. Damien would always politicize social issues, while Thora tended to philosophize. As the time went on they became very close and they too fell in love. The two families had a special connection, and for the twins it felt like one large extended family.

Chapter 20

Nick and Norina, now in their late fifties, were not as busy as they used to be in politics or other social meetings. They chose their activities carefully and spent more time at home. After dinner they frequently sat by their picture window and gazed at the glittering starry space. It was hypnotic; they could stay there speechless for a long time. At other times they would engage in long conversations on many different subjects. Sometimes Nikitas and Thora, now both married with children of their own, would come to visit and the house would burst with young laughter and mischief while the grownups tried in vain to carry on a conversation. Nikitas, as Prime Minister, had a lot on his mind and he would often visit his parents for advice.

It was on one of those visits that Nikitas, Nick, and

Norina withdrew to a quiet place to discuss a subject that was the talk of the whole community. For sometime now they had been looking for a planet that would be appropriate for human habitation. In the last few years they had found several M-type planets but none had adequate oxygen. Even if they were to live in a biosphere they wouldn't be able to cultivate their gardens as easily as they did in the Anastrophe. Anastrophe's gardens had soil brought from Earth, but anywhere they had checked they couldn't even come close to it.

Nikitas was of the opinion that they should look for a planet that was a better match, no matter how long it took. But there was a lot of pressure in the Parliament about expediting things by sharing half of the soil of Anastrophe's gardens and occupying one of the closest planets. The problem was that with the second generation in the ship, it was getting too crowded and they could not extend the size of the ship any more without putting its structural integrity in danger. Sharing the soil, on the other hand, was out of the question. Those who wanted to stay said, and rightly so, that they needed the soil for their well-being for the next and longest voyage ahead.

It was a "hot potato." Norina offered an idea that made sense to Nikitas, although Nick had second thoughts about it. The idea was that from now on they should establish a zero population growth. And if it took longer to find the right planet, they could also curtail new births.

Nick thought that in such an enclosed habitation an unknown and uncontrolled virus could endanger the very existence of the whole community if the gene pool was reduced. Although Nikitas appreciated his father's concerns he nevertheless thought his mother's idea could be a way out of this dilemma. When he discussed Norina's idea with Thora and Damien, they agreed with both Nick's and

Project Anastrophe

Norina's ideas but preferred Norina's at least for the foreseeable future. When the bill was introduced on the floor of the parliament it narrowly passed and became the law.

It was hard for young people who wanted to have children, and caused unhappiness between new and old generations. The younger generation suggested voluntary euthanasia for older people; but that was quickly rejected by the majority of the community.

It was a difficult time for everybody; the overpopulation had caused a strain on available resources and space within the Anastrophe and because of that, they intensified their efforts to find a livable planet. They were now in their fortieth year on their quest for an M-type planet and people were resigned to the fact that they may never find one. So when another planet showed up on their screens they were no longer excited. They routinely sent a scouting team to investigate, but this one was different.

This time they found vegetation and some animal life too, but the most important thing of all was the fact that the air on the planet was breathable. It wasn't anything they had back on Earth or even in their ship, but when the crew removed their breathing masks, they discovered the atmosphere was like it was when one climbed a high mountain on Earth. It was a condition people would adapt to. The instruments picked up signs of life; something they had never seen before. What kind of life? That had to be investigated before they made their move to this new planet.

They sent more scouts and combed the planet from pole to pole. They found a variety of small living things but the two largest species they found were prevalent and rampant. One of them was of the genus Arachnidan, (Spiders). They were about one meter in height. The other was of the genus Myrmecous, (Ants), also about one meter tall.

The spiders appeared to live a solitary life while the ants lived in groups and had organized societies.

Scouts found a clear area for the Dyplopherus to land and about two hundred specialists went down for further preliminary work on security and other important matters. Two shuttles made daily trips to the planet with people and material. In the meantime, guards captured several ants and spiders and zoologists studied them. They also studied other species. They found out that their basic DNA didn't differ much from that of the Earth's animal kingdom including humans. They checked thoroughly all over the planet for possible humanoid species but found none.

When they checked the ants and the spiders they found them to be the most intelligent beings of all the animals and insects on this planet. Both species carried enough poison to kill each other and enough to kill a human being. The one thing they noticed right away was that as soon as they found themselves in close proximity, they formed groups and started to fight each other. They were both underground dwellers. They were omnivorous and ate smaller animals including insects and various plants. When a robot guard went between the two groups they both attacked and stung him. If he had been a human guard he would have died instantly. The scientists were able to come up with an antidote against their poison.

Most of the spiders and ants were females and the scientists spent lots of time trying to find males of the two species. When they finally did find them they were fewer than the females and about half the size. They were very pale in comparison because they were held underground all the time.

After they had been checked and evaluated the scientists let them go; they also sent an electrified robot camera into their dwellings and recorded their everyday life. The

Project Anastrophe

ants had a very complex tunnel system with many intersections and huge rooms as living areas while the spiders lived in underground caves.

The ants appeared to be more intelligent, but the spiders were a formidable enemy. When a secured area was established, many of the Government and the dignitaries were brought to the surface of the planet and Nick and Norina were among them. They showed them the area where they would start building; then they flew them across the planet. What they saw was a planet resembling Earth at a time when vegetation started to form and insects and other animals began to evolve on dry land.

The planet very much resembled the Earth in size and distance from the sun, although the distance was greater, making it a little colder than Earth. However there were a few basic differences. There was more fresh water than salt and more land than water. This planet also had fifteen neighbors, all non-M-type planets, making it the only planet in the area for human habitation.

Many people wondered why the aliens hadn't occupied this planet which was closer to them and had no one to fight. But scientists reminded them that they were here almost five hundred years earlier than the alien's expedition and one didn't know what would happen here in five hundred years in the future. That was a chilling thought no one wanted to contemplate at this time. Many of the officials, those who would stay and even those who would be going away, felt that it was a pity that they couldn't all stay on this planet to prepare for the coming of the aliens.

Billions of Nanos were hard at work under the auspices of the best engineers the twenty–fifth century could offer. This biosphere was going to be built taking into consideration all the problems they had faced back on Earth when radiation was seeping through the ground floor. There were new and better materials to be used now. This was going to be a biosphere to be used not only as a dwelling place but also as a fort to be protected from future enemies.

The work had started in earnest and one could see the first lines of the biosphere being formed by invisible Nano builders. It was amazing how fast the huge piles of material, brought in from the newly discovered planet, were being used by the nanos. They resembled ancient hourglasses with the sand falling down.

By the third month the biosphere was nearly completed although there would be more finishing work to be done as the time went on. It was a huge project by any measure. It was a sister biosphere to the one back on Earth although much smaller. This new biosphere could withstand radiation, erosion, and any adverse weather condition, but most important it could also withstand an attack by an enemy force such as the aliens.

They had an opening ceremony with crowds of people who had already arrived and many officials and dignitaries. Almost fifty percent of the Anastrophe's population of four thousand had already moved in, along with numbers of robots and androids. They had been given a substantial amount of Earth's soil to introduce Earth's biology into the new planet. Soil from the new planet was taken up to Anastrophe to do likewise.

Everybody and everything that was supposed to be moved was moved. Damian was chosen as the first prime minister of the new community. Darna and her friend Varcous went along, but her daughter Chloe stayed behind with Nikitas and her family. The separation was almost equal to death, with hundreds of young people separating from their parents, brothers, and sisters for the first time.

Norina, who was losing her daughter Thora and grandchildren, was deeply affected by the separation. Nick, who was very close to Thora, was heartbroken, but tried not to show it. Norina was given the honor of christening the new planet. It was given the name, GAIA NEA and people liked it because it meant New Earth and reminded them of their beloved planet. Norina was asked to give a speech for the occasion. She said,

"My dear friends, we have lived as a family all these years and it's painful for us to separate, but it's a sacrifice we all must make in order to save our beloved Earth from certain destruction by the aliens. It is a sacrifice that will be remembered by all human beings forever. But let us keep a positive thought in our minds; eventually, in the far future, our children will be able to move back to Earth and live there where they belong.

In the meantime do the best you can in this newly adopted Gaia Nea for this planet is going to be your new home for many generations to come. Thank you very much and may health, peace, and prosperity be always with you."

The people clapped and hugged and most of them could not hold back their tears. Finally the moment of separation came and they said their goodbyes. Those who were destined for the long voyage returned to the ship, while the others remained on Gaia Nea.

With the ceremony now over there were many urgent things to take care of. Prime Minister Damien called his staff to its first meeting and asked for a general report. Among the ministers was Darna, now in her sixties, still beautiful, with long gray hair and a face that looked more like a forty year old. She had retained her vitality all these years and when she spoke she still commanded everybody's attention.

She was the Minister of Internal Affairs and at this

time her job was very important. She started her report by saying,

"I have been told by my staff that our young people are having a hard time adapting to life in our new biosphere and on this planet. Breaking away from their relatives and friends has been more traumatic for them than for the older people. They frequently get into fights and abuse drugs and alcohol. We need to do something to protect our children-- and sooner rather than later. I don't need to remind you that our young people are the very future of this community and that supersedes any other problems that we might have right now."

Damien addressed her as "Minister" and not as a "Mom", and said,

"Minister, you have convinced us of the importance of this matter, do you have any ideas about how to remedy this problem?"

"My staff and I have talked about it in great depth and have come up with a couple of possible solutions to resolve these issues. One is to engage the young people more in state matters and then reward them with every successful contribution to the state or community; the other one goes into moral behavior that involves not only the youth but all of us.

In the past we have experimented with religion, but because of all the different denominations involved, and because most of us are agnostic, it has not worked. We thought perhaps this time we could engage everybody by building a temple and dedicating it to an unknown God. We would tolerate all existing denominations within, but with greater emphasis on the "Force." We think that will be welcomed by the majority of the community, then we must encourage the youth to participate. We think that will go a long way towards building morality within our community."

Project Anastrophe

One of the ministers asked Darna what kind of temple or shrine she had in mind and she said,

"It will have to be something substantial and at the same time beautiful---something that conveys peace, serenity, and communication with one's higher self." It was agreed unanimously and Darna's bill was the first bill to pass in the house. Most people were excited about the new building, but when they were asked where they wanted it built, most of them requested that the new building, being of a spiritual nature, should be built far away from the municipality.

The place chosen was a hundred kilometers away within the biosphere. This time the architects and engineers aimed for beauty and symmetry in addition to structural strength.

While the shrine was underway inside the biosphere, outside, human agronomists and hundreds of farmer androids and robot guards were busy planting conifer trees in a vast area around the biosphere. They would be extending their planting and terraforming, (claiming new land), for years. A genetically enhanced dark moss would be introduced on Gaia Nea. It would be planted between the trees and in other places on the planet to attract and retain solar heat. It would warm the land and help the trees grow, and provide more oxygen in the atmosphere.

In the meantime armies of scientists explored the planet discovering new life and new vegetation, and in time a zoo of local animals would be created next to a zoo from Earth. There would be a nursery of local plants, and next to it, one with plants from Earth.

Damian called the scientists together to discuss an annoying problem the planters had. Dr. Fiodor Yannovich, an agronomist, was the first one to speak. He said,

"We are having a big problem with the ants and the

spiders; we plant during the day and they walk all over the plants during the night destroying them. Then we have to start all over again. We need to do something to keep them out of the cultivated area."

There were many suggestions; from killing any spiders and ants in and around the planting area, to stunning them and then physically moving them to another area. Finally someone came up with a more humane way to keep them out; it called for putting subsonic devices in their tunnels and caves and driving them away. They also installed laser beam devices to protect the planted areas---and they worked.

After the spider's caves and ant's tunnels were vacated, the androids blocked them so that they wouldn't be reoccupied at a later time. Those tunnels proved to be very useful for starting new trees and new moss.

After months of hard work the shrine called "Eunoia" was completed and it was a piece of art. It was built from local stone and the windows and doors were covered with stained glass. It was built in the Doric style with its plain lines, heavy walls, and columns. The architects and artists had delivered what Darna requested from them and she was very appreciative.

During the opening ceremonies many priests of different denominations used the opportunity to speak of their faith. There was a phrase chiseled into a huge monolith that caught everybody's attention; it read "MAY THE SOURCE BE WITH YOU."

Chapter 21

With half the people gone there was now plenty of space on Anastrophe One. There were already petitions from young parents to have more children, but it was decided they couldn't go back to the old days when people were living in the corridors for lack of room. A new policy was introduced and was accepted by the majority of the community; it called for a quota of new births to be determined each year by lottery. This policy would change once they occupied a meteorite some time in the future.

After a few months Anastrophe One had left the last planets and now it was again in deep space. Their next stop would be in the Danerian area where they were hoping to find a large meteorite for their last and longest voyage.

Nick and Norina, like everybody else, kept busy trying

to forget the painful separation from their daughter Thora and grandchildren. Their pain was eased a bit whenever they received holographic messages from them. They were involved in many community projects, and also enjoyed visits from Nikita's family.

Both Nick and Norina decided to write their autobiographies and often they would spend time sitting by their favorite picture window looking at the stars while dictating.

Ner and Vrima kept busy too. Vrima, who was still in charge of all the robot guards, would arrange mock fights with the newest fighting ships out in open space. These exercises were important for the young human cadets. Ner kept busy in the government affairs, but sometimes he and Vrima would charge their batteries together and speak of their daily chores. They would talk of things they had done together in the past and they would be as nostalgic as robots could be.

Ner and Vrima were especially excited because tomorrow they would have their first spinal brain matter transplant; this time they knew who their human donors were. Five months before both Nick and Norina volunteered to go through a simple procedure where a small portion of their spinal brain matter was extracted. Since then it had been cultivated in the lab to the amount needed for Ner and Vrima.

Vrima was to get Norina's cultivated brain and Ner, Nick's. Very few of the robots carried human brain material and those who did, didn't know their donors. But in Ner's and Vrima's case they did and that's why they were so excited. This brain matter would survive in Ner and Vrima long after Nick and Norina were dead. Every so often Ner and Vrima would extract a small portion of it and grow more in a special lab so that a part of Norina's being

Project Anastrophe

would be in Vrima's body and a part of Nick's being would be in Ner's body for as long as they were allowed to live.

The transplantation was successfully done the next day and their old spinal brain matter was replaced with Nick's and Norina's who were there to see them after the procedure was over. Now all four felt like kith and kin.

As the tenth year approached they were closing in on the area where they expected to find meteorites, and they were busy with preparatory work. They had manufactured several huge propulsion engines which were designed to propel the meteorite. Architects and engineers were studying various plans according to the size of the meteorite they wanted to capture.

Eventually they encountered the first small asteroids formed by a thin belt of small rocks. The farther they went, the larger the rocks became, and finally they arrived in an area where they found large meteorites, but not the size they were looking for.

They had had four shuttles scouting for the right size for the last month or so. It took another five weeks until they found what they wanted. The meteorite was approximately the size of Earth's moon.

The first shuttle with scientists landed on the surface for preliminary work. They spent a whole day checking its metallurgical and mineral properties and they were happy with what they found. They also found water in crystallized form, enough for twice the number of the present community. With proper circulation and a filtration system it would last for hundreds of years.

They didn't waste anytime; the next day there were four shuttles on the meteorite with many more scientists and other humans specializing in terraforming. They were accompanied by hundreds of robots and androids. The Anastrophe One was flying a few thousand feet above the center of the meteorite and the shuttles were going up and down with workers and material.

The engineers started building the huge canopy which would eventually cover two thirds of the meteorite. At the same time nanos and androids were working inside, excavating a large enough tunnel for the Anastrophe One to go through. The tunnel was designed to go the length of the covered area and then gradually come up to the open space for incoming and outgoing traffic.

It was a Herculean job; and it would require continuous work by humans, nanos, androids, and robots. But now they had all the time they needed; for this biosphere was different and had to last for hundreds of years.

After a few weeks a much smaller version of the biosphere was built in which humans could live for long periods. It also served as a shop and a warehouse for the ongoing construction. Many people from the government would visit frequently to check on the progress.

Once the excavation of the tunnel was finished, they brought Anastrophe One down, and parked it in a special place prepared just for it. It was away from the main tunnel but it could go out easily if needed. With the Anastrophe One put inside in a secure place, there was no need for anymore shuttling. The engineers had finished mounting the twelve propulsion engines on the meteorite. They were put in strategic places for maximum speed and maneuverability, but were temporarily connected to the Anastrophe main command center to correct the meteorite's trajectory.

The canopy put over this biosphere differed from all the others because the meteorite lacked atmosphere and was more vulnerable here in open space. Because it would travel for decades in dark space there was no need for a clear canopy. Instead it would have a much thicker skin than the composite see-through used back home and on Gaia Nea. Should there be a need for a clear canopy; portions of it could be retrofitted with stronger clear composites.

It took five years of continuous work for the completion of the latest biosphere, but the results were not comparable to any other biosphere built before. It was a fortified, floating city. In addition to the main tunnel there were many others crossing it and they were used as main freeways. The biosphere was made to resemble the one they left back home on Earth before "The Change." The older generation was very appreciative seeing again their old towns, cities, and neighborhoods. The new generations who had heard so much about how their grandparents lived back on Earth, were happily surprised to be living in a biosphere just like it. Of course here they didn't have a real sun filtering through the canopy as they did on Earth, but their artificial sun was just as bright and it followed the same four seasons.

Huge areas were excavated and cleared inside the meteorite, and in them were built block after block of buildings just as they were back at home. When it was done the old timers would walk through the new buildings and say,

"This is where we used to go to school, and that one over there is the university where we graduated in twenty-five-oh-six." Others would find their old neighborhoods and point out to the young ones the places where they grew up. The older generations knew this was a copy of their cities and towns, but didn't mind it at all, because they were happy to walk and live again in a place they knew so well.

Nick and Norina visited the restaurant where they used to meet after work when they were young. In the same restaurant they would find many of their contemporaries.

Norina and Nick often would get into their old-fashioned magneto, and Norina would show Nick the places she hadn't been able to show him back then because they had had to travel through time in the past to save Earth.

It was like living their lives once more, and they were so happy that now they had the time to really live as they would have liked to then. A ceremony was held for the completion of the new biosphere; which was named Z-2 bio, the copy of the first biosphere on Earth. The people were happy to have proper housing on solid ground, and although they were not living on a proper planet, this meteorite would be as close to it as it could be for many generations to come.

There was an important announcement to the community. They were told there was one more week left for holographic correspondence between Gaia Nea and Z-2. After that pictures would become less visible, and within a short time they would lose contact with Gaia Nea altogether. There was a flurry of messages between the two worlds with people showing the completed Z-2 to Gaia Nea, and also showing them the new members of the families, and information about their lives and the way they were now living.

The Gaia Nea people responded likewise and shortly after that there was no more contact between them. As long as the two peoples communicated they felt connected, but now they were completely severed and the feeling of separation was unbearable for both sides. People on Z-2 tried to live as best they could in their new environment keeping busy with their daily chores. There were huge gardens to be maintained and factories were busy making the newest fighting ships; the infrastructure was changing too, with new mass transportation and new communication.

Most of the changes were made in weaponry. They had

adapted several of the alien's weapons, mixed the two technologies and had come up with hybrid weapons.

With the new water they found on the meteorite they were able to use some to create an artificial river and a lake. They planted fish and other water living things. They also planted many different trees anywhere they could find room; even up on the mountains. The artificial sun resembled the one back on Earth, only here it was the sun that moved around creating the four seasons.

They were able to improve the gravitational pull so that it felt almost like Earth, and one had to go outside on the one third of the meteorite that had been left open, to realize they were in a foreign and unfriendly environment. Nick and Norina, now in their nineties, were helped by nurse robots. They were busy attending graduations and ceremonial parties, but always found time to go to the lake and sit on the sand and see the young people swim and play. Nick would often go fishing with his buddies and have a drink or two. It was the best of times. Norina was busy with her women friends, attending seminars, poetry groups, reading and writing in the big library.

Nikitas and Chloe, now in their sixties, would visit them frequently, and sometimes there would be three generations under the same roof. That was when they had their best time together, young and old, having fun.

It was one of those quiet nights, both of them were sitting in their favorite seats writing their memoirs, when Norina felt unusually tired and said to Nick,

"I don't feel well; I feel lightheaded, what do you suppose it is?"

"I suppose it's old age, love; you know we are not young anymore, but I am calling for help anyway."

"Come closer, Nick, and hold me tight."

Nick went close to Norina and held her hand telling her this would pass too, and that she would feel better soon. But he could see this time it was different. Later on while the doctors were working on her, trying desperately to save her, she looked at him, smiled and said,

"Thank you, Nick, for all the wonderful years we had together, you have been the only love in my life." And with that Norina fell into a deep coma and died a few hours later. Nick was devastated by Norina's death; he loved her and found it very difficult to live without her. She was given a state funeral which was attended by all, young and old.

Norina had been their first president and even as old as she was, she kept the people together and they felt secure having her around. She was loved by all and her passing was a loss for everyone in the community.

Soon after Norina's death, Nick's health went into a decline. He spent most of his time sitting in his chair looking at the stars through the picture window, lost in thought. Two weeks later they found him slumped in his chair---dead.

Within two weeks the community had lost two giant personalities; two heroes who had saved Earth from total destruction and who were very instrumental in setting the process to save Earth once more; this time from the aliens. They were buried together in a temple which was built as a tribute to them. The temple bore the inscription:

"THIS TEMLPE IS BUILT FOR OUR BELOVED NORINA AND NICK AND IS DEDICATED TO THE UNKNOWN SOURCE.

The death of Norina and Nick left a vacuum in the Anastrophe community as well as in the political arena. There

Project Anastrophe

were very few of the old generation from Earth; they were the remnants of a life this community never knew and never would know. These old people were the last thread to a mythical planet called Earth, and they were treated with affection. Nikitas Papas, now in his seventies, had been the president of the Anastrophe community for the past eight years, and was anxious to find someone younger to replace him in order to spend more time with his family.

The community had grown and now approached five thousand. This necessitated more building deep inside the meteorite to meet the needs of all the people. At the same time they were finding much needed minerals and other material. The downtown area now looked like a busy metropolis, with magnetos flying above or driving on the main roads. There were hundreds of people using the moving sidewalks going about their business. It was a beehive of people from far away Earth, cocooned in a meteorite on a space odyssey, on their way to the alien's planet Voursa.

As the people became more hybrid, they changed in appearance, attitude, and manner. The younger children were the forth generation since the community had left the Earth's Moon. As the time went on they became more bionic and smaller in stature, but far more intelligent than their ancestors. Their bodies adjusted to a meteorite with a lesser gravitational pull although they used artificial gravity to approximate Earth. They were becoming smaller, smarter, and stronger; a perfect fighting force.

Robots and androids had gone through changes too. Robots had been given more responsible roles in the government and in the fighting force. And androids were now the main working force in the community. Ner and Vrima had adapted to the changes too. But they had retained their special status with the community; they were the only robots that had part of Nick's and Norina's brains, and that gave them special status within the community.

Gaia Nea

The separation from the mother ship was hard on everybody, but especially on the new generation. Darna, as the first Minister of Internal Affairs of the new community, did a good job keeping the young people busy and out of trouble. As hard as life appeared to be for this new community on the planet Gaia Nea, they knew that their friends and relatives were a lot worse; crammed into a spaceship, traveling in deep space to find the aliens on their planet Voursa.

Gaia Nea was similar to Earth in many ways, and it wouldn't be difficult adapting to its climate and environment. With the completion of their biosphere, and the establishment of democratic government, the community turned its attention to the planet. They used the Dyplopherus to scout and explore it, and every day they discovered new things. They mapped Gaia Nea from pole to pole and they found out it was rich in many different minerals, and other useful materials.

The terraforming started right away; first in the immediate area, then farther away. They planted a special kind of fir tree that did well in a cold climate, and in between they planted dark moss to retain the heat and encourage growth. As the climate became warmer they planted other kinds of trees and vegetation. More oxygen was produced which made it easier for people to stay outside the biosphere for longer times. It would take thousands of years to even come close to resemble Earth, and perhaps millions

Project Anastrophe

of years to be like the planet Earth, but they had started the process and it was now a matter of time.

As the community grew in population, they found it necessary to build more biospheres in different places on Gaia Nea, but for now there were only small substations. They also named their biosphere Z-2 and it would remain their main habitation area for decades to come. The community's main problem, so far, had been the native ants and spiders. They were found all over the planet, and were the predominant species of Gaia Nea.

Although the humans had made an antidote to their deadly poison, there were a few near-death incidents with some of the younger people.

The humans established a safe area of several thousand acres around their biosphere and eventually planted millions of conifer and deciduous trees. Whenever the Dyplopherus and other spaceships flew high over their colony, it appeared to be an oasis in an arid land. This would be their homeland away from home for a long time. The nanos, androids, and robots were kept busy on a program of terraforming this alien planet called Gaia Nea, and as time went on, it looked and felt more like Earth.

The Aliens

Millions of light years away, in the cluster of Pleiades identified as M45, Mel 22 14 degrees Northwest of Aldebaran and around the magnitude 4.1 star Merope 23 Tauris, there was a planet called Voursa, which approximated Earth in size and atmospheric conditions. That was where the alien Voursi lived. The humans found out about the Voursi a long time ago, when Nick and his heroic crew traveled into the thirtieth century and discovered that the

Voursis were about to take over Earth in a war with the humans that would last over a hundred years.

Nick managed to steal some of the Voursi's advanced weaponry; he infiltrated the alien's space fleet and recovered important data about their capabilities and culture. The Voursi attacked his ship with superior strength and it was about to be destroyed, but was saved by Dr. Vlasic who used Nephus' famous escape formula.

Half of the original community that left Earth chose to live on the planet Gaia Nea. There they were to prepare themselves in manpower and new weaponry to join the other half of the community hundreds of years in the future when they would go back to Earth to fight together to save it from the aliens once and for all. Now the two human communities knew a lot about the Voursis, but they needed to know more in order to fight them and win.

The Voursi Homeland

During the great Mourdug dynasty, Voursis had no plans for invading any of their neighboring planets, much less a planet like Earth, far away in the outskirts of the Gardana galaxy. The Mourdug dynasty had had dominion over Voursa for eons, and had great influence over the neighboring planets too. Voursa was rich, powerful, and the envy of its neighbors but there was resentment from within and from other worlds. Voursa was a beacon and an inspiration to all with its advanced culture and science.

There had been many dynasties through the one billion years of Voursi civilization and many revolutions through its history. That resulted in many defeated dynasties moving and occupying the neighboring planets. But Voursa remained, through all ages, powerful and rich. The Mourdugnian was Voursi's longest surviving dynasty. The

Project Anastrophe

latest Mourdug Monarch, The Great Throvolan, was in the 175th year of his life and was getting too old and frail to attend to all his duties. But he never missed the annual Mourdugnian celebrations which were held every year in appreciation of the royal family. This time the Voursis were preparing to celebrate the 2000th year of the Mourdugnian dynasty.

Tharnata and Flarnar

Tharnadians were the first to break away from Voursa 1500 years ago when they were defeated in a long and costly war with the Mourdugs. Rather than surrender and submit to the great ruler Mourdug, the Tharnaty revolutionary warrior took his armies and people to the neighboring planet. He named the planet after his name, and started a new colony and a new country. The people called themselves Tharnatians instead Voursis, but they spoke the same language and were culturally like the Voursis.

During the first few decades the Voursis attacked Tharnata a few times, but were pushed back by the heroic Tharnatians. Finally a peace treaty was signed between the two peoples, and since that time a successful commerce started between the two planets, and there were no more wars although Tharnatians never felt at ease with the Voursis. Tharnata was smaller than Voursa and was farther away from the sun which made it a colder planet. But it was rich in minerals and other material needed by the Voursis.

Flarna was an even smaller planet between Voursa and Tharnata which had initially belonged to Voursa. It was sparsely populated mainly by Voursi miners and their families. During the last few hundred years it was populated by Voursis and Tharnatians. Most of the people who migrated to Flarna had one thing in common; they were called

Gaians. They were ridiculed and mistreated by the Voursis and the Tharnatians for their beliefs.

They were followers of the great Gaias, who millions of years ago, established a religious sect believing in polytheism. He taught his followers that his deities were above every monarch or dynasty. That didn't go well with the mortals of that time or any time. Flarnars had established their own government, based on their own religion. Although they were a peaceful people they were powerful enough to protect their planet.

Chapter 22

The small community of Anastrophe had been traveling in space for one hundred and forty- five human years, and they were within five years of getting to Voursa, their final destination. The population of Anastrophe had grown to one hundred thousand people, and it occupied every possible space in and on the meteorite. They had become a complex society, but had kept their forefather's democratic system. But above all they had perfected their weaponry; all they needed now was the same material the Voursis would use a few hundred years from now, when they attacked Earth. The humans had the technology, now they needed local material to make more weapons.

They had been preparing for this war for decades—they were the best fighters the human race could offer. This generation was the one which was training to fight the Voursis. The robots had also been made to be lethal in battle. The shield all around the meteorite had been reinforced to be almost impenetrable. There had been daily mock sorties with their latest spaceships, but they would not be ready until they found local material, and built more of the weapons they now knew how to build.

In the last few months scout ships had explored many large and small asteroids in the outskirts of a new-found sun. Although they found many minerals and other material to replenish their stockpiles, they hadn't yet found the special material needed for weapon production. But this large asteroid was different. It looked glassy and shiny like basalt rock, but it wasn't black, it was green with yellow veins running through it. It was in those yellow veins they found what they were looking for--and plenty of it. Within hours humans, robots, and androids landed on it. The excavation started in earnest. Cargo ships carried the precious alloy to the colony. They worked continuously for months until they had enough, and at the same time they were making the new weapons based on the combined alien's and human's technology.

After years of hard work they rebuilt all their weapons mixing the new-found alloy with other metals and finally achieved the strength of the Voursi's weapons as it would be three hundred years in the future.

Commander Argeris Papas couldn't contain his pride at being in charge of the newly built space force.

These ships were different from any others built before. His Grandfather, Nick Papas, of many decades ago, would have been proud of such a powerful fighting fleet. Commander Papas called his officers to a staff meeting. Ner and Vrima attended as advisors. They were the only robots Argeris had asked for advice. In fact they were considered relatives to the Papas' through all the past decades because they contained portions of Nick's and Norina's brains.

Ner and Vrima were the oldest robot issues and had been repaired many times to keep up with the new changes. Every so often their precious brain matter was organically rejuvenated too. Ner and Vrima were the only living remnants from Earth and were treated with great respect by all. Argeris' first question was directed to Vrima,

"Are all robot and android warriors retrofitted and ready for combat?"

"Yes they are."

"You are going to accompany us on our first reconnaissance expedition."

"I would appreciate that, Commander Argeris."

The meeting lasted two hours with the rest of the officers reporting on the status of the human force and the expedition. It was decided to leave the next day at 8:00 A.M. metric time.

Commander Argeris Papas had been in charge of the space force for the last two years, and was well-liked by all those who depended on him. He had proven to be a good leader during the mock or simulated battles, but tomorrow was going to be different. They were going to approach Flarna, the smallest of the three planets. Until they knew the strength of all three planets they had to be careful not to be discovered.

The plan called for the home base to be kept far away from the aliens. A flotilla of five thousand ships would stay cloaked at a safe distance from Flarna, and then they would initiate first contact by sending several probes. After that they would act according to the information they received. Commander Argeris and his armada left the next day with the whole colony wishing them good luck, but there was apprehension among the people. He had left his young family behind many times in the past; sometimes for two to three weeks. But this was going to be a long trip; perhaps six months or longer. Argeris' wife Nourska, 30, his sons Tounos 10, and Klamos 9, and the two daughters Niria 7, and Kallista 6, worried about him leaving, but they knew it was something that needed to be done.

Ner and Vrima were inherently bonded to the Papas family through the last few decades, and now that Vrima was away Ner felt more responsible for Argeris Papas' family. Ner has seen a lot of changes during the last two hundred years of this expedition which started back on Earth's Moon in that old Anastrophe spaceship. It had been kept intact in a museum through all these years for the benefit of the younger generations--part of the community's short history. Ner had brought all four Papas' children to the old Anastrophe for a visit. The children were excited and asked many questions about the ship and those bygone relatives called Nick and Norina.

Not all Voursis were happy with the Great Throvolan. A great portion of the Voursi population were disappointed when he signed a treaty for permanent peaceful coexistence among all three planets. Those who disagreed thought that both the Tharnadians and the Flarnars were using this peaceful time to buildup their war chests. They were afraid they were losing their superpower status. Their leader Larnos knew that after the Monarch died, next in line to the throne would be his older son Vlog and he had made it clear he wanted to unite the three planets as one empire. That didn't go well with many Tharnadians and Flarnars, but especially with Larnos and his fanatic followers who had their eye on the Monarchy.

Project Anastrophe

The Mourdug Dynasty reigned for many years using their power to maintain peace and commerce with their neighboring planets. The absence of wars made the people on all three planets prosperous and happy. The Voursis had many good reasons to wish long life to the old Monarch Throvolan in the coming annual celebrations. However Larnos and many of his followers thought that Throvolan and his son Vlog were naïve. Larnos had many sympathizers especially in the army. They thought that before long Voursa would lose its superpower status; and feared they would be taken over by the Tharnadians and the Flarnars. They conspired to assassinate both Throvolan and his son Vlog during the coming celebrations and takeover the Dynasty under Larnos' leadership.

As always the Voursis enjoyed this celebration with organized parades and marching bands, dancing, and other merriments. The day had come; Larnos and several of the top generals had worked out the takeover down to the smallest detail. They waited for the time when both father and son would be momentarily exposed to the people; and they struck with lightning speed. Throvolan and Vlog were killed instantly and the takeover was complete. The Monarchy passed to the new leader Larnos and his warmonger generals. They quickly commanded the Tharnadians and the Flarnars to surrender. They both replied with an emphatic "no" and the three planets prepared for an all-out war.

Commander Dranos, in charge of the Flarna's fighting force, called his generals. One by one they told him how grim their situation was. They couldn't sustain a defensive war with the Voursis for long. Naoul, one of the high ranking generals, said,

"The only way we can defend our planet is to join

forces with the Tharnatians, and with a combined fleet, fight the Voursis before they enter our space borders. The Tharnatians cannot fight the Voursis alone." The high priest Shaidor gave permission to go ahead with the plan.

The Tharnatians had similar meetings concerning the impending attack by the Voursis. They put aside the differences they had had with the Flarnars in the past, and were eager to join forces with them and fight their common enemy. The generals from both planets worked out a defensive plan and their combined armadas left their home bases to meet the Voursis. When the two powers met at the appointed area they looked very impressive. Even though the Voursis had a superior force, they knew their enemies were determined to protect their planets.

The Tharnatians and the Flarnars had placed their armadas in strategic areas. They would fight a defensive war; the most they hoped to accomplish was to keep the Voursis from penetrating their established safety zone, and at best, push them back. Victory was out of the question; the Voursis were too powerful for that. The Tharnatians and the Flarnars had admired the Great Throvolan; during his Dynasty they enjoyed uninterrupted commerce and many decades of peaceful coexistence and prosperity.

Throvolan's son Vlog, who was next in line to the throne, was inexperienced and they didn't trust him. So in the last few years they had prepared for a war they knew was going to happen in the near future.

The Voursi generals wanted to use their power to establish an empire while the enemies were weak. With the Monarch Throvolan and his son Vlog gone, the generals finally got their wish. They prepared for a war they knew they were going to win. Their armada outnumbered the enemy's by three to one. While Larnos had the army on his side, he had a hard time convincing the majority of Voursis

Project Anastrophe

to go to war. The people loved the Great Throvolan, and Larnos had to use dictatorial powers to force the Voursis into an unwanted war.

The first probes came back from Flarna and were analyzed by a special scientific team. The results were given to commander Argeris and his generals. They met in the war room and Vrima, as always, sat next to him. The information was unfolding in three dimensions and it was impressive. Kaloneris, a high ranking officer, narrated the information as it was projected. He said,

"What you are about to see just arrived from the planet Flarna. We have sent more probes to the planet and will have more information in a few hours."

Flarna looked similar to Earth in size but had two Moons about half the size of Earth's Moon. It had more oceans and fewer lakes, but its geophysical features were very similar to Earth's. Although Flarnars had a theocratic society; they had a very old and advanced civilization in comparison to Earth's. Then the officer zeroed in on the armada leaving Flarna and followed it to where it met a larger armada about halfway to Voursa and stopped. Then he said,

"If I am not mistaken these two armadas are either engaging in war games, or they are about to engage in real war." Commander Argeris said,

"They wouldn't need to use so many ships for war games; they must be positioning their armadas for war." General Vremos said,

"I agree with you, Commander Argeris, although I am puzzled by how they have positioned their armadas." Several other generals offered different explanations, then Vrima said,

"Commander Argeris, I agree with you that the armadas

are not engaging in war games, but they are not about to fight each other either. Notice how they have placed their ships; they have all taken defensive positions. They are preparing for war, but not with each other.

Chapter 23

It all made sense now; a closer look at the two armadas proved Vrima right. The ships were divided in groups and dispersed in strategic areas. They now could see two different insignias on the ships indicating two separate powers merged into one. There were scout ships in constant movement; these two merged fleets were braced for an attack-- but from where? More information from Flarna showed the whole planet was taking defensive measures. Flarnars were not as powerful as the Voursis or the Tharnatians but nevertheless they were a power to be reckoned with.

Probes sent to Tharnata and Voursa were sending more information from those two planets. Commander Argeris and his generals concentrated first on Tharnata; now they knew without a doubt that the other power merged with the Flarnars were indeed the Tharnatians. They too were preparing their homeland for a possible invasion. Information was coming in from all around Tharnata. Tharnata was about the same size as Flarna, had one Moon about the size of Earth's Moon; but was a richer planet in important minerals, agriculture, and had a more advanced civilization. Its population was almost double that of Flarna. Tharnatians were more warlike in nature and had a superior army and better weaponry than the Flarnars.

The humans had had two hundred years to study and learn about these three planets, thanks in part to Nick and his brave crew who had traveled to the thirtieth century and retrieved vital information from the Voursis. They learned about their past history and now they were comparing notes with their present information. The humans knew that three hundred years from now the Voursis would attack Earth for some reason; they also knew how strong they would be and what kind of weapons they would have in the future. Now they wanted to know how strong the Voursis were at this time.

Commander Argeris and his generals were anxious to get information from Voursa, but didn't want to be discovered by the Voursis. They had to be careful with the probes they sent to Voursa, that's why it took so long. Finally they were rewarded by useful and revealing information. Commander Argeris said,
"The Voursis have a much larger armada than the combined armadas of their enemies. Their weapons are superior too. There is no doubt in my mind they will come out of this war victorious." General Vremos agreed with the

commander although several other generals thought it would be a long war before the Voursis won. All this time Vrima was analyzing the information as it arrived from Voursa. Finally she said,

"Commander, generals, have you noticed the type of weapons and ships they have? They are inferior to the weapons and the ships they will have three hundred years from now. We have been in the future and have seen them. What does that tell us?"

General Phillips said,

"It looks to me as if it will take the Voursis three hundred years to improve the quality and strength of their weaponry and ships."

"General Phillips is correct, but the important thing is that we have copied their future weaponry and ships and have combined our own technology. Even though we don't have as many, ours are superior to theirs at this time." Commander Argeris said,

"That is true, but even with our superiority we are still no match for the Voursis. So we still have to be careful not to be discovered."

General Phanos said,

"They may be enemies now but if they discover us, we will be the alien enemy to them and perhaps they would join together and attack us." Vrima said,

"That might be possible if we attack them, but if we stay away, even if we are discovered, they would probably continue with their war and deal with us at a later time. It would be prudent for us to stay out of their way for now."

Now there was more information coming in from the Voursi homeland. Voursa was the warmest of the three planets, and it was rich in agriculture and minerals. It had the most productive industry and it was culturally more advanced than its two sister planets. It had more of the latest weapons and ships and was a powerful planet. Voursa was the mother planet of the Tharnatians and the Flarnars. It had eight billion inhabitants, far more than those of the two other planets. For hundreds of years the Mourdug Dynasty reigned in peace. Now with the Monarch Throvolan and his son Vlog gone, Larnos and his regime were preparing for war.

Commander Argeris, Vrima, the rest of the generals, were studying the information that was pouring in and were working on a plan of action that would best suit the humans. General Phanos said,

"My feeling is that we should withdraw from our present position to a more secure area. If we stay here any longer we risk being discovered, and at the present time we are not strong enough to fight any of them--much less all of them."

General Phillips said,

"Perhaps this would be the best time to make ourselves known to the High Priest Shaidor of Flarna and convince him that we are here to help them."

Commander Argeris responded,

"That would be a grave mistake; perhaps we could do that later, but not now. I agree with General Phanos, we should move out of here, go to a safer place, keep an eye on the battle, and act accordingly."

Vrima agreed,

"We should let them have their battle and see what happens; it is my feeling that the Voursis will win, but the question is--how strong will they remain? If they have big losses--that would be the time to make a deal with the Flarnars and then attack the Voursis with our superior power." Commander Argeris gave the order to move the armada to a safe area.

Being on a wandering meteorite was good camouflage,

Project Anastrophe

but it was not completely safe. So Governor Diotheos put his community on alert and took defensive measures for possible attack from the aliens. The special pursuit fleet was armed with the latest panoply of weapons and was ready to defend the homeland at all cost. There was a continuous communication between Commander Argeris and governor Diotheos, and he knew in detail of every move of the armada; so it was with great relief to those at home to see that the armada was out of harm's way.

The probes' information from all three planets was forwarded to the home base as well. The Governor and his security staff knew the strength of each planet, but what worried them most was how capable the aliens were of breaking their homeland's defensive shield. Nephus' unique cloaking method was by now perfected to a point that even he would not have recognized it. The Anastrophe community now had the ability to put the whole meteor in cloak mode, and avoid being found by the enemy. Should their shield fail this would be the last protective measure.

Ner's time was spent between the Governor's office and the Papas family. He missed Vrima but took comfort being with the children. Ner had always been a surrogate father to all the Papas children for many generations. He had seen the likenesses of Norina and Nick come and go on the faces of the children and was amazed at the human genes' abilities to carry so much information through the ages. In Argeris' and Nourska's family there was the six year old girl, Kallista, who not only looked like Norina, but acted like her. Ner was close to Kallista and often told her stories about her grandmother Norina who lived a long time ago.

Because of Kallista's likeness to Norina, Ner had an idea he wanted to discuss with Vrima. His idea would apply to a Papas child in the future that looked like Nick. But for now he had to study his theory to be absolutely sure that it would work. Ner started with a small portion of Kallista's saliva; from it he extracted the Papas' and Anderson's D.N.A s and matched them with Nick Papa's eighteen percent brain matter he maintained in his own body. Then Ner matched Kallista's D.N.A. s with Norina's twenty-five percent brain matter which was maintained in Vrima's body. The match was close but not close enough. Ner would have to repeat this process with many of Nick's and Norina's look-alikes in future generations until he found the perfect match; then his theory might work. But for the time being the secret experiment would stay with Ner and Vrima.

Gaia Nea

Under Damian's leadership the little community of Gaia Nea flourished. Hundreds of new biospheres were built all over the planet, and as one flew above, one could see them like oases sprouting on this new-found land. Terraforming continued even in places no one lived. Billions of Eco-nanos worked continuously converting an arid landscape into a habitable ecosystem. There was mass transportation to all biospheres along with thousands of magnetos carrying people and goods to all parts of Gaia Nea.

Darna worked for many years in the newly formed government, but in the later years she worked mainly without portfolio. She was busy with women's needs and aspirations, and with children at risk. She lived a full life and was one of the most celebrated citizens in this new world. She died at the age of ninety-five, and the citizens of Gaia Nea erected a statue to her memory in the center of the first biosphere. Damian and Thora had four children: two boys, Lichnos and Davlos, and two daughters, Daphne and Clima. Thora taught history and languages and in the later

Project Anastrophe

years she was in charge of the terraforming program. Thora missed her parents and she always talked of her father Nick Papas, who had been beamed away five hundred years to the future. Damian became the first President of the new community. When he and Thora died of old age they joined the pantheon of heroes who had started Gaia Nea.

Of the fifteen neighboring planets the closest one, Atalandos, was rich in diamonds but not easily accessible. Governor Lichnos was scheduled to meet a group of civil engineers headed by his brother Davlos who had conceived the idea of mining the precious mineral. Governor Lichnos didn't get to see him often enough because he lived with his wife Doria, and his two children, a son Lathios and daughter Artemis, away in another biosphere called Theta-Biosphere. Governor Lichnos welcomed his brother Davlos and his entourage,

"Well, Davlos, we don't see you often enough lately, how is the frontier land doing nowadays?"

"Doing fine--I suppose you know why we are here."

"Oh, yes, the diamonds on Atalandos; I studied the information you sent me, it looks promising."

"I am going to let Mr. Floupash explain the mining procedure." Mr. Floupash was a capable man in his fifties in charge of the proposed Atalandos mine; he had worked in different mines on Gaia Nea and was considered the right man for the job. He projected the planet in 3-D which was suspended in the middle of the room, then zeroed in on an enlarged area and said,

"Governor, this is the area we are planning to excavate; notice that big-black-mountain, it's solid diamond, and there is enough of it to build our towers."

Davlos again interjected,

"Now I'd like to let Dr. Shindros explain the construction of the two towers."

Dr. Shindros pointed to a flat area of the planet and said,
"We think this would be a good place to build the tower on Atalandos. We have examined the ground underneath and it's solid diamond, we believe that it will hold the weight of the structure. Both towers on Atalandos and on Gaia Nea will be built mostly of diamond. It's the strongest available material and it is plentiful."

"How high will they be built?"

"Both towers on each planet will reach as high as the start of its Mesosphere about ninety-two kilometers from the surface." Davlos explained,

"Here is what we aim to do; once the two towers are built, we will install special elevators to move spaceships up, thereby avoiding the gravitational pull of the planets. This method will be faster and secure and will enable us to bring diamond to Gaia Nea."

"How long will it take to complete the towers?"

"With the workforce and the equipment we have at this time we figure it will take five years."

"Which tower you are going to start first?"

"The one on Gaia Nea."

"Have you chosen the place for it?"

"Yes, in the southern hemisphere."

"You have my permission to start at anytime you are ready."

Most of the preparatory work on Gaia Nea was done ahead of time and as soon as they were given permission to start the project, they began the work in earnest two weeks later.

The Aliens

There were probes on all three planets, and many more covering the area where the battle was about to take place.

Project Anastrophe

The human's armada was hidden, and out of the way, but the atmosphere in the war room where Commander Argeris and his generals were, was electrified. They had a clear view of the three fleets, the Tharnatians and Flarnars on one side and the huge fleet of the Voursis on the other. They had been in that position for the last three days, with the Voursis always on the move bringing more ships all the time and positioning them in strategic places. The Tharnatians and the Flarnars were not bringing more ships but were positioning their ships facing their common enemy. The Voursis went on the offensive hitting Flarnars' left wing with a barrage of bombs aimed to weaken the Flarnars' shield capacity--- they did not respond. It was immediately followed by a second salvo, but this time it was intercepted in midair by a volley of missiles from the Tharnatians. Next the Voursis attacked the Tharnatians but they did not respond either. Another barrage from the Voursis directed to the Tharnatians was intercepted and destroyed in midair, but this time by the Flarnars.

Argeris said,

"It's interesting how they cover for each other, instead of shooting directly at the enemy."

Vrima said,

"It appears that they want to confuse the Voursis and it has a positive effect." The Voursis felt that they had weakened their enemies, and now they started to encircle them and bombard them with thermo kinetic missiles causing great damage. The Tharnatians and Flarnars did not respond to this barrage; instead they gathered closer although they sustained great damage. It looked as if they were about to surrender when both fleets attacked the Voursis' concentrated center annihilating half of Voursi fleet. It was a daring move, but they didn't come out of it unscathed either.

Although the Voursis were reduced to half of their previous power, the Tharnatians and the Flarnars had sustained even more damage and they knew that they couldn't fight the Voursis for too long. The Voursis were now preparing for the kill, but they could see that their enemies were not going to surrender easily. The Tharnatians and the Flarnars gathered their fleets together and waited for the inevitable last fight.

In the Human Armada

General Vremos said,

"I think this is a good time to make ourselves known to the Flarnars and make them an offer to help, what do you think?" Vrima said,

"I disagree with you, General Vremos; this would not be a good time to talk to them. My feeling is that now would be a good time for us to attack the Voursis while we have the element of surprise. If we make ourselves known to the Flarnars they must tell the Tharnatians and I am afraid the word would go to the Voursis. Also we don't know that our offer would be accepted. They know they are going to be defeated so perhaps they might prefer to negotiate to surrender to the Voursis rather than make a deal with aliens like us." Most of the generals and advisors agreed with Vrima and were in favor of attacking the Voursis. Commander Argeris said,

"In the first place we don't know if we would be successful with our surprise attack; and what if they unite and go after us?"

Grounos, a respected old general, said,

"I agree with commander Argeris, the Voursis may know we are here and don't want to deal with us at this time. But I also agree with Vrima. This would be a good time to attack the Voursis. I do have an idea but if it doesn't work it could be the end of our colony." The possibility of their homeland's demise made everyone in the room sober. Commander Argeris said,

"General Grounos, please proceed with your idea."

"Commander, as you said, there is the possibility that they might unite and go after us. In that case we may perish, but our colony will survive and fight another time, perhaps better prepared. I suggest we should use a second armada leaving our home base with a fifty percent fighting capability. But with a second armada as a backup, our attack would be more successful even if they knew about us. On the other hand, if we were destroyed, our homeland would fight a defensive war at best and it may not survive." It was something Commander Argeris had never learned in school or in practice. When he asked for opinions, most decided to postpone for now, and attack the Voursis at a later time with more ships and weapons. One of the proponents for attacking, officer Kaloneris, said,

"Commander, our people have traveled for many decades, and have endured many sacrifices to fight the Voursis. At this time we have superior ships and weapons. They have lost half of their fleet, and the Tharnatians and the Flarnars are in even worse shape. We will never have another chance like this. If we defeat them we will set the rules according to our interest. I say we attack and take our chances." Vrima responded,

"If we are going to attack, we must wait until the Voursis start the last phase of this war. We must deprive them of their victory before the Tharnatians and the Flarnars are about to surrender. This way they will all be more depleted and thus it will be easier for us to defeat them." This time they were more inclined to attack, and finally they all looked at Commander Argeris for a final decision. All this time, he had covered his face with both hands leaning with his elbows on the table listening to his generals and advisers saying nothing; as if trying to avoid the inevitable question. Finally he looked at them and said,

"We attack!"

Vrima said,

"Commander, this is a very courageous decision, but it is the right one."

His generals knew what to do next. For generations they had been practicing to fight this mythical enemy, always improving their weapons, ships, and fighting techniques. For the last few months they had been spying on the three planets, and learned all there was to be known and especially their weapons and ships. They learned how these aliens fought. Now Commander Argeris' armadas were fine-tuned and ready for war.

In the homeland, Governor Diotheos and his advisers were listening from afar, and knew what the Commander had decided. Now it was their turn to fortify their bases and be ready for war. Their fighting force may have been reduced to fifty percent but they were ready to fight and protect their homeland. And if they were to perish, their last act would be to destroy the planet Voursa as well.

The Last Battle

The Voursis' fleet once more encircled the Tharnatians and the Flarnars. In order to inflict the most damage they dispersed in single units and attacked for one last time. The Voursis hit back with precision and the battle was over in minutes. The Voursis again sustained many losses, but as expected, they came out victorious. The Tharnatians and the Flarnars fought heroically but now they were about to surrender to the Voursis.

Project Anastrophe

Humans Versus Voursis

Out of nowhere strange looking ships appeared and this time encircled the Voursis and the remaining Tharnatian and Flarnar ships. The humans quickly arranged part of their armada in the form of a horse shoe. They guarded the one opening and waited for the Voursis' response. Fortunately for the humans the Voursis were unprepared for them; they didn't know what to think. Their first thought was that the Tharnatians and the Flarnars had been reinforced with new ships and were not about to surrender; but on closer examination they appeared to be of unknown origin or alien made. This was a new phase in the war, something they were not prepared for.

Only a few minutes before, the Voursis were about to taste victory, but now they were faced with a new and unknown enemy. A message from the humans got them out of their predicament. Commander Argeris appeared in holographic form to Commander in Chief Larnos and his generals. He spoke in clear Voursi language,

"We are humans; we come from the planet Earth from the outskirts of this Galaxy. We don't wish to fight with you, but you must stop the war immediately and surrender to us. If you do not do so, we will destroy you." The same message was communicated to the Tharnatians and the Flarnars. Commander Larnos and his staff were dumbfounded, but quickly began to make plans to fight this new enemy. They knew one thing; they were not going to surrender to these aliens. The first thing they did was to ask for reinforcements; then they communicated with the Tharnatians and the Flarnars asking them to join forces to fight the aliens. But they declined the offer and went into defensive mode.

Even after their losses the Voursis outnumbered the

human fleet three to one; and there were more reinforcements on the way from home. So far the humans had deployed one armada; the other was under cloaked mode, waiting for orders to engage. The Voursis didn't bother to answer the communiqué; instead they attacked the humans with all their might. And there started a battle of unparalleled ferocity. The Voursis tried to break out and to their surprise the humans let them go. But only a portion of them made it out; then the humans quickly closed the circle again. Those ships which broke lose were surrounded and destroyed. Next the Voursis attacked the human fleet all at once; this time they were able to break out of the circle. Now the Voursis attacked the humans with their numerous ships. The human ships were smaller, faster and had better shielding protection. The Voursi ships were larger and less maneuverable and their weapons were old and less effective. The humans used an ingenious tactic against the Voursis; they formed a large number of their ships into groups, and attacked and separated a small number of Voursi ships. Then they destroyed them and at the same time fought defensively. They did that until they greatly damaged the Voursi fleet; then they went into offensive tactics.

The Voursis fought heroically, but the superior number of their ships quickly diminished and now they were fighting a defensive war. The humans had losses too, but in smaller numbers, and it appeared that they were winning the battle. The Voursi's reinforcements arrived. And now the humans found themselves encircled. The Voursis went on the offensive using the tactic that had worked so well for the humans. They tried to break the humans out of their defensive mode, the humans held together until their second armada arrived. Then there started an all-out war with two enemies determined to come out of this battle victorious. In

Project Anastrophe

the end the Voursis were not a match for the humans who fought just as heroically with better ships and more potent weapons. The Voursis surrendered to the humans without conditions along with the Tharnatians and the Flarnars who had kept out of the fight all this time.

Chapter 24
THE PEACE TREATY

The Tharnatians and the Flarnars went back home defeated; not by the Voursis, as they had feared, but by alien. The Voursis also went home to an unhappy citizenry. The humans sent the second armada back home where they were received with welcoming victory parades. Representatives of Voursa, Tharnata, and Flarnar were sent to the human armada to negotiate a peace treaty among the three planets under human auspices.

Governor Diotheos, representing the humans, opened the meeting speaking in the Voursi language,

"Friends, I am glad to meet with you this time not as a combatant. The war was very unfortunate but as you know it wasn't started by us. We saw an unjust war started by the Voursis, and we felt compelled to stop it. In the process we

Project Anastrophe

also lost many of our fighters. We come from the outskirts of this galaxy, from a solar system similar to yours but many light years away. Our ancestors started this voyage for the sole purpose of meeting you. For generations we learned your language, studied your culture and your long history. In the process we discovered that we are the descendants of the Gaians who left Flarna a long time ago searching for new solar systems; in fact we call our planet Gaia.

But why did we leave our beloved planet searching to find you? We have traveled into the future and discovered that a huge armada from Voursa will take over our planet. That is the reason we came here; to stop them before they started their destructive voyage. Unfortunately we found out that the Voursis we came to stop have already left and now they are on a quest for new solar systems. We know the time they will invade and we want to be there to help our planet. But before we leave for home we want to see peace among your people."

If they were expecting retribution or harsh measures from the humans, they were in for a big surprise. All the humans demanded from them was a long peace treaty among themselves. Nichtas, the leader of the Flarnars, said,

"I have heard of the lost Gaians but I thought they were gone forever; but I am glad to know that you are our distant relatives."

The next one to talk was Flooch, the Tharnatian leader,

"As long as the Voursis have a superior army there will always be the temptation to break the peace treaty after you have gone."

Commander Argeris said,

"We will make sure you have parity in all of your armed forces; you will also have free commerce and peace for an indefinite time."

Mouchda, representing Voursa, responded,

"We wish to live in peace with our neighbors, and we are prepared to sign the treaty as it has been written."

The treaty was signed by all three parties, and it was agreed that the human armada should stay close by as long as it was needed for the three planets to reach armed parity before they left for the long voyage back home.

Governor Diotheos asked the question many of the humans wanted to ask,

"Mr. Mouchda, tell us about the group of Voursis that left Voursa on a quest to find other solar systems."

"They left fifty of your human years ago on a scientific expedition in search of other solar systems like ours; if they found other humanoid species they would introduce them to our civilization. It was to be a peace expedition; their orders were to make contact by peaceful means not to take over another species. We haven't communicated with them for about ten of your years, and at this time we don't know where they are."

"We don't know where they are either, but we do know that they will attack our planet two hundred years from now and we must be there on time to stop them from doing so."

Flarna

If the Flarnars hated the Voursis, they loved their distant cousins the alien humans. After all, if it wasn't for the humans they would have surrendered to the Voursis and they would have been treated like second class citizens. Now they had parity in arms with the Voursis and the Tharnatians and a peace treaty that could last for a long time; thanks to the humans. So when Commander Argeris, his wife, Nourska, Governor Diotheos with his wife Lyfa,

Project Anastrophe

Ner, and many generals and other officials arrived for a first visit to Flarnar, the people were happy to see them and they were rapturously received in the capital. They were taken to the high priest Shaidor, who welcomed them to a state dinner.

Next day Ner and the scientists were shown the capital city of Gourha. Once Ner was identified as an artificial entity he wasn't treated with the same enthusiasm as the humans. There were many robots among the Flarnars but they were not anthropomorphic; instead they were designed specifically for the kind of work they were doing. It was obvious that the humanoids were in charge of the business of the state and war. Ner talked to one of the human technicians called Svengo,

"I wonder why, in such an advanced society, artificial intelligence is not used to its full potential?"

"I have noticed that too; I believe there must be a good reason for this behavior."

"I see that I am not liked here, and would like to know what has caused this antipathy towards artificial intelligence." Ner noticed that there was an automatic screening and he was often cutoff on any of his inquiries. Humans, on the other hand, were free to inquire about everything. Ner was able to penetrate their electronic filtering system without being noticed; and found the reason why they were so careful with his kind. This information was not available in the Anastrophe's data base taken from the Voursis when they visited Earth a little before the thirtieth century.

During the reign of the high priest and great leader Stachtus, in Flarnar, and during the war campaigns with the Tharnatians, robots had been given great powers in state and in the war department. Robots were indispensable to the Flarnars; they were made to look like them and many excelled as political leaders and in the war with the Tharnatians. But at some point their artificial intelligence made them uncontrollably dangerous. They looked down on their masters and started to break away. They reproduced themselves without their masters' supervision. At first they started with small numbers; they were autonomous and would not answer to the humanoids or the rest of the robots. Those who were found were quickly destroyed but the rebellion continued and finally they multiplied out of control and soon there was civil war between the humanoids and the robots. The rebellious robots changed the rest of the robot population and they were well on their way to take over Flarnar.

The Tharnatians and the Voursis were alarmed and were afraid that the rebellion might start on their own planets. Finally the more technologically advanced Voursis were able to introduce an artificial virus into the rebels' cybernetics which put them out of action thus saving the Flarnars from defeat. It took the Flarnars many years to change their robots to their present form. No wonder they looked at Ner so suspiciously. The Voursis and the Tharnatians took similar measures and now their robots were also under complete control.

The next day Ner caught the first shuttle back to the armada and then continued on home to the Papas' family where he felt more comfortable. Commander Argeris, his wife Nourska, Governor Diotheos, his wife Lyfa, and their close associates along with their guards, were asked to join the high priest Shaidor for a special gathering. Even though the humans had become shorter in stature during the last two hundred years they looked like giants to the Flarnars who were a little over a hundred centimeters tall. They were given larger chairs to sit in but they had to be careful going through doors. The meeting took place in a huge temple which was big even by human standards. The doors

Project Anastrophe

and all furniture were normal size for human but looked and felt enormous to the Flarnars. They all sat around the table and the Flarnars looked even smaller in those chairs. The high priest, Shaidor, sat at the head of the table. Before he addressed the humans he murmured a few words at which the Flarnars bowed their heads. Then he said,

"Gaians, I welcome you back to the planet where your forefathers began; I brought you here because it is here where our beloved Gaias met with his brave people before they left for their long voyage many eons ago. At that time the Flarnars, the Tharnatians and the Voursis were all giants just like you. We all have the same D.N.A.; we are of the same species, but you are especially related to us because the Gaians were most of all Flarnars. Unlike the Tharnatians and the Voursis, who believe in mortal emperors and other leaders, we believe in deities and for that we were persecuted through the years. Our forefathers broke away from the Voursis and the Tharnatians and moved to this planet. They made it their home under the leadership of the great Flarnar, the father of our country, many eons ago. Now you came and saved us just as we were about to become slaves to the Voursis once more. You are our lost cousins and you are welcome to stay with us, but we understand that you wish to go back to your planet. We would like to help you in any way we can to make your voyage back home easier and faster."

It was a very welcoming speech Shaidor gave for the humans. Governor Diotheos said,

"High priest Shaidor, on behalf of my compatriots I thank you for your hospitality; but as you said we wish to go home and if you can help us in any way, that would be much appreciated."

The humans were introduced to the state officials. They were treated like deities because of their connection to the mythical Gaians. They were taken to many temples and other sites. The next day human scientists with a "wish-list" met with Flarnar scientists for possible help. Because the humans had traveled two hundred years into the future and had borrowed the Voursis' advanced technology; they were technologically ahead of all three planets. But the humans needed fresh water and a few other minerals which were hard to find. The next and more important thing for them was a faster way back home. They were hoping these people with a billion year history knew a better and faster way of traveling long distances.

While the scientists were meeting the Flarnars, the rest of the humans, with Governor Diotheos, commander Argeris, their wives and other officials, visited the planet Tharnata. The Tharnatians were just as thankful to the humans for liberating them from the Voursis but they were not as welcoming as the Flarnars had been. Both Governor Diotheos and Commander Argeris thought that it was important to establish good relations with all these people to expedite the peace treaty before they left for home. The Tharnadians, like the Voursis, were not religious people but they also had large temples, remnants of the old religions. The Tharnatians were richer and more technologically advanced; they were a warlike race and had a Spartan attitude towards solving problems. During the peace treaty negotiations they were more obstinate than the Voursis. They demanded that they and the Voursis should be given more powers because they were more populous and more technologically advanced. But the humans insisted on parity for all three planets in weaponry and other security. The humans also introduced incentives and checks and balances, to all three people to insure long lasting peace.

However difficult the Tharnatians were during the peace negotiations, they were smart enough to realize that without

Project Anastrophe

human intervention in the war with the Voursis, they would now be a defeated people and subject to Voursa. They were very thankful to these alien humans and treated them almost like messiahs. They were taken to banquets and shown their archaeological sites--the best Tharnata had to offer. They gave the humans fertile soil to take back to their floating world for the long voyage back home.

Now the humans had to visit Voursa, they needed to be delicate with the proud Voursis who had lost the war because of their intervention. The humans were extra diligent with the Voursis because they knew that even with all the checks and balances the Voursis, at some point in the future, could terminate the peace treaty. They were capable of starting a new war and taking over the neighboring planets.

When the defeated Voursis went home, they faced an unhappy population. The new government had to resort to harsh measures to control the people. But that made the people more determined to remove them from power. They brought back the monarchy and reintroduced the Mourgdunian Dynasty. They placed as new Emperor on the throne, the twelve year old Mourgdos, grandson of the murdered Emperor Throvolan. Although the majority of Voursis didn't want the war, they didn't like the humans interfering with it either. They were looked upon as intruders when they arrived on Voursa. But the Voursis also realized that the treaty the humans had introduced would be good for all three planets. They knew that from now on they wouldn't be the superpower they once were, but at the same time they felt safe that no other power would invade them.

Voursa was in parity in weapons and other war technology with Tharnata and Flarna, but they were ahead in any other way, and therefore they still felt like a superpower. The new authorities treated the humans in a civilized manner and showed them most of their important sites. They were also called to the palace and were given dinner by the young Emperor Mourgtos.

Voursa was by far the most beautiful and richest planet; they were many years ahead in science and in culture. However the most impressive thing of all was how similar Voursa was to Earth. No wonder the Voursis wanted to take over Earth and make it their own. At the end of their tour the humans were asked to meet the royal advisors at the palace. The young Emperor wasn't there but there were many of his family. Likewise Governor Diotheos and Commander Argeris had their advisors too. Mouchda, who took part in the negotiations of the peace treaty on behalf of the Voursis, was there too. He started the meeting by saying,

"I hope you enjoyed your visit here on Voursa."

Governor Diotheos spoke for the humans,

"We had a wonderful time, thank you."

Mouchda again took the initiative to speak for the Voursis,

"We have sent fresh water and other materials to your home base, for the long journey back to your planet. But there is a favor we would like to ask from you. Should you succeed and defeat our expedition who will attack your planet in the future, we would like you to replace the current command crew with the one we are sending with you should you accept our request."

Now it was Commander Argeris who intervened,

"It will take many generations of our people before we reach our planet; and even though the Voursis live longer than humans, it would still take many of your generations before your people reach our planet."

"We are not sending live people with you; we are sending the D.N.A. of the future crew in a specially designed unit. It is programmed to start morphing into our people

Project Anastrophe

twenty of your years before your final destination. But it will require you to initiate it at that precise time."

Governor Diotheos, after he talked with commander Argeris and other advisors, said,

"We would like to know what the new Voursi crew would do, once it takes command of the armada."

"It would simply bring the armada home; we don't want them to cause anymore trouble to other species." Governor Diotheos said,

"We accept your request." By Commander Argeris' orders the special unit was not sent directly to home base. It would be taken home in their own ship.

Chapter 25

After the humans left Voursa, they headed for Flarna to pick up the scientific team that had been left behind. Commander Argeris had a long talk with his advisors about the Voursi special unit they were carrying with them. He said,

"Hundreds of years ago, a Greek army was fighting the Trojans. For ten years they were unable to penetrate the Trojan castle; finally King Odysseus, a Greek warrior, built the infamous "Trojan Horse" and in it he hid his best warriors; then he gave it to the Trojans as a present and said his troops were going home. The wooden horse was taken inside the castle, but during the night the Greek warriors broke out, opened the gate to the Greek army, and defeated the Trojans. My question to you is, do we have another

Project Anastrophe

"Trojan Horse" from the Voursis?" Governor Diotheos said,

"I suppose our scientists will be able to tell us if the unit is safe to bring home."

Coming to Flarna was almost as good as coming home; again they were received enthusiastically by the Flarnars and stayed there for another three days before they headed home. However before they left Flarna the scientists were able to check the unit and verify the fact that it was safe, but Commander Argeris went one step further by asking the Flarnar scientists about the authenticity of the Voursi unit. He was told that indeed this was a method used by all, to transfer living things through long distances. The humans were disappointed that the aliens didn't use any faster way to travel through long space journeys. They arrived home with their armada and were received with a hero's welcome. They immediately made preparations for the long voyage to Gaia Nea.

Ner and Vrima, whenever they could, continued to charge their batteries together. Although they had repaired their frames and cybernetics countless times all through the decades, they were considered old issues by any standards and were used mainly as advisors. However they had within them, part of Nick's and Norinas' brain matter, and that made them very important to the community. They were symbols of continuity, parts of Earth still living after ten generations since their ancestors left Earth. They both lived with the Papas family and were acquainted with all of them, living and dead.

Ner and Vrima could not love like the humans; theirs was a Platonic love based in friendship and trust. Although Vrima clamed that she did love Ner with the same pathos humans had. It was on one of those charging get-together times that Ner started to talk about travel,

"Vrima, lately I have been calculating time sequences and travel, and I have discovered that we could travel very close to the speed of time but the pressure would be so enormous that human beings and other living matter would collapse and their constitutions would be irreparable. So organic matter is very sensitive to excessive warp-drive, however I have an idea I would like to discuss with you. The Voursis and their neighbors have been traveling long distances by changing their female and male reproductive cells to their D.N.A. state and then reconstituting them as they are needed. I am sure the geneticists would be better qualified to elaborate on this subject."

"I understand that this is a convenient way to transport great numbers of people and other living things on long distances."

"In the future we will need to resort to this kind of technique when we abandon the meteorite and move into spaceships."

"That will be a long time from now."

"That is true, unless we find a way to travel closer to the speed of time without harming those composed of carbon matter."

"Perhaps you should mention your idea to Governor Diotheos."

"Thank you, Vrima, I think I will do as you say."

Heading Homeward

The humans had accomplished half of their goal; they had acquired the material with which to build the alien's weapons. They had established long term peace among the aliens. The humans had weakened the Voursis' superior power to wage war. The next two hundred years would be crucial for the human species; they had to use this window of opportunity to go back to Earth on time to defeat the other Voursis who were already on their way to Earth and would attack at the end of the 29th century.

With the speed they were traveling now it would take another ten generations before the last generation arrived on Earth to fight the aliens. Their next stop would be Gaia Nea according to the plan; but they wouldn't be able to travel to Gaia Nea with this meteorite as their main means of transport. At some point they would have to transfer their people to spaceships for the last leg of the trip. But how could they transfer so many people to spaceships? Those were problems which the future generations would have to reckon with; but for now this generation had accomplished its goal. Now they had to stay alive and work towards making more and better weapons for the final battle.

Ner eventually met with Governor Diotheos and discussed his idea with him. The Governor, as well as the rest of the community, were resigned to the idea that they had to travel back home the same way they had traveled to Voursa. They were continually working towards finding a faster way back home, but for now there was nothing worth talking about. So Ner's idea interested the Governor and he promised Ner that he would bring it up in their next meeting.

They were in their third month on the way to Gaia Nea, a voyage that would take one hundred and fifty years before they reached their destination. They had fallen into their usual routine, a life without the excitement of war or even preparing for a possible war. If everything went as planned, this generation and the next ones to come; would not see any action in real war. So a meeting that had to do with faster speed was indeed an interesting subject. Governor Diotheos, Commander Argeris, Ner and Vrima, and many other scientists gathered in the Governors office. Diotheos said,

"The reason we are meeting today is that Ner has something important to tell us." Ner began,

"Since your ancestors and I left the dark side of the Earth's Moon two hundred years ago, in search of the aliens, I have never ceased to think of finding a faster way to travel. I had hoped that perhaps the aliens, with over a billion years of civilization, might have found a faster way. But perhaps no one is made to travel faster than the speed of light--or even close to it. However the aliens do something you humans or we the robots have not thought of doing yet; and that is to micro-size your ovum cell and the spermatozoon cell into D.N.A., so that you can travel long distances. This method is far superior to freezing the whole sperm or ovum and then thaw them at a later time. We will not always be able to travel on our meteorite; at some point we will need to travel in spaceships. Perhaps that would be the time for us to use this micro-size method. I only wanted to mention my idea to you, I am sure that the scientists and the geneticists will be able to find different ways to enhance this method in the future." Commander Argeris commented,

"Ner is right, at some point we must transfer all the community into ships; with the number of people and animals we have at this time we would need thousands of them. However if we were to adopt the option of micro-sizing, then we had better start some kind of a plan now to reduce our population. By then we would have the right number of people and other living things to be transferred." It was decided that micro-sizing would be preferable to any of the other options discussed so far and they gave orders to the scientists and geneticists to devise the best possible plan for the future transfer to ships.

They were now far away from any planets and deep into dark space once more. Now with their main goal of finding the aliens' material to build new weapons, and with a long term peace treaty among the aliens accomplished, the community's priorities changed. The production of newer and more powerful weapons continued and it would do so indefinitely. Newer ships and carriers continued to be built. Their second goal was to be a powerful army with the best possible weapons to fight the final battle with the Voursis on the home planet Earth. Their second decisive meeting took place two months later. Scientists and geneticists had used that time to work out a good plan for the transfer of the future inhabitants from the meteorite into ships for the last leg of the trip to Gaia Nea.

In addition to officials, there were many others representing all sections of the community. Governor Diotheos began by saying,

"As you know, we can't live on this meteorite forever, eventually future generations will have to travel in ships; however most of us will live our lives here as we have been doing for decades. The reason we are here today is to set a program in motion that will reduce the population to half of what we are now. I am going to let Dr. Thirion, who is a geneticist, explain it to you in detail."

"In about a hundred years, future generations will arrive in the area where our ancestors found this meteorite; in turn they will have to set it in its exact trajectory as our ancestors found it, and abandon it. All people and animals, as well as those who died and were cremated, will be moved to ships. Of course they will take anything they deem to be valuable at the time. The reason we need to start this program now, is because according to our estimations, we need these years to achieve a normal reduction of our present population." Next one to speak was Dr. Vrionich, technical advisor.

"For the last two months many of us have studied this

plan and found it to be the best there is for our situation. I won't bother you with all its details, but I would like to elaborate on a few of them. In the near future every young couple will continue to have the maximum of two children; however one of the children will be removed in its state of ovum and spermatozoon and will be reduced to its D.N.A. then it will be kept in a special tube until we reach Earth. At that time each future baby will be engineered to intermingle with the contemporary humans and then all of them will be born at different times on Earth."

The plan was adopted by most of the community and became the rule for all of them. At the same time there were many other projects going on. During those decades traveling through the deep space; the Anastrophe community advanced in science, health, and art. Their culture increased far beyond any humans in the past. For most of them the meteorite had been and would be their homeland. They lived a busy and a happy life but no one of the present generation would see Gaia Nea--much less the planet Earth. But they knew that their descendants would be born on the mythical planet Earth and that made them feel satisfied.

Gaia Nea

The two towers, one on the Atalandos and the other on Gaia Nea, were completed sooner than the estimated five years. The Gaians started to use the towers right away; they brought tons of the precious cargo to Gaia Nea which was used for building and tooling, but mainly for weapons. Even after so many years they had not forgotten the threat that might come someday from the aliens. Most of their dwellings were reinforced with the precious diamond and other hard materials. There were now many more biospheres all over the planet; and trees of many different

Project Anastrophe

kinds, in and around the biospheres. Although there was more oxygen in the atmosphere because of all the new trees, it would still take hundreds of thousands of years before the humans would be able to breathe with ease outside their biospheres. The giant ants and spiders were natives to the planet and through the millions of years had adapted to less oxygen. They now lived far away from any human settlement and were not a problem anymore. But for the most part the planet still looked desolate as it had for millions of years. Progress had been made with lots of trees, dark moss, and other greenery planted through the years. There was a transport system that connected all the biospheres and other places on the planet.

It had been three hundred years since the humans had landed on Gaia Nea; all the old timers had gone now. This was the fifteenth generation of humans living on this planet and for them it was home. That other planet called Earth was a mythical place one they learned about in schools. The other people who had left for the aliens' planet so long ago had stopped communicating with them and were almost forgotten. Many thought that they never reached their destination, or most likely were destroyed by the aliens. So when they received a hologram sent from deep space, they were surprised to say the least.

President Nuferious, of Gaia Nea, was alerted immediately and was shown the hologram.

"Well, what do you make of it?" The question was directed to all who were gathered in his office. Mr. Thompson, the Minister of Transportation and Communication, said,

"We should not be surprised that we have received such a message; for if the Anastrophe expedition had successfully accomplished their goal, they would send us a message at this time." The President asked an officer to project the hologram again. They all looked intensely at the message. It showed a man in his thirties of small stature, 157 cm, his face revealed a person who was racially mixed. He had curly brown hair and brown eyes; he looked pleasant but serious. He said,

"Greetings, my name Darmos, I am the latest leader in charge of the Anastrophe expedition to the planet Voursa. We have successfully completed our mission, and we are on our way back to Gaia Nea. We are humans---the progeny of your friends and relatives. If you receive this message, please reply."

President Nuferious said,

"I suppose we need to answer in the affirmative."

Again Thompson said,

"This was only a greeting message; they wanted to know if we have survived on Gaia Nea. We need to reply with a message informing them of our status-quo."

"Are we sure that we are communicating with humans, or are they the aliens using humans to get to us?"

"We will verify that with their next communication, but we must let them know that we are here and that we are doing well."

"How far away are they at this time?"

"According to plan they must abandon their meteorite in the area where they found it, and then transfer into ships for the last leg of the trip to Gaia Nea. It will take another ten years before they arrive, unless they have a faster means of traveling. But they must not be there yet, they will not transfer into ships unless they are sure of their destination." President Nuferious asked another important question,

"How many are they and how are we going to accommodate them?"

Dr. Dimotis, who was a sociologist, explained,

Project Anastrophe

"Even though their colony must have grown by now, they couldn't have grown at the same rate we have, because of limited space on the meteorite. However I am sure that they could live in their ships for an indefinite time once they arrive here." Many ideas were discussed in that meeting, and many decisions taken. They decided to respond as soon as possible and wait for a more detailed reply.

By now everybody on Gaia Nea was aware of the message, and there was a certain excitement among them. Even though the Anastrophe voyagers wouldn't arrive for another ten years, the epic story of their ancestors who left Earth for the long voyage to the alien homeland was the talk of every biosphere on Gaia Nea. The faces of Nick and Norina, Darna and Nephus, and many others who were part of the first expedition, as well as the first leaders, who started the colonies on Gaia Nea, were in every living room.

It was the most exiting thing that had happened in many years. Now there were plans made for the new voyage back to Earth and the big battle to be fought with the aliens. There were two million people living on Gaia Nea, and although there was excitement for some to go back to Earth, most people loved this place. It was the only place they had known all their lives, and they were determined to stay here and defend it if needed. But they never forgot Mother Earth. They knew that sometime in the future they would have to defend her. After all, wasn't that the very reason they had came here? Now the time had come and in the near future they would be asked to make good on their promise they had given to those pioneers who brought them here; to prepare and fight the aliens and defeat them once and for all.

The second message arrived, this time giving them more information. The voyagers would be arriving on Gaia

Nea approximately ten years from now. They would require a biosphere of there own to acclimatize to Gaia Nea. Their fleet would remain in space until the time for departure to Earth. There was more information in regards to their population, technology, culture, and science. There were specifications about the construction of the new biosphere and other requests.

A message was sent from Gaia Nea to the Anastrophe voyagers welcoming them and agreeing to all of their requests. The Gaia Neans told them about the improvements they had made on the planet. From then on there were frequent communications between the two groups that went on for many years.

The Voyagers

One hundred and forty years had passed since the Anastrophe expedition left Voursa, Tharnata, and Flarna. Now they arrived in the area where big changes were about to take place. The biggest change of all was to abandon their meteorite. According to the plan they were to move into huge carriers capable of supporting thousands of people and animals. There were also cargo ships and other carriers fully equipped with a panoply of the latest war machinery.

After they moved every valuable item away from the meteorite, including the ashes of their departed, they moved the meteorite into its previous trajectory and let it float away from them. It was decided to leave the infrastructure as it was; a necropolis inside a meteorite traveling on its ancient route. It was a sad departure, because these people and others before them; had lived on this piece of land for many decades. It was the only land they knew, and leaving it was just as painful as it was for their ancestors leaving their beloved planet Earth.

Project Anastrophe

It was an impressive flotilla going the opposite way from the meteorite. They were determined to follow their plan to the letter; and now their destination was Gaia Nea. After they were well on their way and people couldn't see the meteorite anymore, most of them went back to their duties and so the last leg of their voyage had started in earnest. Governor Darmos sent a message to his people. He said,

"My dear friends, today we switched homes, we are no longer living in the land our ancestors built for us; but we knew that this was going to happen someday. Now we are on our way to Gaia Nea where our friends and relatives are waiting for us. May the "Force" be with us." Most people knew the plan, it had been taught to them since they were children, but now the Governor's message solidified it in their minds. Governor Darmos met with his advisors to discuss the status of the flotilla. The admirals that were on duty participated as holograms; others beamed into the Governor's office. Both Ner and Vrima were there too. The Governor welcomed all,

"Friends, I must tell you that I don't feel as sure and comfortable today as I did a few days ago when we were still in our well-fortified homes inside the meteorite. But I believe that we have built the biggest and strongest ships with plenty of room for all our citizens. However from now on we must be very careful because the Voursis could be anywhere between here and Earth; may the "Force" keep our enemy away from us. We are not ready to engage them before the rest of the humans from Gaia Nea join us."

Everyone in charge of a ship reported in that first meeting and everything appeared to go according to plan. By now there was constant communication between the flotilla and Gaia Nea, and the information was very encouraging. The Gaia Neans had built several formidable armadas and even though their ships didn't come up to the standards of the Voyager's ships in technology and deliverability, they were still powerful. They decided to send them technical information to upgrade their electronic gear, and diagrams to start work on improving their weaponry with the promise to give new material for their weapons upon arrival on Gaia Nea.

There were ships scouting for thousand of kilometers around the flotilla looking for possible enemy ships, and there were daily simulated battles honing their fighting abilities. Admiral Gerakas, in charge of the fighting force defending the flotilla, was an unforgiving commander. He wanted perfection and he got it. He wasn't satisfied to merely look from afar, but participated with his pilots, often scoring higher than the younger crew did. He was the pride of any participating armada. Governor Darmos didn't want to fight the Voursis here, but if he had to, he had one of the best human fighting forces of all times and he wouldn't hesitate to use it to defend his people.

Ner and Vrima had been working for many years on the Papas and Anderson families' lineage. Their aim was to locate the closest matching genes in the Papa's and Anderson's hereditary pools. But finding the specific chromosome that contained the right D.N.A. and R.N.A. of both families proved to be a daunting task. Today, as Ner and Vrima were regenerating their batteries at their usual place, Ner announced to Vrima,

"Eureka! I have found the closest genes possible on both Nick and Norina."

"As far as I know the closest is not close enough to matching Nick's and Norina's chromosomes."

"You are right, Vrima, but don't forget that we are the catalysts; I carry a portion of Nick's brain matter, and you

Project Anastrophe

of Norina's. By inserting Nick's D.N.A. into the male gene matching chromosome, we will create a baby boy who will match Nick at the time of his birth three hundred and eighty years ago---at least 99.9 percent. That is the best we can accomplish at this time. Using the same procedure by using Norina's D.N.A. from you, we will create a baby girl like Norina. The question is when to go ahead with the procedure."

"I suppose it would depend if we need them now, at Gaia Nea, or on Earth."

"I would think on Earth."

"Perhaps not on Earth; it would be wise to have them born in the ships twenty years before arrival; that way they can participate in the final battle with the Voursis, and became the new leaders of our colony on Earth."

"Wouldn't we be taking a chance of them getting killed?"

"That is a chance we have to take, after all they would be human beings, wouldn't they?"

Ner wanted to say something else about what he had been working on lately; something concerning the two of them, but he thought that now wouldn't be the appropriate time.

Five years passed uneventfully with the flotilla reaching the half-way point to Gaia Nea. But being on ships was quite deferent than being on the meteorite with almost unlimited material available at anytime. They badly needed certain minerals which could be found on non–M-type planets. In the next five years they would be sailing in dark space without the possibility of finding planets or any terrestrial bodies at all.

For the last few years scouts had been combing long distances in hope of finding the material, but so far they had had no luck. Now they were approaching the asteroid belt of an unmarked small planet. The debris that was circling the planet was too dense and therefore dangerous to navigate through. But this would be their last chance of finding the precious minerals before they plunged into the deep black space once more. A group of several of their best pilots were used for this dangerous expedition.

They were navigating in small pods, but even that proved to be difficult; in the first approach, two of their pods crashed, killing four of their best pilots. People in every vessel were glued to their monitors watching the tragedy as it was unfolding. They withdrew, regrouped, and tried again; it was a slow and tedious process and took several agonizing hours to finally go through all the debris, but once they were out, they landed on the planet with ease.

They knew that it would be cold out there, but it was worse than they thought. There were thick sheets of frozen methane they had to dig through. Finally they found what they were looking for in great quantities. They drilled a hole and started to pump the precious mineral. They found other needed minerals in solid form; those they excavated but with great difficulty. They beamed everything to the waiting shuttle outside the asteroid belt; but they couldn't beam themselves because this was a contaminated area. They managed to beam the material to the shuttle; now they had to fight their way back home through the dangerous debris. They formed a line resembling a train going slowly between the larger boulders, but the smaller fragments were more difficult to navigate. Again people watched their monitors, holding their breaths as they saw the brave men and women finding their way back.

All the humans were concentrated in the middle of the moving line with robots and androids at the front and back. This time it was the robots and androids that perished; two pods in front and one in the rear. The middle of the line,

Project Anastrophe

where the humans were, managed to survive, but they still had a long way to go to freedom. It was pitch-dark and they were navigating with sensitive instruments. Those who followed them from the ships saw bright lights in the dark anytime a pod exploded. Finally after the arduous passage they got out of that hell and the people in the flotilla were relieved.

With the material secured on board the ships, they could now concentrate on their main task which was to prepare to defend the flotilla and arrive on Gaia Nea on time. A memorial was held for the fallen heroes and both Admiral Gerakas and Governor Darmos praised the dead and the living heroes. Now they were once more in deep space with nothing between them and Gaia Nea. They traveled like a swarm of bees in an unfriendly black abyss.

Ten years living in the ships had taken their toll; people missed their homeland even though it was only a small piece of land--a meteorite. Only those young children who were born in these vessels didn't miss it. For them the vessels were their home, but they were prepared to live on Gaia Nea just as the natives did. Teachers in holographic form had arrived many years earlier to prepare them for their new homeland. Grownups were also introduced to the language with the funny accent and learned how to live on Gaia Nea. The closer they came to arriving, the more excited they became. Today they saw the first Gaia Nean war ships; they looked different from their own, but they noticed the same writing on the vessels. They were followed by other bigger ships; still many smaller ships shuttled between the Governor's carrier and headquarters.

Communications between the two peoples continued; they were exchanging not only ideas but important material too. The voyagers could use some special minerals and food provisions and the Gaia Neans could use more advanced technical information and the alien's weapon building material. So when they met for the first time they already knew each other well. Now they met in the flesh, Governor Darmos and his advisers, as well as several of his admirals, were waiting for them at the arrival port and shook hands with the visitors. Governor Darmos welcomed President Nuferious to the flotilla. Then he proceeded to shake hands with the rest of the visitors. There was more welcoming from the rest of his staff; then they all went to one of his main meeting rooms where they had a more intimate conversation. President Nuferious said,

"I am so glad your expedition was successful, Governor Darmos, our ancestors would be happy to know that you came back to Gaia Nea victorious."

"The glory belongs to our ancestors who fought the Voursis and won; they also found the precious metal. We just survived our voyage back to Gaia Nea."

"We consider all of you victorious and we are lucky to have you back on Gaia Nea." The cordialities went on for a while and after dinner at the Governor's house the visitors were free to visit different carriers of the flotilla. After the visits, the Gaia Neans realized that they were decades back in technology compared to these people. They felt lucky that they didn't have to fight the aliens with their inferior weapons, and they were glad to have the flotilla on their side. The Voyagers were in quarantine for a few days and they were subjected to vigorous hygienic tests until the Gaia Neans were satisfied that they wouldn't harm their colony.

After the Voyagers were given a clean report they could visit Gaia Nea as they pleased. The flotilla stopped far enough away to avoid the planet's gravity and started to shuttle people and material to Gaia Nea using the diamond

Project Anastrophe

tower built decades ago. The first visitors, as expected, were Governor Damos, Admiral Gerakas, and other officials with their families. The Gaia Neans welcomed them with festivities, and there were many common people who came to the President's house to see the Voyagers. After the festivities they were shown their newly built biosphere and Governor Damos and his officials were impressed and astonished how well the engineers had followed the plans sent to them years ago.

No ships from the flotilla landed on the surface of Gaia Nea; the Anastrophe community, or the Voyagers as they were called, preferred to keep their flotilla at the ready to fight the aliens if they came their way. Most of the younger and older people were moved to the new biosphere immediately; and from then on there were people young and old transferring back and forth so that after a few years all of the Voyagers would be acclimatized to the planet's atmosphere and gravity. They maintained their flotilla in good shape and they were always ready to fight and defend themselves and Gaia Nea. In addition to upgrading the Gaia Nean's weaponry, they were renewing their own too. As the time went on both the Voyagers and the Gaia Neans were becoming more powerful and ready to fight the aliens, but so far there was no sign of them.

The Voyagers were smaller in stature compared to the Gaia Neans but they were stronger and more intelligent. They were all hybrid and one could see in them every race on Earth; they were healthy and beautiful. It was a wonderful biosphere resembling in many ways the one they left behind. They had their own government but were also subject to the local laws. The only place they felt at home was when they were transferred back to the flotilla. At first it was difficult for them to adjust to a regular planet's gravity and they walked like drunkards; but as the time went on they became used to the stronger gravity and before long they too walked like everybody else. And that was precisely the idea; to be able to live in the flotilla and on a proper planet.

Within a year's time they were able to intermingle with the locals and many were in universities and technical schools teaching the Gaia Neans advanced technologies and theories they had learned from the aliens decades earlier. The two peoples got along very well and learned from each other. Under the auspices of the Voyagers the Gaia Neans built a very powerful flotilla ready to take off in time of need. But this advanced technology needed experienced personnel; consequently the Voyagers were in charge, which made some of the locals unhappy.

There was a movement by a few lower ranking officers to completely separate the two flotillas but the Voyagers persuaded the government to stick to the plan that called for the two flotillas to be governed by the Voyagers who had more experience with the new technologies. To keep the Gaia Neans happy and maintain cohesiveness within the flotillas; a treaty was signed between the two peoples which dictated that after the battle with aliens and the liberation of Earth the Gaia Neans would gain complete control of their flotilla. The agreement appeased the Gaia Neans and created a better atmosphere within the two forces.

During the last fifty years the Voyagers and the Gaia Neans had intermarried and become one people just as their ancestors were three hundred and fifty years ago. During the last five years the government, which by now was equally represented by all; had started the drums of war. The old stories of Mother Earth and the need to liberate it from the alien Voursis were told over and over. The gov-

Project Anastrophe

ernment never failed to mention that Gaia Nea would be next in line to be taken over by the alien Voursis if they were not destroy. Fear had worked throughout the ages in every civilization, and it worked here too. Many young men and women along with many young families joined the new flotillas; it was a big sacrifice, because they would never see Gaia Nea again.

They were going to fight for a mythical planet called Earth, and if they defeated the powerful aliens their reward would be to live in the land of their ancestors; a land without biospheres, with an open and clean environment. Gaia Nea was not left unprotected; it was now fortified with the latest and most powerful weapons. It was a generation of weapons which was a combination of human and alien technologies. All biospheres and those important exposed areas could be protected in time of immanent attack by an invisible shield.

There were five hundred thousand humans occupying the two flotillas waiting for orders to go. The flotillas would travel separately but they would be controlled by the headquarters which were in the biggest carrier that looked like a large floating city. The man in charge of all the people was Governor Dale Jones. Supreme Commander William Cotton was in charge of the fighting force: humans, robots, androids, and other mechanized entities. Both men were in their fifties, born on the Voyager's flotilla, but educated on both the flotilla and on Gaia Nea. Governor Dale Jones served as Prime minister and as President of Gaia Nea, and after he retired from political life, he became an advisor for building and maintaining the new flotillas. His wife Alice and his two children, son Tom and daughter Teresa, both in their early twenties, went with him. They all inherited the small frame body and intelligence of the Voyagers. Supreme Commander William Cotton lived his formative years on Gaia Nea where he got most of his education; he had a successful career as a young officer in the main base space port. Later he commanded various types of ships in space guard and eventually was moved temporarily to the main carrier. There he took part in many simulated battles and eventually was promoted to commander on a medium-sized carrier. He served there until he retired. When he was offered the position of Supreme Commander; He accepted it without any hesitation. His wife Daltea, and daughter Nalia, who was in her early twenties, joined him in his new career.

Anything that needed to be moved into the flotillas was moved; and for the last two months they had been waiting impatiently for permission to leave. Finally the order for departure was given and once more people were leaving for another epic voyage; but this time back to Earth. The goodbyes and good wishes had taken place two months earlier and people had time to get used to the feeling of separation. But today, the actual day of separation, hit people much harder and sadness was everywhere. It was a melancholy day on both the flotillas and on Gaia Nea.

Paradoxically Ner and Vrima, being the oldest robots made on Earth, were also the only two entities that resembled the humans on Earth because they were made in their image. During the fifty years the Voyagers spent on Gaia Nea; Ner and Vrima spent most of their time on the flotillas, visiting the planet only to teach in various universities. They would speak to them about the "Change" that took place on Earth. They spoke about Nick and Norina and how they and the Anastrophe team had traveled back in time to stop the nuclear radiation from destroying the planet Earth. The students and other people on Gaia Nea learned about Earth, and about their ancestors coming to Gaia Nea and

Project Anastrophe

those who went to the aliens' planets. Now Ner and Vrima lived with the Papas' families working as archivists and advisors.

The two flotillas traveled separately for security reasons but stayed in touch at all times. Scouts would check long distances for the enemy Voursis but so far had found nothing. The production of new fighting ships kept on and war games took place frequently. They never stopped honing their abilities to keep in good fighting shape and be at the ready to fight the Voursis wherever they met them. They had traveled in deep space for twenty-five years and they were half way to reaching Earth. Old people died and babies were born; once more the young people adapted to living inside metal walls and created their own culture which was sometimes not welcomed by the older generations; but life went on.

Chapter 26

In a special secret place in the archives where Ner and Vrima spent most of their time, there were two items that looked like old fashioned books; one had an inscription in Voursi language, the other had an inscription in human metric language. They both bore the note, "top secret." Ner picked up the one with the Voursi letters and walked over to Vrima who was waiting for him. Together they went to a room built especially for this occasion. Ner said,
"It's time." Vrima replied,
"Yes it is." They both sat down, then Ner used a secret combination number and opened it. For a few seconds nothing happened; they waited patiently. Then a hologram in the form of an old Voursi man, stepped out of it and addressed them,

Project Anastrophe

"I am Kalidan, and I am in charge of creating the crew that will bring the Voursi flotilla back home to Voursa; if you wish me to initiate the program--enter the code." Ner entered a code and then closed the "book" and put it back where he found it. He said,
"Now we can go and talk to the Governor."
Vrima said,
"Yes, it appears that the time has come." Ner and Vrima stepped out of the room and locked it.
The Governor's office was a busy place but Ner and Vrima could always find a way to see him. Governor Eric Woo enjoyed talking to them.
"Come in, come in, what a pleasant surprise, sit down; it's been a long time since your last visit, what can I do for you?" Ner was the first to speak, he said,
"Governor, we have been entrusted with a program that has to do with the Voursis. It was in a special container and was given to Commander Argeris Papas by the defeated Voursis before they left Voursa."
"What kind of program is it that is in a special container, and what does that have to do with me, Ner?"
"Governor, in order for us to initiate this program you have to enter a special code."
"Really--and where is this special code that you are talking about?"
"You will find it here in these archives; it is a personal message from Commander Argeris Papas. Governor, I should tell you that this program should start as soon as possible, it has to do with the Voursis' flotilla on Earth."
"Now you got my attention, Ner, I will let you know very soon." Ner gave Governor Woo the code number to the archives and he and Vrima left.
It didn't take long for Governor Woo to get to the archives and find Commander Argeris Papas' holographic

message. Commander Papas appeared in Governor Woo's office as a hologram dressed in his Commander's uniform. He said,

"The defeated Voursis asked us a favor we could not refuse; they gave us a container which contains the needed biological material to produce enough Voursi personnel to take the defeated Voursi flotilla back to Voursa. We have thoroughly analyzed it and found it to be safe to be brought into our armada. The program must be initiated twenty-five years before arriving on Earth to give enough time for the personnel to grow and be at an age at which they could assume their responsibilities.

To initiate the program you must use code, "wz5", plus the commander-in-chief's code. The program is self-contained and the material is easily obtainable; however they should be separated and guarded at all times for their security. Should the Voursis win the final battle on Earth, the Voursi personnel will self-destruct. Good luck, and may the humans prevail in the final battle."

Governor Woo had the container analyzed and after the security staff told him that it was safe beyond any doubt, he asked the Commander-in -Chief, Noi Kinitaki, to enter his code and then he entered the code from the holographic message. The container was placed in the middle of a huge room and they all withdrew to one of the corners and waited for things to happen. A few seconds later a three dimensional picture was projected on the floor. It showed, in great detail, a room that was many times larger than the present room; with incubators having baby Voursis in them, then another hologram with young children and their nanny robots.

The projections went on for a long time showing the various facets in the lives of the children growing up, and all the time being taken care of by their nannies until they

Project Anastrophe

were grown up and assumed their responsibilities as personnel on the defeated Voursi flotilla taking it back home. At the end of the show a long list of material with directions in metric language was given to the humans and then it stopped projecting. It was an ingenious way of telling the humans what was going to happen and what the Voursis wanted from them. The Governor entrusted the job to Ner and Vrima.

Within a few days Ner and Vrima provided the appropriate place and material, and assigned guards. As soon as the program went into effect, things in the area began to change. A large room was created by invisible nano builders, followed by robot nannies and incubators with tiny Voursi embryos. All the material needed was put inside their place and one could see some of the material being used. Human scientists were assigned to follow their progress.

As soon as the alien program was initiated and everything appeared to be working well, Ner and Vrima concentrated on their next important project. Ner had done the entire preliminary work which had taken decades. Now they had to find hosts in the Papas family for Nick's implantation, and in the Anderson family for Norina's implantation. They had to be young, healthy, and intelligent. The Papases and the Andersons were intermarried with other families and now had different names so it was harder to find them. They divided the families for easier access and Ner looked for the Papases and Vrima looked for the Andersons.

They searched for look-alikes to match Nick's and Norina's appearances. Ner had matched the D.N.A. of the two embryos they had kept in suspended animation all these years. Finally after searching for two months in many families, Ner found a young couple with enough of Nick's physical similarities and matching D.N.A. The names of the couple were Nickiphoros and Maria Papas, they were a young couple in their twenties with a one year old daughter. Maria Papas would be the perfect person for a host mother. Now Ner had to wait for the appropriate time for the implantation procedure.

Maria was under surveillance by both Ner and Vrima for the time when she could be found alone and asleep. They got their chance during a time when Nickiphoros was participating in one of the frequent battle simulations which took him away for a few days at a time.

They beamed themselves into her room while she was in deep slumber and implanted her with the embryo. The whole procedure took only seconds. If all went well, Maria would have a healthy baby boy. It would look like both the parents even though the father's spermatozoon or the mother's ovum were not used in the infusion; the child and the parents would share genes from the same Papas families' pool that went back for many generations. Ner made sure that even though Nickiphoros and Maria came from different families, Nickiphoros Papas was part of Stelios Papas' genealogical tree. Maria Serifiotis was a direct relative of Meropy Artemidu, Nick's grandparents who came to America from Greece to escape the Second World War in Europe.

Finding the Anderson couple proved to be more difficult because they were working with a smaller gene pool; finally Vrima was able to isolate ten families that were good look-alikes for Norina. Now Ner and Vrima were looking into their genealogical tree to find the couple with the most matching D.N.A. of her grandparent's lineages. They found the perfect couple although they were a little older than the Papas. His name was Ted Robinson, 29 year's old, and her name was Judie; her maiden name was

Project Anastrophe

Vinson and she was 27 year's old. They lived on a different carrier which made it a little difficult to transport, but not impossible. They were both directly related to Norina's grandparents. In the next three weeks Ner and Vrima were able to transport themselves to the other carrier, and again waited for the right time and implanted the embryo into Judie following the same procedure.

When a few months later both women appeared to be pregnant, Ner and Vrima were delighted; now it was a matter of wait-and-see. They arranged the proper connections with the doctors who took care of the young mothers, and they were informed about the health of the mothers and their unborn babies. The last project was one of the most important they had done in their long lives; now it was only a matter of a few weeks to find out if they had been successful. Ner and Vrima were recharging at their usual place when Vrima said,

"Ner, have you prepared their profiles, and are you going to install them in their fourth year as usual, or are you going to wait longer?"

"At this point, the sooner the better, I will incorporate their profiles in their implants in their fourth year when they are about to receive them."

"And at what age are their profiles going to be downloaded into the rest of their programming?"

"When they reach the age of their parents; I think that would be the best time for them to know who they really are."

"Ner, I am envious. I wish we were humans and could live with them--you know--be like them."

"Vrima, we are robots and we will never be humans, but we could live with them and share their happiness vicariously."

"I know."

"Vrima, I have been working on an idea that concerns the two of us; I meant to talk to you a long time ago about it, but I wasn't sure it would work. I am now positive that it will work."

"It sounds interesting, especially if it has to do with the two of us. Tell me, I would like to know."

"We are robots, we can repair, change parts, update and download new files, and if they let us, we could live almost indefinitely. As you know, we are who we think we are because of our profiles; but there is something we could do to change that. We could also find two human hosts; download our profiles into their implants, and be who we are, only this time in hosts that have flesh and blood."

"It sounds like an excellent idea, but wouldn't that be illegal?"

"Not at all, humans already have professors and many other personalities programmed in their implants; I believe that once the hosts learn to live with us, we would have a successful symbiotic life."

"You mean that I would be able to love like a human being?"

"You would feel jealousy, hatred, anger, and yes, love. In short, you would be mortal but those are the properties that make a human who he or she is."

"I would do anything to be able to love."

"Then we should proceed with my idea."

"Yes, yes, let us do so."

Within days from each other both Judie and Maria gave birth to their babies; Judie had a healthy and beautiful boy and Maria a healthy and beautiful little girl. Ner and Vrima were even happier than the biological parents because they could see the fruits of their labor realized. Ner and Vrima had no problems being close to the Papas family and they had easy access to the baby boy. It was more difficult to be

Project Anastrophe

close to the Robinsons; but because Ner and Vrima were so well respected by the authorities, and well-known to many people, they eventually became good friends with the Robinsons too. Ner and Vrima saw to it that the Robinsons were moved to the carrier where the Papas family lived, and both families were given priorities to better jobs and housing.

The Voursi children were growing in their special laboratory under the auspices of Ner and Vrima and their Voursi robot nannies.

The baby boy Nickiphoros, or Nick for short, and baby girl, Norianna, or Norina for short, were growing with lots of love from their parents and especially Ner and Vrima who in the last four years had become good friends of their parents and visited frequently. With those two important projects accomplished, Ner and Vrima could now concentrate on their own project. They found two families with boys and girls who were friends to the Papases and the Robinsons. They chose the four year old boy called Bart, from the Thompsons, for Ner's host. And a four year old girl called Artemis or Artie for short, from the Napolitanos, for Vrima's host.

At the appropriate time Ner downloaded his profiles into Bart's implants and Vrima did the same thing with little Artie. Then they proceeded to download Nick's profiles into little Nick's implants and then they did the same thing with little Norina. All those procedures were done secretly from the parents or the authorities. Those four profiles would be blocked within a special code and would be unreadable by any authorities. When the children became twenty-eight years old their profiles would open simultaneously and they would realize that they were hosts to important entities.

George Karnikis

The two flotillas had been traveling now for forty-nine years and they were approaching the Earth's solar system. Seldom had the two flotillas met to participate in simulated battles; but when that happened it was considered the ultimate war games. The coming one was to be their last before they reached the Kuiper belt region; an asteroid belt consisting of many small-sized meteorites that both flotillas had to navigate through. Their next engagement, in all probability, would be a real war with the alien Voursis. The preparations on both sides were enormous and although they considered themselves one people with one common goal to destroy the aliens and liberate Earth; when they participated in war games they were different groups. There was pride involved with those two flotillas; for those who conducted themselves in a heroic and professional way would be given prizes and promotions.

Governor Roy Miller was understandably excited with the war games; as a politician he knew that a good performance on both sides would secure him victory in the coming elections and he wanted to be in charge when they engaged the Voursis. Nick and Bart had been good friends since they were toddlers. In school they were always above average and they were among the top few cadets. Later in the space force they did so well that they became the darlings of their armada. Their armada belonged to the main flotilla and they were eager to compete with the armadas of the visiting flotilla. There were young men and women in the visiting flotilla who were just as eager to compete.

The stage for the war games was set and everything was real except for the ammunition. Both forces were trained equally well, so there was little room for mistakes or successes. Those few who excelled were the best of the bunch and were treated like heroes by both sides and especially by the higher brass. That's why every young man and woman in the force wanted to be counted as one of those few heroes. Because of their families' closeness, Norina and Artie were also good friends. They had played together since they were little girls, and they too were above average in their early school years and as cadets. Now they had to prove what they were made of.

Since they were young children all four of them had often played together and the girls hadn't given an inch to the boys; they had held their ground especially when they competed in sports. As grownups they had other friends but they felt more at ease when they were together. Now they were together once more but this time in the same armada piloting the latest and fastest fighters. It wasn't an accident that all four of them ended up in the space force; their parents were in it too. In any gatherings they had, the conversation inevitably centered on the newest ships or weapons. When Ner and Vrima were around they were like walking encyclopedias, better than anybody's implants. So from early on they heard stories of real battles and war games. All they wanted to do when they grew up was to join the force and be like their parents or better.

Unbeknownst to Nickiphoros junior, or to anybody for that matter, save Ner and Vrima, he had the physique and character of his grandfather Nick of many generations ago. To Ner and Vrima it was like looking at their master Nick. It was hard to believe, but they were very happy to see him. And then there was Norianna or Norina, she also looked like her grandmother Norina many generations ago. To see them walking together was like being in a time-warp. Bart and Artie were their best friends but they had no special lineage in them; they had been chosen by Ner and Vrima to be their hosts at a later time.

The Voursis who were born in the laboratory especially made for them were also in their 24th year---all one hundred of them. They were raised and educated by their Voursi nannies; and their only purpose and function was to take the defeated Voursi flotilla back home to Voursa. If the humans lost the war to the Voursis, these one hundred Voursis would have no reason for living and they would self-destruct. They were all under constant observation by special human staff and in addition to that, Ner and Vrima would check on them periodically.

The war games started in earnest; with the two flotillas at their appropriate distances. The fighter ships were flying every which way and there was controlled pandemonium. Small and large groups of fighters would attempt sorties against the enemy's vulnerable areas only to be driven away by well- coordinated counterattacks by the defenders. The war games went according to plan and the brass on both sides were happy with the results. Nick and Bart, as always, scored high points and once more they were noticed by their superiors. What set these war games apart from the previous ones in their armada, was an incident that drew the attention of many high ranking officers. Norina and Artie were in a group of two dozen fighters executing a "Dourvie" maneuver; the two of them broke away from the company and flew close to the enemy lines. As expected they were chased away by enemy ships. That was their intention, because the rest of their company attacked and compromised the enemy's defense line. It was a successful maneuver but something went wrong. It appeared that two of the enemy ships collided and the jettisoned pilots were sucked away in the void of space, quickly disappearing. Norina and Artie went after them, putting their lives in danger, and retrieved them alive. It was a heroic move on their part, and it was appreciated by their company and the commanders on both sides.

Except for a few mishaps here and there, these last war

Project Anastrophe

games turned out to be their best. Everybody was happy and the commanders knew that they had a fighting force that could fight the aliens and win. The next time the two flotillas would meet, they would be on the same side fighting the Voursis. But now they had one more obstacle to overcome; they had to be careful to avoid colliding with the smaller asteroids of the Kuiper belt. Although the two flotillas were sailing far apart, they were both vulnerable to catastrophic collisions. Finally the passage close to an asteroid caused damage to several of their ships, but there were no fatalities, and those ships were repaired quickly.

They were approaching the ten dwarf planets which were still a long way from the sun approximately, 5,913,520,000 Km. In a few months they would see the three dwarf sisters Pluto, Eris and Ceres. But for now they went back to their routine which was to hone their abilities to fight the alien Voursis which could happen anytime now; even though they were still so far away from Earth.

Besides the election for a new Governor the floating community had many other changes. Many of the older commanders were replaced with new ones; the two flotillas exchanged carriers and smaller ships, as well as newer weapons. The flotillas were separated into eight small ones and were placed in different strategic areas; in short they were preparing for an offensive war whenever it happened. The main and largest flotilla was placed in the middle, and in there was the largest carrier, the head quarters and the nerve center of the community and war theater. It was very well protected and one felt safer there than anywhere else in the fleet. A new Governor was elected. His name was Dave Zebigos, an experienced politician. The new commander of all forces was Commander in–Chief, Kent Derral; a well-known man who had worked his way up with bravery and experience. Among the older commanders who were placed in the headquarters were Nick's father, Nickiphoros Papas senior, and his friend Bart Napolitano.

Nick, Bart, Norina, and Arty were given Commandership and now each one of them had their own carrier. They were in the flotilla that was sent to the front line. That flotilla had some of the best fighters and that was the reason they were sent to guard the most exposed area. If there were aliens around they would be the first to meet them and they were ready and eager to find them.

Even though the four heroes now were busier and had more responsibilities, they found ways to meet and spend time together especially when the Commanders met at the headquarters. They would talk about their responsibilities and the coming war with the Voursis. Sometimes they talked about dating people but Nick and Norina had always had a special place in their hearts for one another. Bart and Artie felt the same about each other. There was an unspoken feeling that all four of them, sometime in the future, would spend more intimate time together and perhaps on a more permanent basis.

Ner and Vrima spent some time with the old Papases and the young children of the family as they had always done through the decades. But now with Nick, Norina, Bart and Artie being in charge of their own carriers, Ner and Vrima found themselves visiting them more often. They were excited with the four young people being Commanders on their own carriers and with all the preparations and the possibility of an early engagement. They were always welcome even though they weren't needed, except as advisers.

Ner and Vrima were considered antique robots by today's standards. The new issue robots were less humanoid and were built to be single-function and not multifunctional

Project Anastrophe

like they were. But whatever they were assigned to do they did it well. The latest robot soldiers were armed with a panoply of weapons that were not in existence even five years ago. Their outer skin was made of diamond and other fireproof material that could fight through an inferno. They could fly and fight in dark space-- they were valuable war machines. The androids were also medics and technicians; they did thousands of other jobs including cooking and cleaning. Other robots were given important work in government and other functions in the community. But Ner and Vrima had something the other robots didn't have; they were walking encyclopedias, and they had some of the brain matter belonging to the ancient Nick and Norina. Ner and Vrima knew their limitations and they stayed out of the way. Besides, they felt superior to the other robots because they were closer to humans.

The flotillas had left behind the dwarf planet Pluto and now they were well into the solar system heading for Planet Earth. The 8th flotilla where Nick, Bart, Norina, and Artie belonged had the responsibility to guard the frontier. They sent many scouts inspecting the area in front of them, but so far they had fount no aliens.

This was going to be their last meeting in the main headquarters, there were many high ranking officers and Commanders representing all the flotillas and armadas. The meetings had been going on for days and this was to be the last day when both Governor Dave Zebigos and the Commander-in-Chief Kent Derral were to give speeches that would be heard and seen throughout the fleet. There were dinners and parties for all the participants. The women officers and Commanders were encouraged to dress in a more feminine way and both Norina and Artie looked beautiful. Ner and Vrima watched Nick and Norina dancing and again they couldn't believe their eyes. They looked like the couple they used to know so long ago. Both girls were dressed in the fashion of many years ago. Norina wore a royal blue taffeta waltz-length dress; Artie was stunning in yellow satin. Both couples whirled around the dance floor. Vrima looked at Ner and said,

"If everything works out according to plan, three years from now we will be part of their lives. I can hardly wait to feel like she does right now."

"All in good time, Vrima, trust me---everything will be all right."

"Ner, there is one thing I haven't asked you yet."

"And what would that be, Vrima?"

"Will we be able to talk to each other when we are merged with them?"

"Of course, Vrima, we just have to wait until they are asleep; then we will be able to talk all we want. If there is an emergency, we could all converse at the same time."

Nick and Bart were dressed in their Commander's uniforms; Norina said to Nick,

"You realize this is the last time we will meet like this."

"Maybe our next dance will be on Earth, if we win we will have a lot to celebrate."

"It's not going to be an easy war, the aliens are just as powerful as we are; remember we only recently caught up with them. They have the latest weapons and from what I heard from those who fought them, they are powerful warriors."

"Our technical staff has analyzed their weapons and not only copied them, but integrated human technology. Now our weapons are far superior to theirs. Our warriors have been practicing for this war for years and are in top shape. I have no doubt that we will win this war."

"I am of the same opinion, but we cannot under estimate our enemy."

Project Anastrophe

"I agree with you, Norina, we must not." They stopped dancing and walked to their table where they were joined by Bart, Artie, Ner, and Vrima. All six of them enjoyed being together, taking advantage of that precious time. Nick raised his glass and made a toast to victory and they all clinked their glasses. The music stopped and everyone sat at their tables waiting for the Governor to speak. He rose and walked to the platform; his image was shown simultaneously to the room and to the whole fleet at large. He smiled and said,

"It is with pleasure and pride that I am your Governor at this crucial juncture of our destiny; we are about to fulfill a goal that our ancestors had put into motion hundreds of years ago. Back then they decided to liberate Earth from the alien Voursis. In the twenty-fifth century they had just saved Earth from complete catastrophe caused by radiation poisoning. You all know from your schooling how brave Dr. Dylos, Nick, Norina, and our beloved robots, Ner and Vrima, along with many of their contemporaries were at the time. They could have stayed and lived the rest of their lives on Earth knowing that they had done their best and saved Earth. But when they traveled into the future and saw what was about to happen to their people; they disregarded their own well-being and started on an epic voyage to the alien's homeland. They knew that they, and many of their future generations, would never see Earth again. They lived like vagabonds traveling in the deepest and darkest space on a quest to find material for making the powerful weapons, and to learn from their enemies so that they were better prepared to fight and defeat the future Voursis. After an odyssey of almost four hundred years, my friends, the responsibility rests squarely on our shoulders. We are the fruit of their efforts. The labor of millions of our ancestors, as well as our contemporaries, makes us who we are today.

If our ancestors could see us today they would say it was all worth it. Because today we have the best fighting force and equipment the humans of Earth or the Voursis ever had. My friends, we are going to find the Voursis and destroy them and liberate our Earth once and for all, thank you.

They had passed Pluto, Neptune, Saturn, and the giant Jupiter, and now they were approaching another asteroid belt and then Mars. This time they sailed through a safe distance from the asteroid belt. Commander in-Chief Kent Darrel called all his high-ranking Commanders to a meet again. Nick, Bart, Norina, and Artie were among them. Ner and Vrima were there too. Commander Darrel said,
"In one month's time we will be approaching Mars. Our scouts have discovered that Mars is taken over by the Voursis. It goes without saying that they have taken over the Earth's Moon too. We never thought that we were going to surprise them; so by the time we approach Mars they will know we are here but they don't need to know the full size of our force right away. The Eighth Flotilla will engage the Voursis alone and they will proceed to occupy Mars, liberate the humans and guard Mars until new orders." Commander Nick Papas was asked to elaborate on the occupation by the aliens. He said,
"We have searched the area for months now, and we had our first contact about a month ago. The Nephus cloaking device has made it possible for us to go close enough to observe and obtain information. We surmise that they have only a small occupying force with one carrier with the strength of two hundred ships, and a police force of two thousand on Mars. Although we are sure of the number of their ships, we are not sure of their occupational force on land."

Project Anastrophe

A question was asked by a chief commander of the Second Flotilla named Sveng Papovich,

"Do you know what the human population is on Mars, and why they keep such a small force?"

"From information we have obtained from the Anastrophe crew back in the twenty-fifth century before the "Change," the population was about ten thousand people. We have no records of the population residing on Mars now, Commander. As to your second question, I can only guess that by now the aliens have complete control of the space and they know that the humans can't help their people on Mars."

"Thank you, Commander Papas; I would say that's a good guess."

It was decided that Commander Nick Papas would engage the aliens with one carrier followed by Commander Bartolomeo Napolitano with a second carrier. The rest of the flotilla would standby in cloaked mode. There were many other important decisions taken at the head quarters and they were to meet again after they had taken Mars from the aliens. The next few weeks passed with the Eighth Flotilla preparing for real war; Nick's carrier had disengaged from the main flotilla, followed by Bart's from afar. Hundreds of small fighter ships surrounded both carriers and others shuttled in and out. The scout ships had given the exact locations of the alien's ships and now the carriers were coming closer by the minute.

It didn't take long for the aliens to discover the human carrier which was coming at them at full speed. Their reaction was quick; they sent a group of fighter ships towards the approaching human ships. The two combatants were coming closer to each other at an amazing speed.

In the human headquarters, Commander-in-Chief Darrel, with his high-ranking commanders, was in the war room watching the war theater as it was taking place in front of them in three dimensional mode. It looked and felt as if they were right there.

The Alien Voursis

The Voursis had never fought the humans in open space; the humans on Earth, realizing from the beginning that they were fighting a superior opponent, chose a defensive war; they never sent fighter ships to meet them. Their defense worked well for many years keeping the Voursis away from planet Earth; it was only lately that the Voursis had managed to penetrate their defenses and occupy small portions of Earth. Now the humans fought the alien Voursis on land too. Their weapons proved to be no match for the superior Voursis; they continued to fight a defensive war on two fronts while they were working for the first time on building nuclear bombs.

When Nick Papas and his crew jumped from the twenty-fifth century to the end of the twenty-ninth, using the newly found time-travel method, they were horrified to see the humans using nuclear weapons---this time against the aliens. They had to stop them; that is the reason the Anastrophe community decided that they should arrive on Earth before the humans developed and used nuclear bombs. So neither the humans on Earth nor the Voursis, had adequate experience in "dog fights" with small fighter ships in open space. On the other hand the humans of the Anastrophe and Gaia Nea had been practicing this type of battle from the beginning. The whole aim of their lives was to defend themselves from the aliens and to destroy them. And now they had their chance to prove their superiority against a powerful enemy. Vrima was next to Commander

Project Anastrophe

Papas on the bridge of the carrier watching the info-grams coming from the front.

"Vrima, do you think they will use Flash bombs?"

"Yes, Commander, that is their tactic."

"Well, let them do that and see how far they'll go." Every move the aliens did was registered on Nick's carrier bridge and in headquarters. At this point it was Nick's war and he was giving orders.

Hun Tsu was in charge of the fighters. He was the best captain Commander Papas could use in the first battle with the aliens. Commander Papas appeared on Tsu's monitor, "Prepare for N.C. jump on my mark!"

"Aye, aye, Commander, ready for N.C. jump." (Nephus Cloaking was a device made by the infamous Nephus; he used it to escape the Anastrophe ship four hundred years ago; then Nick Papas, the great, great, grandfather of the present Nick Papas, used it against the aliens and escaped with his ship).

Just as the ships were about to engage in combat the aliens released a cluster of flash-bombs; at that precise moment Commander Papas said, "Now!" What happened next was a battle for the text books of the new generation cadets. Both the aliens and the humans executed their first maneuvers with ingenuity and accuracy. The slightest delay in Captain Tsu's reaction could have cost the obliteration of his fighter ships and the lives of his crew. But Commander Papas and Captain Tsu had practiced on this and other maneuvers and the Commander knew he could trust him. The flash-bombs created an inferno right where the human ships had been a split second earlier. But they fell into a void; there was nothing left for the aliens to burn, they had vanished. The aliens must had been surprised to see the ships disappear; but their biggest surprise was when they reappeared, this time divided in three groups, and attacking them from multiple sides. The aliens put up a good fight but in the long run the surprise attack from the humans was too quick and too deliberate. They didn't have a chance. Those who tried to escape the onslaught were chased and destroyed before they reached their home base.

This was a first victory for the humans and it was sweet retribution for all the human killings the aliens had done. The aliens had lost the first battle, but not the war. There were two more carriers that lifted up from Mars with hundreds of fighter ships. Now there was a huge alien force coming at Nick's carrier but Commander Papas didn't ask for more help just yet; he had a few more surprises for the alien Voursis. The aliens must have communicated with their superiors on Earth and help must be coming to Mars. The human scouts were reporting that the Voursis were preparing their defenses on Mars for possible invasion by these unknown invaders. But how could they hide two huge carriers from the human scouts, and how much more do the Voursis have that cannot be detected? Those were questions that concerned Commander Derral and his advisors in the headquarters; they wanted to clean Mars of the Voursis without committing too much of their force.

Now they were all waiting to see how Commander Papas would deal with the next Voursi attack. All this time Bárt's force was waiting for the right time to come into the fight. They were all in Nephus' cloaking mode and so far the Voursis had no idea of a second carrier, much less the rest of the flotilla, or flotillas farther away. Their first carrier didn't move from its position but the two extra ones were coming towards Commander Papas' carrier; they were much larger than the human carriers. Hundreds of fighter ships accompanied them forming a barrier and at the speed they were traveling, they would reach the hu-

Project Anastrophe

mans in ten to fifteen minutes. The officers on the bridge were looking nervously at Commander Papas for his next move. He knew that this time the Voursis were coming at him better prepared and with more force than before. So this time he would have to engage with them closer and hoped that he wouldn't have great losses. Just as the Voursis were getting dangerously near, Bart's forces joined with the humans and matched the Voursis speed. Then both enemies stopped at a safe distance and the battle started in earnest.

In previous mock fights both Commander Papas and Commander Napolitano, as well as other Commanders, had to follow the protocol of engagement directed by the headquarters. Now the only difference was that they were fighting a real war. This time it was Commander Napolitano's force which attacked first; his fighters met the Voursis in mid-air and the battle began. This time there were human losses, the Voursis were prepared and fought well. There were hundreds of robots flying like tiny planes collecting human fighters, dead or alive, who were floating helplessly in their spacesuits. The Voursis collected theirs in pods but it was harder and inevitably they lost many who floated away in the unfriendly, cold space.

It looked as if the Voursis were inflicting great losses on the humans, not because they were better fighters, but because they outnumbered the humans two to one. Several of the officers in Commander Papas' war room started to wonder what the Commander-in-Chief had in mind. It was sad to see so many human ships destroyed and so many of their comrades dead. Vrima said,

"I think the Chief is going to go for the twisters."

"It appears so, but with great loss to our fighters." It was now Commander Papas' fighters that sprang out of their nests like mad hornets and the fight became more intense. Now the fight began to favor the humans, but not for long. Still many Voursi fighters kept coming, trying to compensate for their lack of experience in "dog fights."

Then all the human fighters withdrew at once. Jumping into Nephus' cloaking mode, they were thrown into another dimension completely undetectable by the Voursis. Then the human carriers bombarded them with twister bombs; it was as if the Voursi fighters found themselves in a tornado moving them like matchboxes and crushing them. The human fighters reappeared---this time far behind their carriers.

The Voursis responded with flash bombs directed at the carriers followed by kinetic bombs which were like cluster bombs with the ability to penetrate the strongest shield. Both human carriers sustained heavy damage but regrouped and fought back by hitting the Voursis with a barrage of new weapons that created such vibration inside the Voursis' carriers, that most of their electronic equipment was destroyed and their oxygen was reduced. At the same time they were bombarded by the human fighters inflicting heavy damage to their carriers. Those Voursi fighters who managed to come out and fight were quickly destroyed; in the meantime hundreds of robot warriors penetrated the carriers killing and/or taking many Voursi prisoners. Next the human carriers attacked the last Voursi carrier which had stayed out of the battle all this time.

They also put up a good fight but in the long run they succumbed to the human's superior strength. All three heavily damaged Voursi carriers were gathered together and were put under human control. The Voursis on Mars accepted their fate and surrendered without resisting. It didn't take long for the humans on Mars to realize who their benefactors were; when they were told where they came from, and the reason they were back, they were thrilled. All the Voursis were held as war prisoners, the three carriers were

Project Anastrophe

brought down on Mars and the prisoners were put under human supervision. Several of the cloned Voursis who were especially made for taking the defeated compatriots back home to Voursa, assumed responsibility.

Commanders Nick, Bart, and Vrima came down on Mars and met with the newly appointed human leaders: George Vrionis Governor; Roy Jensen, Lieutenant Governor; Jennie Southerland, Supervisor; and Susan Gregory, Supervisor. The Governor said,

"On behalf of all humans on Mars I welcome you and thank you for giving us back our freedom."

Nick said,

"The Mars colony was only the beginning, next will be the planet Earth, but we need your help to communicate with the proper authorities on Earth. They need to know who we are and why we are here. All we need to know is who is in charge of the war against the aliens."

"The war is fought on many fronts on Earth and in space. Many leaders are in charge of their regions; however the United Federation of Earth is now represented by a newly elected President, Annan Hurou." Commander Bart said,

"We expect you to treat the alien prisoners in a humane way until they are sent back home; this is a requirement from our leaders."

"Even though they have mistreated us, I promise that we will treat them in a civilized and humane way, Commander." A large enough force was left on Mars, to protect the humans from possible Voursi attack.

Commanders Nick and Bart were asked to join a meeting requested by the Governor at his office. Commander-in-Chief Derral was there along with several other high-ranking commanders.

Governor Dave Zebigos said,

"I congratulate you for your victory; you and your staff executed your duties in battle with the aliens in the most honorable and heroic fashion. We all thank you very much." Then the Governor proceeded to award them the prestigious Medal of Bravery. They both thanked him.

Then Nick said,

"Governor, Commanders, we accept these awards on behalf of our staff and especially for those fallen heroes." Then the Governor asked Commander Derral what was next on the agenda, Commander Derral said,

"We have a secured line of communication with the President of The United Federation of Earth, Annan Hurou. We will be talking to him soon, Governor."

"Excellent, what would you like me to do, Commander?"

"Not much, Governor. You have already sent them a personal message along with the story of our people and the reason why we are coming back. So they know by now who we are. After the usual salutations; my staff and I will discuss special technical perimeters of the rules of engagement with their Generals and technical staff pertaining to our involvement in the war against the aliens."

"Very well, Commander, but how soon is soon?" One of the Governor's advisors said,

"You are scheduled to talk with President, Annan Hurou, in precisely two hours, Sir."

"Splendid, then I will see you gentlemen in two hours in the conference room."

Earth's Response

Governor Vrionis had a safe way to communicate with the proper authorities on Earth ever since he joined the insurgents against the alien Voursis. The insurgents formed

Project Anastrophe

their secret society decades ago as soon as the aliens took over Mars. Vrionis had been a member of the society for the last ten years; he was respected by all humans and tolerated by the aliens because of his position as a leader. It was natural for him to become the new Governor; and one of his first duties, as soon as he took office, was to get in touch with the authorities on Earth. He told them what had transpired during the last few days, and asked to speak directly with President Annan Hurou. This time he called him on a secured line directly from his office and said,

"Mr. President, it's true---we are free. All the Voursis are now our prisoners, thanks to a powerful group of humans who came from far away to destroy the aliens and liberate Earth. They said that we were their first stop and that their next stop was going to be Earth."

"How do you know they are humans and not a ploy by the aliens to gain entrance to Earth by devious means?"

"They do look a little different from us; they are shorter and more hybridized, resembling different races, but otherwise they look just like you and me. They wish to talk to you and tell you what they will do when they arrive on Earth. Mr. President, I have no doubt of who they say they are. They are our liberators here and judging by the powerful weapons they have; they will liberate Earth too."

"Thank you, Mr. Vrionis, I will ask my staff to arrange a meeting with them; in the meantime keep us posted of any changes out there." After the conversation was finished, the Governor talked to his staff,

"I don't think he believes me, what do you think?" Roy Jensen said,

"Governor, if someone told me that some so-called human beings liberated you, and they are on their way to liberate Earth; I would have a hard time believing you too."

"Yet we know that they are telling us the truth don't we?"

The next day the Governor was told from Earth that the President would be willing to talk with this group. Two hours later the Governor arrived. All the important personnel were there. The line between Earth and the Anastrophe's headquarters was turned on and right in the middle of the floor appeared a group of humans in holographic form. They looked bigger and not as hybridized as the Voyagers. Governor Zebigos started the meeting

"Greetings, my name is David Zebigos and I am the Governor of Anastrophe. Over here are my Government representatives and over there are the Commanders of our force. We are coming in peace to you, our human brothers and sisters, but our aim is to destroy our common enemy the aliens."

President Annan Hurou said,

"Greetings to you, Governor Zebigos, this is my staff and these are some of my generals; we welcome anyone who comes to us in peace. We are grateful to those who wish to destroy our enemies, the aliens."

"We forwarded the story of our people so that you would know who we are; the reason our ancestors left Earth, and the reason we are coming back. Do you have any questions before our Commanders ask your generals some important questions of their own?"

"We want very much to believe what you have told us so far, but we find your story incredible and difficult to comprehend."

"President Hurou, we don't expect you to believe us just from learning of our odyssey and from our short visit. May I present my Commander in-Chief-Kent Derral?"

"Greetings--our ancestors traveled to the future, specifically to the end of the twenty- ninth century. They saw

Project Anastrophe

what was about to happen to Earth and decided to save it. In the near future the aliens will take over Earth and you will live like your people lived on Mars before we liberated them. The nuclear bombs you are building now will not save you; all you will accomplish is the introduction of a very dangerous substance into the Earth's environment. We told you our story and we hope that you will believe us. But we will attack and destroy the aliens with or without your help; we have come a long way and our people suffered too much during the last four hundred and fifty years. Our ancestors have entrusted us with the responsibility to save Earth from the aliens and we intend to do that. If you decide not to help us, please stay out of the way and let us deal with the aliens. President Hurou, I hope that we have conveyed to you our purpose for coming to Earth and that we are not your enemy but your friends who want to help you." There was some discussion between the President and one of the generals. Then President Hurou said,

"I will let General Peter Johnson respond to your statement, Commander."

"We will never allow anyone to tell us how to fight our war with the aliens, and we will use any weapons if we think they will help us win. However, if we find it to our advantage not to interfere with your war then we will stop firing of our own will. But the minute you fire at us we will fire back."

"General Johnson, that sounds fair to us; we don't want to fight you; however should you decide to help us, all we need from you is to concentrate your forces on the aliens on Earth. My staff will give you the perimeters of fighting and assistance, should you need it."

"We will decide on that, and let you know, Commander Derral."

Chapter 27

Before the Voursis were captured on Mars, they must have had communication with their headquarters on Earth about a new and powerful human force. The Voursis now increased their bombardment of Earth and committed more weaponry and warriors to captured areas. For the humans on Earth, fighting the Voursis on two fronts proved to be increasingly untenable. The alien Voursis were using newer weapons and had destroyed most of the infrastructures on Earth. The humans were fighting a defensive war in space and an offensive war on land, but they were losing on both fronts. It was now a matter of time before they would be taken over by the Voursis. In time the humans would use nuclear bombs but those weapons would only slow them down and would introduce radiation on Earth

Project Anastrophe

again. That was the reason the Anastrophe travelers wanted to come to Earth earlier; to defeat the Voursis before the humans used nuclear bombs.

It was obvious to the humans on Earth that the Voursis were building powerful bases on land, not to fight them, but to fight the other humans who were on the way to Earth. General Peter Johnson had an emergency meeting with President Annan Hurou; they met in his office,

"Mr. President, we need to get in touch with our human friends as soon as possible."

"According to our last report they are due to arrive in two weeks; what's the big hurry general?"

"Mr. President, in two weeks it will be all over for us; we must use nuclear bombs against the aliens before they build anymore bases on Earth. In the last two months they have acquired twice as much land on Earth, and they have fortified their bases with more and newer weapons. We think that their strategy is to turn their new weapons on us to weaken us before they engage with the other humans."

"General, you know how they feel about us using nuclear bombs; we will use them only as a last resort."

"Mr. President, this is our last resort; if we wait any longer there will not be much left of us for them to save; we must act now."

"The least we can do is to let them know; they may have a better idea. After all, they want to save Earth as much as we do."

"Mr. President, bear in mind that the longer we wait, the stronger the Voursis get."

"General, I will get in touch with them as soon as possible; and I will let you know right away."

"Thank you, Mr. President." The conversation between Annan Hurou and David Zebigos was short and to the point,

"Governor Zebigos, we are about to use nuclear bombs

against the Voursis and I thought you should know about it."

"President Hurou, our scouts have informed us about your dire situation and we have taken measures. You will see the results in two days; do not use nuclear bombs, we will be there in two weeks."

"General Johnson has informed me that the Voursis are preparing a big offensive on land and I am afraid in two week's time it will be all over for us here unless we go nuclear."

"We will never allow the Voursis to take over Earth; we have ways of slowing them down even though we are not there yet."

"Two days is all you have, after that we go nuclear." President Hurou called General Johnson and told him he had decided to wait for two days before he would allow him to use the bombs; he also told him to concentrate his forces on the Voursis' bases on land rather than in space; things would happen for the best within two days. General Johnson wasn't happy but promised to wait.

After Mars, the Voursis took over Earth's Moon. The humans had fought them bravely but lost to the powerful intruder; that was decades ago. Since then the Voursis had built huge bases on the Moon and used the human prisoners for slave work. But just as on Mars, the humans managed to keep those on Earth posted with what was happening on the Moon. At times they even managed to sabotage the Voursis causing great damage to the factories that were making weapons and fighter ships. It was this group that Nick's scouts were able to get in touch with. The humans on the Moon knew about this new force that was on its way to liberate them and Earth. They were ready to help in the cause in any way they could.

The scouts landed on the Moon commanded by Andreas

Project Anastrophe

Karn, a young man in his twenties. They were in cloaked mode; they were taken to a secret place by the human resistance. Andreas talked to the leader of the group, Dannie Brooks, a man in his sixties who had been with the Resistance most of his adult life. Andreas said,

"We need to know when the next freight is leaving for the Voursi bases on Earth."

"In the last few weeks they have been leaving daily, and from what we are hearing they are fortifying their bases on Earth for an all-out attack to weaken Earth before your forces arrive."

"We are aware of this; that's why we need to act fast."

"It's impossible to go near their bases; they have infrared detectors and other detection gear that sets alarms."

"We have ways to avoid their alarms, show us where the freight is."

"If we can bypass their alarms we can inflict heavy damage on them."

"That is precisely the reason we are here." Andreas' group, accompanied by a few selected humans, arrived at the main base. They were covered by the Nephus' cloaking device and were completely undetected by the Voursis. Andreas and his group got busy right away; they installed explosives inside the freight that was destined for Earth. Before Andreas and his group left, they were replaced by another team of scouts who would coordinate the coming fight. At the end of the second day, explosions occurred on all the Voursis' bases on Earth; the explosions were so catastrophic that they damaged the bases to the extent that they could not be used.

On top of that, the humans launched a surprise attack on the aliens. The Voursis held their bases but at a great cost in life and material. Now they were weakened, not the humans. The Voursis would never launch their attack on

Earth; they could barely hold onto what they had. After the near destruction of their bases, the Voursis changed tactics. They now concentrated their fire on the big cities on Earth; they used new and more powerful weapons. The humans kept their promise not to use nuclear weapons at this time; they were able to concentrate most of their power in space. The two powers were now at an impasse and that was fine for the humans for the time being; at least until the other human force joined the war.

Two days before they were to engage in the final battle with the alien Voursis, there was another conference of the high-ranking commanders at the headquarters. Most of the day was spent going over plans for the coming battle; so by the end of the day there was no doubt in their minds as to how they were going to approach this coming war. After the meetings were over; Nick, Norina, Bart, Arty, Ner, and Vrima, had dinner together. The conversation was mainly about war and the possible fatalities on both sides. Nick and Norina wished their friends good luck and left. Bart and Arty stayed longer talking to Ner and Vrima. As Nick and Norina were going to their separate rooms, Nick asked Norina if she would like to have a drink in his room to celebrate a little before the coming battle. They had been together before, but this was different. She said,
"I was hoping you'd ask me to come in."
"Will you take your usual?"
"Yes, Please."
"I have been meaning to tell you of a feeling I have had for you, Norina, for a long time, but I was afraid that you wouldn't understand me. But with the possibility of either one of us getting killed in this coming battle, I thought I had better get it off my chest tonight."
"That's interesting, Nick, because I have had special

feelings for you too, and I didn't know when or how I was going to express them; but lets hear yours first."

"I have had relationships with other women, but with you it is different. It is as though I knew you even before I met you; and I loved you from the first minute I saw you when we were young children. And now I love you even more. If I am one of the fallen ones, at least you will know how I felt for you. That's all I wanted to confess to you and I hope that you understand me."

"Nick, I am so glad we were able to meet tonight. I have the same feelings for you, but I can't explain why; perhaps we are destined to love each other and be together." That night Nick and Norina slept together and made love and they felt that they belonged to each other.

Humans versus the Alien Voursis

The final orders were given to attack the Voursis as soon as they arrived. They didn't come all at once; they appeared a few armadas at the time, which thoroughly confused the Voursis. They had made special preparations for this new human force; they were also tactical and methodical warriors. In the last few decades they had build a powerful fleet with many armadas; they had bases on the Moon and on Earth. The Voursis were upgrading their weapons all the time making it very difficult for the humans on Earth to catch up with them. Even if the humans were to use nuclear weapons it would only have slowed them down. They were here for the long run, and they were determined to take over Earth and interbreed with the humans and start their own empire on Earth and beyond. Although the Voursis suffered catastrophic damage on their Earth bases, they didn't lose them; in the last few days, before the new human force arrived, they were able to reorganize, regroup, and fortify their bases. Now once more they were ready for what they thought would be a decisive battle. Vourook, the Chief Commander of the Voursi fleet, called his staff to a pre-battle meeting, he said,

"We have superior warriors and weaponry than those Savages down there on Earth; we are a superior race and we are going to win this war. Our bases on Earth will keep the Savages busy; we only need to concentrate on these new invaders in space. Once we defeat them, the Savages will fall easily. Now what do we know about this new force?" Porvas, a high-ranking leader and second in command to Vourook, said,

"We know very littler about this new force, we think they are of the human species but are far more intelligent than their savage relatives. We don't know where they came from but they are good warriors; they have superior weapons from those of the Savages, and they defeated our forces on Mars."

"Do we know how large their fleet is?"

"We do not; they have the ability to cloak using a formula unknown to us.

"Are you sure they are Savages and not another species?"

"They appear to have all the human characteristics but they are a little shorter than those on Earth."

"If they are relatives to the human Savages, where did they come from?"

"Until we catch some prisoners we won't know who they actually are."

"We should assume that they are as strong as we are, and fight accordingly."

"There is one thing we do know for sure and that is, they have weapons similar to ours with some small differences."

Project Anastrophe

"How can that be? They couldn't find the material they need in this solar system to construct weapons like ours."

"If they were able to make synthetic metallurgical substances to match our alloys, then they are far more intelligent than we are giving them credit for."

"If they are humans, they are Savages, no matter how intelligent they are; we are going to defeat them."

"Commander Vourook, we don't know the strength of our enemy, and that puts us at a disadvantage."

"We will fight them as equals; they can't be better than we are. Now go back to your posts and fight like Voursis; we will destroy those Savages." The Voursi leaders left their headquarters determined to fight and win this war, but they were apprehensive about these unknown human Savages.

With the arrival of the new human force, all the people on Earth felt relieved; they knew that now, for the first time, they could fight the aliens on a more equal basis than before. Although they didn't know their strength, they knew by now how they fought and beat the aliens on Mars; they assumed, and quite rightly so, that if they initiated a fight with such a powerful enemy they must have had substantial strength. Nick and Norina, Bart and Arty, and Ner and Vrima all communicated with each other before the battle began and wished each other good luck and a quick victory.

It had been a long wait for the little Anastrophe community since those pioneer days. Generation after generation, they had built their fighting forces and their weaponry to be able to fight these alien invaders. Their ancestors would be proud to have seen the powerful warriors they had created; and now the day had come. Through many years the alien Voursis had the upper hand with the humans on Earth; but now they were up against a new enemy as powerful as they were.

Preparations for Battle

The Voursis were frustrated not being able to know the strength of their enemy, but they were working feverishly to unlock the human's cloaking formula. In the meantime they took a defensive posture and their fleet was on high alert. The Eighth Flotilla of the human fleet was the closest to the enemy line. Nick, Norina, Bart, and Arty were in the same armada; Ner and Vrima were on Norina's carrier. Bert Gamble, the commander of the Eighth Flotilla, was waiting for the order from head-quarters to attack. When it came, hundreds of fighting ships from the first four armadas attacked all at once. They were met midway by a determined enemy and there started a "dog fight" like the Voursis had never fought before.

They had seen their forces fighting these humans on Mars and had an idea of their fighting techniques, but to fight them in real life was something else. The human ships were smaller and faster and more maneuverable than those of the Voursis. Their outer skin was covered with black diamond that had been excavated from the planet Atalandos. The humans were winning the first battle until more Voursi reinforcements arrived; that's when the humans were ordered to leave. They disappeared all at once; seconds later the Voursis left the area too.

They had seen what had happened to their forces on Mars when the humans disappeared like that, and they didn't want to be incinerated. Now it was the human carriers bombarding the Voursi carriers; thousands of missiles hit the Voursi carriers inflicting heavy damage. They responded with missiles of their own destined to hit the humans. But they hit a void; the humans were able to make whole armadas disappear only to reappear momentarily thereby inflicting damage on the Voursi ships, then disappearing in split seconds. The human armadas used the same method of "hide and seek" all around the alien fleet. It was taking a toll on the Voursis. However after a while they were able to adjust their firing responses and hit many human ships as they reappeared. It was a battle fought by two skilled groups of warriors, who were using every trick of the trade to destroy one another.

The humans on Earth had better luck fighting their war on land. The Voursis in space had finally met their match with the new-comers. What little they could do to help their forces on Earth was compromised by their powerful opponent in space; so the Voursis on Earth were left alone to fight the humans on land. The war had gone on for two weeks both in space and on Earth. There were fatalities on both sides but little by little the Voursis were losing the war. It became worse for the Voursis when the humans launched an all-out attack on their bases on Earth; it was orchestrated by General Peter Johnson when he realized that the Voursis didn't have much help from space. It was a well coordinated attack from space and land; while the humans in space prevented the Voursis from helping their forces on land, the humans on Earth bombed the Voursi bases by land and air. What the humans had not been able to accomplish in decades, they were able to do in two days. The first day the Voursis put up a good fight, but during the night, and well into the next day, the humans broke into their bases and defeated them. It was the only defeat of the Voursis and the only victory for the humans.

Although there was a lot of hatred against the aliens, General Johnson kept the promise he had made to the newcomers and put the aliens in prison and out of harm's way.

When General Johnson asked Commander-in- Chief Kent Derral of the human fleet in space, if he needed help, the answer was,

No--we alone will fight the Voursis in space--keep out of it!"

The Voursis expected the humans from Earth to join the fight in space. When they didn't, they realized that their enemy had to be stronger than they thought to decline help from Earth at such a crucial time. And so the fight continued for a third week without anyone being able to declare victory. Both sides had underestimated their adversary; the Voursis thought these human Savages were not intelligent enough to fight them and win. The humans thought that they were superior fighters and that they had superior weaponry. They were wrong; the Voursis had newer and powerful weapons, and they proved to be equally good fighters.

At the end of the third week, Commander Kent Derral, after discussing the state of the war with his strategists and advisors, wanted to break the impasse in which they found themselves. He said,

"Evidently we have been underestimating the aliens; they seem to adapt to any new tactic we use in this war, and they always surprise us with new tactics of their own. Something has to give---or we will be fighting them for years. They have an inexhaustible supply of material, weapons, and fighters, and we don't. At the present rate they can win this war just by maintaining the status-quo; we have to do something to break out--I am open to new ideas."

Commander Erik Napavo, a high-ranking commander and advisor in the head office, said,

"We have three options we could use to break this impasse. One is to ask for help from Earth; another, to destroy their bases on the Moon, thereby depriving them from material and new weapons; the third one, and the most daring, is to fight them head-on and count on our pilots to penetrate their defense line. I think our pilots have proven that they are superior to theirs, and they can do the job." There were many ideas discussed that morning in the war room, but all of them came with great sacrifice in lives, weapons, and fighter ships.

Chief Commander Kent Derral said,

"I would like to use the Earth option as a last resort. Destroying their Moon bases would prolong the war because they would defend it with all they have. Even if we were to destroy it, they could still fight us for months, resulting in great losses to our forces. I would prefer to attack them head-on, and then ask for help from Earth, should we need it. I also believe that our pilots are capable of breaking their defense line; once we are in, we could use kinetic bombs and incinerate them." Again Commander Napavo said,

"Commander, are we going as far as to destroy their non fighting people---the young and the old?"

"I believe that they would surrender before we attack their big carriers; besides have they spared any of the human population on Earth? They are killing everybody indiscriminately, aren't they?" It was decided to take the third option which called for an all-out attack, and preparations for the final battle started right away.

The Voursis knew that something big was happening with the Savages because they had not attacked them for the last three days, and that was very unusual. They used this unexpected break to regroup and reposition themselves for the next Savage attack. Commander Vourook used this time to meet with his and advisors to discuss what the Savages were up to, and what else they should do to better prepare for what might come their way.

"We all sense that the Savages are planning something big, do you have any idea what they may be up to?" The

Voursi leaders discussed many scenarios the human Savages could take, and although they didn't all agree, they did agree that the Savages weren't about to stop the war. One Voursi leader by the name of Couvas, said,

"Perhaps they are preparing to use a new weapon on us and they are clearing their people away from the war zone."

Vourook said,

"If they were to do something like that, are we prepared enough to protect ourselves?"

Porvas responded,

"Of course that would depend on what kind of weapon they use; the most powerful weapon they might use would be a nuclear bomb. We know that they have been working on it for a long time, and if they are ready to use it; that would explain the reason they are pulling their people away."

"Can we protect ourselves from such a weapon?"

"It's a powerful weapon and if it hits a carrier it would be demolished, but we could protect ourselves from the radiation that would be released from it. However the radiation would sooner or later settle on Earth and that would cause greater damage to them, plus the fact that we would inherit a sick planet."

Another leader called Fleegas said,

"We can't afford to underestimate these new humans we are fighting; they are matching us in weaponry, in the battle, and in ingenuity. Maybe they are humans but they are not Savages like the humans on Earth. My feeling is that if they are going to use such a weapon that, in the long run, will damage their own planet; they will use it only as a last resort. Why should they use such a weapon now? They are not losing the war, we are." It was a sobering statement, one everybody was aware of, but did not want to acknowledge. Commander Vourook responded violently,

Project Anastrophe

"We are not losing the war to these Savages; I realize that we lost our bases on Earth, but when we defeat them in space we will get our bases back, and then we will defeat them on Earth too." Vourook's thinking wasn't shared by all his officers, but they didn't dare say otherwise.

Porvas advised,

"At this point all we can do is to strengthen our defenses and respond accordingly." It was a strategy that was accepted by all and soon after that they dispersed.

The Final Battle

The human fighter ships appeared out of nowhere, not by the hundreds but by the thousands; they came at the Voursis' defense line. They expected an attack from the humans, but nothing like that. However the Voursis counter-attacked with thousands of their own fighter ships and there started a space battle, the biggest the Voursis or humans had ever had. The human fighter ships were smaller and their outer skin was protected by the special alloy which they brought from the Voursa area, just like the Voursi ships. However the human fighter ships had an additional protective layer of diamond. This extra protection enabled them to better endure the toxic fireballs that were thrown at them by the Voursis. On the other hand the Voursis didn't always survive the kinetic bombs of the humans. Although the alien pilots fought bravely, the human pilots proved to be superior. After two hours of continuous fighting, the human fighter ships broke their defense line and started to attack the carriers. Soon after that, the human carriers broke through the Voursi defenses and started bombarding their carriers with kinetic bombs. The Voursis were now losing the war, but they had inflicted heavy damage on the human fleet.

George Karnikis

It was one of those counter-attacks by the Voursi fighters that hit Commander Norianna Anderson's carrier; it was a well-coordinated attack. They destroyed a good portion of the carrier, and then the Voursi robots and live army boarded the carrier. A fight began between the humans and their robots, and the invaders with their robots. They fought in the corridors, and on decks. The human's robots were so massive and so lethal they contained the enemy, for the most part, in the area in which they arrived. The war room where Commander Anderson was at the time was hit badly and she was caught, along with several other officers, under some twisted metal beams. Ner and Vrima, who were there too, sprang into action.

Ner said,

"Vrima, cover the corridor until help arrives; I am going to free Norina from that beam that trapped her in the war room." There was fire and smoke in the room and it was very hot. Ner yelled to Norina,

"Are you all right?"

"We are O.K. Get us out of here!"

"I am prying a piece of beam that's blocking the door and I'll be there soon." As Ner was trying to free Norina and the other officers, a battle started in the hallway between Vrima and the invader robots. Vrima put up a good fight but she was an old issue robot; she couldn't keep the enemy away for long. Within minutes she was destroyed. Ner was able to fight them a little longer, but then he too was destroyed. The invader robots were about to kill Norina and the other officers when help finally arrived. A group of the human's robots started fighting the enemy robots and destroyed them. Soon after that android medics arrived and took Norina and her officers away to safety. As she was taken away she gave orders to the androids to collect the charred remains of Ner and Vrima and keep them

Project Anastrophe

in a safe place. Both Ner and Vrima had sacrificed their lives to save their beloved Norina.

For every human carrier destroyed by the Voursis, three of theirs were destroyed by the humans; and it was getting worst for them. The human pilots were gaining the upper hand minute by minute; among the many carriers that entered the dangerous zone were Nick's, Bart's and Artie's. Norina's carrier was taken back for repairs, and she, along with many of her injured crew, was in the hospital. Their carriers with hundreds of fighter ships were ordered to go closer to the biggest Voursi carrier which housed their headquarters. This carrier was defended by many of their best pilots and the humans knew that this was going to be the most decisive battle of all. The closer they came to the Voursis the more they were attacked, and they were wondering if they would arrive in one piece.

Nick, Bart, and Artie were in constant communication; their aim was to encircle the Voursi carrier and then send thousands of robots and human fighters to board it. The Voursis fought determinedly and heroically to save their headquarter carrier, but they were up against a superior enemy. But as long as they were getting help, which was coming endlessly, they could fight for a long time causing great damage to the invading human forces.

Finally with the help of more carriers the humans managed to separate the Voursi carrier and it was boarded. For a while the Voursis fought the invaders bravely, but eventually the humans captured the war room and all the high-ranking commanders. Vourook, the Chief Commander, Porvas second in command, and two other high-ranking commanders, committed suicide rather than surrender to the Savages. The battle was over. The humans had won a hard-fought war with many losses; but the victory was sweet for the entire human race.

"There were other high-ranking Voursi commanders and officers who were willing to discuss the surrender of the remaining Voursi fleet. They were taken to Nick's carrier and he was personally involved with the official surrender of the Voursi fleet. There were four Voursi commanders and many lower-ranking officials in the war room. The Voursis were Chief Commander, Vrofnoof, Commander Nichtos, Commander Mougro, and Commander Flaflox. Nick welcomed all and spoke to them in Voursi,

"Commanders and officers, I welcome you to my carrier; the war is over and we are here to discuss peace. You are all brave fighters and you have fought admirably. We know your people and your country, well. Hundreds of years ago our ancestors were able to travel to our times and could see that you were about to take over our planet and make it yours. At the time they knew that the humans on Earth would lack the material and technology to fight you. So they traveled to your homeland where they found the material they needed and combined your technology with the human to produce superior weapons.

Our ancestors lived in ships and on a meteorite for hundreds of years. For many generations their goal was to build weapons and to practice the art of war so that when the time came, we could fight well and defeat you--and that's what we did. Commanders, let me assure you that we are not Savages as you were led to believe; we are civilized and we will treat you with dignity and respect. We are not going to keep you as our prisoners, but we are going to send you home where you belong.

When our ancestors went to your homeland, they told them that in the future your people would try to take over Earth. The people from your homeland said that you were sent to meet other worlds and establish peaceful communi-

Project Anastrophe

cation; not to engage in war with younger civilizations. They gave us a special unit that produced Voursi clones which would be your new commanders that would take you home. We were told that you are acquainted with this practice and that you would transfer power to them." Then Commander Papas asked for the clone Voursis to be brought in. Three young Voursis stepped in and saluted the humans; then they saluted the Voursi Commander by touching their foreheads with each other as was their custom. Then one of them said,

"I am Gouga, and I have orders from the Emperor of Voursa, his Highness Mourgdos, to assume leadership over the Voursi fleet and take it, and all its occupants, back to our homeland Voursa. You shall be replaced by my High Commanders, Warmeck and Zoboch. And you shall live the rest of your lives as plain citizens." Commander Vrofnoof and his high commanders were disappointed that they would be replaced with new staff by orders of the Emperor, but they accepted their fate without complaints. Then the new Chief Commander Gouga put on the table a unit resembling a regular book; and they proceeded to put their right hands on it, thereby surrendering biometrically their fleet to the new Voursi staff. The humans gave the Voursis four weeks to gather their people from their bases on Earth and from the Moon; then the Voursis left for Mars, where they joined their remaining carriers and the Voursi prisoners. After a few days they left Mars for their long voyage back to Voursa.

After the war was over Nick, Bart, and Artie visited Norina at the hospital; Nick was happy to see Norina again,
"How are you feeling, Norina?"
"I am feeling much better; I only had a small break on my left forearm. Did you hear about Ner and Vrima?"

"Yes, it's very sad that they were destroyed so close to our victory; they were an institution in the whole fleet and now they are gone, very sad indeed." Nick, Norina, Bart, and Artie were decorated for bravery. During the ceremony Norina spoke for those of her crew who were lost in the war. She said,

"I would like to express my deep sympathy to the relatives of those who lost their lives defending my carrier. They fought well and they successfully eliminated or captured the aliens that boarded the ship; and my special thanks and gratitude goes to the two old issue robots known for hundred of years throughout the fleet and Gaia Nea as Ner and Vrima. They lost their lives fighting bravely and delayed the aliens from coming into the war room, thereby giving time to our fighters to save me and my officers.

Humans versus Humans

The humans on Earth were happy to see that the defeated Voursis had gone back to their homeland and left Earth forever. The victory was celebrated all over the planet and the humans on Earth were thankful to the newcomers, the so-called "Anastrophe people", for defeating the Voursis. Mr. Annan Hurou, the President of the United Federation of Earth, General Peter Johnson, and other officials were waiting anxiously for the arrival of the Anastrophe's Governor, David Zebigos, Commander-in-Chief, Kent Derral, Commander Nick Papas, and other Commanders from the victorious fleet. Their meeting was held at the President's office; their first contact was an official one and was kept secret from the rest of the people. President Annan Hurou shook hands with Governor Zebigos and General Derral. After the greetings they all sat down and the conference started in earnest.

Project Anastrophe

President Annan Hurou said,

"On behalf of all humans on Earth I want to thank you for delivering us from the alien Voursis. During the last few decades the war has destroyed many of our cities, drained our economy, and has killed and maimed millions of our people. But now thanks to you, our enemy has been defeated. We will again rebuild our cities and once more live and prosper. Governor Zebigos, my government and many people are wondering what you will do next."

"We sent you the history of our people well in advance, before we arrived on Earth. I realize that it is difficult to believe our story, but it is the truth. I would like to let Commander Papas elaborate on the history of our people before I answer your question.

"We are humans like you; we are your brothers and sisters and we are tired of living as vagabonds on spaceships. We have told you in detail the history of our people; now I would like to tell about the personal sufferings our ancestors had to endure.

It was my grandfather and grandmother of many generations ago, along with others at the end of the twenty-fifth century, who were sent to stop the production of nuclear bombs. Their project was called "Anastrophe", which means to turn things back. Our ancestors traveled to our time and saw that our planet was about to be taken over by the aliens. They could have lived the rest of their lives on Earth and let future generations deal with the aliens. However they knew that you would have lost the war, that's why they decided to commit their lives and many generations of that small community to a four hundred and sixty-five year long voyage. They wanted to get the material and technology they or you could not find on Earth at that time. We are their and your descendants, we have fulfilled our promise to save Earth; now we are home where we belong and we want to live with you in peace. The Governor and the Commanders are going to tell you how we can best achieve that."

Nick was received well by the President and his government and if there were any doubts before now they were believers. Still, there was that superpower over their heads that worried them a lot.

General Kent Derral said

"Our main goal was to defeat the aliens and we have succeeded in doing so. Now all we want is to settle on Earth, be part of this world, and fulfill the wish our ancestors had for us to come back home. However there a few things that must be understood; the first thing that we need to make clear to you is that we don't wish to take over the Earth or your government, Mr. President. On the other hand we are not going to surrender our fleet to you either. What we would like to do is to incorporate our forces in a fair and just way; we have done this before with the humans that now live in Gaia Nea and I see no reason why we can't do it here too. We can have our commanders and your generals, admirals and air force officers, work out the technicalities and come up with a powerful force that will belong to all of us. I am sure our governor would like to elaborate on this subject too."

"Thank you, General Derral; Mr. President, we have technologies in industry, medicine, and farming that would greatly improve your standard of living. We will help you rebuild your cities; then we can all live together in peace and we can all prosper from this union."

"Governor Zebigos, my government and I appreciate all the sacrifices your ancestors and you have endured and we believe that this planet is yours as much as it is ours. We have no objections to your living with us if we can achieve a fair and just division of our forces. Therefore I propose to have our staff start negotiations as soon as possible." Their meeting lasted for many hours but in the end they were all happy with their preliminary agreement and withdrew to have a state dinner.

The Vagabonds Come Home

The new comers and the humans on Earth worked continuously for many months and in the end they managed to merge their forces in a way that satisfied both groups. Now Earth became a super power that belonged to all human beings. Cities were built for the thousands of the Anastrophe people. Because they had been living in space for so many years the cities were especially built for their particular needs. They were to reside in those special cities until they adapted to the Earth's gravity and were acclimatized to their new environment. The big day for the move from their spaceships to the cities started with a few hundred people at a time. They were welcomed as heroes by thousands of people expressing their appreciation for defeating the aliens.

One year had passed since the time they had arrived on Earth, and just as their ancestors had done when they had arrived on Gaia Nea more than a hundred years ago, they too adapted to Earth. At first people would stop and look at them, mostly from curiosity, because they were smaller by a few centimeters than the average people on Earth, and were hybrids of all races. They were also known to be very intelligent and physically strong.

Most of the carriers and the thousands of fighter ships were now landed except those which were destined to go back to Gaia Nea. Now there were preparations for yet another separation. Many of the middle-aged people had been born on Gaia Nea and for them that was their homeland.

George Karnikis

Many of them were homesick and signed up for the trip back to Gaia Nea. Most of those born on the ships readily adapted to the easier life on Earth, and were happy to stay. A few of them decided to go to Gaia Nea with their parents. Young volunteers who were born on Earth also signed up to go to the New World. A much smaller fleet was now ready to depart for the long voyage and the people once more felt the pain of separation. However this time people knew where they were going and as the time went on, people would learn to travel faster, and the time of separation would shorten. There would be many trips to Gaia Nea in the future, but for now the separation would be for life; and it would be very painful. Andreas Karn was chosen as the Chief Commander of the new fleet, with Lee Lum as its new Governor. Those who were to go and those who were to stay had a farewell party and a few days later they left for the long voyage back to Gaia Nea.

Chapter 28

Discovery

One hundred and twenty–five years ago the little community of Anastrophe were on their way to Gaia Nea; at that time part of their plan was to reduce their population. The plan went into effect right away calling for each young family to have a maximum of two children; one was allowed to develop the other was reduced to its D.N.A. and was hibernated. They were to be reconstituted and allowed to develop if and when they arrived on Earth. There were hundreds of thousands of them, and the time had come for them to be born, a few thousand every year, in those special cities made for the new-comers.

George Karnikis

Bart and Arty, who were now married, retired from the force and were in charge of that project. Nick and Norina, also married, chose to stay in the force as high ranking Commanders and were now teaching in the space academy in Seattle. It was one of those sunny days in the North West and Norina had called many of her friends to celebrate her twenty-eighth birthday. Her parents, Nick's parents, Bart and Artie, and many other friends from the service and from the academy were all there having a wonderful time.

Ner and Vrima who had put the special implants in all four youngsters twenty-four years ago had programmed Norina's implant to initiate first, then Nick's, Bart's, and Artie's seconds later. They had different birthdays but they were all now twenty-eight years old. It was late at night and all of the friends and relatives had left. They were working on their last drink and Bart and Artie were about to leave when Norina froze in mid-sentence while talking to Artie. Seconds later they had the same experience;

Norina looked at them surprised and said,

"Do you feel what I feel?"

They all nodded in the affirmative, and then Nick said,

"I have a feeling that we all have someone within us. He then turned to Norina and asked her, "Norina, who do you have?"

"I have my grandmother of many generations ago, her name was also Norina and her last name was Anderson. Who do you have, Nick?"

"My grandfather, Nick Papas, of many decades ago."

Bart and Artie, almost at the same time said, "I have Ner."

"And I have Vrima." Nick was about to say something when Bart said,

"Wait a moment, Nick, Ner is communicating with me." That night they spent many hours listening to Bart telling them what Ner had told him. After Bart and Artie

Project Anastrophe

left, Nick and Norina looked at each other for a long moment; then they embraced for a long time and Nick said,

"That clearly explains the attraction we had for each other; according to Ner we are made of ninety-nine percent of our grandparent's D.N.A."

"They must have loved each other very much and that explains the feelings I have for you, Nick."

"I feel the same way about you, Norina, now we are them and they are us, and the four of us are one."

"Thanks to Ner and Vrima, this is the best present I have had in my life. I love you, Nick."

"I love you too, Norina."

Bart and Artie left for home happy to have Ner and Vrima back again and this time within them as best friends and advisers. That night Bart and Artie made love, and Vrima was ecstatic.

THE END

Names of the Characters

35-A: robot
35-B: robot
Anderson, Norina: Nick's girl friend in the 25th century
Atalandos: closest planet to Gaia Nea.
AZM, BZM, CZF: Enemy robots.
Biosphere Z-2: built on Gaia Nea.
Davidson, Edward: oil Baron.
Dericton, Charles: Prime Minister of England 1942 Derral, Commander, Kent: in charge of all human fighting forces.

Project Anastrophe

Diotheos: the Governor of the Anastrophe's community at the time of the arrival close to planet Voursa.

Dorgovich, Dr. John: scientist in charge of the conspirator's group.

Dylos, Dr. George: in charge of the team to save Earth.

Dyphus: Norina's and Nick's third robot "mainly for security."

Dyplopherus: the newly rebuilt spaceship by Nephus' scientific staff.

Eastman, Mary: Vrima's cover name.

Eastman, Roy: Ner's cover name.

Fillmore, Lisa: Scientist.

Flarna: a planet close to Voursa.

Flarnars: citizens of Flarna.

Gaia Nea: a planet occupied by half of the Anastrophe's community.

Gardana Galaxy: where the humans live.

Hamilton, James: American President.

Johnson, Robert and Loretta: Nick's and Norina's cover names.

Karn, Andreas: leader of the scouts on the Moon.

Larnos: Commander of the revolutionary army, and later the new Monarch of Voursa.

Lavoutis: underworld character, employed by Narky.

McMiness, Jim: the President of the Sentunian club

Megacephalos: robot

Mourdug, Vlog: son of Throvolan.

Mourgdos: the new young Emperor of Voursa.

Mourgdunian: member of the Mourdug Dynasty.

Napolitano, Artemis: Artie for short, hero, and future host for Vrima's profiles.

Narkilos or Narky: underworld boss.

Narthur, Dr. Neal: Specialists in weapons and security.

George Karnikis

Nazer, Mary: the governor of the Z- Biosphere.
Ner: Norina's robot.
Nomarchos, Lefteris: the captain of the Anastrophe one.
Northmount, Chloe: daughter of Nephus and Darna.
Northmount, Damien: son of Nephus and Darna.
Northmount, Nephus, Taly: unstable, genius.
Papas, Commander, Argeris: in charge of the human armada.
Papas, Kallista: (6), daughter.
Papas, Nick: from the 21st Century.
Papas, Nickiphoros Junior: or Nick for short, hero, genetically engineered.
Papas, Nikitas: son of Nick and Norina.
Papas, Thora: daughter of Nick and Norina.
Paterson, John: American President.
Phylios: chief of all robot guards, (himself a robot.)
Preston, George: U.S. Secretary of defense.
Robinson, Norianna: Norina for short, hero genetically engineered.
Sheldon, Michael: general in the U.S. 1940s.
Smith, Anna: Reporter / correspondent.
Tharnatians: citizens of Tharnata.
The great Mourdug Dynasty: on the planet Voursa.
Thomas, Peter: scientist.
Thompson, Bart: hero and future host for Ner's profiles.
Throvolan: the Monarch on Voursa.
Varnether, Darna: Nephus' girlfriend/ cover name Susan Robinson/ teacher.
Varnether, Flavia: Darna's mother.
Vlasic, Dr.: a scientist who saved Nick's crew from the Aliens.
Vourook: chief Commander of the Voursi fleet.
Voursa: the aliens' home planet.

Project Anastrophe

Voursis: the aliens.
Voyager A-5: spaceship gone wrong.
Vrima: Nick's female robot. Secretary and body guard.
Zebigos, David: newly elected Governor of all flotillas.

Credits

(1) Merriam Webster's Collegiate Encyclopedia.

(2) Merriam Webster's Collegiate Encyclopedia.

(3) Merriam Webster's Collegiate Encyclopedia

(4) Wikipedia.

www.ingramcontent.com/pod-product-compliance
Lightning Source LLC
Chambersburg PA
CBHW021103020225
21278CB00019B/45